The Witch With No Name

The Witch With No Name

KIM HARRISON

HARPER Voyager

An Imprint of HarperCollins *Publishers*

Harper Voyager and design is a trademark of HCP LLC.

THE WITCH WITH NO NAME. Copyright © 2014 by Kim Harrison. All rights reserved. Printed in the United States of America. No part of this book may be used or reproduced in any manner whatsoever without written permission except in the case of brief quotations embodied in critical articles and reviews. For information address HarperCollins Publishers, 195 Broadway, New York, NY 10007.

HarperCollins books may be purchased for educational, business, or sales promotional use. For information please e-mail the Special Markets Department at SPsales@harpercollins.com.

FIRST EDITION

Library of Congress Cataloging-in-Publication Data

Harrison, Kim, 1966–
    The witch with no name / Kim Harrison.
        pages   cm
    ISBN 978-0-06-195795-6 (hardback)
1. Morgan, Rachel (Fictitious character)—Fiction.   2. Demons—Fiction.
3. Witches—Fiction.   4. Vampires—Fiction.   5. Werewolves—Fiction.
I. Title.
PS3608.A78355W53 2014
813'.6—dc23   2014007793

ISBN 978-0-06-236931-4 (signed edition)

14 15 16 17 18   OV/RRD   10 9 8 7 6 5 4 3 2 1

To Tim, the "guy in the leather jacket"

Acknowledgments

I'd like to thank my agent, Richard Curtis, who understands that big things start out small, and Diana Gill, my editor, who knows how to make small things big.

The Witch With No Name

Chapter 1

Neck craned, I squinted up between the shadowed apartments. High in the sun, dragonflylike wings threw back the glow with the transparent sheen of glittery tissue paper. The sporadic traffic at the end of the alley was enough to cover the sound of Jenks's wings, but I could hear them in my memory as the pixy hovered before a pollution-grimed window.

The moist-dirt smell of damp pavement was a hint under the light but growing scent of frightened vampire coming from near my elbow. I doubted Marsha was having second thoughts, but disobeying your master vampire could have lethal consequences.

Still watching Jenks, I surreptitiously edged away from Marsha's tense, middle-class office professionalism. Her heels were this year's style, but she wouldn't be able to run in them. Her hair was a luscious handful that spilled over her shoulders in an ebony wave—again, it made her an easy target in a close fight. A curvaceous figure sealed the deal that she was beautiful. But as a living vampire, her looks had been selected for over the last two generations, and not for Luke's benefit, the man she'd unfortunately fallen in love with. But she knew she was vulnerable. That's why Ivy, Jenks, and I were here.

My neck was getting a crick, and I dropped my gaze to the passing cars, confident that distance and recycling bins would hide us from casual sight. A tight hum jerked my attention back in time to see Jenks dart from a winged shadow. A blue jay squawked, and the tips of five feathers spiraled down between the buildings. Flapping wildly, the sheared bird managed to get across the street before thumping to the sidewalk.

Having already dismissed the bird, Jenks cupped his hands around his face and peered through the window. His skintight, thief-black tights and knit shirt helped him blend into the shadows, and the red cap was to tell rival pixies that he wasn't there poaching, a real issue this close to Eden Park. So far, no one had bothered him, but birds were a constant threat.

"I shouldn't have to do this," the woman at my elbow complained, oblivious that a third of the team here to keep her alive had just had a narrow miss. "It's my apartment!"

I took a slow breath when Jenks lifted the flap to the bathroom vent and vanished inside. "You want to risk running into Luke?" I said, and she made a sound of frustration. Yes, she did, but to do so would mean her death.

A lingering sensation that something was off dogged me, despite—or perhaps because of—the ease of the run so far. Restless, I resettled my shoulder bag. I wasn't a slouch when it came to looks, but next to this woman's structured beauty, my frizzy red hair and low-heel boots fell flat.

Ivy's confident steps against the hush of the side-street traffic tightened my gut. The vampire next to me stiffened at my increased pulse, and I gave Marsha a look to pull herself together. "Stay here," I said, not liking that Jenks was still inside. "Jenks will tell you when you can come in." Hiking my shoulder bag higher, I headed for the sidewalk.

"The hell I will," Marsha said, then stepped as if to follow.

Spinning, I shoved her shoulder, sending her thumping back against the wall. Shocked, the woman stared, not a hint of anger thanks to a lifetime of conditioning. "The hell you will," I said. "Stay here until Jenks says you can move, or we turn around and walk. Right here. Right now."

Only now did her anger show, her pupils widening and the scent of angry vampire prickling my nose. Wanting to nip this show of dominance, I stretched my awareness out and tapped the nearest ley line. Energy flowed in, making the tips of my hair float as it spooled in my chi. My skin tingled, and I leaned into her space, proving I wasn't scared of her little fangs or her greater strength. "You're under a conditional death threat, sweetheart," I breathed. "Once I verify that Luke isn't in there, you can come get what you want. But if all you're looking for is a way to die that doesn't invalidate your life insurance, do it on your own time."

Sullen, Marsha dropped her eyes, the rim of blue around her pupils returning to normal.

I rocked back, thumbs in my pockets, satisfied that she'd wait. It was unusual for a vampire to listen to anyone outside her camarilla, but she *had* come to us. Nodding, I looked up and made a sharp whistle. Immediately, Jenks peeked out of the bathroom vent and gave me a thumbs-up. "Park it," I muttered, and the woman shrank against the Dumpster and out of sight.

Appeased, I started for the front entrance. The run had sounded simple enough when Ivy had brought it up over grilled cheese sandwiches and tomato soup last night. Helping a woman get her things out of her apartment was a no-brainer—until she told me the separation was being forced by two rival vampire camarillas and if Luke and Marsha didn't comply someone was going to end up dead. No way was Ivy going to do this one alone.

This was doing nothing to bolster my already low opinion of the undead vampires, the masters who manipulated everyone and everything in their decades-long games. Once they noticed you, the only way to avoid being a victim was to die and become a player yourself.

But not Ivy, I thought as I emerged from the alley and she angled toward me. I wouldn't let that happen to her. Unfortunately, the harder you squirmed, the more they squeezed.

Ivy's pace hid a thread of tension I never would've noticed if I hadn't been sharing living space with her for the past three years. Sleek in her black slacks and top, she strode forward with her arms free and swinging. Her long black hair was up in a hard-to-grab bun, and even from here I could see the rims of brown around her eyes were nice and steady. She jumped at the distant sound of a door closing two streets over, though. She'd noticed something was off, too.

Her shoulders eased as she fell in beside me, and we took the steps up to the front common door together. "Luke's car is still in the lot," she said as I pulled the door open and we walked into the foyer of the old apartment building as if we belonged. "By the smell of it, it's not been run for two days."

"So he's doing what he's been told and is still alive." I glanced up at the camera. Jenks had been through the common areas, and according to him, they were fake. The scuffed tile floor was dirty in the corners, and I leaned against the stairway as Ivy leafed through Marsha's mail, pulling out everything she might want before putting the rest back in.

"They won't let one of them die without killing the other," Ivy said as she made keep and toss piles. "Otherwise the dead will claim the living as his or her scion."

Which wouldn't do at all, I thought, looking up the dimly lit stairwell. It reminded me a little of my first place. "I don't like this."

A rare smile came over Ivy, and the letter box snapped shut with a click. "You worry too much. These two aren't that important."

My eyebrows rose. Despite my comments, Marsha was gorgeous. It would be hard for a master to let that much beauty go. "Worry? I only worry about you. I don't like this run."

Ivy handed me Marsha's mail, and I tucked it in my bag. "You just don't like the undead," she said, and I pulled my splat gun out and checked the hopper.

"Golly, I can't imagine why."

Making a soft sound of agreement, Ivy started up the stairs. I knew she wasn't interested in the mail, but it had given us a chance to stand at the foot of the stairs while she breathed the air and decided if anyone was waiting for us on the way up—Jenks's assurance or not. "Relax," she said as I fell into place behind her. "They agreed to not see each other. We go in, get her stuff, get out. End of story."

"Then why did you ask me to come with you?" I said, rounding the first landing.

Not looking back, she whispered, "Because I don't trust them."

Me either. The door downstairs clicked open, and I spun. My hold on the ley line zinged through me, but it was just Jenks and Marsha. I put a finger to my lips, and she closed the door behind her to seal out the *shush* of cars. Even three stories up, I could see a new, healthy fear in her. Maybe Jenks had talked to her.

The pixy's wings softly hummed as he rose straight up in less than a second. "We're clear," he said, the silver dust slipping from him making a temporary sunbeam on my shoulder.

Clear, sure, but he couldn't detect charms unless they were active. "Keep her in the hall till I say," I asked. "And let me know if anyone pulls up."

Jenks nodded, dropping down to where Marsha was trying to creep up the stairs without her heels clicking. Ivy was waiting for me at the end of the hall, and I closed the gap quickly, eyeing the new detector charms on my bracelet. It had been a pain in the ass to make them that small, but if they were on my bracelet, I could watch them and point my gun at the same time. The wooden apple detected lethal spells, and the copper clover would glow in the presence of a strong charm. The two were not always synonymous.

Ivy was starting to smell really good, a mix of vampire incense and leather. I tried to ignore it as I gripped my splat gun tighter, amulets clinking. Marsha's front door had a corkboard for leaving notes, decorated with flowers and a smiley face with fangs. I could hear the woman's heels scrape on the stairwell, and I grimaced. It was noon, a time when most day walkers would be at work and the night walkers safely underground—but there were ways around that.

The amulets were a nice steady green and I nodded, splat gun level as I crouched opposite the door's hinges. Ivy worked the key and pushed it open to stand in the opening. Jenks flew in, confident that his first look was sufficient, but I listened as Ivy tasted the air, running it through her incredibly complex brain. "Hi, honey. I'm home," she said, and I followed her in.

I had to walk right through Ivy's scent, and even with my breath held, I shivered at the touch of pheromones she was kicking out—wafting over my skin like the memory of black silk. Though still sharing our investigation firm's letterhead, she'd been pulling away from me the last six months or so. I had a good idea why, and though I was happy for her, I missed working with her on a more daily basis.

My old vampire bite tingled at the obvious aroma of amorous vampires that permeated the one-bedroom, open-floor-plan apartment. *Or maybe I just miss the intoxicating mix of sexual thrill and heart-pounding adrenaline she pumped into the air when she got tense.* Frowning at my own shallowness, I looked over the small, plush, well-decorated sunlit apartment and the evidence of their love. I knew what it was like having people tell you who not to fall in love with, and my thoughts pinged on Trent before spinning away.

"Stay there," I said to Marsha, now at the door. My amulets were still green, but I was only five feet into the place. "There could be person-specific spells."

Person-specific spells: a nice way of saying a bullet with your name on it—and Jenks couldn't detect them. They were a necessity when making lethal, illegal charms. Vampire politics would keep the hit quiet, but if the spell took out an innocent, they'd track down and jail the black witch who'd made the lethal charm.

Senses searching, I did a quick walk through the living room before checking out the small kitchen. Ivy was in the bedroom, and I slowed, eyes on the amulets. It was easier to hide stuff among the gleaming metal and new appliances, but if there was anything here, it'd show.

"Hey!" Ivy exclaimed, muffled from the walls. My head snapped up and I lurched to get in front of Marsha. Shit, I'd been right.

"Jenks!" Ivy shouted, exasperated this time. "Why didn't you tell us about the dog?"

I slid to a stop, peeved as Jenks dusted an embarrassed red. Marsha had come in, eyes alight, and I waved for her to stay where she was.

"Sor-r-r-rry!" Jenks said as the jingle of a dog collar became obvious. "It's just a dog."

No one had been here for two days? The place smelled like candles, not dog crap.

"Buddy!" Marsha called out, exuberant as she pushed around me to drop to her knees, and I eyed the small, scruffy pound puppy that timidly walked, not trotted, into the living room. "Come here, baby! You must be starving. I thought Luke had you!"

My eyes narrowed. I'd never had a dog, but I knew they generally underwent the throes of delight when their owners came back after checking the mail, much less two days. "Ah, Marsha?" I said as the dog took a hesitant step in, his tail just hanging there.

"I think we're good," Ivy said as she came out of the back room. "You want to sweep it with your charms?"

"Sure," I said slowly, something ringing false.

"Buddy?" Marsha called again, and the dog gave me a sideways look as he passed me, a mix of excitement and hesitancy I wouldn't expect from an animal.

At my wrist, an amulet flashed red.

"Shit, it's the dog!" I shouted.

Marsha looked up, her beautiful little mouth in an O of surprise. Her hands were outstretched and the dog was almost to her. I'd never get there in time.

"*Rhombus!*" I exclaimed as I pulled on the ley line, feeling it scream into me, harsh from my demand. The energy pooled and overflowed, and I shoved it out again, my word tapping into a hard-won series of mental handsprings that harnessed the energy into a molecule-thin barrier. It took the easiest form—a sphere with me in the center—and the dog predictably ran into it.

But instead of the expected yip of surprise, the energy levels spiked.

It was the only warning I got, and I cowered as a bright flash of energy exploded inside my circle, coming from the dog! The loosed power reverberated, making my circle chime like a sour bell, and I froze, skin crawling as the illegal death spell flooded over me, then fell back into the dog when it didn't find its intended victim.

"Buddy!" Marsha screamed as Ivy shoved her into the wall, covering her with her body.

"Get her out of here!" I shouted, afraid to move. The spell had been invoked, but it hadn't fastened on its intended victim. It was a loose cannon, and it was trapped in here with me.

"That's my dog!" the woman protested, wild with fear as Ivy manhandled her into the hallway. "Buddy! *Buddy!*"

Slowly I realized I was unhurt. Buddy, though . . . Wincing, I looked at the dog, prostrate and beginning to shake. He wasn't dead, and he wasn't a dog. It was her boyfriend, Luke.

I hate vampires, I thought, realizing what had happened. Someone had turned Luke into a doppelganger of their dog and tacked a secondary spell on to him that would kill them both when Marsha touched him. Luke was halfway gone, but until the spell found Marsha, it wouldn't invoke fully. I had a chance.

"Marsha!" I stood, carefully watching the energy flow as I broke my own circle. "Where do you keep your salt?"

"Stay put," Ivy snarled. "Tell me."

"In the cupboard beside the stove!" the woman sobbed from the hallway. "What happened? Buddy? Buddy!"

I ran to the kitchen and snapped on the faucet. "It's not your dog, it's your boyfriend."

Maybe that had been a mistake, since the woman totally freaked out. "Luke!" she screamed. "Oh God, Luke!"

"Stay in the hall!" Ivy shouted, and the sounds of a struggle grew louder.

Salt, salt . . . I thought, pulse fast as I found a mixing bowl and dropped it into the sink. "Don't let her touch him! If she touches him, they both die!"

"Luke!" the woman sobbed, and I triumphantly found the salt. I wedged a nail under the spout and ripped it right out. Hands shaking, I shook it into the mixing bowl.

"Is he going to be okay?" Jenks asked, his dust pooling on the surface and running like mercury, but I didn't know.

"Oh God. Hurry!" Marsha begged, and I gave the salt water a quick stir, tasting it before I picked up the bowl. The woman was hovering over the dog, terrified. My heart went out to her. Vampire masters were sons of bitches. Every last one of them. "Help him!" she screamed, her perfect face twisted in terror. Ivy held her, and I moved fast, bowl of salt water before me.

"Stay back," I warned as I stood over the little white dog and dumped it. Water splashed, and Marsha backed up, white faced and breathless. I had no idea if the entire concentration was optimum for breaking earth charms, but there'd be enough to not just turn him human, but to break the lethal charm as well.

As expected, the dog vanished behind a thick puff of brown-and-blue aura-tainted energy. "Luke!" Marsha screamed, and Jenks frowned at her. He'd seen enough spells break to know this was normal. I backed up, tense as the cloud grew to man size. Slowly the mist broke up to show a naked, bruised, and beaten man huddled on the soggy white carpet.

Luke took a sobbing gasp of air. He was going to make it—for now, and I eased back to sit on the edge of the cushy couch, elbows on my knees and head dropped into my hands. The amulets on my bracelet clinked, and I sighed. The salt water had ruined them. I'd tack it on to Marsha's bill, but I didn't think she had the money. Besides, she was going to be a little busy trying to survive.

"You can touch him now," I said, realizing that Marsha was still hovering over him.

Frantic, she dropped to her knees. Water squished from the carpet, and she pulled him to her. "Oh, baby!" she gushed, oblivious that he was covered in salt water. "Did he hurt you?"

By the bruises, clearly someone—probably his own master—had, but he raised a shaky hand and brushed her cheek. "I'm okay," he rasped, a flash of ugly memory finding me at the sight of him, his black hair plastered to his face and his eyes not quite open. It hurt like the devil to shift with earth magic, but his toned, athletic, and beaten body covered in easily hidden scars looked as if it was used to pain.

Crying, Marsha cradled his head to herself and rocked him. I wondered how many scars were hidden behind Marsha's expensive clothes. This sucked. Vampires looked as if they had everything, but it was a lie. My eyes shifted to Ivy, seeing her inner struggle. *A big fat ugly lie.*

The clatter of Jenks's wings was a short warning as he landed on my shoulder. "He looked like a dog to me," he grumped.

"That's because he was one." I plucked at my wet shirt, sticking uncomfortably to me. The question wasn't how, but why. Why had two minor vampire camarillas spent this much on a double-whammy spell like this on a simple Romeo and Juliet? It was expens-s-s-sive.

Ivy was in the hall to convince the neighbors nothing was going on. It didn't take much. Clearly they were familiar with the situation. Not happy, Ivy shut the door and stomped into the kitchen to turn the faucet off.

"I'm sorry, Marsha," Luke was saying, and the crying woman stretched for a blanket to cover him. "When they told me I couldn't see you again, I went to a witch. She said she could turn me into a dog so I could be with you. No one would know it was me."

I watched as Ivy pulled the living room blinds. Her expression was empty, hearing far past what the man was saying. Closing the last, she sat across from me in the shadow light, worried.

"I didn't care if I was a dog," Luke continued, his eyes still not open as his hand gripped hers. "I knew you wouldn't leave Buddy." His eyes opened, and I stared. They were the clearest shade of blue I'd ever seen. "I love you, Marsha. I'd do anything for you. Anything!" Crying, he pulled himself into a ball in her arms. "I'm so sorry."

My God, they'd tricked him into buying the charm that would've killed them both. Ivy and I exchanged a worried look. This was bad, but we couldn't just walk away. Jenks, too, was looking ill, and he moved to the decorative bowl of pinecones on the coffee table. He'd loved and lost more than Ivy and me combined, and this wasn't sitting well with him either. But it wasn't one master vampire we'd have to outwit, but two.

Ivy was still silent, and I sourly thought of my bank account. "You think we should help them?" I said softly, and Jenks's dust shifted to a hopeful yellowish pink.

Ivy didn't look at me. The couple on the floor was silent.

"You think we should help them," I said again, this time making it a statement.

Ivy's eyes flicked up. I could see her tremendous need to give, to make it right. She'd done so much wrong, and it chewed on her in the small hours. My heart ached for her skewed view of herself, and I wished she could see herself as I did. This would rub the guilt out—for a time.

"Okay, we'll help them," I said, and Marsha gasped, her tear-wet eyes suddenly full of hope where there'd been only despair. Jenks's wings hummed his approval, and I sat up, gesturing weakly. "But I don't know what we can do."

"You can't," Marsha said, voice harsh as she held Luke. "They know everything."

Unfortunately, she was right. We couldn't simply set them up in a nice house out of state and hope that they wouldn't be found and made into an even bigger example. Ivy had been trying to wiggle out from her master her entire life only to become more entangled, so much so that they'd ensnared me, too. *Trent, maybe?* I thought, but as it was, he was struggling to keep his head above the political sharks.

"Maybe," I said as Luke sat up, muscles beginning to work again. "Changing into a dog was a great idea." Actually, it had been a lousy idea, but unless you practiced magic, you wouldn't know how easy it was to circumvent it. My gaze went to the soggy carpet. Obviously.

"We'll run," Marsha said, tensing as if ready to walk out that exact second.

Ivy shook her head. "You won't get past the city limits."

"Marsha, sweetheart," Luke whispered. "You know that won't work."

But I'd given her hope, and the woman wouldn't let go. "We can use the tunnels!"

Ivy looked toward the shuttered windows at the sound of a horn. "They built the tunnels."

"I can't live without you. I won't!" the distressed woman cried out, and I wondered if the place had been bugged. But if it had, Jenks would have heard the electronic whine and disabled them. We had a moment to catch our breath, and then we'd have to move.

It wasn't as if we could stake their two master vampires; there were laws against that kind of thing. Unless Marsha and Luke could come up with ironclad blackmail, they were stuck.

"Okay," I said, feeling the need to get moving. We'd been here too long. "There might be some law or something you can tap into. Ivy's going to need access to every document your names are on. Birth certificates, property deeds, insurance, parking tickets, tax returns, everything."

Marsha nodded, that same glow of hope back in her eyes hurting me. This wasn't going to work, but we had to try something.

Ivy rose to look out through a crack in the blinds. "Do either of you have a safe house?"

"None we trust anymore," Luke said, and Ivy let the blind fall.

"I've got one," Ivy said, coming back to help Luke stand. "You should be okay for a few days. Especially if you help out a little with the other guests coming in."

Wrapped in the blanket, Luke awkwardly got to his feet, pale and shaking. "Anything. Yes. Thank you."

Jenks took to the air, humming out under the crack in the door to check the hallway. Almost immediately he darted back in with a big thumbs-up.

"We can't just walk out with them," I said, and Ivy gave me a glum smile.

"They won't try anything new until sundown," Ivy said, catching Marsha's arm before the woman went into the bedroom and shaking her head to leave everything. "They'll want to be present the next time."

God help me. I hated vampires. "Okay, let's move out."

"But he needs his clothes," Marsha was saying as I collected my splat gun from the counter. Ivy was almost carrying Luke to the door, and tears began to slip again from Marsha. I totally understood. The entire place was a perfect blending of their love. It was sucky when happiness became this costly. But if they'd fought this hard for it, then it would last their entire lifetime. I just hoped that lifetime would be longer than a week.

The hallway was quiet, smelling of dust and old carpet. Eyes were watching through peepholes, and it made me edgy. Marsha took Luke's elbow to help him shuffle down the stairs in his blanket, and Ivy dropped back to talk to me.

"Jenks, you're going with Ivy, right?" I asked, knowing she wouldn't tell me the address of her safe house, much less take me there. Jenks, though . . .

Jenks's wings hummed into invisibility, and he rose up a hand width. "Yeah."

"No," Ivy said, frowning, and he made a face at her. "You're not coming, pixy."

"Tink's a Disney whore, like you could stop me!" he shot back.

Smiling, I edged around Ivy to keep Marsha and Luke from heading out without us. "I've got my phone on," I said, pushing them back to the mailboxes until I could look at the street.

"I'll be fine. See you at home," Ivy said, ignoring Jenks and his sword pointed at her nose. "Hey, you doing anything tonight?"

"Listen to me, you broken-fanged, moss-wiped excuse for a back-drafted blood bag!" Jenks said, a silver-edged red dust slipping from him.

I looked back inside from the street, thinking this had been nice, even with the near miss. I liked working with Ivy. Always had. We did well together—even when it had gone wrong. "I'm working security for Trent," I said, lips quirking as I saw her mentally smack her forehead. "You want me to bring you back something? It's probably going to end somewhere with food."

"Sure. That'd be good," she said, turning to give Marsha and Luke some last-minute instructions on how to get from here to there alive. "I'll call if I need help."

I touched her arm, and her eyes met mine in farewell. Smiling, I turned away remembering something Kisten had once said: I was there when she had her morning coffee, I was there when she turned out the light. I was her friend, and to Ivy, that was everything.

"Jenks, I've got this!" I heard, and then I shut the door, my steps light as I headed for my car. Ivy would get home okay. She was right that the masters would want to be there when they brought their children in line. Besides, everyone in Cincinnati with fangs knew Ivy Tamwood.

Head up, I stomped along, eyeing the few pedestrians. Slowly my good mood was tarnished. Love died in the shadows, and it shouldn't cost so much to keep it in the sun. But as Trent would say, anything gotten cheap wouldn't last, so do what you need to do to be happy and deal with the consequences. That if love was easy, everyone would find it.

I turned the corner, my head coming up at the clatter of pixy wings. "She said no, huh?" I said as Jenks landed on my shoulder, his wings tickling my neck as he settled himself.

"Tink's little pink rosebuds," he muttered. "She threatened to dump insecticide on my summer hut. Besides, she's got it okay. God! Vampires in love. The only thing worse is you mooning over Trent."

My smile widened. Maybe I'd make cookies. The man loved cookies.

He made a rude sound, his silence telling me he was unhappy. "Sorry about the dog."

I lifted a shoulder and let it fall. "You didn't know."

"I should have."

I didn't answer, thinking about my date tonight with Trent. Well, not a date exactly, but I had to get dressed up as if it were one. I was still trying to decide whether to put my hair up or wear it down. *Chocolate chip is his favorite.*

"Oh God," Jenks moaned. "You're thinking about him. I can tell. Your aura shifted."

Embarrassed, I halted at the crosswalk, waiting for the light. "It did not."

"It did," he complained, but I knew he crabbed because he couldn't say he was happy for me lest he jinx it somehow. "So it's been like what, three months? Does he still curl your toes?"

"Totally," I said, and he made a rude noise at my blissful smile. "He's a total toe curler."

"Awww, this is sweeter than pixy piss," he said with false sarcasm. "All my girls happy. I can't tell you the last time that happened."

My smile widened, and I pushed the walk button as if that might hurry it along. "I think it was when—"

The unmistakable sound of tires screaming on pavement iced through me. My breath caught, and I turned. Jenks was gone, his white-hot sparkles seeming to burn an airborne trail back the way we'd come. A woman screamed for help, and I jumped back when a black sedan roared past me, the front fender dented. Somehow I knew, like when a picture falls off the wall, or the clock stops ticking.

"Ivy," I whispered, then turned and ran.

Chapter 2

The thumps of my feet on the pavement jarred up my spine. Dodging people turning to look, I followed Jenks's fading dust. My heart seemed to stop when I turned the corner and saw Ivy crumpled in the street. Marsha and Luke were standing looking down at her, dazed. A car stopped even as I watched, and a man got out, white faced, his phone in hand.

"Call 911!" I shouted as I slid to the pavement beside Ivy. *Shit. Ivy.* She had to be alive. *I shouldn't have left you.*

Jenks was a frantic, darting shape as he dusted the blood from a scalp wound. She'd hit her head. Her chest moved shallowly, and her legs were twisted. I was afraid to touch her, and my hands hovered over her, reminding me of Marsha standing over Luke.

Pain charm! I thought frantically as I searched my bag. Fingers fumbling, I dropped the charm over her head. I was putting a Band-Aid on a concussion, when she took a clean breath.

"Did you call 911?" I exclaimed as a pair of Meris dress shoes scuffed before us.

"No hospital."

Her voice was soft, almost not there, and both Jenks and I looked at Ivy. She was pale, and pain pinched her still-closed eyes. That was good, right? She wasn't unconscious, even if her eyes were closed. *Damn it, I should have learned how to make a healing curse!* But Al was gone and it was too late.

"Ivy." I brushed her hair back, my fingers trembling. They came away warm and red, and my fear redoubled. She'd hit her head badly enough that Jenks's dust wasn't stopping it. "Ivy!" I called when her eyes didn't open. More people were ringing us. "Look at me, damn it! Look at me! Can you move your fingers and toes?"

"I think so."

Her eyes opened as I took her cold hand. The pupils were fully dilated, scaring me. I wasn't sure if it was from head trauma or my fear. The circle of people around us whispered, and when a smile of satisfaction edged over her pain, panic took me. "Ivy?"

Her hand squeezed mine, and she moved her legs, wincing as she straightened them. She could move, and I remembered how to breathe.

"Marsha and Luke are gone," Jenks whispered as he hovered by my ear.

Like I freaking cared?

She was trying to sit up, and I gingerly helped her as the heat from the stopped car bathed us. "Little fish," Ivy said, hair coming out of the bun as she held her middle. "They weren't after them. Oh God, I think I cracked a rib."

"Don't move," I said, stiffening as a siren lifted into the air. "The ambulance is coming."

"No hospital." Her black eyes fixed on mine, and she went whiter still as she tried to take a deep breath. "No safe house. I've been marked."

Marked? Her gaze went to the pain charm around her neck, and she gripped it tight, shocking me. She never used my magic. Avoided it. "You need a hospital," I said, and she hissed in pain as she tried to turn her head.

"No."

"Ivy, you were *hit* by a *car*!" Jenks had dusted her cuts until they were only a slow seep, but her eyes were dilated and she hadn't taken her other hand off her middle.

"Cormel," she said softly, hatred temporarily overriding her pain. "I told you Marsha and Luke weren't worth all of this. I wasn't supposed to walk out of that apartment alive. That charm was aimed at me, too. He wants me dead . . . so you . . . will figure out how to save the souls of the undead. The car was a last effort to salvage their plan before going back with failure."

My heart seemed to catch, then it raced as I looked at the surrounding faces for anyone watching too closely—their eyes holding fear. Ivy moaned as she breathed in my alarm, but I couldn't let go of it. I couldn't distance myself. The lethal charm had been aimed at all three of them. If I hadn't been there to break it, Ivy would be dead and I'd be getting a call from the second-rising morgue.

"I don't want to become a dead thing," she whispered, then clenched in pain. "Rachel?"

I closed my eyes. Ivy groaned, her pain doubling as my panic pulsed through her, bringing her alive even as she struggled to stave off death. I couldn't do this. I couldn't be her scion. But I knew I would if it came to that. Cormel had grown tired of waiting for his soul. If Ivy was dead, me finding out how to return the undead their souls would move way up on my to-do list.

We had to get out of here. Even the safe houses held death, and the hospitals would only make her passing smell of antiseptic. *Why had I worked so hard to save their miserable existences?* I wondered as I found my bag and looped it over my head. But it hadn't been just the undead in the balance when I'd freed the mystics last July, it had been the entire source of magic.

Jenks dropped down as I gathered my resolve. "They're everywhere, Rache," he whispered, his fear easy to read on his narrow, pinched features, and Ivy nodded. Surrounded by onlookers, we had a small space to breathe, but we couldn't stay here.

Slowly I began to think. Trent. He had a surgery suite, one that wasn't staffed by people who could be bought. I wasn't sure where he was, but I could text him. Ivy was sitting. Maybe she could move. "Ivy," I said, blanching at the blackness in her eyes when she looked at me from around a stray strand of hair. "Can you move?"

Her boots scraped as she shifted them under her. "If I can't, I'm dead."

A few in the crowd protested, but they backed up when Jenks rose, his fast, darting shape and the sharp sword in his grip making him a threat.

My stomach turned when every hold I tried to help Ivy with only brought more pain. Teeth clenched, I tucked my shoulder under her arm and rose, staggering until we found our balance. Ivy's eyes closed. We hung for a moment, waiting to see if she was going to pass out. In the nearby distance, a siren rose—but it brought death, not life.

"Okay, nice and easy," I said, and Jenks kept everyone back as we started for the curb. Ivy's head was down, and she moved in sudden, painful limps. Step, pause. Step, pause. Her weight on me was solid, and her scent was tinged with sour acid. Tears threatened, and I ignored them. I couldn't live with Ivy if she was dead. I couldn't be her scion, but I knew I'd do it, even as it would destroy me. I'd try to keep Ivy sane, knowing it was a bitter fallacy. I couldn't kill her a second time as she would want me to. I was a bad friend.

"I'm sorry," Ivy said as we reached the curb and she took her hand from her middle long enough to use the lamppost to help her step up.

"This isn't your fault," I barked so I wouldn't cry. "We'll get you to Trent's, and you'll be fine." His compound was almost deserted since the serious inquiries into his illegal bio labs had begun, but he probably had a surgeon on call.

Seeing her standing to catch her breath, I dug in my bag for my phone. "Can you hold this?" I said, giving her my splat gun, and she held it loosely. My fingers shook as I scrolled for Trent. He was the last person I'd called, and knowing he might not take a call but would always check a text, I wrote 911 and Eden Park and hit send.

My stomach was twisting as I tucked my phone in my back pocket. It was all I could do. But we couldn't stay here. Each moment seemed to weigh more heavily on Ivy. She was slipping, and her living vampire endurance would mean nothing if she gave up.

"You can't go to the car, Rache." Jenks hovered before us, watching us and our backs both. "They'll run you down."

Shit. He was right. Tears of frustration pricked, and Ivy leaned against the lamppost. Behind her, people were turning away, leaving us to die.

"Where else can I go, Jenks?" I shouted, frustrated. "Nowhere on earth is safe from them!"

He shrugged, even as his dust grew dismal, but behind him was Eden

Park, and a flash of hope lit through me. Ivy sensed it, and her eyes opened, glazed with pain.

"The park." I wiggled under her again, and we staggered into motion. "Ivy, hold on."

"The park!" Jenks echoed in disbelief, and then he nodded, rising up to fly five feet over us where he could keep watch.

The park. There was a ley line in it, thin and broken, but it was there. I couldn't jump the lines without Bis. He wouldn't be awake until the sun went down, but I could shift realities if I was standing in a line. The ever-after was a poor choice, but no one could follow us there, and maybe we could walk to the church's ley line and pop back into reality.

Ivy stumbled as we found the grass, and we almost went down. Her moan sounded almost like pleasure. Old toxins were being pulled from her tissues to cope with the pain as her body struggled to stay alive. But this time it wasn't a master satisfying his blood urge that was killing her, and her breath quickened as she took in my fear and kindled her own long-suppressed desires.

"Almost there," I panted, struggling under her weight as I scanned the open grass between us and the footbridge. It was exposed, but they probably wouldn't shoot her and risk hitting me by accident. Cormel needed me alive and Ivy dead. They only had to wait.

This was partly my fault, and I felt the helpless tears trying to start as I took more of Ivy's weight. There was no way to bind a vampire's soul to his body once he died, and as we slowly limped across the green space to Twin Lakes Bridge and the broken ley line, a warm tear ran a trail down my cheek.

"Don't cry," Ivy slurred. "It's going to be okay."

I wiped my eyes between our lurching steps, my stomach roiling. "Almost there."

Jenks dropped down, worry pinching his features. "Her aura isn't looking good, Rache."

"I know!" I shouted. "I know," I said again, softer.

"It hurts," Ivy said as I took even more of her weight. "It's not supposed to hurt, is it?"

Oh God. I knew the pain amulet was outclassed, but that the damage was too much for even the vampire toxins to mutate was scary. "Almost there. Hold on," I whispered, eyes fixed on the statue of Romulus and Remus. "You can rest when we get to the line."

But I didn't think we were going to make it, especially when Jenks's dust went an angry red. "There're two blood bags on the footbridge," he snarled, his blade catching the light. "Keep going. Don't stop no matter what you hear. I'll take care of them."

"Jenks!" I cried out as he darted away. Beside me, Ivy wheezed. Her fingers rose to touch her mouth, coming away red with blood. Immediately she curled her fingers up in a ball to hide it, but a flash of fear lit through me. Internal bleeding. My gun, too, was gone, left behind somewhere on the summer-burnt grass.

"Almost there," I said again as we moved another few feet, but inside, I was despairing. There were no hospitals in the ever-after, only demons who didn't care. I didn't think we'd make it all the way to the church. If Trent didn't show, I might have just killed Ivy by trying to save her.

Ivy's breath became labored, and the sudden shouting at the bridge yanked my attention up. With a quick flurry of motion, a woman swung wildly at Jenks, falling down the embankment and into the water, harried the entire way by the pixy. Suddenly she was screaming as Sharps, the resident bridge troll, rose up, swamping her.

Without a second look, the other vampire continued toward us, leaving her to sort herself out. He was vampire-child, beautiful, graceful, and sure of himself—and when he looked at me, I shuddered.

Jenks darted in and away, distracting him.

"Move faster, Ivy," I begged, knowing Jenks couldn't hold off a determined vampire. Eyeing the statue of Romulus and Remus, I brought up my second sight. A faint haze, ill looking and sporadic, hung at chest height. It was Al's line, half dead because of the shallow pond someone had dug out under it, but unable to die because the other half of it lay in the dry, desolate ever-after. It reminded me of the demon himself, having given up on life but clinging so tightly to the memory of a love he had once had that now he couldn't live or die.

He would never help me. Not now. And an old guilt pulled my brow even tighter.

From the water came a gurgling scream as the woman fought to be free of Sharps. Ivy moaned and I dropped my second sight. My eyes jerked to the controlled anger and grace striding toward us despite Jenks's darting flight and bloodied blade. The vampire knew the line was there and was trying to cut us off.

Crap on toast. I wasn't going to make it. I'd have to beat him off.

Ivy hung on my shoulder as I came to a heart-pounding halt, her head down and her breathing frighteningly raspy. A lousy twenty feet was between me and the line, and the suave man smiled when he rocked to a silent stand before us. He was the expected eight feet back, his hair moving in the light breeze as he assessed my determination, feeding off my fear even as I found a firmer stance. Eight feet. He'd fought magic users before. It was just far enough that he could dodge anything I might throw at him.

Fine. He was between me and the line, but I could still pull on it, and I allowed the line's energy to funnel down to my hand and gathered it in a tight ball of frustration. He was stunning in his black suit, but it was more than his sculpted, carefully bred-for beauty. It was his attitude of a complete and utter lack of fear. He was wearing sunglasses, and an old scar on his neck said he was someone's favorite. Behind him, the woman screamed at both Jenks and Sharps as she tried to get out of the water.

"Morgan," the living vampire said, his voice holding layers of emotion, and Ivy stirred, drawn awake by either the screams at the lake or the pull in his voice.

"Go to hell!" Ivy managed, and Jenks joined me. Together we faced him, my knees shaking and Jenks's wings clattering in threat.

The man's eyes flicked to Ivy, then back to me. "Give it up."

Not happening, and I found a better grip on Ivy, my bellyful of everafter waiting for direction. "Come and get me," I mocked, trying to lure him a foot closer.

"You're not who I'm interested in. She's almost dead. All I have to do is wait."

Son of a bastard . . . This wasn't the original team sent to kill Ivy. It was probably the one sent to collect her body, and they'd be eager for the extra kudos killing her would bring them. Behind me, a car door slammed. I didn't dare look, but from the edge of my sight, three more men in suits started across the grass. Damn it, I couldn't fight off four of them and protect Ivy, too, even with Jenks.

The living vampire's beautiful brown eyes went black as he breathed in my fear. "Let us finish the job, or we beat you up and we finish the job anyway. She's dying her first death before the sun goes down."

"Over my dead body." The sun was nearing the horizon, but there were hours left in its path.

"And my broken wings," Jenks added, dusting Ivy's scalp again as blood began to mat her hair.

They were almost to us. I had to do something, his being out of range or not. I thought of Trent. Had he gotten my text? Was he on his way?

"Dead?" the vampire said, recapturing my attention. "No, he wants you alive. For now."

My frustration rose. The hazy read smear of the ley line was just behind him. Twenty lousy feet. "It can't be done!" I shouted, Jenks's dust tingling against my skin. "Tell Cormel it can't be done!"

"Then you owe him for the year he's kept you both safe," the man said. "Watching you suffer Ivy's second life will do."

"I already saved him once! I'm not paying the same debt twice."

The man chuckled, motioning for the arriving thugs to circle us. I could smell them, the rising scent of vampire incense bringing Ivy's eyes open and a new tension to her face. "You prolonged his misery is all."

He gestured, and I moved, throwing a single burst of energy at the beautiful man before turning my attention inward. "*Rhombus!*" I shouted, relief a slap when Jenks, contrary to his instinct, dropped down, safe inside my circle.

The rushing vampires skidded to a halt, stymied. Before me, my black-and-gold fist-size unfocused magic slammed into the head vampire, throwing him back four feet to hit the ground hard.

Nothing could get through my barrier unless it held my aura: not bullet, not vampire, not demon—unless he was very determined and I'd left an opening. But we were trapped in it, trapped twenty feet from safety. Damn it! This was so not fair. Every other demon could shift his aura to slip into a line, but I couldn't jump on my own, couldn't jump a lousy twenty feet. The line was so close I could almost feel it humming.

Dazed, the vampire found his feet, his beauty ruined by his snarl. "She's going to die in there!" he shouted, stalking forward to halt so close the barrier hummed a warning and I could see the first wrinkles about his eyes. "She's going to die, and then she will fall on you!"

Ivy stared up at me, clearly in pain, clearly feeling the pinch of instincts and desires she had lied to herself were under control. Tears filled her black eyes, and she reached out, her hand shaking as it found mine. "I'm sorry," she said, and anger filled me that they had brought her to this. "Please don't let me wake as the undead. I won't remember why I love you. *Promise me.* Promise me you won't let me wake as an undead."

My throat closed, and as Jenks's dust sifted red between us, I dropped down, my arms going around her. She wanted me to kill her if she should die. I couldn't do it. "I promise."

"Liar." She smiled at me, hand shaking as she touched my cheek.

Panic renewed, and I felt unreal, dizzy as I looked at the vampires ringing us in the late afternoon. There was no one to help me. I had to find a way.

"She won't last an hour," the beautiful man said, anticipation making his eyes black. "She will wake undead. You will fix her soul to her, or die at her own hands."

Ivy shook, and I let her go, resolve filling me as I stood until the shimmer of my circle hummed just over my head. "Jenks, I need you to do something," I said, and his face went white.

"I'm not leaving you, Rache."

I eyed the twenty feet and four vampires that separated us from the line. "I'm going to kick some vampire ass and get to that line. Ivy and I can wait in the ever-after."

"With the surface demons?" Jenks barked, his wings clattering harshly.

I had no choice. "Go try to wake Bis up. He can jump us to Trent's." I looked at the pixy, seeing his fear in his tight, angular face. He didn't want to leave us, was terrified we would die without him. He was probably right.

"No!" His wings clattered as he understood what I was saying. "It's hours until sunset. Don't ask me to leave you!"

I dropped down to grab Ivy's elbow to help her stand up. "I'm sorry, Ivy. You have to help me get you to the line."

"But she can hardly walk!"

"Which means she still can!" I shouted, and Ivy clutched at me, halfway to a stand and heavy in my grip. "Jenks, please," I said softly, and he hovered, helpless and angry, before us. "I can't jump on my own and Bis can't find me. You have to tell him where we are."

Slowly his expression shifted from anger to a frustrated understanding. "Keep her alive," he said, and I nodded, again making promises I couldn't keep.

Scared, I turned to the vampires watching suspiciously. Behind them, Cincinnati drowsed in the late afternoon sun. Al could have jumped us right to Trent's, or the hospital, or the church. But I wasn't one of them any longer. The break with the demons had been clean—even if the jagged edges of it still dug into my soul in the quiet parts of the night.

Breath held against the pain, Ivy got her weight over her feet and wavered to a rise. I felt her clench in agony as she fought to keep from coughing, her grip on me hurting. She took one breath, then another. Head up, she stared at the men ringing us. At the bridge, the woman finally got out of the water, dripping and bleeding from scratches and with a malevolent gleam in her eye. Five now.

I sucked in the line energy, feeling it hiccup and stutter. *Does Al know I'm using his line?* I wondered, feeling Al's utter abandonment of me again—jealousy, heartache, and hatred too much for him to forgive.

"Let me go, Ivy. I have to fight," I whispered, and after the briefest of hesitations, she did, her eyes closing as she uncrimped her fingers from around my arm. I could tell it had taken all her resolve, and she swallowed her saliva back, refusing to give in to her instincts—but instincts die last and hard.

"I like it when you say my name," she said as her eyes opened. "It doesn't hurt anymore."

Shit. This wasn't good. Not good at all. "I'm glad," I whispered, wishing my knees weren't shaking. "I'm going to have to kick some ass. Can you get to the statue on your own? Maybe critique me when it's over?"

"Over a beer," she said. Her hand wasn't so tight against her middle. I didn't know a charm for this. I had nothing.

Ivy slowly lost her balance and leaned into me again, unable to stand on her own. She wasn't going to make it, no matter what happened, and I shoved my panic down deep. "Thank you, Jenks," I whispered.

His wings clattered, and he wouldn't look at me, that same black dust sifting from him and making my skin tingle. I held Ivy close, the chill of her pressing into me as her head hung down and her breathing grew shallow. She was close to passing out. Slowly I lifted my chin and found the eyes of the waiting vampire.

"You first," I said, yanking a wad of ever-after into me. My breath came in with a sharp sound. Ivy stiffened in my grip, and I wondered if she felt it as I pulled everything I could handle into me. "Jenks, grab something!" I shouted as the building energy crested, lapped the top of my abilities, and, with a spasm that seemed to shake me to my core, edged into pain as I took even more. I had to take it all. All.

"Rache!" Jenks shrilled, tugging on my hair as he wound himself up in it. "What are you doing?"

I had one shot, and I wasn't going to waste it, even if it burned my synapses to a twisted mass. "*Corrumpto!*" I shouted, letting the energy explode from me.

My knees buckled. I felt airy, light and unreal. The line hummed through me, smelling of ozone and stardust. A soundless wave sped out, flattening the grass and bowling the vampires head over heels, making them look like crows. Ivy shuddered, her eyes opening black and deep. Together we straightened as a distant bell rang, and then another. Across the river, the basilica's bells tolled, and tears threatened when I recognized my own church bells ringing an echo from the force of my blast.

My skin was tingling, and I almost went down as Ivy's weight suddenly became my responsibility. "Ivy!" I called, bringing up my second sight and looking for the ley line. The vampires were down. We had to move. "Come on! Just a few steps!"

But then panic took me, not that the head vampire was getting up off the pavement, but that the ley line was gone! It wasn't running where it should, through the man-made ponds and beside the statue the vampire was leaning heavily against.

"Where is it?" I shouted, and Ivy sagged in my grip. Bewildered, and head humming as if it held a hive of bees, I strengthened my second sight until reality wavered under a broken landscape of dust, cracked rock, and bloated sun hazing an empty landscape and dry riverbed. The desolation of the ever-after was complete, and the gritty wind lifted through my hair even though I still stood in reality. But there was no line. *What have I done?*

Jenks hovered before me, blinking in shock. "You're in it," he said, a weird greenish dust sifting from him. "How did you move it, Rache?"

My mouth dropped open, and I spun, shocked. I moved the line? How?

"Get her!" the vampire screamed, and the present rushed back.

"*Rhombus!*" I shouted, staggering under Ivy's weight as my circle sprang up heady and thick since I was standing right in the middle of the line. *I'd moved it? How? I had only tapped it.* But Jenks was right. I was standing in Al's flimsy line, and it was growing stronger, no longer dampened and drained by the ponds. I'd shifted it. I had moved it to me.

The vampires slid to a halt, one of them screaming as he touched the circle and a snap of energy struck him like lightning. We were in the line. Ivy was with me. I looked past the angry vampires, knowing the line had been behind them, knowing it couldn't be moved. But it had.

And somehow, I didn't care that I'd done the impossible.

"Sorry about the beating," I said as I melded my aura around Ivy's to shift her with me to the ever-after.

"Beating?" The vampire leaned closer, not knowing what had happened. "That wasn't a beating."

I tightened my hold on the line, feeling it start to take us. "No, the one your master is going to give you." *Thank you, Jenks. I will keep her alive.*

The man's eyes became round, fear shimmering his motion for the first time, making him somehow more captivating with the contrasting shadows of fear and power. We'd bested him, and he was going to be punished.

"No!" he shouted as I shifted my aura and the world moved around us. The red of sunset became the harsh red of the ever-after sun. His howling cry of denial evolved, peaked, and became the scream of the gritty wind. The image of his crooked fingers reaching for us dissolved, and I saw it mirrored in the broken rock surrounding us. The sound of Jenks's wings was gone. We were alone and the world was broken—just like me.

My heart thumped and I shifted Ivy's weight until she hissed in pain. I squinted at the distant, red-smeared horizon, then brought my eyes closer, sending it over the remains of the Hollows, already in shadow. The spires of the basilica rose over it all, the bastion carefully preserved where most everything was left to crumble. The space where my church would have been was nothing but rock and grass. My idea to walk to it vanished. Ivy was done.

"You can rest now," I whispered. "It's going to be okay." Heart aching, I eased her down against a boulder, and she gripped my arm, refusing to let go. My eyes shot to hers, and the utter blackness in them stitched all my fears into one smothering black piece. I couldn't kill her to prevent her undead existence. If Bis didn't find us in time . . . I . . . I didn't know.

My throat was tight as I sat beside her and pulled her head to rest against me. She could move no farther, and this was as good a place as any, better than some. Whatever happened, we would face it together, away from the filth she'd struggled her entire life to escape.

Chapter 3

The gritty wind had rubbed the skin between my short boot and pants leg raw. I huddled closer to Ivy, trying to get into the lee of the stone, but the boulder wasn't large enough. Ivy didn't move as my weight shifted, and I twisted my leg almost under myself to hide it. It would be asleep in about three minutes, but the respite from the wind was worth it.

Ivy's shallow breath came and went, her scent obvious under the choking burnt amber reek that permeated the ever-after. I listened for the clink of rock or sliding rubble that would mean a surface demon as I looked over the dry bed of the Ohio River and to the crumbled remains of the Hollows below. The sun was almost down, and the light was vanishing from the basilica's steeple inch by slow inch. Elsewhere the shadows were already thick. Behind me where Cincinnati would be, things moved, howled, and hooted as the sun vanished.

Surface demons. The large circle I'd put around us would keep them at bay, but they were gathering. No one, not even Newt, stayed still on the surface after dark—and we'd been noticed.

The horizon was still bright, but directly overhead the sky was that peculiar ever-after shade of reddish black that reminded me of old blood. A tiny sliver of moon would set just after the sun, and it glowed an eerie silver. It was the only pure thing, but so distant as to depress rather than uplift.

Experience told me the wind might abate with the sunset, a prospect I both welcomed and dreaded. It got cold when the sun went down, and Ivy was suffering, drifting in and out of consciousness. We were both thirsty, but she'd never said a word, happy that I was here with her.

Vampires suck, I thought, not for the first time as I rested my head against her shoulder and closed my eyes against the upwelling grief. How had we gotten here, playing a deadly game of waiting where Ivy's life hung in the chance between time and pixy wings?

Black traces of smut ran over the gold glow of my aura hazing my protection circle, arching like electricity between poles. The surface demons were gathering outside, not so patiently waiting for my circle to fall. One of them stood so his silhouette would be obvious against the darkening sky. He was taller than the rest, and the way he held his staff made me wonder if he was the same one Newt had tormented last summer in her calibration curse.

"You should go," Ivy whispered, and I started, not having realized she was awake.

I tugged her coat closer around her, careful not to hurt her. "No," I said simply, and she turned her black eyes to me, unblinking and catching the faint light from the sky.

"I'm going to die compromised," she said, as if she were talking about cutting her hair. "Without medical intervention, I'll wake hungry and incoherent. You should leave. I don't want to hurt you."

My thoughts flashed to the one time we'd tried to share blood. She'd mistakenly taken her feelings of love from it and had nearly killed me. I'd seen the beast of hunger in her before, and she hurt me because I would hurt her to stop it. "No," I whispered, and she sighed.

Silent, I watched the tall surface demon elegantly swing his staff to drive another from his rock, and the smaller demon scuttled sideways. "Bis will be awake soon," I said, but it sounded like a prayer even to me. Ivy wasn't shivering anymore, scaring me. "It will be okay. Jenks went to get Bis. He can jump you right to Trent's surgical suite. It won't be long now."

But I knew she heard the lie as well as I did.

"I'm sorry," Ivy slurred, and a lump filled my throat. "I know you wanted things to be different."

I stared ahead, trying not to blink. They weren't going to make it here in time. Forcing a smile, I adjusted her blood-stained coat. "They'll be here in a few minutes."

"I'm scared."

I eased closer, not liking the chill she had. "I'm not going anywhere." Damn it, I didn't have anything to help her. Nothing. She was going to die, and all I could do was hold her hand. The tears slipped down, cold in the chill wind. I didn't bother to wipe them away. Sensing the end, the surface demon with the staff moved, easing down from his rock to hunch just outside the barrier. He looked like an Aborigine, wise, gaunt, and cautious where his kin were simply thin and hungry.

"Promise me you won't be my scion. I want Nina to do it."

Surprised, I stilled my hand against her hair. I'd thought she'd been sleeping. "Nina?" My voice had been bitter, and I couldn't help but wonder if some of this was Nina's fault. The young woman liked risks, was clever, and was in love with Ivy—and so addicted to the sensations that her master vampire could pull through her that she'd do just about anything to escape him even as she crawled back for more. If Ivy was an undead, she could claim Nina as her scion. At least that way, someone Nina loved would be abusing her instead of a half-mad, dying undead. Felix was insane from the sun already, and his children would soon be orphaned, vulnerable in the extreme unless another undead claimed them. No one would contest it.

"I can't do that to you," she said, and heartache filled me when I realized she was crying. "I don't want you to spend the rest of your life trying to keep me from walking into the sun. If you can't end my second life, then promise me that you'll walk away. That you won't try to help me. Understand that I'm lost."

Throat tight, I held her close. "I promise," I lied. The wind gusted and died, making the surface demon's tattered clothes shift. "I shouldn't have brought you here."

"I'm feeling better," she said, her breath becoming shallower. "Really."

"That's good," I said, my hand moving against an unbloodied part of her hair. My throat was tight. She'd tried so hard to be the person she wanted to be. She'd given me friendship, kept me from pain, sacrificed her goals to keep me alive. And I couldn't stop this. I couldn't give her anything back. I could only hold her hand.

Maybe it's enough, I thought miserably. The smallest things meant the world to her.

But then the head surface demon jerked straight. In a breath, he turned and vanished, rocks clinking to mark his passage. Another was an instant behind him. Tense, I pulled myself up, tasting the gritty night wind. Something had scared them off.

"Bis?" I whispered, the sound of my voice echoing back off the flat, rocky earth. But the sun was still up.

"I should have known," a bitterly proud and slightly accented voice said. "How did you do it? Elf magic?"

My pulse thudded. Breath held, I sent my eyes searching. A soft glow blossomed, and I found him. Just outside my circle and between me and the ruins of Cincinnati, Al stood in a soft puddle of light. His velvet frock coat was elegant, and his stance sure. The glow leaking from the archaic lantern hardly made it past his silver-buckled shoes, but I knew it was all that could get through the thick layer of smut on his soul—and I knew it bothered him, for once he'd been able to light an amphitheater to bright noon.

"Do what?" I whispered, not moving—hardly breathing. Al had tried to kill me. Okay, he'd tried to kill me a couple of times, but this last time I think he'd really meant it.

"My line is no longer in that stinking puddle of water," he said, nose wrinkled. "I came to find out why before the sun set. It was you?" Lip curling, he dusted a nearby boulder with a silk cloth and set the lantern down. "Trying to curry favor makes you weak."

"Al . . . ," I breathed, and pain flashed across his face, ruddy from the setting sun.

"*Do* not call me that. My name is Gally."

"Al, please," I said again, carefully extricating myself from Ivy, hoping she would remain asleep. The heartache of his bitter abandonment hit me hard, my emotions already paper thin because of Ivy. I felt new tears threaten, hating them. "It was an accident. I was trying to . . ." My throat closed up. Ivy slumped behind me, but he wouldn't help, and that hurt even more.

"Oh-h-h-h," he said in mock distress. "Your sad, sad little friend is dying."

He could save her with a word, but I remained silent, standing before him, hating his bitter callousness. He was better than this. I'd seen it in unguarded moments.

"You smell like carrion," he said, nose wrinkled. Behind me Ivy stirred but didn't wake. "Butterflies like carrion." He paused as if in speculation. "No, that's elf. I can smell the stink from here, even over the putrid reek of burnt amber."

Nothing in him had changed. I knew it wouldn't have. My finding love with Trent hadn't hurt him this bad. I was a symptom, not the core of what brought this hatred out. The fear that he might kill Trent just to spite me was real, though, and I backed up a step.

"Silent?" He sniffed, looking disgusted. "Miracles *do* happen."

Why is he still here? I heard the scrabbling of claws and I glanced at Ivy. "I could use your help," I whispered, knowing he never would.

"Demons don't help," he said bitterly. "Demons torment. Can't you *tell* the difference?"

"That's not how I saw you."

Al eyed the thin bands of smut crawling over the surface of my circle, his lips twisting in jealousy. "You did at first."

"Because that's all you showed me," I shot back. I'd thought he'd understood me. I'd trusted him, and he'd turned his back on me because Trent was an elf, the same as the woman he'd once loved and hadn't been brave enough to fight for. "What did I ever do to you?"

Al uncrossed his arms and leaned forward, anger shining from his eyes. "*You hurt me!*" he yelled, giving in and punching my circle.

With an inward rush of energy, my circle fell into him with a pop.

Not expecting it, Al lurched, his hat falling off as he stumbled back and caught his balance. I stared at him in shock as his hat rolled to a stop almost at my feet. There'd been an instant of connection between us, an undeniable spark. He looked just as surprised, his eyes wide in disbelief.

"H-how?" I stammered, then renewed the circle as claws scraped in the ugly red light.

His lips parted to show his blocky teeth. Al put a careful finger to my bubble. The black crawled to him, and when he touched it, my circle fell.

"Stop that!" I shouted, heart pounding as I set it anew, but he was already across it and in here with me. Something was wrong. He'd broken my circle, and he hadn't even tried.

"That little bitch!" Al shouted, and Ivy stirred.

I gasped as Al strode to me, halting with an unexpected shortness when I raised my hand in threat. "She changed your soul, yes?" the demon demanded, fidgeting and so close I could smell the smoke from his fire on him. "Newt changed it so that puking elf goddess couldn't find you by your aura?"

I nodded, not breathing until he took three steps back. Okay, he was pissed, but he wasn't choking me.

"The crazy bitch changed your aura to mimic mine!"

My mouth dropped open. Horrified, I looked at my circle. Jenks had said my aura was different, but he never said it looked like Al's! But then, mine wasn't covered in as much smut and probably looked brighter. That's why the demon had been able to drop my circle with a touch. Great. Now I had nothing to block his spells with!

"She patterned your new aura after mine. The bitch!" Al wasn't looking at me, hands on his hips as he watched the surface demons throw rocks at the lantern he'd left behind until it shattered and Al's globe of light rolled in the dust. "That's how you were able to move my line."

"But why?" Had it been the crazy demon's perverted attempt at a joke? Or maybe she thought it would bring us back together. But then a new thought sparked through me. "If our auras are the same, then Treble can teach me how to jump the lines."

Al spun, coattails furling. Expression hard, he pointed a finger at me. "I share my soul resonance with *no one!*"

My skin was prickling. He was pulling on the line, gathering energy to him. Our eyes met, and he grimaced when he realized I could feel it. He took a breath, and frantic, I dove for cover. "Knock it off!" I shouted as a ball of black-tinted energy exploded against the ground, peppering me with bits of rock. "It wasn't my idea!" I added, scrabbling to my feet.

But he was already deep in a chant, a glowing mass of forced power stretching between his fingers. Crap on toast. He was using old battle magic. "Al!" I protested, then stiffened when Al's lantern light rolled into my circle and it fell with the sensation of sparkling tingles.

"Ivy," I whispered, turning to see a surface demon creeping to her.

"Son of a bitch," I muttered. Ignoring Al, I dove for her. Howling, I pulled a massive wave of energy from the line. Al lurched to get out of my way, his goat-slitted eyes wide when I threw the unfocused energy at the surface demon instead of him. The surface demon skittered back, scuttling away with an evil chatter.

"And don't come back!" I shouted, shaking as I reinstated the circle. "Or I'll give you more of the same!"

My skin prickled. I spun back to Al. But the demon wasn't even looking at me. Relieved, I turned to Ivy, seeing her eyes black and beautiful. "You okay?" I asked her, and she smiled.

"I'll miss watching you work," she said, more alive than I'd seen her in two hours.

Pissed, I pulled the hair out of my mouth and glared at Al. "You're a prick for standing there when I need help, you know that?" I said, then ducked as something flew over my head.

"Rachel!" Bis called, the cat-size gargoyle winging in a tight circle to drop down onto the rock Ivy was slumped against. "Jenks said you were going to walk to the church. Hold on. I'll be right back. Trent's at the wrong line."

Trent? I took an elated breath, but the little guy was gone. The sun had gone down unnoticed, and his pebbly black skin was hard to see against the night. I'd hardly recognized him before he'd vanished.

My knees were shaking, and I turned to find Al was gone. *Coward.* "*You* left *me!*" I shouted. "And I can love anyone I want!" I added, but there was no one there but Ivy to hear me.

"Son of a bastard," I muttered, hope a quick flash as a figure stepped from nothing in the soft sound of displaced air. There was the quick pulse of leather wings, and Bis was gone again.

"Nina!" I had expected Trent, but it was Nina, the athletic woman in her classy dress suit and black nylons bolting to Ivy with a vampiric quickness despite her high heels.

"You've been here for hours!" Nina exclaimed, black eyes angry as she fell to kneel before Ivy and covered her with her jacket. "Why didn't you give her any blood?"

It hurt when she said it like that. "She doesn't want any," I said, my relief overwhelming.

Ivy pushed weakly at Nina, eyes slipping shut. "No. I'm okay. Rachel did what I asked."

"She doesn't want blood. Stop forcing her," I said.

Hunched over Ivy, making her Hispanic elegance into a frightening shadow, Nina all but hissed, "This is what she is. What she wants means nothing when it comes to keeping her alive."

But if she quit striving for who she wanted to be, Ivy might as well be dead.

I took a breath to tell Nina to back off, startled when Bis jumped back into existence. The little gargoyle was on Trent's shoulder, and he immediately popped back across the lines, for Jenks, probably.

Thank you, God. Trent shuddered as the stink of burnt amber filled his lungs, and something flip-flopped in me. My eyes darted to where Al had last been to be sure he was gone. *Trent was here.* I didn't have to do this alone. He wouldn't let Ivy die. We'd be in time.

"Rachel." Trent's usual slacks and dress shirt looked out of place, sheened with red from the glow in the sky. His dress shoes slipped on the dust, and he caught his balance effortlessly. His pace crossing the dust was fast, and his eyes were quick. Sunset, even in the ever-after, was truly his best time. "Thank God you're all right. Jenks told me what happened. Is Ivy okay?"

"She's hurt bad," I said as he reached me. Nina was trying to get her pearl button undone from a silk cuff, but Ivy wouldn't let her, insistently promising she was okay. "She's got internal injuries and a concussion." I hesitated, surprised at the sudden lump in my throat. "I probably shouldn't have moved her, but I had to get to a line . . ."

"Why the hell am I always last!" Jenks complained, joining us in a bright flash of pixy dust. His bright sparkle sifted down like a temporary sunbeam over Ivy, making her smile and lift her hand to give him a place to land. She was whispering to Jenks, comforting him when it should have been the other way around.

Bis landed on the rock above them, clearly anxious to start jumping us out. His lion-tufted tail wrapped around his feet, looking both submissive and protective—dangerous even as the white tufts on his ears made him cute.

We had to go—but I nearly lost it when Trent pulled me close, smelling of green things and spice, his touch real and loving, reminding me of everything I wanted but was afraid to call my own. Suddenly I was fighting the urge to cry as fingers strong from pulling in unruly horses and tapping out keyboard commands gentled me closer. I'd had to keep it together, and now there was someone to help. Ivy was going to make it. She'd make it! *She had to.*

"You did the right thing," Trent whispered, the deep understanding in his voice bringing my defenses down. I'd never have expected it a year ago, but now . . . after seeing him lose everything to follow his heart, I could. I could accept his comfort, show my vulnerability—even if it might not last. The undeniable truth was, he was meant for better things than me. One day Ellasbeth would have him, and I'd be left with the memory of who he had wanted to be.

"Rachel?"

But I'd be damned if I didn't take what I could of the time we had. Catching my tears, I wiped my face, giving Trent a thankful smile as I pulled back and looked for Bis. The little gargoyle had his wings draped around him, looking like a devil himself. "Bis? Can you jump her to Trent's?"

"Not until I give her some blood!" Giving up on her sleeve, Nina used her little teeth to rip the button off. "She can't be moved yet," the living vampire said as she pushed her sleeve up. Her naturally dark skin showed the scars even in the dim light, and her panic at finding Ivy this close to death obvious. "I can't believe you let her sit here on the cold ground!"

"Easy," Trent said when I stiffened, and he lifted my chin, reading the strain I'd lived with for the last few hours, the fear. "Why is it harder when those we love are in danger than when it's just us?" he whispered, and I blinked fast. I wasn't going to cry, damn it. I wasn't!

"No," Ivy said again, her eyes black as she found Nina's. "No," she said more stridently, and Nina hunched over her, aching with her need to help her.

"Ivy, sweetheart, please. Let me make you stronger so we can move you."

Bis waited, wings half open, unsure and unwilling to do anything that might hurt Ivy. Trent, though, was grimacing. He knew it for the lie it was as well as I. Oh, I was sure blood would help stabilize her, but it would be an unredeemable step backward, back to where Nina, in all her expensive perfume and trendy clothes, was—back to where Ivy was striving to pull Nina from despite Nina's assurances that she wasn't allowing Felix into her mind anymore. The clever woman was too in control most days not to be.

"No." Ivy's voice was stronger. "No blood. Not like this. I'd rather die twice."

"But, Ivy . . . ," Nina protested, breaking off when Ivy fumbled to pull Nina's sleeve down and kissed her fingertips. Frustrated, Nina knelt over Ivy. "It doesn't have to be this hard!" she begged, but Ivy only smiled lovingly, feeling good that she'd resisted, that she'd won again for another day. "Why do you do this to yourself?"

I turned away as Ivy patted Nina's back, comforting her. In Ivy's eyes, Nina was the one who needed help.

"Bis. Go. My surgical staff is waiting," Trent said, and the gargoyle awkwardly hopped from the rock. "We need to get out of here before the surface demons find us."

"Too late." My eyes lifted to the surrounding rocks, glad they hadn't shown themselves yet as they evaluated the threat Nina and Trent might be.

"I thought so." Trent sighed, turning to watch my back. "I'm sorry about the church."

"My church? What's wrong with the church?"

Jenks's blur of wings shone against Trent's fair, almost transparent hair, glowing red as it picked up the red ever-after dust. "The pixy-piss vampires have overrun it," he almost snarled. "Stinking up the place and stomping everything like fairy maggots looking for spiders. They thought you might jump to the line in the garden, and they've got enough manpower there to make Piscary puke—if the putrid pus pile of vampire piss were still alive."

Ivy chuckled, the laugh choking off in a pained sound making Nina's eyes go black again. Bis carefully reached a clawed foot out to touch her, and when Bis and Ivy winked out of the ever-after, the tight knot around my gut finally began to ease.

Nina hunched over the space Ivy had been in for a moment before rising to lean dejectedly against the rock. Slowly her expression changed as she realized where she was. Tension wound through her, turning her from uneasy to a threatening shadow, smeared red with the remaining light in the sky. When I'd first met Nina, she'd been lively and eager for anything new. Now, after almost a year under a failing master's warped attention, she was still looking for thrills, but she was also twitchy and unpredictable—her jealousy of any attention I might show Ivy becoming increasingly violent. I didn't believe for a second that Felix was ignoring her, but every time I brought it up, Ivy got mad, wanting her happy lie rather than the inconvenient truth.

"Word got out you were finding undead souls," Trent said softly.

"That's not true!" I exclaimed, but he was nodding as if already knowing it.

"Even so, every undead vampire in the city now believes you can," he added. "Especially after what happened last July. In their minds, they don't understand why you haven't done it."

No wonder they were camped out at my church. "I don't think you *can* tie a soul to a mind when the body is dead," I said. "That's why souls leave after the first death." I was tired, but I didn't dare relax, and I strained for any clink of rock, any sliding of dust.

"They don't want to believe that." Trent cupped my elbow. Tingles spread from there to the small of my back where his other hand had gone to pull me closer to him. "We'll figure this out. I'm not entirely penniless, you know."

That he was there to help without my asking was a guilty relief, but I didn't know how he could. He'd lost almost everything in discrediting the truth of his illegal manufacture of genetic medicines and the very drug that the vampires depended upon for survival. It didn't sit well that both the vampires and the elves had gone after him because of me, and I bowed my head when I realized I'd done the same thing to Al, bankrupting the demon before he'd had enough and left. I was an albatross, pulling down those who meant the most to me. Maybe I should leave before I brought Trent down, too.

Trent's arms were around me, but I couldn't speak, unwilling to breathe in his clean scent and feel the whisper of wild magic that sometimes rose from him like aftershave. But the guilt of him losing almost everything because of me was a sharp, insistent thorn.

"He still cares for you," Trent said, and I looked up, confused. "Al, I mean. He was here, wasn't he?"

Oh. That. Grimacing, I turned in Trent's arms, feeling his grip ease as I looked at Al's line, knocked off its path by my desperate pull on it. Al's jealousy wasn't born of affection, but from a weird kinship and maybe a little envy. I'd stood against the demons to keep who I loved, and Al had worked within the shadows of their hatred for a thousand years for the same reason, ultimately failing. He was bitter. "How can you tell?"

Smiling, Trent tucked a gritty strand of hair behind my ear. "You have that 'I yelled at someone who deserves it' look. He'll come around."

Sour, I bobbed my head and pulled entirely from him. "That's what I'm afraid of."

Bis jumped back in, and Jenks yelped, taking to the air and dodging the winged gargoyle until the bigger flier snagged him. "I'm going last!" Jenks protested. "I'm going last with Rachel, you overgrown worm!" And then he was gone. It was just me, Nina, and Trent.

The scrape of wood on rock jerked my eyes to a surface demon, its gaunt shadow rising up black against the still-darkening horizon. *And the surface demons,* I thought, setting up a new protection circle and wondering if it was too late.

Behind me, a rock clinked. Slowly Trent moved to put his back to mine.

Yep, it was.

"Rachel?" The air tingled at the pull Trent drew on the ley line.

"There," I said, flicking a tiny pop of energy at a swiftly moving shadow. Shit, there were two of them in here. Heart pounding, I turned to the first. "*Detrudo!*" I shouted, and he pinwheeled back, crashing into the inside of my circle. His staff lay on the dirt, and I ran forward, scooping it up before running back to Trent.

Hissing, the larger surface demon jumped from rock to rock, looking alien as he circled us. Nina was white faced, pressed up against that rock, and I beckoned to her. Scared, she inched closer, but she was moving too slowly, and there was a demon creeping up behind her.

"Nina! Get down!" I shouted, leaping to get between them. Without thought, I pulled on the line, sending it from my chi to my hand, condensing it as it took fewer and fewer pathways until it finally reached my fingertips and ran down the staff. "*Dilatare!*" I shouted as it exploded from the end, the rod acting like a rifle bore to focus it into a finite point that slammed into the surface demon with a thunderous ache of release.

Nina screamed as she dropped, the burst of light showing surface demons doing cartwheels into the rocks and pebbles. The shock echoed back up my arm, and the staff fell from my senseless fingers. Shaking, I looked at it, wondering what the thing was made of.

And still . . . a hunched shadow found its feet, not giving up as it began to creep forward again, low to the ground and hissing.

Slow with surprise, Trent helped Nina up before coming to stand beside me. His jaw was set, and he looked fantastic, eyes bright and a glow of magic about his hands. Seeing him as he wanted to be, not the careful businessman he was so good at being and that others had forced on him, I felt my heart swell. I'd had something to do with it, and I was proud of him for finding the courage to be what he wanted. *Why can't it last?* I thought, aching.

"Together?" I said, and Trend nodded, eager to blend our strengths into one. I quashed the fear that Al was watching. If he'd known Trent was here, he'd be trying to kill him.

Pale, Nina scooped up the staff, holding it inexpertly. My hand found Trent's, and my breath came fast as his energies mixed with mine like shades of gold twining together. The rank taint of burnt amber eased, overpowered by the clean scent of grass and trees and sweet wine. My chin rose. This wasn't wrong. I didn't care that the demons and elves said it was. *This wasn't wrong!*

The surface demon hissed, his ragged clothes hanging like a tattered aura. He hunched, preparing to jump, and Trent and I gathered our power.

"Now!" I shouted, exhilarated as our joined energies wound together and struck the demon, sending it rolling back into the darkness. Trent's eyes were alight, his hair almost floating as he inhaled, bringing with it a wash of sparkles through me. My God, it was almost better than sex with the man.

Nina's scream iced through me, and we spun. The second demon was on her, the staff the only thing keeping it from her neck. Snarling, the twisted form fought to wrench the staff away. My heart thudded. I reached out, fingertips aching as I made a fist, unable to use my magic for fear of hitting her. "Nina, get him off you!" I shouted. "Let him have the stupid staff!"

But she couldn't let go, afraid. Her gasping breaths cut through the air, and I jumped when Trent blasted the first surface demon behind us. Jaw clenched, I ran for her, feeling as if my hand sank into the demon when I reached for it.

It screamed at my touch, and I stumbled back, ripping it off her as I fell on my butt.

It didn't do much good, as the age-twisted thing went right back at her.

"Oh God!" Nina cried, and then both surface demons were on her, smelling the blood.

Son of a bitch! I stared, flat on my ass, aghast and panicking as they covered her. I could *not* go back to Ivy and tell her Nina died in the ever-after.

"Trent!" I shouted, head hurting as I pulled in a massive amount of ever-after. This was going to end right now.

"Get! Off!" Nina thundered, and I froze, halfway to her, when first one, then the other surface demon flew through the red-tinted air to land in the rock-strewn shadows.

Someone touched me, and I jerked, pulling my energies back when I saw Trent. "Trent . . . ," I started, words failing when I realized he was dragging me away from Nina.

My eyes darted to her, and my mouth went dry.

I didn't think it was just Nina anymore.

She'd rolled to her feet, hands still holding that staff as she hunched into a ball and bared her teeth at the surface demons still shaking off the fall. Her eyes flicked to Trent and me, and I shuddered as I recognized the second presence smothering her psyche. It was Felix. And it had happened far too fast.

In a smooth, unhurried motion, Nina rose, her feet placed wide to bind the skirt about her knees. An almost visible charismatic power spilled from her in the new dark. Black eyes glinting, she whirled the staff in a dangerous arc, making it smack into the earth in a clear threat.

Anger tightened my resolve, and I pulled myself straight. Nina had lied. She had outright lied to Ivy, telling her she'd made a break from Felix. There was no way the master vampire would've known she was in danger if she hadn't already had him in her, balancing her emotions and soaking in her thoughts of sunlight and love.

From the darkness, a surface demon hissed.

Trent spun, his shoes grinding the grit as his magic tugged at my energies. The smaller demon was running at her, Nina screaming at it, egging it on, whirling the staff again as if it were a sword.

But it never reached her as that second, larger surface demon plowed into the first.

"Look out!" I cried, pulling Trent back as the demons rolled in the dirt, grappling, hissing and howling, clawing at the tatters of their clothes and gouging each other's eyes.

"Get back!" Trent said when, with a scream of outrage, the larger demon finally beat the first away. Standing between Nina and the darkness, the tall surface demon raised his hands to the sky, howling as if making a claim. His cry echoed against the flat spaces, dying away to leave the demon staring at us, his chest moving up and down as he panted, thin hands clenched.

Trent's fingers tightened in mine, his uninvoked charm hovering just under his skin. "Wait," I said as the surface demon spun to Nina. "No, wait!" I demanded as the silence was broken by the soft clicks of rock and the whisper of dead grass as the surrounding surface demons skulked back, leaving us. "I think he drove the rest off."

With a high-pitched whine, the tall surface demon fell prostrate before Nina, burbling and groaning, the tattered remnants of its aura smearing the dust to leave patterns. Nina/Felix stared, inching backward.

"What is it doing?" I whispered as the demon closed the new gap, his wizened arm black with age or disease, stretched out as if wanting to touch her but afraid to.

Bis popped in, winging up for altitude when he saw the surface demon writhing at her feet, gibbering like a monkey. I'd never seen anything like it, and the noise it made crawled up my spine like ice.

"Go away, you putrid thing," Nina threatened, her voice dropping into the lower ranges. It was Nina, but not, and I started when Bis landed on my shoulder to wrap his tail around my back and under my arm for balance. He wouldn't dare jump her out. Hell, I think he was scared to touch her, much less share mental space with her.

But the surface demon cowered like a beaten dog as it couldn't move forward, couldn't move back, snatching glances at Nina and the blood dripping from a scratch under her eye. I'd never been this close to one before and not been fighting for my life. It was almost as if I was looking at him through a fog. His features were indistinct, but gaunt, as if starved. The tattered remnants of his clothes gave no indication of color, and as soon as I looked away, I couldn't remember if his hair was long or short. Again, I was struck by the feeling that he was there, but not, and I shuddered at the memory of how it had felt when I had pulled it off her.

"I said, *go!*" Nina/Felix shouted, and the surface demon scuttled back at her swinging foot. Feet spread in a way no woman in a skirt ever would, Nina threw the staff after it to clatter into the dust.

My circle was long gone, but it didn't matter. The surface demons had left, even the ones at the outskirts. I exhaled, relieved. But another part of me was seething in anger. Felix had taken Nina over far too easily. The woman had been lying to Ivy, lying for *three whole months*. The worst part was, I think Ivy knew it.

"I ought to leave you here to rot," I said, talking to Felix, but if I did, Nina would be the one to suffer.

Nina stiffened, her lip curling to show tiny pointed canines. She wouldn't get the extended fangs until she died, which—if I got my way—would be tomorrow.

"Rachel," Bis whispered as his feet pinched my shoulder in worry. Trent, too, wanted to leave, but I couldn't. Not yet. The son of a bastard was playing Ivy for a fool.

"Get out of Nina," I said, shaking off Trent's hand and moving a step closer.

"I don't know what you're talking about," Nina said, foolishly trying to hide the fact that it really was Felix, but young women in dress suits do not tug their sleeves down in agitation.

"Do we have to do this right now?" Trent said, eyes on the darkening shadows.

"Yes," I said, coming another step closer. "Felix, get out of Nina. Get out and don't come back. Right now, or I'm telling Ivy."

The woman bared her teeth, dark eyes going darker. "Ivy? She doesn't matter!"

"Maybe not to you," I said shaking from the spent adrenaline. "But if Ivy knows, she might give up on Nina."

"That's fine with me." Nina's eyes narrowed, making the woman look dead already in the last of the light.

"Me too," I said, heartsick for Ivy even as I hated Felix. "But if she does, Nina is going to find the balls to kick you out for good."

Beside me, Trent made a sound of understanding. Nina's expression twisted up in a snarl, hearing the truth of it.

"Love is funny like that," I added.

Nina's expression darkened, anger bubbling up until she was as ugly as the monster seeing the world through her eyes, wallowing in Ivy's love as if it was his to have. My chin lifted, and seeing my determination, he suddenly left her.

Nina staggered, collapsing like a puppet whose strings had been cut.

Sobbing, she huddled on the ground, exhausted and hyped up on the hormones Felix had pulled into her blood system. She touched her face, shocked at the blood, and my heart just about broke for Ivy. God, I hated the master vampires.

He might be gone, but the flash of evil intent that had crossed her left me shaking.

He'd be back.

Chapter 4

The coffee smell coming from the wax-coated cup was nauseatingly familiar, and I held it listlessly as I sat in the chair I'd pulled into the carpeted hallway. The oil-like sheen on the surface caught the fluorescent lights, showing the shake in my hand. I'd managed a few fitful hours of sleep after Ivy had come out of surgery, and though the beds in Trent's surgical suites were comfortable, I'd been too worried to do more than doze. Besides, the smell of antiseptic and stainless steel kept waking me up.

Nina had crashed right in Ivy's room. She was in there still, the guilt that I'd found out her secret making her noticeably passive and pliant. It pissed me off that she'd been lying to Ivy all this time, but I think Ivy had known it, her belief that she didn't deserve anything good or lasting keeping her mouth shut and her eyes blind. I hoped that Bis and Jenks were doing better, the two of them having returned to the church to try to get the squatters out.

My breath came in with a harsh sound, and I listened to the voices echoing down from the third floor where Trent had his living quarters. I'd always wondered what took up Trent's second floor. Now I knew. Two well-outfitted hospital suites were tucked between the ground floor and the third story, but the surgery itself was downstairs, closer to his labs.

Hand trembling, I sipped the coffee. It had no taste. I'd just been in to check on Ivy. She'd been sleeping: clean and sanitized between ivory sheets. The angry red suture lines and orange antiseptic stains had been hidden behind a cotton nightgown, but I'd seen them before I'd lost it and cried from relief. Now I just felt numb.

And yet something sparked in me at the sound of Trent's footsteps on the unseen stairway, and I sat up straighter when Jonathan's voice twined melodiously with Trent's. I didn't like Jonathan, but I'd be willing to bet Trent's number two adviser had a singing voice that could make angels weep.

I managed a smile as the two of them came around a corner. Trent looked as confident as always with his hands in his pockets like a *GQ* model, his smile faltering as he took in my tired misery. His hair was free of the ever-after dust, and he was smooth shaven. I'd taken the time to shower, but I felt scruffy in a pair of jeans and clean sweater I'd left over here a few weeks ago. Jonathan wrinkling his nose at me in disapproval didn't help, and I checked to make sure all my hair was back in a scrunchy, the frizzy red tamed with a band of elastic instead of a charm.

A lot had changed since the allegations of drug running and illegal genetic research had been levied against Trent. It had been ages since I'd seen him in a full suit and coat; his business meetings had dropped to almost zero and the research campus had been closed. On the plus side, he was more relaxed, more apt to crack a dry joke, more often smelling like ozone or his stables than the boardroom. He was doing more on his own, needing me less and less for security.

My focus blurred, and I looked into the depths of my coffee as I imagined what it would be like to go to the mall with Trent, catch a bad movie and dinner. Maybe I should ask.

The one-sided conversation between Trent and Jonathan was clearly coming to an end, and their forward progress halted. Trent gestured elegantly as he made his point, and I stood, leaning heavily against the wall as I waited. I knew he got lonely, even with Quen and the girls keeping him occupied. Falling out of high society had been good for him and his family, if you ignored the increased number of death threats and his loss of income. Trains still ran, though, and farms still grew food. He wasn't destitute. Yet. Ellasbeth was still working on that in her effort to gain control of the girls, and through them, Trent.

Not going to happen, I vowed, but after having witnessed the four of them on a good day, the girls playing happily and both Trent and Ellasbeth as loving, though not united, parents, a questioning guilt slid through me. Quen, too, seemed to regard Trent's and my relationship as a phase tied to Trent's newest preoccupation with furthering his magical studies. It was irksome, but every time Trent spoke of Ellasbeth and the girls, it left me wondering why I was delaying the inevitable.

"Thank you, Jon," Trent finally said, touching the tall, almost gaunt man on the shoulder as he gave him a grateful smile. "That makes my day a hundred times easier."

Contenting himself with a short nod and a dry look at me, Jonathan turned and went back the way they'd come. I knew the girls loved the man, but I liked him just as much as he liked me. Which was to say not at all.

"Is Jonathan going gray?" I asked as Trent closed the few steps remaining between us.

"I haven't noticed. But that might be why he's cutting it so short lately." Trent stopped before me, worry creasing his features. "You could have slept upstairs. You did sleep, yes?"

"A few hours." I fell into step beside him when he gestured for us to continue down the hall past Ivy's door. "I'm not a spare room kind of girl."

"It wouldn't have been the spare room you would have been in," he said, matching our steps and giving me a sideways hug. "Life is too short for bad coffee," he said, taking my cup out of my hand and setting it on a table in the hall. "How's Ivy?"

"Okay, thanks to you," I said, not wanting to talk about it. My arm went around him and my head fell onto his shoulder. Trent eased us to a halt and I pulled him to me, resting my head against his chest. The light scent of his aftershave was a bare hint, just enough, and my jaw finally began to relax. I could hear the sound of his waterfall downstairs, past the great room, and my eyes closed.

The relief that he came to help me in the ever-after had almost hurt, even if he'd risked his life and an already failing reputation. There hadn't been a wisp of regret in him, and I shoved the coming heartache down because even though he meshed with my life perfectly, I did not mesh with his.

Trent had been moving toward bringing his people back from the brink of extinction his entire life. The path had been laid out. He'd willingly sacrificed for it—and he would again. The ugly truth was, I couldn't help him accomplish what he needed to do, I could only hinder it. That was why Jonathan disliked me and Quen disapproved even as he agreed that this was the happiest Trent had ever been despite his dwindling fortune and the lawsuits piling up like cordwood. Trent was all about duty—and I was dragging him down.

"You okay?" he asked, and I tilted my head and turned the hug into a brief kiss.

"Yes." I dropped my head again, needing to feel him next to me if only for this space of time. "I don't like leaving her in that ugly white bed."

"It's going to be okay." His voice rumbled up through me.

I didn't want to move. Ever. "I don't know what I would have done if she had—"

I couldn't even say it, and my eyes warmed as the tears spilled over.

His grip strengthened, and I blinked up at him, feeling like a wimp. "But she didn't," he said firmly, understanding in his eyes. "You did good. You got her out of immediate danger, and more important, gave her a place to meet her future with dignity and peace. If she had died, she would've done so with the person she loved most in the world with her. No one can ask for more than that, even kings."

How could he understand so clearly? "When you put it like that . . ." I sniffed back the tears, letting go of him to wipe my eyes. "Sorry," I said with a sad little laugh that really wasn't one. "I haven't gotten enough sleep. I don't know how you do it, getting up at daybreak like this. This is crazy."

He eased me back into motion, heading down the hallway. "Coffee helps. Have you found the staff break room? There's a mini kitchen. Frozen waffles . . . ," he coaxed.

I remembered the homemade ones Maggie had made for us. It had been the first meal we'd ever shared. "Sure, thanks." His hand lingered about my waist, and I dropped my head onto his shoulder again, breathing him in, gaining his strength. I wished things were different. Ivy was going to be okay, but that Trent had saved her life wasn't going to help his political standing. Keeping her alive was going to be even harder. Cormel didn't want money, he wanted his soul.

The click of Ivy's door brought me around, and we hesitated when Nina came out looking exhausted and rumpled—worse than the day after she and Ivy had come back from a five-day backpacking adventure in what was left of a Turn-ravaged Guam.

"Coffee?" the bedraggled woman rasped, her hair still dull with dust and hanging in strands about her creased, worried face. The scratch the surface demon had given her was red rimmed and swollen, looking worse than it probably was.

"And waffles." Trent gestured for her to join us. "Right this way."

Relief flickered across her face. "Thank you," she whispered, shuffling forward in her torn nylons. She hadn't even taken the time for a shower, and was still in the same clothes she'd had on in the ever-after. The faint scent of burnt amber lingered even now. Her clothes were a monochromatic orange from the dust, and guilt kept her head down. That was fine with me.

"We keep this stocked for the medical staff," Trent was saying as we found the comfortable, if somewhat sterile, break room, open to the hallway. "I'm assuming that you'd rather eat here than upstairs?"

I nodded as I took in the clean counters, homey tables, and fresh flowers in vases still beaded up with condensation. Four monitors hung from the ceiling, three dark and one lit with Ivy's vitals. An entire wall was taken up with one of those floor-to-ceiling vid screens showing a deck and a garden, and I collapsed at a table, thankful for the small comfort.

Nina took a chair across from me, easing down with a little more grace and a cautious glance. There were dirty dishes in the sink from the doctor and nurse on call. I'd put them in the dishwasher later.

I loved watching a man cook, even if it was only toast, and I collapsed my head onto the cradle my arms made on the table, exhausted, as Trent took waffles out of the tiny freezer in the top of the fridge. "If you want to come upstairs, I can make them from scratch," he said as the door sealed with a sucking sound. "The girls are at the stables with Quen. I thought it better to keep them occupied out of the, ah, house."

"Frozen is good." I smiled as he ripped the box open, letting my head hit the table as the toaster went down. I liked the girls, but Lucy, especially, was inquisitive to the point of exhaustion.

"I never thought I'd ever eat anything out of a box from the freezer," Trent said, his voice distant in thought, "but the girls want everything *now*, and frankly, these aren't half bad."

My breath was coming back stale from the table. It sounded as if he was in the fridge again, and curious, I pulled my head up as he set butter and cold maple syrup on the counter. Nina had fallen asleep in the chair, her head lolling back and her breath even.

I had said I wasn't going to tell Ivy, but I couldn't ignore the fact that Felix had been dipping into her Nina as if she were his personal thirty-one-flavor shop. My anger was a slow, steady burn for the lie she was living. Ivy was trying to *help* her, damn it. Ivy *loved* her. And Nina wasn't even trying.

A muffled thump echoed through the walls, and Nina snorted awake. For an instant, we froze. Alarm slid through me at Nina's expression. She was scared. It wasn't fear for Ivy, it was fear for herself. *What have you done, tricky little vampire?*

My eyes went to Ivy's monitor: elevated pulse. Panic dribbled through my thoughts, and I stood.

"Rachel?" Nina quavered.

Fear slammed into me, and I ran.

"Jonathan!" Trent shouted, but I was already sliding to a halt at Ivy's door. Heart pounding, I yanked it open. Fear bubbled up, acidic and paralyzing. Ivy was on the bed struggling with a man all in white.

Jaw clenched, I silently grabbed his arm and flung him off her. His mask pulled free and he crashed into a bank of low cupboards, arms and legs askew. Ivy's face was creased in pain. Her eyes met mine as she held her middle and slid off the bed and out of the way.

The man's black shoulder-length hair stood out strongly against the white of his suit, and the annoyed expression on his young face ticked me off. "Who let you in?" I said, and he smirked as he got to his feet.

Living-vampire fast, he made a dart for the door. I jumped for him, careful not to hold him long enough for him to turn and get a grip. It had been years since I'd sparred with Ivy, but hard-won lessons die even harder.

My foot jabbed out to hit the back of his knee. He went down, pissed when he caught himself with his palms on the floor. Tossing the hair from his eyes, he shook his head, the promise of hurt in his eyes.

He came at me fast and hard. I blocked, the sudden pain in my arm vanishing when his second strike made it go numb. I retreated, pulling the side bar from the bed and slamming it into his next swing. He hissed in pain, and I spun with it in the bare moment he hesitated. It hit him square across the temple, and he reeled backward. My heart pounded as he staggered, hand to his head. I still had my magic, and as he shook the stars from his sight, I pulled the line to me.

"Ivy!" Nina shrieked from the open door.

"No!" I cried, reaching out when the attacker dove for her instead.

Trent was a dark blur, yanking Nina into the hall and out of danger. *"Celieano!"* he shouted, hand outstretched, and I felt a drop in the ley line. It was a simple circle, and Ivy's attacker ran right into it. He staggered back into the room, his nose broken and bleeding, unable to see through the blood and tears.

I dropped the bed bar. Hands in fists, I spun for momentum and sent my foot into his exposed middle. His air huffed out, and he hit the floor and slid into the built-in wardrobe.

Panting, I looked at Trent. We had to take the vamp alive, or we'd never find out who'd sent him.

The vampire, though, was finding his feet.

"Detrudo!" I exclaimed, shoving a wad of energy through my palms. It blew him back onto the bed and sent Trent stumbling into the wall. Ivy rose, shaking and pale. The vampire's eyes widened upon seeing the needle in her fist.

"Right," he said, and with no warning, he lunged at Trent, jabbing out in a rabbit punch at the last moment. Trent shifted to avoid it, falling when the vampire hooked his foot behind Trent's and pulled. Trent went down, silent even as he pushed back up.

The damage, though, had been done, and the vampire dove for the hall and his freedom.

"Get him!" I shouted as I lurched past the bed. Trent was three steps faster. My breath came in with a gasp at a sudden pull on the line. Trent stopped short, and I ran into him.

"Down!" he shouted, shoving me.

We hit the hallway's floor in a tangle. Trent's elbow slammed into my gut even as my shoulder took most of the fall. Wiggling, I tried to shove him off, only to have him grip me tighter. I found out why when a heat-stealing wave of force pulsed over us, and was drawn back, tingling like frost in my nose. It was Jonathan, and only now did Trent slide off me.

I propped myself up on an elbow and tossed the hair from my eyes. The vampire was clenched in a ball, either in pain or from cold. Jonathan's aura danced over him like little waves of electricity. Jonathan stood in an aggressive hunch, the charm still dripping from his stiff fingers.

Crap on toast, he'd done it again. I was sure the vampire was alive despite it looking otherwise; Jonathan enjoyed wringing information from people more than he should. I had a pretty good idea of how word got out where Ivy was, but confirmation would be nice.

"Oh God, Ivy!" Nina exclaimed, and she passed me in a wave of burnt amber and vampire incense.

I pulled my knees together and wiped my mouth. "Thanks, Jonathan," I said, reaching up for Trent's hand. He yanked me up, and I stood, catching my balance against a brief wave of vertigo. Felix might not be actively in Nina, but a master that skilled could lay low, take in the world without even being recognized. Damn it all to hell and back. Like it or not, Nina was a threat to Ivy's life. I couldn't let Ivy pretend anymore.

Jonathan lifted his eyes from the contorted vampire on the floor and tugged his shirt straight. "Why is it every time the Sa'han is with you, someone tries to kill him?"

"He wasn't trying to kill Trent, he was trying to kill Ivy." *Ivy.* Anger bubbled up as I turned to Ivy's room. Pissed, I strode in. Nina was there, crying as she tried to get Ivy into bed.

"I'm okay. Nina, I'm okay!" Ivy protested as she slid into the rocking chair instead. She wasn't okay. She'd sat there because it was too hard to make it to the bed.

Shaking, I grabbed Nina's shoulder and spun her up and away from

Ivy. "Get away from her!" I shouted as Nina fell back against the bed, her shock shifting to a black-eyed hatred.

"Rachel, no!" Ivy protested, but I pushed her hand off me, not caring that both vampires' eyes had gone pupil black.

"This is her fault!" I exclaimed, my hand shaking as I pointed at Nina. "She let him in!"

"I did not!"

She wasn't a very convincing liar, especially when she scooted across the bed to get closer to the door and away from me. "How else would Cormel know where we were?" I demanded, and Trent took her shoulders. If it was to keep her unmoving or to keep me from smacking her, I didn't know.

"I wouldn't help Cormel!" Nina objected, eyes darting. "I've not even told my sister where I am!"

But if Felix was as good as I thought, she'd never know he was there. I hadn't in the ever-after.

Ivy's hand was cold on my arm, her fingers making a tingling path. "You don't have to," I said softly, and Nina's face went ashen. "Tell her. Tell Ivy, or I'm going to."

"I . . . I . . . ," Nina stammered, pulling away from Trent to stand alone. She wanted to be caught in the lie. She wanted it to end. She could be innocent—but I didn't trust her.

"Rachel . . ." Ivy's voice held heartache. It ticked me off. Ivy knew she wasn't clean.

"Tell her how you've been letting Felix in," I said, and Nina dropped her head, her beauty marred by fear. "As long as he stays quiet, you've been letting him see the sun and remember what it's like to love someone."

Her head snapped up. "Stop it!" she protested, but she wasn't nearly angry enough.

"You don't have enough control," I said, carefully gauging her mood as I goaded her. "He's been doing it for you! Ivy's been risking her life, everything, to help you get out from under him, and you're sneaking behind her back, pretending you're clean, but you're nothing but a filthy vampire doll cutting lines in your own arm to suck on!"

Nina stiffened. "How dare you!" she exclaimed, eyes black.

I rocked back to put distance between us. "How dare I?" I echoed. "If he wasn't in you now, you'd be at my throat. You don't have enough control on your own—not with all the power he's dumped into you. Little girl whining about how hard it is. You need to decide if you love her or him, and make your choice. Frankly, I don't care about you, but I *will not* let you drag Ivy back down into that slime. He's in you now, isn't he? Isn't he!"

Nina's eyes widened, but it wasn't me she was afraid of. Trent wisely eased back as Nina shuddered, a violent spasm taking her. I swallowed hard, tensing when her trembling ceased. I could hear people whispering nervously in the hall, and I prayed they didn't come in.

For three seconds, Nina didn't move, head bowed and hands clenched. Slowly, as if settling into her skin, she drew herself up into a confident stance and cold mien. When her eyes met mine, it wasn't Nina anymore. I was starting to wonder if it ever had been.

Behind me, Ivy groaned, heartbroken.

"You're becoming a pain in my ass," Nina said, but though the voice was the same, the cadence was not. It was Felix: devious, soulless, politically powerful, and yet still Cormel's ward. Cincinnati's master vampire was required by law to chaperone him until old age and madness picked away the last of him and he walked into the sun. It looked close now. Nina would go with him. I could see no other path, and my heart ached for Ivy. She had wanted to help her so badly, saw her own redemption in saving Nina. That's what hurt the most.

I backed down with a show of deference if only to save my skin. This was all I had wanted: Ivy to see so she wouldn't blind herself any longer. "Get Ivy out of here. I want to talk to Felix alone," I said, and Ivy protested as Trent helped her out. Nina shifted her gaze to Ivy as they passed, and I stiffened.

"Leave the door open," I said softly, and Nina snorted, the sound both scornful and masculine. I didn't care if Felix knew I was scared. I was, and I didn't want that door shut. I could hear doctors, and my worry for Ivy eased. She'd be okay. Me, however . . .

Finding a firmer stance, Nina tugged the sleeves of her trendy, soiled jacket as if it was a business suit. Glancing down, she frowned at the state of her untidiness, a soft *tsk-tsk* escaping her as Felix noticed the hole in her nylons and that she was pretty much barefoot and filthy.

"Tell Cormel that I'm working on how to fix souls to the undead and to back off," I said, wishing I had that bed bar in easy reach.

"I'm not your messenger boy." She was looking at Ivy's chart, again shaking her head. "We are so fragile." Her head came up, and a cold wash went through me, making her eyes dilate. "And yet we cling to life long past what should be possible."

I took a breath and held it. "If Ivy dies, I'll never give you what you want. You can tell Cormel that, too."

Nina twitched, and I wondered if Nina was trying to regain control. "If we don't get what we want, Ivy dies. If we still don't get what we want, you die. Give us what we want, and everyone lives. Why do you hesitate?"

Again, she twitched, her knees almost buckling. Hope, unexpected and almost painful, pulled through me. *Nina?* Ivy had never given up on Nina. Maybe I shouldn't either.

"It's impossible," I said, wondering. "It can't be done."

Nina put a hand on the dresser, her head bowing in pain, and my pulse thundered. "That's . . . what you're good at," Felix said through her. "Doing the impossible. Blind. The living are so blind. Why do you fight this? That you love her burns like the sun itself. You could have everything, and yet you still fear it?"

My breath came in fast, and I held it. Felix was talking about Ivy. Yes, I loved Ivy, but I couldn't give her what she craved, deserved. The one time I'd tried, it almost killed me. *But that's not why I'd said no.* "I'm not afraid," I said, my resolve faltering when even the last rims of brown were lost behind the utter blackness of her eyes. The air seemed to haze, and my skin tingled from the pheromones he was pulling from her, sophisticated and far beyond her living-vampire abilities.

"You're afraid to love," she said, pushing back from the dresser and tossing her hair from her eyes. Felix was regaining control, and a thread of doubt pulled through me. "Ivy still waits for you. Nina knows it. She knows Ivy loves you best. *That's* why I will win."

"I'm not afraid to love someone," I whispered, but the pain in my gut said he might be right. I'd said no to Ivy, not because she'd almost killed me, but because I was afraid that by saying yes, I'd lose my own dreams, my own self. *Would I lose them now if I stayed with Trent?*

"Shut up," I whispered as Nina began to laugh. "I said shut up!" I shouted, and her chortling glee took on a hysterical sound before it eased into a happy *mmm* of sound. My jaw clenched. I didn't care that he was feeding off my anger, relishing it. I wasn't afraid to love someone. I wasn't! I'd loved Kisten. *And he had died.*

"Nina is too weak," she said, running an ever-after-stained finger across Nina's neck in a motion of seduction. "Her love isn't strong enough to best me. Leave me alone."

"Perhaps," I said, chin high. "But Ivy's is strong enough for both of them."

Nina eyes flicked to mine, her expression suddenly blank.

Seeing it, I felt my resolve strengthen. *Ivy. It had always been about Ivy.* "Nina," I said suddenly. "You love her. Don't let her think she doesn't deserve you! She needs you, Nina, more than you need her! More than she needs me. You know that!"

"You stupid little . . . bitch . . . ," Nina choked out, suddenly wavering. She stiffened, stumbling back. "No. You're mine. You're mine!" Nina cried, a hand reaching as her eyes went wide. A silent scream came from her, mouth open as she gasped, and then her eyes rolled to the back of her head. I sprang forward to catch her as she went limp, her sudden weight almost bringing us both down.

"Trent!" I shouted, managing to at least break our fall. Maybe Ivy was right. Love had given Nina the strength when nothing else had.

"Oh God!" Nina sobbed, her voice high and panicked as she huddled on the floor beside the bed. "Someone help . . . me. Someone *help me!*"

"I've got you, Nina," I said, wrapping my arms around the panicked woman as Trent skidded in. He must have been just outside the door, and my face flamed at what he'd overheard. "Ivy is going to be so proud of you."

Trent reached to help us up. "Ivy's okay. What happened?"

My foot was twisted, and I wedged it out from under me. "Nina kicked him out," I said, truly proud of her as Trent helped me get her up. I'd call her a wimp, but what she'd done was incredible. "Upsy-daisy. That a girl!"

Her wailing suddenly ceased, and Trent's hands sprang away as her head lifted, a snarl on her face. "I hate you!" she screamed, jerking from me. "I hate you! You don't know anything! Leave me alone! Ivy is mine. I hate you!"

Yep, Felix was gone. She was on her own now, and out of control.

"Watch it!" Trent warned, and I danced back when she swung at me, her fingers crooked into claws. But it was only Nina, and I ducked under her arm, pinning her arms to her sides and tilting my head when she flung her head back to hit me. Ivy was at the door, eyes holding love and pride, slumped in one of the doctor's arms. I waved her back, but she knew better than to come in yet.

"That's better," I soothed, trying to keep Nina facing me. The hormones that Felix had been turning on in her brain were running like a bad drug trip. He'd been keeping her calm and under control before, and now she was alone, tossed into the deep end of the pool with no life preserver. "Slow breaths. Calm down. Ivy's right next door," I lied.

"Let me go!" She began to twist, going limp and then wildly kicking out. "I *hate* you! Where's Ivy? You can't keep her from me! I'll fucking kill you! I'll kill you both!"

"My God." Trent glanced at Ivy as he jerked out of reach of Nina's swinging foot. Tears spilled from Ivy, and she held a hand to her mouth. "Is this normal?"

Ivy nodded, still a silent witness. I'd seen this before. Actually, I'd seen worse. "Breathe, Nina," I said, tossing my head to indicate the drugs on the side table. "No one is attacking you."

"*Ivy!*" Nina raged, her voice raw.

"It's going to be okay," I soothed as Nina stopped fighting and began to sob. "Ivy loves you. She needs you. She doesn't need me anymore. I'm not going to keep you apart. She's resting. You can see her in a minute." My face flamed. How much had Trent heard? All of it?

At the door, Ivy closed her eyes, aching. The doctor holding her upright finally stopped trying to get her to leave, and the professional woman watched with sympathy as Trent readied a syringe. I made my hold on Nina even looser as he took her arm. Those veins of hers were popping up like mole trails, and Nina watched through the tears as he angled the needle to her inner elbow. As out-of-control vampires went, this wasn't half bad. Guilt had tempered her.

Snuffling, she said, "I didn't mean to let him stay. I thought I had this. I wouldn't hurt Ivy for anything. Ow! I love her. What did you give me?"

The spent adrenaline and lack of sleep were making me shake. "I know you do," I said as Trent silently backed up to dispose of the empty syringe. "It's going to be okay now. Take a deep breath. You want to lie down?"

She didn't answer, the drug already hitting her. But she was looking at the pillow, so I eased her down, pulling her feet up as if she were a child and drawing a blanket over her. Eyes already closed, she clutched Ivy's pillow, breath fast as she fell into a medically induced sleep.

Slowly and in pain, Ivy shuffled in with the help of that doctor. Worried, I stood over Nina as Trent moved the cushy chair right to the bedside. No one said anything as Ivy sank down, and I put a hand on her shoulder. The doctor fussed about getting her back into a proper bed until I gave her a dark look, and she finally left in a professional huff, leaving the door open behind her.

"Wow," Trent said, and I took a long, slow breath. "I'm totally out of my depth here."

"She'll be fine now," Ivy whispered, and Nina whimpered as Ivy intertwined her long fingers in Nina's broken-nail, red-dust-smeared perfection. "Everything will be fine. The hard part is over." Tears spilled from her, and she kissed the top of Nina's hand. "I'm so proud of you."

Hard part over? I wasn't so sure.

It smelled of frightened vampire and the ever-after, and my neck was starting to tingle. *I'm not afraid to love someone, am I?* I turned away, and Trent caught my elbow.

"Rachel, I can kill the vampire virus, but I don't know how to treat someone coming off a master high."

"Soon as Ivy's stable, we're leaving," I said, not really answering his concern. "It's not safe here."

Ivy nodded, and deciding they were okay for now, I went into the hall. I didn't think anywhere was safe anymore. I didn't know what to do, and frustration tempered with fatigue rose up, swamping me.

Turning from the closed door, Trent ran a hand over his chin in thought. "Let me ask around," he said softly as we started down the hallway. "See who owes me a favor."

But no one owed Trent Kalamack favors anymore. Again, sort of my fault.

My guilt thickened, and sensing it, Trent looped his arm in mine, slowing our pace. "Rachel, you aren't afraid to love. He was saying anything he could think of to put you on edge."

Crap. Embarrassed, I tried to quicken my steps back to the kitchen and hopefully some coffee. "I think that's the last we're going to see of Felix for a while," I said with forced cheerfulness, desperately trying to change the subject.

Beside me, Trent sighed in acceptance. "I hope so. But really, Rachel, what are the chances? Twice in one night."

My pace slowed, and I nodded at the doctor as she passed us in the hall on her way back to Ivy and Nina. "The chances were never good," I admitted. "But it feels better now. Nina kicked him out. The longer Felix sulks, the more stable she will be when he tries again." Because he would try again.

But thin as it was, it was still hope, and my heart ached for Ivy as we found the kitchen. Tired, I sank back down in my chair, glancing at the newly lit monitor before letting my focus blur and my head hit the table.

Trent sighed, and I heard him take the cold waffles out of the toaster. "You ever see anything like that before? With the surface demons?"

"You mean that one fought the others off?" I lifted my head. "Only when they wanted to eat me by themselves."

"That's not what he was doing, though." Trent's lips twisted as he looked at the waffles. "These are awful. I'm making you some from scratch."

"I'm not hungry," I said, and he turned from throwing them away, his eyes pinched.

"Coffee?" he asked, and I nodded just so he'd lose that sad look. His reach for a mug hesitated at the sound of men in the hall, but it was just Quen setting up additional security. A faint smile twisted my lips. I imagine a white-clad vampire sneaking into the common rooms had put Trent's head of security in a tizzy. Thank God Jonathan had been there.

I blinked. *Thank God Jonathan had been there? Never thought I'd think that.*

Trent set three full mugs on the table, and I pulled the nearest closer, a flutter going through me as I felt as if I was a part of something—Trent expected Quen to join us, and I was a natural part of the conversation—even if Quen acted as if he was humoring us.

"What strikes me as the oddest is that the demon who defended Nina was the same one who tried to chew her face off not thirty seconds earlier," Trent said, gaze unfocused as he held his coffee and breathed in the steam. "One moment she's breakfast, and the next she's a god."

I tapped the mug with a finger, not liking the red dust under the nail. "I think I'd do a little groveling myself if I'd never seen a master vampire before."

"True." Trent bobbed his head. "But the rest didn't seem to care."

"You noticed that, too?" I took a sip, startled by the rich warmth, but my thoughts were on Ivy. She was going to be okay, but the panic of sitting with her on the cold ever-after ground, holding her hand as she died, was just under my skin. I thanked God I hadn't had to make that choice of following her desires and killing her again before she rose as an undead.

Oblivious to my thoughts, or more probable, aware and trying to distract me, Trent said, "I've never seen a surface demon with a weapon before. Apart from rocks."

"I have," I said, turning my mug in a revolving circle. "Newt used a surface demon as a marker in a time and space calibration curse. It had a sword. That's how she knows which one it is and how long it lived."

Kisten, I thought, sighing. Kisten had died twice within moments of his first death. I'd been there, but thankfully I hadn't had to make that choice.

I had held Kisten's hand and he had died happy, telling me that God had kept his soul for him. *Stop it, Rachel,* I thought miserably, wiping a tear away before it could brim as I recalled Kisten's laughing smile. God! My emotions were all over the map. I had loved Kisten. I *could* love someone without fear. Felix was wrong.

Trent's eyes were pinched, and he fidgeted. "Calibration curse?" he asked, desperate to get my mind on something else.

Smiling faintly, I reached out and gave his hand a squeeze. "Ask me some other time," I said, remembering the pain of the surface demon living its entire existence in the span of three heartbeats. I was starting to think that surface demons weren't much more than ghosts, living, breathing ghosts who lusted after the living like the undead only without the shackles that a consciousness imparted. How could anything survive five thousand years without magic?

Clearly relieved, Trent scooted his chair closer to mine. "You think it's the same one? Newt's, I mean?"

Tired, I shook my head. "Newt's had a sword. This one used a staff." Felix used a staff, too. Maybe that was why the surface demon liked him. But the question remained, why had it done a one-eighty and turned into a groveling love puppy? "You know, it was almost as if the surface demon knew Felix already," I said slowly. "And didn't recognize him at first."

I stopped, heart pounding as I looked up. It hadn't been Felix in the ever-after in the beginning. It had been Nina. The surface demon hadn't groveled in front of Nina, it had groveled in front of Felix. Like it knew him. Which would be really hard since the undead never go into the ever-after.

Lips parted, I stared at Trent, a new idea sifting down through my brain. "I think I know where vampire souls go when they die," I whispered, seeing Trent's face as white as mine felt.

"The ever-after," we said in unison.

Chapter 5

I'm *trying* to *help* you," I said, phone pressed to my ear as I sat in Trent's car, parked across from the church. "But I need to get into my church, and I need you to take the hit off Ivy. I've found your souls, so back off!" *Calm, composed, relaxed.* The litany was no help. Coming home to find my church full of vampires was harassment, pure and simple. It had scared the crap out of me, too, but that had probably been Cormel's intent.

"You've had over a year to work on this." Cormel's New York accent fell flat, when I usually found it charming. "You expect me to believe that today, only when I threaten you, that you have a viable plan. Just like that?"

Nervous, I picked at the window stripping until Trent made a pained sound. Beyond the tinted glass of his sports car, my church looked as if it had been hosting an all-night Brimstone party with toilet paper in the trees and what I hoped were just tomatoes smeared on the stained-glass windows. Bis was a lumpy shadow on a hard-to-reach eave, and I hoped he was okay.

"How often do the undead go into the ever-after?" I asked, and he rumbled a soft agreement. "Even *I* wouldn't have figured out the connection between surface demons and vampires if you hadn't chased me there with Ivy. Nina showing up with Felix in her unconscious was the trigger."

Cormel was silent, probably unwilling to acknowledge why Felix had suddenly become raging and erratic—freaking out over having been tossed out on his ear by Nina—and with that doubt resonating in him, I put my last card on the table, shaking and glad we had thirty miles and probably two stories of dirt between us.

"Cormel," I said softly. "I'm not making this up. Surface demons do not defend people, they tear them to shreds. That surface demon was Felix's soul. It recognized Felix's consciousness lurking in Nina. I can do this, I just need time."

"Felix has not been dipping into Nina's mind. He has promised me. He's working again. A productive member of society."

"Seriously?" Disgusted, I slumped to put my knees up against the dash, then took them down when Trent cleared his throat. "Look. I need time to prep the charms to capture it and then affix it to Felix. If it works, then we can all go back to normal. If it doesn't, I'll tweak it until it does, but I can't do anything if I'm protecting Ivy. I'm doing what you want, but if you kill her, this all goes away."

I glanced at Trent, drawn by his fingers slowly tapping in concern, not all of it for me and Ivy. It was his opinion that giving the undead a soul might not have the effect the vampires were looking for. Frankly, I didn't care. I just wanted them to leave Ivy and me alone.

"Excuse me," Cormel said. "I'll be right with you."

"Cormel?" I called, but he was gone. The line was still active, and I put my phone on speaker so we both could enjoy the happy, light sounds of dulcimers that Cormel had on his hold button. *What a crock.*

Peeved, I set the phone on the dash and unkinked my fingers. Someone was looking at me from the belfry and drew back when our eyes met. I was glad Nina and Ivy were still at Trent's. Ivy had a hard enough time when a repairman came over. Seeing this invasion would jerk her instincts to the breaking point.

"Thank you for waiting with me," I said to Trent as I pulled my shoulder bag onto my lap. It was dusty from the ever-after and smelly, and it didn't have much in it anymore.

"I wasn't about to drop you off and leave. I'm looking to chip some vampire fang before I go." His smile became charming. "It's much more satisfying than my political boardroom shuffle."

"I'm hoping it doesn't come down to that." Worried, I rubbed the tension from my fingers. Sure, I could drive them away with a charm, but Jenks and Belle were in there.

The dulcimers cut off and I scrambled for the phone. "One hour," Cormel said tightly.

"An hour!" I exclaimed, not bothering to take him off speaker. "Mr. Cormel, I have to wait until sunset before the surface demons even come out! I cannot, nor will I, go any further with this if I have to guard Ivy against your assassins."

My heart pounded, and Trent and I waited, breath held.

"Ivy is safe until sunrise," Cormel said. "I'm leaving a chaperone."

"No chaperone," I countered. Maybe that was asking a lot, but the last thing I wanted was an amorous vampire lurking in the corner, filling the air with sexy pheromones and innuendo.

"Then you have until midnight." Cormel waited as I silently protested, but when I kept my mouth shut, he ended the conversation by hanging up. Midnight. I had until midnight to show real progress, or it would all start up again.

Exhaling, I ended the call. Trent took the keys out of the ignition; we could walk from here. "You think I should have gone with the chaperone and the extra time?"

"No."

"Me either. Good thing I work well under a deadline." Feeling sour, I reached for the door. Getting them to leave was going to be a treat, but with Cormel's word, I had the clout.

"That was fast," Trent said, and my head snapped up.

Surprised, I got out as the church's double door banged open and a steady stream of thin bodies staggered to their cars and vans. There were a lot, and I hoped Jenks was okay. Our phone conversation this morning hadn't instilled much confidence.

Motions graceful with a slow deliberation, Trent got out, his book on how to put souls in baby bottles tucked under an arm. It was an elven charm, so in theory I shouldn't have much trouble with it.

A flash of guilt took me, and I looked back at the church—anywhere but at that book.

Doors thumped and engines raced. My neighbors watched behind twitching curtains. It was obvious by their unkempt state and untied shoes that my visitors weren't assassins per se, but they could still kill someone— and with Cormel running the city, there'd be no inquiry, no notice. Ivy would be a warning, or worse.

"Hey!" I shouted as a woman with a bad case of bed hair shuffled to the last car. "That's *my* coat!"

Head hanging, the woman stopped right in the middle of the street, took off my red jacket, and dropped it with a tired indifference. The rest of them were complaining and wanting her to hurry up, and not bothering to open the door to the car, she dove in headfirst through a back window. The car accelerated in a noisy squeal of tires.

I slammed Trent's door, stalking to my jacket. It reeked of vampire, even worse of her perfume scented heavily with pine. I'd have to air it out for weeks, maybe send it to the cleaners. Vampire incense stuck to leather worse than burnt amber in my hair.

Trent scuffed to a halt beside me, one hand in a pocket, the other holding that book. "I think I just turned a profit on this one party alone," he said, squinting up at the steeple, and I gave him a dry look. But my mood improved dramatically when a familiar glint of pixy dust arrowed out from the fireplace's flue.

"Rache!" Jenks shouted as he came to a dust-laden halt before us, his sparkles continuing forward on momentum, making me sneeze. "Tink loves a duck, how did you get them to leave?"

I held my jacket like a dead rat. "Cormel gave us until midnight."

Jenks flew backward as Trent and I started for the open front door. "And then what?"

My steps slowed. "He gets serious about killing Ivy."

"Yesterday wasn't serious?" Jenks said as he alighted on Trent's shoulder, but it was obvious we were on borrowed time. My stomach clenched as Trent and I took the shallow steps, and I blanched at the smell wafting out the door.

"Nice." Holding my breath, I went in. "What did they do? Have an orgy?"

The whine of Jenks's wings increased as I propped the door open. "Uh, something like that. But no one died. Hey, I tried to keep them out of your stuff. I'm sorry. It was just Belle and me after the sun came up and we had to pick our battles."

"Don't worry about it. It's not your . . . fault . . ." I stopped just inside the sanctuary, lips parting as I took in the empty bowls, smeared glasses, crushed beer cans, and chips bags. The furniture had been rearranged, and someone had drawn a mustache and beard on the TV, presumably on someone's face at the time. Kisten's pool table had a cooler on it, and a dark stain spread under it as water dripped from the long crack running the width of the plastic. It was worse than the time my high school boyfriend had volunteered my house for the homecoming party because he knew my mom was working.

"Is Belle okay?" I said as Trent made a sorrowful noise. "Jumoke and Izzy?"

I could re-felt the table, but I knew I never would. I'd have to look at that stain on Kisten's memory for the rest of my life.

"They're okay." Jenks hovered by my ear, a depressed bluish-orange dust slipping from him. "Jumoke and Izzyanna kept to the garden, but Belle was with me. I couldn't have saved the kitchen without her. That fairy is something else."

A faint smile found me, and I started to think again. It was a God-awful mess, but I almost didn't care if it meant Jenks and Belle had attained a deeper level of respect. "Ah, sorry about your room," Jenks said as I ran a hand down the smooth finish of the pool table's bumper. "I figured you'd rather I save your kitchen, and ah, they really wanted the bed."

Oh God. My bed. "Don't worry about it. You saved the kitchen?" Tired, I started for the hallway. I'd send Cormel the cleanup bill if I thought he'd pay it.

Sure enough, the bathrooms were trashed. I think every vampire in the Hollows had used my shower. I'd probably just throw what was left of my soap away. Even so, it wasn't as bad as my bedroom.

"I'm really sorry, Rache," Jenks said as I peeked in, nose wrinkled as I hustled to prop the stained-glass window open. I couldn't deal with this just yet, and Trent went across the hall to make sure Ivy's window was open as well. Someone had been through my closet and my clothes were everywhere. My perfumes, too, were knocked over, most of them empty. More clothes spilled from my open drawers, and I began to get mad. Multiple someones had had sex in my bed by the look of it. There were nasty scratches in the headboard and the top of the footboard had been snapped off as if someone had kicked it in the throes of passion.

"Oh, Rachel," Trent breathed, his words making a warm spot on my shoulder. "This was totally uncalled for. I am so sorry."

Angry, I turned to the kitchen. "Not half as sorry as Cormel is going to be."

Belle, looking small without Rex beside her, stood at the threshold to the kitchen. She slumped, clearly fatigued as she leaned on her six-inch bow. "Rachel." Her lisping, raspy voice, too, lacked its usual flair. "Is-s-ss Ivy well?"

Damn it, Cormel, if your people have hurt my cat . . . "Yes," I said, again finding a drop of good in the ugly. "Your sister and brothers are keeping her safe."

Jenks's wings cut out for a brief second. "Holy pixy piss, really?"

Trent nodded, a faint smile on his face as he put a hand on the small of my back and almost shoved me into the untouched kitchen. "I've let most of my security go, and at Quen's urging, I've come to an agreement with the clan that's been living in my gardens. I've been told that pixies would have been better—"

"Not likely," Belle interrupted as we came in.

"But I appreciate their unobtrusiveness and good manners," he added, and Jenks frowned.

Slowly my shoulders eased. After the disaster of the rest of the church, the dishes I'd left in the sink yesterday looked like heaven, even if everything was covered in pixy dust. Da-a-amn, Jenks must have worked his wings to bare veins to keep them out.

"You guys are the best," I said, miserable as I stood beside the center island counter and looked at my spelling supplies hanging from the rack, the twin stoves sporting a thin layer of sparkles, and the huge antique farmhouse table shoved up against the interior wall. Ivy's latest research was in her usual careful disarray, and the bag of cookies I'd had for breakfast yesterday looked untouched. "I can't believe you kept them out of here." Crap on toast, I was almost crying, and Jenks's wings shifted to an embarrassed red.

Trent set his book on the center counter with a soft thump. A thin cloud of spent pixy dust rose and vanished into nothing. "So is the rest of the church as bad as the front?" he asked as I slid the single window open. *Thank God Al's chrysalis is still here.* The church stank, far worse than if it had simply been living vampires. It had been an all-access party. The sanctity of the church had been broken by Newt three months ago. I should have gotten it reinstated, but it was expensive, and insurance wouldn't cover it a second time. Cheaper to just move. *I can't move, this is my home.*

"I've yet to s-s-s-survey the damage in the garden," Belle said, having snaked up a thin line to stand on the counter. "We kept them from the kitchen, though it was a mighty task."

I shook my head, imagining it. "Thank you. Thank you so much. I can't ever repay you."

Jenks looked pleased, but Belle scowled, sullen. "If I had a flight under my direction, the entire church would have been untouched."

"They would have just burnt it to the ground," I said, eyes on the ceiling. "You chose what I would've saved." It was going to be hard to find any sleep tonight, but then again, I probably wouldn't *get* the chance to sleep. My face scrunched up as I thought of my bed. No way. I was buying a new one.

"I'll check everything out if you make coffee," Trent offered, and I nodded. He wasn't being sexist, he just didn't want me to see anything until he had a chance to maybe fix it. Half of me wanted to go through the church from the belfry to the most distant tombstone and use that anger to get through the next twelve hours, but the other half just wanted to get my sheets in the washer, ignoring the rest until I could deal with it.

The cat door in the back room squeaked as Belle went into the garden. I ran a finger across the pixy dust, head coming up in surprise when Trent pulled me into an unexpected hug. I went willingly, and for a moment, we just stood there, taking strength from each other as I breathed him in, finding his cinnamon and wine scent under the chaotic vampire mashup. The sound of Jenks's wings grew loud, then vanished as he followed Belle out. Trent's grip was firm without being binding, and the faintest hint of energy slipped between us as our auras tried to mix.

"You going to be okay?" he said, and I nodded, pushing back even as I made sure he didn't slip away completely. Oh, I was still pissed, but after enough people try to kill or imprison you, the stuff that can be fixed and forgotten in a week tends not to matter as much.

"Thanks," I said, and his smile became devious. "Could you do me a favor and open the windows in the belfry first? With them and the back door open, the place airs out remarkably fast." Most of it was surface stink. They hadn't been here long enough for the pheromones to soak into the paint and woodwork.

"You bet." Trent rocked back, and my hand slipped reluctantly from his waist. He was looking at my lips as if wanting to kiss me, but then he turned and headed down the hall. Just the idea that he was thinking about it was almost as good as the kiss would have been, and I found a smile. I could tell the instant the belfry windows opened as the pixy dust vanished in the fresh air. I could never repay Jenks for keeping the kitchen untouched, and as I ran the tap for warm water to make up some suds, I pulled Trent's book closer.

It wasn't the first elf spell book I'd ever seen, but again I was surprised that most of the charms I browsed past had the same mix of earth and ley line magic that demon magic did. I'd be willing to bet the two branches of magic had developed hand in hand despite the long-standing anger between them.

Remembering that I'd promised coffee, I set the book aside. The charm to capture a soul looked easy, I thought as I dumped yesterday's grounds and changed the water to cold. Easy, but I wasn't sure how I was going to do it without asking the Goddess for help. Lots of elves didn't believe and still got the job done. Landon, for example, though he probably believed in her now.

Landon. My lips twisted in disgust. He'd used Trent and me to try to destroy the vampires. That the elven muckety-mucks of both the religious-oriented dewar and the political-faction enclave had disavowed any knowledge of his plot made it obvious that they'd each backed him. Though still in charge of the dewar, Landon had lost credibility. Trent had lost more.

At least no one had died, I thought, my mind going to Ivy, still at Trent's mini-hospital.

Apart from the quiet and the vague unease, it almost felt like a normal, quiet Saturday as I measured out the grounds, the scent of it reminding me of how much I enjoyed living here with Ivy, even as hard as it was sometimes. Understanding didn't come cheap, and I blinked back an unexpected surge of sadness at the thought that it might be ending. I wasn't moving in with Trent, but this latest snag made it feel . . . over somehow.

"Stop it, Rachel," I whispered. Nothing was really ending. Jenks, Ivy, and I had been through worse. We'd get through this, and everything would return to normal. Better even.

But how many times can we get back up as if nothing has changed?

I folded the bag of the grounds down and fastened it shut with one of Ivy's binder clips. I wished I had a reset button. How far back would I take it? I wondered. To the day I made that deal with Cormel? Farther?

I snapped the coffeemaker on, then found a smile when I heard Trent and Jenks in the hallway. "Coffee ready yet?" Trent called loudly.

"Give it five!" I shouted back. Smile fixed, I leaned against the counter and waited for them to come in. But they didn't, and I tiptoed to the archway, stopping when I heard Trent mutter, "I know how to wash sheets, Jenks. I've got two toddlers."

He's doing laundry?

"Hey, okay, cookie man," Jenks drawled. "It's your funeral if you shrink them."

There was a hesitation, and I leaned closer. "Shrink them?" Trent asked.

"Those are one hundred percent cotton," Jenks said importantly, "not your richy-rich linen stuff. If you use the sterilize cycle, you'll not only shrink 'em, but set the oils carrying the vampire pheromones into the fabric. Look, Ivy's got a bottle of no-nose up here."

My brow furrowed. *No-nose?*

A cupboard creaked, loud over the sound of water filling the washer, and then Trent's bemused "I've never seen this."

"Put a splash in. It'll take care of the vampire cooties and the pheromones, too."

I could almost see the pixy preening in that he'd known something Trent hadn't. Sure enough, Trent's voice held a smidgen of humor and humility when he next spoke. "Thanks. I shouldn't be so quick to prove I know what I'm doing."

"Don't sweat it," Jenks said, and I eased back into the kitchen. "That's why Ivy has silk sheets. Me, I don't like silk. The dust makes them as slippery as all hell."

Smiling, I busied myself with Trent's book. I felt bemused and loved. Trent was washing my sheets, the one thing that I wanted most and didn't have time for. And I hadn't known about the no-nose, either.

The coffee was gurgling its fragrant last when they came in, the book splayed open before me as my interest in it went from pretend to real. "Smells good," Trent said, Jenks a humming shadow behind him.

"You want the rainbows or the smiley face?" I asked, reaching for the mugs.

Trent eyed the two overly happy mugs. "Ah, whatever. You need a fresh stick of yew. I'll be right back."

"I'll get the yew, cookie man." Hands on his hips, Jenks yo-yoed before him. "I want to make sure no one peed on it."

"I can get it," Trent insisted, and Jenks darted forward, rocking the larger man back.

"I said . . . I'll get it," Jenks said, and I rolled my eyes as the pixy bristled. "Sit and drink your coffee. If I need your help, I'll whistle. I want to check on, ah, Jumoke, anyway."

Eyes wide in question, Trent took the rainbows. "I'll sit and drink my coffee."

"Good man." With a relieved sigh, Jenks flew out the back door's cat flap, whistling and calling coaxingly for Rex.

Eyebrows high, Trent leaned past me to look out the window. The scent of cinnamon and wine dove deep, and I almost sighed. "Ah, why doesn't Jenks want me in the garden?" he asked.

I sipped my coffee, thinking the scent went well with content elf. "My guess is he's looking for his cat and he doesn't want you to scare her off."

"Mmmm." Expression concerned, Trent dropped back to his heels, steaming mug behind his laced fingers. "Cats like me."

My head slowly shook. "Nah. A pixy dancing an inch off the ground is a lot more enticing than a man she barely knows. Besides, how often do we get the church to ourselves?"

His eyes flicked to mine and held for a telling moment. Introspective, he went to the large table, turning one of the chairs halfway around before sitting sideways in it. "My cleaning crew could be in and out of here in two hours."

Again, I shook my head. The thought of more people in my church made my skin crawl. Besides, I should wait until I knew if I was going to survive the next couple of days. Book in hand, I set my mug next to his before I shifted Trent's arm and sat right in his lap, curving his arm around me. He grunted in surprise, holding me almost in self-defense as I dropped the book open before us. "Oh, I like this," he said, tugging me into a more comfortable position.

"I bet you do." Smiling, I thumbed to the proper page. I felt vulnerable, and this helped. "I've been looking at the charm you dog-eared. Changed aura or not, I can't imagine the Goddess won't recognize me if I petition for her help."

A memory of the Goddess shivered thorough me. Al had tried to kill me because of her, believing it was the only cure for the voices in my head. I'd had to trick Newt into admitting the Goddess was real. It wasn't my fault the Goddess's mystics liked living in mass better than the space between mass. If they ever found me, the only way to survive would be to kill the Goddess—turn her into something new.

Trent's fingers were tracing a delicious path along the top of my waistband, and I jumped when he found my skin. The memory of the first time with him surfaced like bubbles in my thoughts, breaking with little tingles against the top of my mind. It had been in the kitchen. Well, we'd started in the kitchen. We'd ended in the back living room.

He was smiling when I turned to him, and I let the pages shift so I could trace the outline of his ear with a slow finger. "You want to find a different charm?" he asked, a new thought hazing the back of his eyes.

I slowly leaned in and found his earlobe with my lips, tugging suggestively as I breathed him in, waves of sensation spilling through me. "No," I whispered, shivering when his fingers gripped the back of my neck. "I want you to do it. You've done it before. Right?"

I hadn't meant to put a sexual innuendo in there, but there it was. "Sort of."

His sour tone slumped my shoulders, and I pulled back. His eyes wouldn't meet mine, but his hands never fell from around my waist and kept me where I was. Wincing, he glanced at the book. "The charm I'm familiar with affixes souls based on aura identification. Felix doesn't have his natural aura anymore." My balance shifted as Trent flipped to a new page, his long fingers moving the paper like fingers over a keyboard. "We can use the first part to capture the soul, no problem," he said when he found it, "but we'll need to tinker with the second half to find something to affix it to, something not altogether alive and coated in someone else's aura."

"Al and Newt have collections of souls. I bet they have a way to affix them."

Trent stiffened under me. "You're not asking Al."

"I know." I leaned to put my head on his shoulder. It was awkward, but I didn't care when his arms went around me again. "I'll ask Newt unless you have something in your library." This was nice. I didn't want to move.

"Newt isn't any better than Al," Trent muttered, but we had little choice. Elves and witches seldom worked with souls, and never to affix them to a nonliving thing. *The Were's focus was kind of like a soul. Maybe I could use that curse?*

Trent squirmed, and I got up knowing he probably wasn't altogether comfortable. "We'll find something." I needed professional guidance, but my professional guide was pissed at me. Fidgeting, I looked at the cookies, wishing I had something better to offer Trent. I'd seen his taste in cookies, and I was a bohemian by his culinary standards. "You don't have any more books on the subject, do you?" I asked as I pulled the bag to me and snapped one to check for staleness. *Flat.*

"No."

"Maybe simply capturing Felix's soul will buy us enough time."

Depressed, I set the open bag down and sat in the chair next to him. He was silent, waiting until I took three cookies before he reached in and pulled out five. I swear, I didn't know where the man put his calories. Maybe a box in his basement. "Al would know," I said softly, and his eyes jerked to me. He took a breath to say something, then hesitated.

"Is that really how you eat those?"

I looked at the bite out of my cookie and flushed. "Yeah," I lied, brushing the crumbs off. To be honest, I usually separated them, eating the cookie part first and scraping all the frosting into one gigantic wad. But I wasn't going to in front of Trent.

"Huh." Trent screwed his cookie open and scraped the frosting out with his teeth. "I thought everyone opened them up."

Damn it, I was flushing, and saw him file my lie away for later. Trent leaned closer. "Don't call Newt," he said. "We're not out of options yet. Landon owes you a favor."

"Landon?" I said around a mouthful of crumbs. "The man is slime!" I exclaimed, and Trent bobbed his head, ruefully agreeing. "Nothing but a . . . politically perfect engineered piece of backstabbing elf slime who thinks only of himself and the hell with the rest."

Leaning back and looking uncomfortable, he nodded. "I know."

"He tricked his predecessor into suicide!" I said, hand flying up into the air.

"I know."

Frustrated, I stood up. "Trent, I'm *not* asking *Landon* for help. I don't trust him. If it wasn't for him, I never would have damaged the Goddess to begin with!"

"I know. But it all worked out."

Worked out? I sputtered, trying to find the words, and Trent took my hand and pulled me closer. "Rachel, I agree it's risky. The elven dewar and enclave would still like to see the vampires die out—and you and me with them—but I'm not asking the elves, I'm asking Landon. He owes you, and I've got a little blackmail left in me."

Expression sour, I pulled my hand from him, arms around my middle as I moved to stand beside the sink. Trent silently waited. I knew how much it had hurt Trent going from everyone's owing him to his owing everyone. He was still making his genetic medicines in his basement labs, but now it was more to keep his customers from turning him in than the other way around.

"You think Landon knows how to fix souls to bodies?" I asked.

Sighing, Trent unscrewed another cookie, stacking the black cookie with the rest he'd already scraped clean. "Positive. If I can convince him that success will mean the end of the vampires, he'll tell you." Jaw clenched, he stared at nothing.

"You think he'll believe that?"

Trent's gaze sharpened on mine. "Why not? It's a distinct probability."

"But . . ." I thought of the chaos that had taken Cincinnati and the Hollows when the undead had fallen asleep for four days. Head cocked, I leaned back against the counter. "Remind me of why we're doing this if you think it's going to topple the vampires' power structure." Not like I really had a choice.

Trent put an ankle on his knee, looking totally yummy with that cookie in his hand. "The charm Landon would know works one to one, not en masse. One vampire going insane and walking into the sun isn't going to have an impact on the world. And when Cormel understands that having his soul will send him into the sun, they'll all accept that it's not a viable way to extend their undead existence."

I didn't like the idea of even one vampire committing suncide because of a charm I twisted, and seeing it, Trent stood, coming to me and taking me in a hug. "Rachel, Felix won't survive more than a few more months regardless of what happens." Leaning back, he caught my eyes with his own. "Or it will work with no ill effects, and we'll have a different issue to deal with. Either way, Landon will help if only for the chance to see the end of the undead."

But I didn't trust Landon. "What's to stop them from just killing them all, then? I mean, after we prove it works? Elves can go to the ever-after, same as witches."

Nodding, Trent reached into the bag of cookies. "True, but whoever was going to try would have to not only *catch* a surface demon, but catch the right *one*. It's a miracle we found Felix's. Besides, if elves can't make money on it, they won't do it, and witches know better than to try."

He put a cookie in my hand, and I ate it, thinking it over as I chewed and swallowed. But as the only alternative beyond Landon was Al, the choice was easy. "Fine. I'll ask him."

Trent's arm around me tensed. "Ah, you mind if I ask him?"

Ahhh, I thought with a smile, thinking this might be why Trent was so hot to give Landon a shot at this. If it failed, then Landon would lose face in the dewar and the enclave. "Sure."

Immediately Trent went back to mowing down those cookies, slowing when he realized I was staring at him. *What are we up to now? Ten?* "Great. I'll go give him a call," he said, dusting the crumbs from his fingers and reaching for his phone.

There was only the faintest flicker of unease as I dunked my cookie into my coffee. Even if Landon caught a flight today, he wouldn't be here by sunset. "I don't like doing this by phone. Too much chance for someone overhearing it," I said, but Trent was already scrolling for the number.

"We won't have to." Trent stretched and yawned, reminding me that this was his usual down time. "He's in Atlanta trying to win his position back," he said as he rolled his shoulders. "He can be here in a couple of hours."

"It's not going as well as he'd like?" I prodded, and he smirked.

"Getting old men and women to agree on anything new is like wrangling cats, and he has no practical skills." He hesitated. "Yet," he amended. "But things change. I get better reception outside. Back in a second."

His hand trailing across my cheek raised tingles, and I darted my tongue out to tag a knuckle, making him jump and smile. "Wicked demon," he muttered, and I watched him leave.

My smile faded fast. I didn't trust Landon. The last spell he "taught" me nearly killed me. I was sure the demons would have a curse that would do the same thing, and after listening to make sure Trent wasn't going to walk back in, I pulled my scrying mirror from between my cookbooks and spelling tomes.

The cracked glass was cool, and as soon as I set my hand atop the calling glyph, I felt the hint of connection to the demon collective. Tapping the line out back strengthened it. Heart pounding, I reached out with a soft thread of awareness, lacing my thought with enough regret to choke a horse. We had the same aura resonance, damn it. Al could at least be civil.

Al?

Rage boiled up through the folds of my brain, and I jerked my hand back as the wave crested, threatening to swamp me. His anger fell back into my mirror, and the sudden snap of the cracked glass breaking made me gasp.

"You okay?" Trent shouted from outside.

Shit. "Ah, just dropped a cookie," I lied, face flaming as I looked at the broken shards. "I'm good!"

But I wasn't good, and I took the broken pieces to my saltwater vat and dropped them in one by one, watching them ride the currents of their passage to the bottom. They lay there, sending glimmers of light sideways out their broken edges.

Depressed, I stared out the window and watched Trent meet Izzyanna, Jumoke's young wife. I couldn't help but wonder if Al was angry because Trent and I reminded him of what he'd lost long before I knew him—a woman he'd once loved enough to risk everything for, give everything for, but was too afraid to fight the anger of two worlds for. Maybe Al was angrier at himself than me.

But as I washed my hands free of the salt water, I didn't think it mattered.

Chapter 6

The chill of the coming September evening seeped into me, the cold as real and enduring as the damp grit of the earth pressed into my fingers as I lifted the last stone and replaced it in the low wall that separated the graveyard from the more mundane garden. It had been knocked out of place, and though Jenks had permanently taken up residence in the church walls, I knew it would be something he'd want fixed.

Straightening, I wiped my hands off on my jeans and looked at the red light of sunset shining against the familiar stones I mowed around every week. Well, not *every* week. The grass had gotten long, catching the leaves that had shifted color and dropped early. My weekends were a lot more interesting now that Trent had more free time, and the yard was beginning to show it.

"Sorry, Jenks," I whispered as my gaze lifted to the church. I knew it bothered him that the graveyard was going fallow apart from a small space Jumoke and Izzyanna had claimed. The garden felt empty, and my mind wouldn't stop circling over the thought of endings. It was why I was out here moping in the garden. That, and Trent had been underfoot ever since getting up from his noon nap, driving me to distraction as he went over that charm he'd brought.

The bright sparkle of pixy dust glowed at the far side of the garden. It was joined by a second, and the twin trails of dust wound around each other in breathtaking beauty until they both arrowed to me. It was Jumoke and Izzyanna, but my welcoming smile faded when two car doors slammed on the street. *Landon.* Apparently he'd brought a friend.

Izzyanna reached me first. The little pixy looked about ten, a late age for a pixy to become a bride, but her eyes were as dark as well-turned earth. It wasn't the typical death sentence that Jumoke's hair was, but it had obviously prevented a more traditional joining age. Her smile, though, was cheerful, and her eyes shone with an impish humor that balanced Jumoke's stoic, introverted personality. I couldn't help but wonder if there was a slight swelling at her middle. It was unusual for pixies to be born in the fall, as they wouldn't make it through the winter. Izzy's children, though, wouldn't have to hibernate, and a fall birth would give them a head start in the spring.

"Rachel, your guests are here," the pixy said, her flush spilling into her dust.

"Guests, huh?" I said, glad she was starting to slow her speech down. The first week she'd been here, I hadn't understood a word she said. "Who did Landon bring with him?"

Please not the I.S. Anyone but the I.S.

"It's a woman," Izzy said, hand protectively over her middle as she hovered backward before me as I headed for the church's back door.

"Woman?" I said. "Thanks for the heads-up."

Immediately she flew away with Jumoke, winding about themselves and talking so fast and high that it might as well be another language. It wouldn't be long until the garden was again noisy with life, and that gave me more peace than I would've expected. I liked beginnings better than endings.

But it wasn't meant to last, and I jerked to a stop when I recognized Ellasbeth's haughty voice coming through the open kitchen window. Ellasbeth? What in *hell* was she doing here, and with Landon?

"She is a *demon!*" Ellasbeth exclaimed, her tone accusing. "Your father *made* her!"

"He did *not* make her. He enabled her to survive. There is a difference."

Trent's voice was soft in anger, and I stayed where I was, my hand reaching for the back door faltering.

"Which might get you killed if it gets out," she huffed, and I stiffened.

"Is that a threat?" Trent's voice was hard. "Are you sure you want to do that? Again?"

Landon cleared his throat, but the words had been spoken. Crap on toast. Trent had a ruthless streak as wide as Jenks's. He'd once stopped me from killing Nick, claiming he wanted one clean thing in his life—me. I'd since agreed that killing Nick for the hell of it would have left a mark I didn't want, but Trent . . . He felt as if he was already lost and had no such compulsion against "doing things for the hell of it."

And Ellasbeth had just called him out.

Why is she here? Why now? Wings clattering, Jenks landed on the doorknob, probably to keep me from going in. "Hey. Eavesdropping is my thing, not yours," he said.

"Shhh," I demanded, leaning to the open kitchen window.

"You are *forcing our daughter* to associate with a demon!" Ellasbeth exclaimed. "If you were anyone else, Lucy would be mine by the child abuse laws!"

My lips parted, and I felt my face go white.

"Lucy doesn't care what Rachel is," Trent said, his voice barely above a whisper. "*That's* the world I want her to grow up into, and by God, Ellasbeth, if I find out you said *anything* to make Lucy or Ray question Rachel's worth, I will never let you see either of them again."

"Then . . ." Ellasbeth's voice went wobbly. "I thought . . . you were very clear on your stance at the zoo."

"Ah, Ellasbeth?" Landon said, as if not liking the hope in her voice any more than I did.

"You were trying to take her by force, demanding I sell Lucy to you for a birthright that was already mine. Stop pushing me into a corner, Ellasbeth. Stop trying to control the situation. You are *not* in charge. I am."

A cold feeling started in my middle. I knew who Trent was, what he was morally capable of doing, seen it firsthand and tried to pretend it wasn't there. *Don't call his bluff, Ellasbeth. Don't.* But . . . if Trent and Ellasbeth found a way to make this work . . . *Damn it, that was why she was here,* I thought, seeing everything Trent and I had found ending far too soon.

"I just want to see my child," Ellasbeth pleaded.

Jenks snorted, his dust shifting to an irate orange. "What a little squirrel sack."

"I find that hard to believe when you show up with Landon," Trent said, and I waved Jenks off the doorknob.

Jenks flew up, startled. "They aren't done yet!" he protested, and I tugged the door so it would squeak. "Rache, you need to work on this spying thing. Your timing sucks fairy dust."

"I need to get in there before he does something dumb, like open up joint-custody talks again," I said, and the pixy snickered. From inside came a shuffling of motion. I knew my face was red, and I took a slow breath as I paced through the back living room, trying to get the ugly look off my face before I went into the kitchen.

But it was obvious I'd heard something. Ellasbeth's cheeks were a bright red against her straw-blond hair. She sat stiffly at Ivy's big farm table, her hands clenched on a trendy purse, knees tight together, and a cream-colored skirt showing a respectable amount of leg. Her coat was still on, and it matched her heels. If I had to describe her in a few words, it would be professional, smart, classic beauty, and probably in that order. Devious, backstabbing, and self-serving would also be on the list.

On the surface, she was a perfect match for Trent's perfection—except he didn't love her. It hadn't mattered before, but after having gotten a taste of freedom, he was resisting going back. I felt a flash of pride that I'd been a part of that. But now . . . I wasn't sure.

As if sensing my emotion, Trent looked at me from where he was standing at the sink. The tension rose as the silence stretched. Trent was unusually ruffled, and as soon as he looked from her, Ellasbeth frowned at his casual shoes—then my wild hair.

"I was fixing the wall," I said, not knowing why I felt the need to explain myself. "Landon," I added, trying not to show my distaste.

Needless to say, I wasn't going to shake his hand, and I stiffened when the young man started forward from the fridge to do just that. Trent cleared his throat, and Landon changed his motion to stand behind Ellasbeth, placing his unworked, tan hands on the back of her chair. The center counter was more or less between us. I'd rather have it be a continent. God! I'd give a lot to know why Trent trusted him enough to do this.

Landon looked uncomfortable in a gray suit that set off his blond hair and green eyes. A traditional cylindrical hat of his clergy profession marred his young-businessman look, but it did give him an exotic air. I was sure he had an even more traditional prayer hat under it and probably a ribbon in his pocket. I knew Trent did, though I seldom saw it unless we got into trouble, and that hadn't happened in almost three months.

Why are Ellasbeth and Landon here? Together?

Landon smiled, but the emotion behind it felt dead. "It's good to see you again, Rachel."

Jenks snickered as he landed in the hanging rack. "I'll bet," he said under his breath, and Ellasbeth's forced smile faltered.

"Ellasbeth," I said next, reaching for a damp cloth by the sink to clean the dirt from my fingers. "I wasn't expecting you." I wasn't going to shake her hand either.

"Neither was I." Trent's head was down over his phone as he texted something. I'd be willing to bet it was to Quen or Jon to double security on the girls.

Ellasbeth stood as I tossed the rag into the sink, and I froze when she stood, hand extended. Great. My hands were clammy from the cloth, and I wiped them dry as she crossed the room.

"My apologies for dropping in on you like this," she said, and I watched her face as we shook, thinking that her hair looked fake next to Trent's transparent wispiness, and her voice had lost its musical cadence.

Her hand slipped from mine, and I said nothing. The last time I'd seen her, she'd been flanked by a dozen magic users and hired guns with the intention of forcibly taking Lucy and Ray. And Ray wasn't even her child.

"Well, this is about as comfortable as finding a naked fairy in your eldest son's bedroom," Jenks smart-mouthed, a silver dust slipping down and pooling on the counter like mercury.

Ellasbeth's eye twitched, and she dropped back a step. "Lucy is my child, too," she said, gaze darting to Trent as he closed his phone with a snap.

"Then you shouldn't have forced that barbaric, outdated tradition on me in the hopes I couldn't fulfill it," Trent said, showing more emotion than he usually allowed himself. "You brought this on yourself. The church can't help you. It's a legal issue, not a moral one."

Landon cleared his throat. "Perhaps I should come back later."

"Or not at all," I said, frustrated. I could figure this charm out. I didn't need elf magic. I needed someone in the ever-after to pick up the damn phone!

"Ahh . . . ," Trent hedged, shifting sideways until he could touch the small of my back. Ellasbeth, too, had a minor panic moment—for a completely different reason.

"Please," she said, eyes wide. "I asked Landon if I could come with him." Her gaze landed on Trent's hand touching me in reassurance, and she swallowed hard. "You won't take my calls. You refuse any dialogue. You say I forced your hand, well, you're forcing mine!"

I saw Trent's sigh more than heard it, but what caught my attention was Landon's sour expression. It was more than watching Ellasbeth beg; he seemed to have an interest here. My eyebrows rose as I suddenly got it. Ellasbeth hadn't stumbled into this meeting between Landon, Trent, and me. She'd been with Landon when the call had come in. *She'd been with Landon.*

Euuwww, I thought. There should be limits to how far one should abase oneself in the search for power, but if the "prince of the elves" had fallen, perhaps the head religious leader was a good second.

"I apologize for my actions at the zoo," Ellasbeth said, pleading with an indifferent Trent. "It endangered both girls and was foolish, but you weren't listening to me!"

Jenks sniffed. "As if you could ever hurt them while I'm around."

"It was wrong. I was desperate," Ellasbeth said. "Lucy is my child! I didn't know what I was risking when I forced you into it. I love her. Please! I'll do anything you want."

Anything? My arms fell from my middle. "Maybe you should talk to her," I suggested, hating myself for even saying it, but I knew I'd never stop until I got my child back if it was taken from me. That, and I didn't think Ellasbeth would give *anything*, and when she balked, Trent could tell her to leave for good.

Trent turned to me, his hand making tingles on my waist. "I thought you'd be against this," he said, and Ellasbeth took a fast breath, hope almost painful in her.

"I'm not for it, no," I said, nervous when Landon's eyes narrowed as he realized Trent and I were so close, functioning as a couple. "But I don't want to be looking over my shoulder the rest of my life. Lucy and Ray shouldn't either. Find out if she means it."

"Of course I mean it!" Ellasbeth's trendy heels ground the leftover salt from a circle into the linoleum. Her eyes were alight, and the only thing that kept me from taking it back was that it was love for her daughter. She was a tricky woman.

"I don't trust her," Trent said softly, his hands now holding mine. Both Ellasbeth and Landon were seeing more than I wanted them to, but I leaned into him, forcing myself to be more open with our relationship. We'd been hiding our feelings from ourselves and the public for so long, it was hard to show them in front of anyone else.

"If she's serious about seeing the girls, she can damn well move to Cincinnati," I said.

Ellasbeth's breath came in a panicked sound. "Cincinnati!" she said, her face reddening. "I am *not* moving to Cincinnati."

Jenks's wing hum came loud from the overhanging rack, and I swear, Trent almost smiled as he gave my fingers a squeeze and let go. Behind her, Landon rubbed his fingers into his temple. I could nearly see the distaste coming from the woman, but Trent was warming to the idea, if only because Ellasbeth didn't like it.

"I thought you said anything." I put my shoulder to Trent's to make a united front. "Talk is cheap, which might be why that's all you do."

Her perfectly painted lips parted in outrage, and from the rack, Jenks snickered. Ellasbeth scowled up at him. Her fingers were in a tight fist, and I was glad she didn't know much magic. "Trent, perhaps we can take a walk," she said stiffly, clearly wanting to get Trent alone and hopefully sway him where I wouldn't be around to sway him back.

Trent's shoulders slumped as he realized he was going to have to deal with Ellasbeth instead of helping me with the charm. "I'm not leaving Landon alone with Rachel."

"I'll be fine," I protested, and a faint but real smile eased his features.

"It's not you I'm worried about," Trent said, and concern flickered over Landon. Trent brushed past me with the scent of cinnamon and wine. "We can talk in the back room," he said, taking Ellasbeth's elbow.

"It's not very private," Ellasbeth protested, but she was moving. "I'd rather take a walk."

Trent glanced at me over his shoulder. "Yes, I know," he muttered, clearly surprised I was okay with this. They left, looking good together, better than Trent and me. Slowly my jealousy evolved into guilt. *I'm not self-sabotaging my relationship with Trent,* I thought, cursing myself as their voices twined together.

No one wanted Trent and me together: not the elves, not the demons, no one. I didn't give a rat's tail about that, but the guilt . . . Seeing Ellasbeth here, begging to renew her ties with her child? I could do nothing to further Trent's grand design to save his people, and he was so *damn good* at it. If there was the chance that he and Ellasbeth could make a go of it, I had to let it happen—if only for the girls.

But it hurt.

Jenks was hovering, waiting for direction, and I made a nod to follow them. He darted off, and my focus shifted to find that Landon had caught the motion. Uncaring, I shrugged.

"Why should Landon not want to be alone with Rachel?" Ellasbeth said faintly.

"He tried to kill her using the Goddess."

Ellasbeth gasped, and hearing it, Landon cracked his knuckles, unrepentant as he sat sideways to the table and pulled his cylindrical hat off his head, leaving his short hair mussed. No spelling cap, but it could have been woven into the top of the ceremonial hat.

"Jenks?" Trent's voice came, loud. "Get out."

"Aww, for ever-loving toad piss," the pixy complained as he flew backward into the hallway, an embarrassed green dust slipping from him. "How did you know I was there?"

"Out!" Trent said again, and Jenks flashed me a grin and vanished down the hallway to the sanctuary. He'd most likely go listen in through the flue, but at least Ellasbeth would have the illusion of privacy.

The coffeepot sat cold on the counter, an inch of old brew in it. I wasn't going to offer Landon any. Being tricked into merging my mind with a goddess bent on taking me over had left a bad taste in my mouth.

Landon seemed to gather himself as the muted, musical voices of Ellasbeth and Trent dissolved into a rise and fall of sound. "You have a nice spelling area. You cook here, too?"

My attention flicked to his and held. "Not at the same time."

Sucking his teeth, Landon shifted his feet. "Bis around?"

I nodded, glancing at the ceiling. "He's sleeping, but he wakes up occasionally." Especially when I was upset, but Landon already knew that.

From the back room Trent's voice rose. "I'm willing to die for Lucy's safety. I'm not about to sell her to you for a little less blackmail or my returned standing. You don't have anything I want, Ellasbeth. Get used to it."

My God, Trent could be callous when the situation called for it, and I propped my elbows on the stainless steel counter between Landon and myself.

David had once told me I'd saved Trent's life, not while being his security, but by causing him to grow, to lose his at-any-cost outlook that the needs of the one outweighed the needs of the many, that the ends justified the means. I'd seen it. Hell, I'd lived it while a mink trapped in his office, watching him kill his head geneticist to preserve his secrets and his money flow. But he'd tempered himself. Because of me, if David was to be believed, and it had saved his life because, as David had said, he wasn't going to make the world live through another Kalamack bent on elven supremacy. Perhaps Landon had risen to fulfill that role instead, and I stifled a shudder at the thought because where Trent had a conscience, Landon did not.

"Why are you here helping me?"

Landon rose, his mood guarded as he spun the book Trent had brought over to face him. "Trent told me he thinks the undead will walk into the sun if they get their souls back. I tend to agree with him. I think it's fitting that giving the vampires what they want will bring about their end. I don't mind being a part of that." He hesitated, and my heart thumped at his still-ness. "My question is, why are *you* doing this if you think it will drive them into suncide?"

"Because Ivy's life is more important than one lousy vampire who's already on his way out." Uneasy, I rubbed a watermark on the counter. Fear that the vampires would take their revenge out on Ivy and me if things didn't go the way they wanted was never far from my thoughts, coloring my hopes—and my decisions.

Landon made a sound deep in his throat, and I jumped when he shut the book with a snap. "Trent's charm won't work."

"Why not?" I said, not liking that he'd startled me.

"Because it uses the auratic residue left in the mind and body to adhere itself with, and the undead have completely polluted theirs with the auras they take in to survive."

It was exactly what Trent had said, and grimacing, I steadied myself for some major boot licking. "You have another way?"

Landon pulled his attention back from the soft conversation in the living room. "In theory. The charm dates back several thousand years. I've never heard of anyone trying it."

He was lying. I could tell in the way he was standing. "So . . . it's a black charm?" I prompted. Elves were reluctant to label their charms as black and white—but a white charm never went out of style. "I won't kill anyone."

His eyes came up, mocking. "Lucky for you you're dealing with people already dead."

Oh God. It *was* a black charm. "What does it do?" I asked, my gut tightening. *I can do this without trusting him. Hell, I used to work with de-mons.*

Landon shifted the book between us until it was perfectly square with the counter. He was thinking, and my mistrust deepened. "In theory? It fixes the soul of an elder to a newborn. It was said to have been used to extend our collective knowledge past the grave." He looked up, jaw set. "I'll write it out for you."

"Let me guess. You have to destroy the newborn's soul to do it." Yeah, the demons probably had a version of this. Ugly. It was just ugly the things magic could do.

Neck red, he didn't say anything, finally turning to pull a few sheets from Ivy's printer. "Pretty much," he said as he took a pen from his pocket and began to sketch a pentagram as I might draw a smiley face. "The original soul must be forcibly ripped away and the old soul fixed into its place. Most times, the recipient became psychotic, which only added to the mystique of being a high priest back then, I suppose." He looked up, reading my disgust. "I did say there's no record of this charm being performed for several thousand years."

"But you still know how to do it," I accused.

"Aren't you lucky for that," he shot back. "You can't get a soul to spontaneously attach itself and hope it sticks, even if it's his own soul and his own body. It left once, it will again."

He was right, and I tried not to look so pensive. The thought occurred to me that he might be giving me a black charm in the hopes of damning me with it. It wasn't illegal to know black magic, just to do it. And destroying the soul of a newborn so an old man might live again was about as black as it got. "No wonder the demons hate you," I said under my breath.

"Oh, are we going to compare past atrocities now?" he said even as he began writing a list of ingredients beside the pentagram.

I cocked my hip and watched him; his penmanship was as precise as his dress. "Stealing healthy babies and substituting your own failing infants is pretty nasty."

"So is a thousand years of slavery. Or creating a species for your own pleasure, one that necessitates acts of perverted brutality to survive, acts committed on the people you love."

He was talking about the vampires. "No worse than destroying your enemy by attacking their unborn children."

Landon stopped writing. "They did it first."

But who really knew the truth? I couldn't solve a puzzle two thousand years dead.

His motion cocky, Landon spun the paper to me. Listed was a mix of plants, objects, and ley line equipment designed to sympathetically harness intent: blood, hummingbird egg white, sunrise spider silk, aspen sap, a copper Möbius strip, silk scarf, salt—probably to scribe the pentagram with—and a familiar phrase of Latin. *Tislan, tislan. Ta na shay cooreen na da.*

My lips parted and a wave of disconnection flooded me as the words rose from my mind. "That's the phrase Trent used to move my soul," I said, my voice sounding hollow, as if from outside myself.

Landon frowned, actually doing a double take as I blinked to find myself. "Trent has done this? Are you kidding me?"

"Not this one," I reassured him. "But he held my soul in a bottle for three days while my aura replenished itself. I remember the words."

Ta na shay cooreen na da. It flowed through me, and I held the counter as if it wasn't real. I'd been trapped in my mind, standing at this very spot making cookies that faded away until Trent and I worked together, a symbol of us joining our minds so he could pull me out.

"Kalamack put your soul into a bottle?" Landon said, his disbelief obvious.

My breath came in a rush, as if I'd forgotten how to breathe. "My aura was burned off when I fought Ku'Sox. My mind thought I was dead, and he kept me on life support until my body was recovered and my aura was strong enough." It had taken a kiss to break the spell, seeing as it was a very old charm to "wake the princess" from a lifesaving coma. I was starting to think that was when I'd begun to love him.

Oh shit. I love him.

The realization fell on me hard. My knees went wobbly, and I held the counter as a surge of emotion rose. *I loved Trent.* Sure, I'd toyed with the idea before, but now, after seeing him with Ellasbeth and giving him the foolhardy chance to make amends with her, I knew it was true. Damn it, this wasn't the way it was supposed to happen. It was supposed to be romantic, with flowers and sun or moonlight, his touch on my face, and the scent of our hair mingling as we kissed. But no. It was me in my kitchen standing before a man I loathed, listening to the muted strains of the man I loved persuading his ex to get over herself and play by his rules.

Perhaps that means it might last this time.

"Rachel?" Landon said, and I shook myself.

"He's better at magic than you think he is." Head down, I locked my knees. Love shouldn't be scary, but whenever I fell in love, my life fell apart. I didn't want anything to change, but how could I stop it?

"He'd better be," Landon muttered, looking at me as if trying to figure out why I was so distant. "Same words? Are you sure?"

Think about it later, Rachel. "It circled my brain for three days. What does it mean?"

Head down, he crossed off and rewrote things. "Most of it is to gain the Goddess's attention."

Swell. "And the rest?"

"I don't know."

It was more likely he just didn't want to tell me. *Tislan, tislan. Ta na shay cooreen na da.* It hung in the back of my brain like a whisper of awareness—slowly gaining strength.

"She is a *demon*," Ellasbeth said from the back living room, her voice breaking through the singsong litany in my mind where nothing else could. "Do you have any idea what people are saying? What this does to our child's chances at success?"

"Lucy doesn't care," Trent said back. "Why do you?"

Landon cleared his throat, pushing his sketch across the counter so I could see it right side up. He was uncomfortable, and I didn't think it was because of Ellasbeth and Trent. I wasn't keen on any charm he had to remember, but it wasn't as if I had much choice.

"Pay attention," the man said, cementing in my thoughts that it was his skills he was nervous about. "I agreed to help you, but I'm not going to do it, and if anyone asks, I was here with Ellasbeth helping her petition Trent for the right to see her firstborn child."

"Sure." His stubble was starting to show, and I could smell the cold plastic of airport on him over his faint woodsy scent. Distant, I looked down at the curse. "Did the parents know you were doing this, or did you just steal the babies, too?"

Landon pulled himself straight, the width of the counter between us. "You want to be held accountable for the sins of your forefathers? Just keep throwing stones, Morgan." Expression closed, he looked me up and down. "I'm assuming you can get a soul into a bottle?"

I scanned the spell, thinking it looked easy. But most of the bad ones were. "Yes." I didn't like trusting Landon and his memory-recalled charm, but he did want an end to the vampires.

"Good." He leaned over the counter and tapped his pencil on the instructions. I knew the moment he caught my scent when he froze, then pulled back. "The, ah, spell calls for removing the original soul from a healthy body. I skipped that part."

"You mean killing a baby," I prompted, and he stared at me until I looked away.

"Step one," he said tightly. "Sketch a pentagram onto a square of silk using salt. If you can match the scarf's color to the recipient's original aura, that's even better."

"I'll ask Nina if she knows," I said, tucking a strand of hair back.

"Second, anoint the feet of the pentagram with the sap, and do the same for the soles of the recipient's feet."

"Using what?" I interrupted, shocking myself when I looked up and found him too close. "The vampire recipient is like what, lying down?" This wasn't good. There were too many variables to remember, and he clearly hadn't done enough magic to know what was important and what could be fudged. "Are you sure there isn't a book it's written down in?"

"No." His voice was tight. "I won't misremember it. I've got it okay."

"You've got this okay?" I accused, and there was a sudden silence from the back room. "You said no one's done this for thousands of years. How do you know if it's right or not?"

"The charm is fine," he said, face red. He was lying; they did this charm at the dewar—more often than they wanted to admit—and that sickened me.

"Then what do I use to anoint the scarf and his feet? My finger?" I asked snarkily. The reason it wasn't written down was plausible deniability. You couldn't be brought to justice for a black charm there was no written evidence of.

"Ahh, I would think an aspen rod," he said, and I took the pen out of his hand and added it to the list. "I'm destroying that before I leave," he said, meaning the paper.

No you aren't, I thought, but was smart enough not to say it. Damn it all to the Turn and back, people were crap. How can you respect a group who sacrificed babies to lengthen their own pathetic lives?

"Aspen rod," I said, setting the pen down with an accusing snap. "Then what?"

Landon was eyeing me in distrust, and I gave him a sarcastic smile. "You do the same with the egg white, anointing the arms of the pentagram first, and then the recipient's palms."

"Using the same wand?" I guessed, and he nodded, flushed. "Can I use a chicken's egg?"

"Not if you want it to work," he muttered, and I took that as a fact. Eggs were a symbol of rebirth, but the Mayans used to believe that humming-birds were the souls of warriors and would make an even closer tie. I could probably pick up one at one of the more exclusive charm shops.

"So let me guess," I said, pulling the paper to me. It looked funny see-ing the clearly old charm on fresh white paper. "Step three is to anoint the point of the pentagram and his forehead with his own blood?"

He grimaced, shifting from foot to foot. "I'd use the same wand again."

"Then what?"

Landon hesitated, as if trying to decide only now if giving me this info was a good idea.

"What next, Landon . . . ?" I intoned, and he tugged the paper back to himself.

"Roll the scarf into a cylinder and run it through the Möbius strip. Both loops."

Big Möbius strip, check. I had one of those. I had two of them, actually. "What's it made of?" I asked, and I almost saw him kick himself.

"Shit, I forgot that part," he muttered. "Copper. Yes, copper."

My fingers drummed on the counter. "You know what? I think I'll just go to the library and find a nice reincarnation spell. Take my chances."

Landon glared. "I know how to do this."

"You sure?" I snapped, and both of us looked to the hallway at a pixy guffaw. No one was there, but a tiny whisper of pixy dust was slipping down.

Landon rolled up the paper, clearly ready to take his ball and go home. It was the lure of being the one who brought down the vampires that kept him here, kept him honest. "Most of this is all just to get the Goddess's attention. It's the thought that counts."

I sobered at the reminder of the Goddess. Newt had assured me that the mystics and the Goddess herself wouldn't recognize me even if I stood in a ley line and shouted for her, but she wasn't called a goddess because she was impotent. "Okay, run the pentagram through the Möbius strip. Then what?"

My sudden meekness bolstered Landon's mood, and I frowned when he tucked the paper into an inner pocket and went to get his hat from the table. "The scarf finds a neutral flow from the copper ions it picks up, so now you can shake the salt out and drape the scarf over the recipient's face, blood spot at the forehead right where you anointed him. From there, you simply open the container holding the soul. Chanting the phrase will draw it forth, and the soul should go to him and fix into place. At least until he dies again. Burn the scarf to break the pathway and prevent the soul from escaping the body."

He put on his hat, clearly ready to go. I nodded, still uneasy in that he might have forgotten something—intentionally. "You never said where the spiderweb fit in."

"Oh! Right." He hesitated in the archway. "Drape it over your shoulder for protection against an aggressive soul."

Aggressive soul. Yes, I'd run into one of those before, but Al hadn't used spiderwebs to help protect against them. Come to think of it, I'd never seen a spider in the ever-after, and I thought it pathetic that the elves and demons had polluted their world to the point where even a spider couldn't survive.

"Ellasbeth, are you ready?" Landon called as he stood in the threshold between the kitchen and the hallway, and I heard her ask him for a moment. Frowning, Landon leaned against the frame of the opening.

"You sure you don't want to add anything else?" I said, trying not to look at the pocket he put the charm in. I wanted it, wanted it bad.

"No." Mood sour, he looked into the living room, then pushed himself forward. Steps fast, he came three paces in, eyes intent as he pulled the paper from his inner pocket, taunting me with it. I jumped when he tugged on the line out back, tossing the paper into the sink and igniting it with a single word.

Son of a bastard, I thought, grimacing at the sudden rush of shoes in the hall. Trent slid to a halt when he saw Landon standing over the fire in the sink, and he exhaled in relief. Ellasbeth click-clacked in behind him, coat over her arm, and Trent frowned. "Thanks for your help. You both have a flight out of here tonight, right?" Trent asked, clearly eager for them to leave.

Landon chuckled, turning the taps on to wash even the ash into the sewer system and out of my reach. "I've got a reservation at the Cincinnatian. Ellasbeth tells me it's the only decent live-in hotel in the area."

"Even if the staff is surly." Ellasbeth's mood wasn't good, but it wasn't bad either. Trent must have given her something, but I bet it had cost her. Suddenly I felt as if both of us had been manipulated, even if it had been us who had called them.

"Do you have what you need?" Trent asked, and I nodded. The more satisfied Ellasbeth and Landon became, the more uneasy I felt. It technically wasn't a curse if I didn't have to kill anyone to perform the magic. There hadn't been any indication that it required direct contact with the Goddess to do the curse either, but he could have left that out. He had before.

Smile stilted, Ellasbeth turned to Trent. "Thank you," she said, and my pulse hammered. "I'll be in touch as soon as I get a permanent address."

My expression froze. Crap on toast, the woman was moving to Cincinnati. Shit, shit, shit! Why had I gone along with this? Made it sound like a good idea?

"I'll wait for your call." Trent put a hand on her shoulder and gave her a cold kiss good-bye on her cheek. My gut tightened. I knew I gave myself away when Ellasbeth leaned in to accept it, her eyes on mine and a mocking smile on her thin, lipstick-red lips. The tension rose. Landon clearly wasn't happy either. *I'm an idiot.* My clear conscience wouldn't keep me warm at night, hold me when I cried, or smile when I made a joke.

"Landon," Ellasbeth said as she held her coat out to him, and he slowly moved to settle it across her shoulders.

"Bye now," I said as I leaned against the counter and tried not to grimace. "Thanks for the soul-stealing charm."

Her coat on, Ellasbeth waited a telling moment for Trent to escort them to the door, but when he ignored them, she turned on a heel and stalked off, shoes clicking on the hardwood floor. Landon lurched to catch up, already digging in a pocket for the car keys.

A shower of pixy dust sifted down from the overhanging rack. I hadn't known Jenks was up there, but I wasn't surprised as he gave Trent a thumbs-up and darted out after them.

Trent sighed heavily, and together we listened to Ellasbeth's heels aggressively striking the floor in the sanctuary. "That woman is plotting," I said softly, and Trent pulled me into a sudden, unexpected hug.

"Oh God," he almost moaned, his arms tight around me as I scrambled to shift gears. "I think you are the only thing keeping me from going insane sometimes. You and the girls."

But he had kissed her. "Really?" I mumbled. From the front, the door slammed, making the curtains over the sink drift.

Breath catching, he nodded, still staring at the ceiling as if the words he wanted to say were imprinted up there with pixy dust. "When everything seems to impact everything and there's no easy answer, I ask myself: Will this decision take me closer or farther from you? And then it's so clear. Even if it doesn't make sense at the time."

He thought this would bring us closer? My heart thudded. He had meant that kiss as show, but fear still lingered. Ellasbeth had brought everything back that I'd been ignoring, everything that Trent had been working his entire life for and lost because of me, everything his father had begun, everything that I couldn't help him with and she could. I could do nothing as a flash of heartache lit through me. *I love him. I can say that now.* "You're going to let her see Lucy? Trent, that's so dangerous."

"It was your idea." He exhaled, pulling me closer so my head was against his shoulder and I could feel every inch of him pressed against me. "You're right, though. It would be more dangerous not to," he said, his words making my hair move. "Besides, I'm angry, not cruel, and I'm confident that Ellasbeth is now cognizant of what she gambled and lost by casually tossing that all-or-nothing choice down before me. If she wants to see

Lucy, she's going to make every sacrifice she would've made if she had married me in the first place, but now all she gets is to be a part of Lucy's life, not mine. She will hate Cincinnati for the very things I love about it. My revenge is complete."

He's giving her a chance to fulfill her original role, I thought, tension winding through me. Trent wasn't seeing this as a way for Ellasbeth to wind him around her finger, but I did.

Trent gave me a squeeze, but I couldn't get myself out of my funk. He was bringing pieces back into play to try to regain his standing. I knew he wouldn't sacrifice me to reach his end, but there was no way he could do it if I was beside him—and someday he'd realize that. He'd grow cold, indifferent. I'd seen it before.

"I don't trust Landon," I said, feeling my breath come back from him as my fingers defined the lines of his back. "I don't trust Ellasbeth, and I certainly don't trust them together. As soon as we're no longer useful to Landon, and she realizes she won't get what she wants, she'll try to gain custody with a more permanent means, you know that, right?"

Trent let me go, avoiding me. Damn it, he did know, and yet he was giving her the very chance she needed to stick a knife in his ribs. "Trent—"

"You think Landon's charm is true?" he interrupted.

He was still holding me, and I pressed into him. "I don't like using a charm passed down by oral tradition for two thousand years," I said, then added, "But I think they use it enough that as long as Landon remembered it right, it will work. Are you sure you don't have anything in your library? He could be setting us up. That charm might take our souls for all I know."

His reassuring smile only made me more concerned. "He wants an end to the vampires more than an end to me or you. We can trust that."

"So we're safe until the undead vampires are dead. I should probably write it down before I forget." I reluctantly pulled from him to get a pencil and paper from Ivy's desk. "Even if it will be in my handwriting and not his."

"I think Jenks has it," Trent said, looking out at the garden. "Jenks!" he shouted, startling me. "Where's the charm?"

Pen in hand, I turned from the table to see Trent stretching to the hanging rack to turn the few hanging pots as if to empty them. "You had him copy it? Why didn't I think of that?"

"Because you—" Spent dust spilled out of one, covering Trent in silver. He sneezed, missing the postage-stamp-size scrap of paper now drifting to the floor. It had to be the copied charm, and I picked it up, recognizing Jenks's handwriting and the glyph of a pentagram. "There it is," he said, seeing it in my hand and smiling. "Because you aren't used to dealing with civil servants disguised as religious leaders."

A smile found me. "Have I told you lately how wonderful you are?" I tugged at his belt, pulling him to me again. My arms went around his neck, and I beamed at him, the copied spell in one hand, the fingers of my other hand playing with the hair at the nape of his neck, stretching until I could just brush the arch of his pointy ears. Heartache swept me. How long could I hold on to him? A year? Two?

"Repeatedly, but I'm open to hearing it again," he said, eyes alight with possibilities as he tilted his head and our lips met in a kiss.

Emotion spilled through me, heat tingling from our lips down to my middle, all the sweeter for knowing it could never last. My hand fisted in his hair, and his breath caught at the tight demand. He pulled me closer, his hands at my waist almost lifting me off my feet. *The kitchen,* I thought as my back hit the counter and his hand slipped under my shirt, his fingers both smooth and demanding, tracing over my skin. What was it about the kitchen that seemed to get both of us in a rush?

My eyes opened as our lips parted, but the tingling he'd started continued, making me move against him in time with his ever-moving hands, searching, rising to hint at finding my breast and send new tingles down to my spine. "You know what to do when you think of me, huh?" I said, thinking it was one of the most telling things anyone had ever said to me, making me feel loved and needed all at the same time.

"Always," he breathed, looking at my lips.

"What are you thinking now?" I teased.

"I'm trying to remember why you haven't moved in with me," he said, and we slowly stilled, pressed against each other and content to just be.

Because I can't take that hurt again, I thought, unable to say it. *Because anything this good can't last. Because I love you.* Because Ellasbeth and he were talking again, and I knew that was what everyone wanted. Quen would be so-o-o pleased.

"Tink's titties, you two aren't pressing flesh again," Jenks griped as he flew in at head height, saving me from answering. "God! I'm glad pixies dust instead of sweat. You should see the heat waves coming up from you."

Trent started to let go, but seeing the doubt my silence had made, I pulled him back and found his lips, hungry almost as soon as I closed my eyes and let my fingers drift down his back to his tight, grabbable backside. Trent responded, and I don't know what happened to Jenks's copied spell as I suddenly found myself spun around and plunked on the counter.

"Oh God!" Jenks complained as I wrapped my legs around Trent, imprisoning him. The bare hint of stubble pricked over my fingertips as I traced his jawline. "Stop it, will you?" Jenks griped. "Just 'cause there aren't any more kids in the church doesn't mean you can . . ."

Breathless, I pulled from Trent. My lip unexpectedly caught between his teeth for a bare instant, and a flash of passion lit through me even as we parted. "Can what, Jenks?" I said, letting my feet fall from around Trent so he could turn to look at the disgusted pixy hovering before us. I'd found Trent to be a surprisingly attentive lover the last three months, the tabloids going crazy at kisses over sparkling wine at Carew Tower, and his casual touch as he tried to teach me how to golf, and though the passion had been real, I knew the intent behind the last thirty seconds had only been to shock Jenks. It made me love him even more—he was a part of my life, and I hadn't seen it even happen. Now all I had to do was hold on until it fell apart.

Trent's smile slowly faded as reality came slipping back, drawn by Jenks's orangish dust and the spell in his hand. "Thanks, Jenks," he said as he moved away. I suddenly felt alone as I sat on the counter, the bitter smell of cold coffee coming from the coffeemaker. I slid down, having to tuck my shirt in before I opened a drawer for my magnifying glass. I had like three of them, and I handed Trent the largest.

"No problem," Jenks said as he got over his huff and set the spell on the counter. "You guys never look up, and Jrixibell had a pencil lead stashed up there already."

Jenks's wings seemed to slow their hum at the reminder of his youngest daughter, now out on her own and raising a family. Jax, too, had left again after only a few weeks. I intentionally bumped into Trent as we clustered over the scrap of paper, and I relaxed at the scent of cinnamon and wine hiding under Trent's aftershave. Jenks's sketch was more precise than Landon's, having none of the crossed-off instructions and with the ingredients in order. Even better, it would be harder to link this to me since it was in Jenks's handwriting.

"I'm not liking the spiderweb," Trent said, frowning as he used one finger to hold the paper from moving from our breath. "It's the only thing that doesn't match from what I remember when Bancroft taught it to my mother."

"You know it?" I exclaimed, following that through to an uncomfortable conclusion. "You know how to strip an infant's soul from it and paste someone else's on it? Why did you make me go through that?" But what disturbed me most was why he knew it at all.

Trent was grinning when he looked up. His expression flashed to panic as he guessed my thoughts. "Oh, Rachel, I was ten when I heard it, listening at a door where I shouldn't have been. I'm sorry. I didn't even remember it until seeing this." He hesitated, and I frowned when he touched my arm. "Really, I didn't. But I don't remember the spiderweb."

My shoulders eased, as much from Trent's obvious distress as from Jenks's shrug. "Maybe you should skip that part," Jenks suggested as he took it and rolled it into a tube.

"Maybe," I said, when Trent ducked his head and winced. "Aren't spiderwebs supposed to be for protection, though?"

"Protection through concealment." Trent dropped back to lean against the counter in thought, looking especially yummy when he crossed one ankle over the other. "I think it's okay. I probably just forgot." His focus shifted to me. "I still think giving an undead a soul is a bad idea, but if you don't, Ivy will suffer. Be careful what you wish for, yes?"

"Because it might come true," I said softly. At this point, I honestly didn't care if they all died out, but having seen the chaos in Cincinnati when the undead had been sleeping was a stiff lesson to swallow—or whatever.

I jumped when Trent's arm went around me. "We'll see it through," he said, and Jenks rose up with the charm, presumably to hide it. "No matter what it takes. Soon as we get the charm prepped, we'll go collect Felix's soul. It's probably still lurking about the ley line at Eden Park. We could have this done by the end of the weekend, no problem."

Somehow I didn't think it was going to be that easy. "Thank you." I turned into him, head falling to his chest as he wrapped his arms around me and held me, grounding me in a way that no one had for a long time. I felt his certainty, but my doubts lingered even as I soaked him in.

I hadn't wished for Trent in my life, but now that I had him, I was more confused, more heartbroken than I'd ever been. Trent was willing to sacrifice everything for me, but I didn't know if I could let him.

Chapter 7

Ellasbeth's light perfume lifted from Trent in the tight confines of his car. My head hurt, but if it was from that, or Cormel's vampires tailing us, or Nina fidgeting in the back, or that I was on my way to Eden Park to capture a master's soul with an elven black charm that *Landon* had given me, I didn't know.

"So much to choose from," I whispered, my grip on the wheel tightening as I glanced at Trent. He was slumped against the window, eyes shut and chest moving slowly in the faint light reflected from the twilight-gloomed sky. My irritation eased, and I stifled the urge to rearrange his hair. He looked charmingly vulnerable when he slept, and because of his nature, I often caught him catching a few winks around noon and midnight. It made me feel loved every time.

The scent of angry vampire was growing stronger, and I opened a vent. Behind us, Cormel's thugs accelerated to close the gap as we neared the interstate's off-ramp. The window would have been better, but that would've woken up Trent for sure.

"I shouldn't have left Ivy," the nervous woman said, expression tight as she looked out the window. The car following us was almost on my bumper, and I flicked on my turn signal way ahead of time hoping they'd back off a little. Cormel knew where we were going, and I thought the escort was a bit much.

"They might try to kidnap her," Nina said, her motion vampire fast as she fiddled with her hair, pulling the heavy wash of rich black out of its thick clip and redoing it. "He said he wouldn't kill her. He never said he wouldn't kidnap her."

Grimacing, I took the curve off the interstate, pumping my brakes to get the vampires behind me to friggin' *back off.* Trent took a deep breath as I slowed for a stoplight, blinking himself awake. His flash of confusion vanished as he sat up, looking entirely accessible in his rumpled, relaxed state.

"Kalamack's security has too many holes," Nina muttered, and Trent's smile vanished.

"I didn't mean to fall asleep," he said as he looked out at the shadowed Cincinnati riverfront and placed himself.

"I like it when you do." Eyes forward, I eased into motion when the light changed.

Trent's hand landed on my leg with a contented pop. I let go of the wheel to take it, giving his fingers a squeeze even as I kept them right where he'd put them. My pulse quickened, but it wasn't from his touch. The distance that he'd always kept between us had gradually—almost shyly—dissolved over the last three months, evolving into a surprisingly tactile nature. Casual touches and meaningful looks had become as natural as breathing. But it was different now because I wanted it to last forever.

And burn my cookies if I didn't think he sensed the change when he cocked his head and leaned across the space between us, whispering, "What?"

The thought was still painfully new, and I shook my head, flustered. "Nothing."

His eyebrows high in question, he glanced at Nina as if she might be to blame for my mood, and I shook my head, staring straight out the front window as we wound through Eden Park's outer drive. I wished things were different, that my life was easier. But then I might never have had the chance to see Trent slumped against his car door, smiling as he opened his eyes and found me watching him. *Good with the bad,* I thought, hoping they would equal out in the end.

"Leaving her alone was a bad idea," Nina said again, stewing as she filled the car with the scent of unhappy vampire.

"She's not alone," I muttered, thinking that between Quen's security and Cormel's promise, she ought to be safe. My mood lifted when we passed the town houses and then where I'd left my car yesterday and I saw it waiting. It hadn't been towed, but it wasn't as if we could stop and get it. Frustrated, I cracked my window, neck tingling as the draft pushed everything to the front. "Ivy is fine," I grumped, glad when Trent opened his window as well and the cloud of pheromones finally found a way out. And if Ivy wasn't fine, I was going to spend tomorrow polishing my stakes and amulets.

I had to believe that Ivy was okay—at least until midnight—and I didn't mind at all that Nina wasn't with her, the edgy vampire coming with us to be the bait in the Felix-soul trap. I had a lingering concern that Nina was out for what was important to Nina, not Ivy. That she loved Ivy wasn't in question. What she'd do to keep her was.

Trent sat up as we wound up the long drive to the overlook and the limited parking. Head down over his phone as he texted, he said, "Not very subtle, is he?"

My gaze flicked to the rearview mirror and the big black car. There were at least five heads in there, maybe more. Nina's slow growl made me more nervous than the car did.

"Where does he get off interfering like this?" the woman said, clearly feeling threatened.

I met Trent's eyes in concern, thinking the woman was a dangerous roller coaster of emotions without Felix's finger in her thoughts, all the power and expectations he'd left in her out of control and beyond her emotional limits. Trent's slight twist to his lips said he agreed with my unspoken desire to get out of the car, and I took the first parking spot I could find. There were a few people up here walking their dogs, feeding the ducks, or just enjoying the first shadows spilling over the Hollows. We'd have to take the footbridge to get to the ley line, just on the other side of the tiny twin ponds. The memory of being here almost exactly twenty-four hours ago—fighting for Ivy's life—flitted through me.

"They promised midnight!" Nina fumed, head almost touching the ceiling. "If they're following us now, what makes you think Ivy is even safe?"

"Nina, shut up!" I shouted, and her eyes flashed black.

Trent smiled at my frustration, and I hit the brakes hard. His head swung and he reached for the dash, but his amusement was undimmed as Nina bolted from the vehicle, her heels snapping sharply on the pavement as she strode to the car following us.

"What are you doing?" she demanded, hands on her hips as she stopped them right in the middle of the road, her knees almost touching the front bumper.

"Ivy is fine," Trent said, but I wasn't convinced. "Shall we set up? We've got a few minutes until Jenks and Bis get here."

Trent turned to Nina, standing in the headlights, her silhouette obvious and shapely as she reamed them out. "Is that Felix or Nina?"

"Nina." It would have been easier if it had been Felix, but I'd swear that Felix hadn't taken her over. Nina was beginning to show the power Felix had taught her. It made her dangerous, more unreliable. But we had no choice.

Sighing, I dropped the keys into my shoulder bag as I got out. Trent moved a little slower, his motions gracefully methodical as he collected the briefcase that held the equipment to capture Felix's soul. My stomach was knotting as I stood between the car and the open door, breathing in the new night as Cormel's vampires got back in their car, tires smoking as they backed up to the farthermost reaches of the long, narrow parking lot. They weren't leaving, but at least we had some space.

Nina didn't move, remaining in the middle of the street in her business skirt and collapsing hairstyle. I could tell by her bowed head and shaking hands that she was trying to bring herself back down without the help of Felix's steadying hand. *This* was why master vampires seldom dropped into the living, and never to the extent that Felix had over the past few months. The reminder of what they'd lost tore at the dead. The connection unbalanced the living, forcing them to deal with emotions they had no practice in handling. The longer it went on, the more addictive and dangerous the experience was. Ivy had promised to keep Nina alive, a thin hope that was likely to fail and cement in Ivy's mind anew that she deserved nothing good in her life.

Pity sifted through me as Nina's hands slowly unfisted. *How many times have I seen Ivy do that?* I wondered when Nina looked at the sky and closed her eyes as if in prayer—just like Ivy coming back from the edge of control.

The goons at the end of the parking lot had gotten out, shouting at everyone that the park was closed and to leave, but I think it was Nina shaking silently in the middle of the street that made the most impact. No one wants to be around when a vampire loses it. Sure, there's compensation and apologies, but that doesn't go very far if you get bitten. A vamp scar is forever, fading in time but able to flair into full potency if properly triggered.

Trent slammed his door, and I yanked my hand from my neck, not even realizing I'd covered it. My head jerked up when Bis flew overhead, wings flashing as he awkwardly slid to a halt on one of the shadowed picnic tables. His eyes glowed red as they found me, and the cat-size gargoyle resettled his leathery wings. His skin had gone entirely black in embarrassment for the ungraceful landing, and the white tuft of fur on the tip of his lionlike tail stood out like a beacon as it flicked nervously.

Pleased, I ambled over, smiling as his skin returned to its usual pebbly gray. If Bis was here, Jenks wasn't far behind.

"Nice of you to wait for me, snot breath," Jenks snarled, clearly out of breath as he dropped heavily down onto my shoulder in a wash of silver dust.

Bis shrugged, touching his wing tips together over his head and flushing again.

"I see we got a posse," Jenks added, tugging on my ear as he settled himself. "Bis, I'm more tired than a pixy on his wedding night. *You* check around. See if we got vampires hiding under that lame bridge."

Grinning to show his black teeth, Bis took to the air. I pulled the hair out of my face and looked to see Nina and Trent, the woman nodding at his soft question. There was a whiff of honey and pollen as Jenks replenished his energy, the scent mixing with the more earthy smell of ducks and the nearby barrel of garbage. He'd probably tried to impress Bis by flying the entire way instead of hitching rides.

The vampires had begun throwing stones at Bis. I took a breath to yell at them, only to snicker when Bis caught one and threw it right back, making them scatter and swear.

Nina's steps slowed to a stop, and when Trent continued on, I rocked into motion, respecting her need to be alone. Three more steps, and Trent came along my side. He looked like a businessman on holiday with his briefcase and shiny shoes peeping out from under his slacks. A pinch of worry marred his attempt at a smile, and I slipped my arm around his waist as we crossed the footbridge. I slowed, wondering if Sharps was around. He'd been a big help last time. But the ripples on the surface were only from the wind and current, and tension began to wind its way up my spine and give me a softly throbbing headache.

"I think I'm going to puke at all this sweetness," Jenks muttered, and I tossed my hair to get him to leave. I didn't care anymore who saw us together, but Trent was tense.

"You've done this before," I said, thinking he was stressing about the charm. "No sweat."

"Your soul wanted to be saved," he said as our steps became one at the apex of the bridge. "You gave me permission to take it. I doubt that is what's going to happen here."

"It'll be fine," I said. "It has a containment circle, right? Then all we need to do is lure him into it."

He nodded, but he still didn't look convinced.

"Hey, ah, Rache?" Jenks said, dropping down in a column of gray dust. "We've got company."

Bis whistled from twenty feet up, pointing at two cars roaring into the park, one at either end to block anyone from going in or out. Cormel's vampire thugs had turned, shouting at them as, like a clown car, the vehicles began to empty of more men than could possibly have fit in there. All of them looked eager for a fight—all of them were headed our way.

"How dare they . . . ," Nina whispered, her hiss making my skin crawl.

Trent slowed, his gaze on the footbridge and Al's line beyond it. "I don't think those are Cormel's people," he murmured.

"Hang close, Jenks," I said, and he alighted on my shoulder. Everyone had slowed, the original vampire guards making a front at the base of the bridge. I didn't like that half of the second group was jogging around the small lake to encircle us. Worried, I scanned for Bis. "Come on. Let's get into the line before they make it around the pond."

Trent nodded. What did they think I was doing out here? Having a picnic? "Stop her!" one shouted. "She's almost at the line!"

Okay. That was enough for me, and I grabbed Trent's elbow to run for it. Nina, though, had turned to face them, shaking in anger.

"You fools!" she shouted, feet spread wide. "She isn't fleeing. She could have done that from her church. Interfere, and Cormel himself will tear his revenge from your skin!"

"We don't work for Cormel," one shouted back, and I heard a crack as someone broke a tree branch for a makeshift club. "Stay out of that line, Morgan, or Ivy dies!"

Suddenly it was making a lot more sense. Great. We were right in the middle of a freaking vamp war. Apparently Trent wasn't the only one who thought giving the undead their souls might be a bad thing. "Come on," I whispered, tugging at him. "We have to get into the line."

"And I thought the press was bad," Trent muttered as he started to jog beside me. "What is the line doing over there? I thought the tail of it was in the water."

I flushed, looking up for Jenks. "I accidentally moved it."

"You moved it? How?"

"By accident," I said again, not wanting to talk about it. "Nina!" I shouted. "If you're coming with us, let's go!"

The soft give of the grass became the hard thump of concrete, and I spun as the warmth of the line cascaded over me. Trent slid to a halt beside me, eyes bright and a smile lifting his lips. Nina was slower, backing up as she glared at the vampires jogging to a slow stop before us. Bis landed on the statue of Romulus and Remus. At the bridge, a pitched fight had broken out, but some were wading across the shallow pond to join the few who'd run around it.

"Don't do it, Morgan," a vampire threatened, dripping from the pond and stinking.

More cars were driving up, angled to light the brawl with their headlights. This was going to either make the international news or be buried so deep the lost-dog-found would get more hits. Nervous, I looked at Trent on my right, then Nina on my left, her eyes a worrisome black. I quashed the sudden fear that she might betray us all. We were in the line. The vampires hung back a safe eight feet, but that wouldn't last. I didn't care if getting their souls back would kill them or not.

"Can you get there yourself?" I whispered to Trent, and he nodded. He had shifted realities before, and that's all he had to do, not jump to an entirely new line. "Good. Bis, you've got Jenks. I'll take Nina. Now!"

"What? Wait!" Nina shouted as I grabbed her arm and shifted her aura to that of the line.

"No!" I heard someone shriek, but it was too late, and their cry of outrage rose, echoed, and vanished. The rank smell of burnt amber filled me on my next breath.

"Let go!" Nina exclaimed, tugging away, and Trent coughed. We'd made it.

Hand over her face, Nina squinted into the dusky night as the gritty wind lifted her hair. Bis hunched on a rock, and Jenks darted into my hair, muttering about pixy piss and bloody daisies. The light was dim and red, and it put an unreal haze to everything as it reflected the early night sky. The scorch marks from our fight earlier looked like wounds.

Trent spun around at the clink of a rock, and my pulse thundered at the glowing eyes peering at us from the dark. A second set of eyes joined the first. They had found us already?

"Oh, this is much better!" Jenks snarled from beside my ear. "God, it's going to take me forever to get the stink out of my clothes. Remind me again of why I wanted to come?"

Immediately Trent knelt and used his hand to smooth a place to spell in. There was another shifting of rock, and Nina spun, eyes becoming black. The bluster she'd shown with the vampires was gone. It was a sucky way to live, never knowing if what you felt was real and if you could back your words up, or if you were about to find yourself pinned to the floor and your neck ripped out by someone stronger than you.

"Oh. Yeah. Right," Jenks grumbled. "Save the world, blah, blah, blah."

"Bis?" I asked, and he took to the air in a single downward thrust.

"On it!" he called out cheerfully, and still grumbling, Jenks went with him. There might be two surface demons here, or there might be twenty. Bis and Jenks could find out.

"I'm going to set a perimeter circle," I whispered to Trent, and he nodded, his expression grim as he used a silver knife to carefully scrape a six-foot spiral into the ragged earth. I strained to hear any sound as I moved to the outskirts and used the heel of my foot to make a shallow groove enclosing both Trent's spiral and the rock that Nina had her back against. I didn't set it, concerned that Al would feel it and show up like last time—not with Trent here.

My skin prickled. Trent's magic was beginning to rise. Face pale, he backed away from his finished spiral. His soft chanting tugged at the recesses of my mind, and I steeled myself against the lure, shivering as the chill of the night seemed to cut right through me.

Uneasy, I hastened back to Nina and set my shoulder bag down beside her. "You think Felix's soul is still nearby?" I said as I scanned the horizon.

Neither Trent nor Nina answered me. Trent was fumbling to put his cap on, his red-stained fingers leaving marks everywhere. Lips moving in a silent prayer, he put his ribbon about his neck. Seeing him, I was amazed again at his mix of professional businessman and magic user. His motions were quick and decisive, but there was a new solemn thread to his every action that screamed his belief in the Goddess. It was no longer a game of pretend. He believed, and it made his magic stronger than a demon's, and more variable than a dandelion tuft in the wind—dangerous and unreliable.

"What if he's gone?" Nina said, and we all jerked as a tiny pebble rolled almost to our feet. From the tufts of grass, eyes showed. A silhouette rose, ragged, as if he wasn't real. My breath quickened as I felt Trent pull more heavily on the line and the spiral glowed to make a puddle of green light. The glow stretched all the way to the surface demon, seeming to shred the first layer of reality from it to expose the spirit it really was.

I reached behind me for the solid feel of the rock as Trent's magic pulled at me. It was a call to go home. I'd been there once, vulnerable to its summons.

Scared, I looked up at the black dome the sky made. "Bis? Jenks!" I shouted.

"I don't think that's Felix," Nina said, and I agreed. The hatred shining from the dark was too deep, too enduring. But he was someone. Cormel, maybe? Luke's master? Ivy's mother? They weren't demons, they were lost souls, shoved into the hell of the demons' making until the body died and mind and soul became one again.

Oh God. Don't let me do anything stupid.

Stepping carefully to not touch his spiral, Trent set a thumb-size bottle at the very center, upside down and still stoppered with a black wax. A faint glow raced from it to fill the spiral. Nina gasped, and I winced at the almost unheard whine. It set the bones in my ears vibrating. It was coming from the spiral itself, waves of glowing light pulsating from it like the heart of creation.

Even more carefully, Trent backed out.

"Ah, it's working," I said as more eyes showed, rising up from the grass like lions.

Crouching, Trent touched the red-drawn circle around the spiral, and a not-there shimmer seemed to rise straight up, not arching closed to make a dome but making a perfect column with the spiral glowing within it. It was his containment field, and the ache between my ears grew.

"Nina," he said, hair falling into his face and a glow about his hands that made him look nothing like himself. "Once he shows, lure him into the spiral. You can pass in and out of it, but don't touch any of the lines. The spell should ignore you, even if you touch the spiral, but no need to take chances. Once the surface demon touches any part of the spiral, he'll have no recourse but to walk it. That will force his essence into the bottle."

Is this how he captured my soul? I wondered, a faint memory of chant chilling me.

"Are you sure?" she warbled, clearly ready to break.

"Pretty sure."

I looked at the glowing eyes inching closer, my unease growing. We'd come into this knowing what to do, but not what would happen. Trent's magic was attracting every surface demon within a hundred miles. "Trent, how can I help here?" I asked, and Nina made a hopeless cry of despair.

Something dangerous plinked through me as our eyes met. He could sing souls to him, mine included, and I wouldn't be able to stop him. "Keep the rest off us," he said, words having an odd cadence, not quite chanting, but oh so close, and it pulled at me. "I don't like what your aura looks like. Stay out of the column," he added, then more sharply, "Nina! On your right!"

The woman shrank away, hand to her mouth as a surface demon edged in, emboldened by the others behind him. I could hear them creeping closer, and I itched to invoke the outer protection circle. "Jenks!" I shouted, searching for the sound of wings. "Talk to me!"

But the surface demon had hesitated, his eyes fixed on Nina. "Try holding out your hand," I suggested, and she shook her head, eyes almost entirely black as she retreated.

"That's not him," she whispered.

I turned to Trent for his opinion, and in that instant—the surface demon moved.

Nina shrieked. Adrenaline slammed through me. I jerked Nina out of the way, my other hand extended toward the slavering soul coming at us. "*Detrudo!*" I shouted, locking my knees against the surge of power.

The surface demon skidded to a halt, but my magic caught him square in the chest, bowling him back into the darkness in a flurry of long bare limbs and tattered clothes.

Shit. "Trent!" I shouted, feeling his chant rising through me. "There're too many of them!"

"Look!" Nina screamed, pointing at the dark.

I couldn't see crap. Jenks and Bis were still AWOL, and frustrated, I made a fist and pointed it at the sky. "*Leno cinis!*" I shouted, funneling a crapload of energy through me and into the faintest imagined circle above us. A burst of amber-tinted light lit the entire area in a flash.

Nina cowered as the surface demons hid from the light. I didn't want to invoke the perimeter circle unless I had to, and I breathed a sigh of relief as the grass rustled like dead cornstalks on All Hallows' Eve as they faded back. But they didn't go far.

"I don't think he's here," I said softly, not wanting to interrupt Trent's chanting.

I turned, lips parting as I saw him crouched before his circle, the amber light from my slowly drifting spell making him look covered in old blood. A memory of seeing Al like this flashed over me, shaking me.

Shit, what am I doing getting Trent involved in this?

Nina cried out in fear, and I spun. But it was only Bis and Jenks, and I yanked the energy from a rising spell back, feeling it burn as I dissolved the outer edges and it collapsed.

"Do what you need to do and be quick," the pixy said, then did a double take at Trent, still chanting. "It's like someone yelled free lunch."

And we're the entrée, I thought, flicking the mostly spent charm at the circling demons.

"How do you know you're not chasing Felix away?" Jenks said.

My lips pressed tight. "I don't." Frustrated, I watched two surface demons skulk closer. Maybe Trent should tamp down his siren song a little. But then my eyes narrowed as they stopped just outside my easy magical reach. I turned to the right, seeing five more doing the same. Three were to the left, but more were coming up to fill in the blanks. Crap on toast, they were staying exactly out of my range. That's why the first had been so bold. They'd been learning my reach. Toast. We were toast.

Concerned, I edged to Trent, hesitating when his pull on my soul became . . . tantalizingly alluring, whispering of peace and contentment.

"Trent," I whispered, attention riveted by the glowing spiral, but he was deep into his spell. "Trent!" I said louder, nudging his foot. I didn't want to interrupt, but we had enough souls to choose from now. "They know my reach," I said, feeling as if we'd just left this scene in reality with the vampires. "Can you tone it down a little?" This had been a mistake. I never should have involved Trent. Newt said the Goddess couldn't hear me. I should have done this myself.

Jenks's dust shifted to an ugly black. "They're focusing on Nina," he whispered, and the vampire paled.

"You noticed that, too?" I muttered, then flung up a hand when five rushed us from three different directions. "Get *down!*" I shouted. Nina shrieked, and I threw wads of unfocused energy at them. Again arms and legs flailed as they were blown back, and I spun, making sure no one was sneaking up behind us. They were testing me, and my heart pounded.

"Rachel!" Bis shouted, and I whirled back around.

"No!" Trent exclaimed. His chanting cut off and pain iced through my head as something I hadn't know was there was suddenly ripped away with his voice. I gasped, stunned and dizzy, unable to react as Nina was dragged screaming into the darkness. Jenks and Bis were slowing their progress, and when one let go to swing at Bis, Nina fought back, bucking and twisting until she got free. Sobbing, she lurched back to me.

Trent's spell had sunk deeper into me than I'd realized, and my pulse thundered as I pulled heavily on the line. "Trent! Fire in the hole!" I shouted as I threw a wad of energy straight up. "*Dilatare!*" I exclaimed, exploding it with a twist of my wrist. Surface demons went flying. Nina pressed into the ground, her desperate clawing motion to get back to me never stopping.

Eyes alight, I pulled myself straight. "*Rhombus!*" I shouted as I set the outer circle. Satisfied we'd have a moment, I reached to help Nina stand.

Face grim with anger, she looked up at me, her expression shocked, and changing to fear as she snatched her outstretched hand away, her eyes wide and black.

My heart pounded, and then I was on the dirt, choking as the dust of the ever-after blinded me. Something . . . was on me. Pain jerked through my scalp, and I fought to breathe as bands of steel wrapped around my neck. Sinewy brown arms pinched me to the earth. Thin wiry fingers choked my throat closed.

Panicked, I spun the line through me. The demon howled like a desert wind, but he hung on, even as his skin peeled back and began to char. I could feel the vampire soul soaking into me, trying to take over my body, to merge his soul with mine. Trent's chanting swirled through both our thoughts, making the edges blur where normally they couldn't touch.

"Enough!" Nina raged, her demand a harsh whip.

The fingers around my neck sprang away and I gasped, rolling prostrate as I coughed and felt my neck. The line I'd used to try to burn the demon from me hummed through my synapses, scorching my brain and making every motion hurt. My heart thundered, and every pulse sent needles through my fingers. I got a clean breath in and shoved the line back into the earth as I exhaled in a half sob. It was gone. The demon was gone. I was still myself, but I could feel its alien nature on me, like red dust I had to wash off.

Gritty tears blurred my eyes as I looked up in the fading light from my charm. Nina stood over me, wisps of hair from the demon she'd pulled off me still in her fist. Trent was behind her, white faced. The demon Nina had flung into the rock beside him slid, unmoving, to the earth.

Had she killed a soul? Was that even possible?

"You will not!" Nina raged, spinning a tight circle in warning, finger crooked, all angles and ugliness. It was Felix. Nina had broken and Felix had slipped into her, freeing her from fear, from any thought at all. "You will not because I say so. *She is mine!*"

Not sure if he meant me or Nina, I sat up, glad the surface demons had withdrawn to an unsettling twenty feet back, their eyes glowing and blinking. Nina's lips were pulled back, her posture ugly with her feet spread wide and her head at a weird angle so she could see the sky and earth at the same time.

"Rachel?" Trent's whisper made Nina twitch, and I raised my hand to tell him I was okay. Bis was beside him, black in fear but ready to act. Jenks was there, too, stuck within the circle Trent had made to protect them.

"If you ever trap me again in a circle when Rachel needs me, I will kill you in your sleep, Kalamack," Jenks said, the unsettling black dust sifting from him and making the red dirt turn white. Wiping the grit from his mouth, Trent nodded and dropped his circle.

Jenks darted to me, and I staggered to a stand. "I'm fine," I rasped. "Go see how many we're dealing with." The rock under my hand hurt. It was as if I could feel the accumulated damage from two thousand years of smut raining down on it.

"No," he said flatly, his wings moving so fast they hurt my ears.

Shocked, I looked up, realizing how scared he'd been. For me.

"They're leaving," Jenks added, rising up a few feet and spinning to get a three-sixty. "Get ready for something."

"I get that feeling, too." Ignoring Felix/Nina, I flexed my hand to rid it of the last of the pinpricks. Trent was scrambling to repair his spiral, his chanting half heard and motions hasty, but all I wanted to do was get out of here and back to the vampires waiting to beat us to a pulp.

Nina stumbled, throwing a white hand to the ground to stay upright. My attention shot to the horizon when a surface demon became obvious, seeming to appear from nowhere.

"Trent, it's him!" I whispered loudly, and his magic rose again, the elven drums pounding a chant into my psyche, demanding I submit, become.

Become. It had been what the Goddess had been terrified of, becoming something new, something else, destroying her as she . . . was reborn. Adrenaline pulsed through me, and the sharp stab of pain from Jenks's sword on my earlobe jerked me back. Damn, I had been headed right for Trent's spell.

Nina had fallen to her knees, eyes fixed on the surface demon as tears rolled down her face. "Oh God," she moaned, the pain in her voice telling me it was Felix. "Please . . . I can't."

Beside me, Trent's chanting rose, strong. Nina reached out to the demon. "My soul!" she screamed, the sound echoing back from the roof of the world. "I can't . . ."

Jenks's wings felt like fire. "Rache, you think them touching is a good idea?"

No, I didn't. I shook off my shock and stumbled forward. It was obvious that the surface demon in front of Nina was Felix's soul; the bruises I'd given him were still red and ugly. He hissed as he saw me, but he'd almost reached Nina and I didn't dare let them touch. The woman was crying, afraid to move, I think, and I pulled her to her feet, dragging her backward to lure the soul into following us. This hadn't been the original idea, but we were down to quick and dirty. As long as I didn't touch the spiral, I should be okay. *I'd be okay, wouldn't I?*

Nina took a step, completely unaware or uncaring as the surface demon closed the gap. Her hand went out, shaking as she enticed him closer. "Please . . . ," she moaned, the sound going to my center and aching.

"Little to the right, Rache," Jenks whispered, and my foot cramped with tingles when my heel touched Trent's outer circle. I hesitated, knowing I shouldn't be here. Knees shaking, I remembered the peace the curse promised, the release from fear, from pain. But it was too soon, and I refused it. My sight dimmed with sparkles as I took another step back, dragging Nina over Trent's spiral. The demon followed, writhing, afraid to follow, but unable to resist.

Nina didn't seem to notice when she crossed the first of the spiral lines, even when her foot touched it. The demon, though . . .

The undead soul's eyes widened. His outline wavered, and my grip on Nina tightened as she reached for him, tears streaming down her face and glinting black in the green and red light. Trent gasped when the demon reached out as well, his hand passing through Nina's. He'd become insubstantial. It was working!

Nina and the demon both shook, touching but not. "Oh God, what have I done?" Nina moaned, and my heart thudded as I realized Felix's soul was trying to merge with Nina's. "What have I . . . Please. I didn't know. I had to!" she sobbed. "Let me die, please God, let me die!"

"Get out of the charm!" Trent almost hissed. "Jenks, get Rachel out of there!"

I jumped when Jenks's sword poked my ear, and dizzy, I began backing Nina across the spiral. The soul followed, his feet stepping precisely where mine had been, avoiding the glowing spiral. Trent was right. The undead couldn't have their souls and survive. Felix was sobbing not from the joy of finding his soul, but from the guilt for the hundred years of brutality he'd committed—enjoyed. Cormel wasn't going to believe me. *I'll make him believe.*

Nina pleaded, arm stretched as I backed her up another careful step. My skin tingled, and I shivered as I reached the last arm of it and dragged her to the other side of the outer circle.

"One more step, Rache," Jenks said, and I held my breath against the lure as I hesitated . . . breathed . . . and finally pushed myself out of Trent's spell.

"No!" Nina moaned when I yanked her through it as well. My pulse thundered, and the zing of Trent's field seemed to lick up the edges of my skin, trapping the demon inside. We had him.

"Oh no," Jenks whispered, and Trent glanced at me. His face went ashen.

"What?" I said, his fear kindling my own, but neither one said anything. "What!" I said again, vertigo hazing me as Nina collapsed, sobbing. My fingertips were tingling, but they looked okay.

"Nothing." Jaw clenched, Trent turned back to the charm. "Keep Nina back."

"Give it to me!" Nina howled, and I suddenly found myself three feet away and gasping for breath on the hard dirt. Nina had shoved me, and I watched as she hammered on the column. Within it, the twisted shape of Felix's soul was doing the same, both of them freaking out as their brief moment of connection was sundered.

"Holy pixy piss, Trent, finish it!" Jenks shouted.

"*Ta na shay cooreen na da!*" Trent said, horrified as the demon tried to dig his way under the energy barrier. "*Ta na shay!*" he said again, to no effect.

The demon howled at the sky, then turned to Trent, hatred in his eyes. And then the demon's foot touched the spiral.

Shock reverberated through the surface demon, and his howling turned from anger to fear, and then panic as he suddenly dissolved, vanishing into a quicksilver pulse of light that spun through the spiral to the tiny endpoint.

The demon's last cry echoed, but he was gone.

Nina stared, shocked as Felix's soul was suddenly not there. In the new silence, the bottle slowly rocked, spun, and fell over, clinking against the pebbly dust.

Had it worked?

"Give. Me. My. Soul."

It had been Nina, and I stared at her as Trent, oblivious to everything, struggled to find himself, head down and panting as the ends of his ribbon shook. He'd done it, and it looked as if it had cost him dearly. *Why was I doing this with him? I was going to get him killed.*

"Give it to me!" Nina shouted again, and I scrambled up as she jumped at Trent. Bis flew up in fear and Jenks darted away. Scared, I grabbed Nina's shirt and jerked her off Trent.

"Nina! Kick him out!" I demanded, and she snarled, her hair wild as I pinned her to a tall rock, my hands feeling as if they were on fire.

"There is no Nina," she howled. "I want my soul! Give it to me!"

"I'm sorry, Nina." I couldn't find a hint of her in the woman's glazed, fierce expression. I made a fist, grabbing it with my free hand and swinging my elbow at her head.

It hit her with a resounding *pop.* Pain flashed up through me and was gone. It was a phantom pain. I'd done it right and all the force had gone right into her head, knocking her out.

Elbow stiff, I caught her before she fell and eased her down. If Felix had been himself, I never would have been able to do it, but he was half out of his mind, lost and adrift from having touched his soul.

"Are you okay, Rachel?" Trent whispered, and I nodded. He was slumped beside Bis, exhausted, shaken by what he'd done. I knew he'd have no regrets and would do it again if I asked. But I wouldn't.

Seeing Felix with even the hint of his soul had been enough to convince me that giving the undead their souls would send them walking into the sun. I'd seen Cincinnati without her undead. As much as I hated them, it would be the beginning of the end.

"You can't give him his soul," Trent said.

Saying nothing, I crossed the space between us, kicking dust and dirt into the spiral as I went to get the soul bottle. The spiral was dead. It held nothing anymore.

"You saw what it did to him," Trent added.

The bottle felt small in my hand, and my stomach twisted as I remembered the demon who'd taken shape from Felix's soul, bitter and savage. Without the mind to temper it and the body to cushion it, the soul became warped and broken. *How long had they been apart? A hundred years? Two hundred?*

"Rachel?"

I scooped up my shoulder bag and dropped the bottle inside. Today I felt like a demon, and I wiped my hands off on my pants, shaking as I looked at them and the red dust like blood. "We need to get out of here," I said, seeing the eyes beginning to close in around us again.

Slowly Trent got to his feet. He looked at his spell for a moment, then away—but not at me.

I could *not* fail Ivy. If I failed to convince Cormel that this would be their ruin, then I'd finish the charm and fix it to Felix. And if Cormel still didn't believe after Felix walked into the sun to end his torment, I'd find Cormel's soul and fix it to his putrid, decaying body.

But I'd never ask Trent to do this again.

Chapter 8

J enks tugged at my hair as he struggled to be free of it. We were back in Eden Park, but little had changed. Living vampires were in front of us, staring in the shadowy light from the nearby streetlamps. They were bruised, several sporting bloodied noses and lips, and the ground was torn up. A quick look behind us confirmed my suspicion that we were surrounded by whatever camarilla had won the fight we'd left earlier.

"Sweet ever-loving humping Tink. Can't you jump us somewhere where we don't have to fight for our lives?" Jenks took to the air with the sound of dry leaves.

I reached to set a circle, but Trent's hand on my arm stopped me. "Best not show any fear," he whispered. "I'll keep a tight hold on the line to set a circle if we need one. It might be better if you laid off the magic for a little while."

Laid off the magic? "Are you serious?" I said, not liking the sullen faces looking at me. But they weren't advancing, and I eased my hold on the line until it was the lightest of touches. He was right about one thing: showing fear always brought out the worst in vampires, living or dead.

I thought of the little bottle in my bag and held it closer. They weren't getting it. Then I grimaced, wondering why I was trying so hard to do a black elven charm that might get me killed. The last one Landon had given me nearly had. *Cormel will believe me, and then I won't have to risk it,* I thought, but when Felix's cry of agony and despair raged out to echo against the town houses, I had a bad feeling that Cormel was going to be just as blind.

"What, by Tink's little pink rosebuds, was that?" Jenks said, and Bis made the short hop from the statue to me, wrapping his tail under my armpit and shivering.

Trent scuffed his feet into the pavement. "I think it was Felix looking for his soul," he said. Tired, I dropped my shoulder bag, ready for a fight. Nina was still slumped on the ground and I hoped she didn't wake up.

Never dropping my eyes, the vampire in front leaned to a scared woman who looked as if she'd come from the office, heels scuffed and dress jacket torn. "Tell him she's back," he said, and the woman retreated, her shadowy form swallowed by the crowd. They were just staring at us, giving me the creeps.

"Cormel wants to talk to you," the vampire said, his voice carrying well. He was dressed casually, but his glasses were top of the line, costing more than my last trip to the spell shop.

"Good, because I want to talk to him," I said. My stomach hurt, but a knot had eased. Cormel's people had won. The man might be reasonable. He'd ruled the free world during the Turn, after all.

I'd have known there was a fight even if we hadn't jumped out at the start of it. It was also obvious that a good portion of them weren't Cormel's usual strong-arm force. There were shopkeepers, students, and salespeople among the bouncers, street dealers, and security. Cormel had called in whoever would respond, making sure that when I popped back into reality he would control my next move. Which begged the question as to how big the faction was that didn't want the undead to have their souls. *Ally?* I wondered, dismissing it. Cormel would listen, but as Felix's laments rose anew, doubt stained my conviction.

The vampires around me were an unsettling mix of hope and fear, hope that I had a way to keep them from losing their souls, fear that it might cause them even more pain. Should I give them what they wanted, knowing it might bring an end to their undead existence and plunge the world into chaos until a new balance could be found? One that might have an elven master?

I glanced at Trent as he checked his phone. A power struggle might elevate him back to his original clout, even if he was against the entire thing. Guilt for his drop in status bothered me keenly, but he wouldn't thank me if I handed it back to him by destroying the current balance. There was no easy answer, and as we waited for Cormel, I began to fidget. I wasn't the only one anxious, and Jenks bobbed up and down, fidgety.

"Relax," I said, seeing someone drive a scruffy white dog away. It looked like Buddy, which sort of answered my question of what had happened to the original dog. "It's just a conversation. No one has ever died from a conversation."

Jenks's wings looked silver in the light from Trent's phone as he landed on the man's shoulder. His dust blanked out the screen, and Trent blew it away. "Uh-huh," Jenks said sourly as he took to the air again.

Trent stiffened, his concern obvious. "Ivy's been taken."

"What?" I spun, leaning to read his screen. "We were gone only half an hour!" My thoughts went back to the rival vampires, and my heart almost stopped. *They had her.*

Trent's expression was grave. "It was Cormel. The girls are fine. Ellasbeth is having hysterics." Punching a few buttons, he closed his phone. "I told them to stay put."

My relief was short-lived, and I looked over the surrounding vampires circling us like zombies. *Where is the I.S. when you need them?*

"Think we're going to have to fight our way out?" Jenks said, looking ready for it, but I was weary of it all. Three vampires, sure. Four, maybe. Two dozen—not happening.

Trent, too, seemed more eager to solve this by action than words, but his fake, political smile faded at the rising sound of approaching voices. Rynn Cormel was making his casual, unhurried way to the front of the crowd. Jenks's wings clattered, and with a nod, I sent him up and away for reconnaissance. Bis went with him, and I breathed easier. The farther away they were from me, the safer they were, and my stomach hurt at the ugly truth of it.

Cognizant of my anger and worry—enjoying it, perhaps—Cormel stopped before us, a confident smile on his thin lips. The somewhat small man took his hands from the pockets of his knee-length wool coat, removing his hat and handing it to an aide. His eyes never left us as he fixed his hair, and my skin crawled when Felix's soulful cry rose to an angry demand before it fell into a sob. Several vampires cringed, and I held my shoulder bag tighter. The bottle with Felix's soul clinked. Maybe I was overthinking this. If I didn't give them what they wanted, they'd kill Ivy. What did I care what happened next?

"You shouldn't have taken Ivy," I said, and Felix cried out again, the sound chilling.

"You shouldn't defy me, Morgan." His voice was even, his Bronx accent obvious. He was angry, but his voice lacked any vampire persuasion.

"It's a personal choice," I said flippantly, rethinking my approach when Trent winced. "Cormel, I'm sorry, but giving the undead their souls isn't a good idea."

"You might think differently in the morning," he threatened, and my face went cold. Trent grabbed my arm, and I pushed him off me. Fear mixed with anger, and I watched every vampire's eyes dilate. Cormel smiled at the titters of laughter. They thought they had me by the short hairs. And they sort of did.

"You just keep thinking this is funny!" I shouted. Damn it, what had happened to my midnight deadline? "If you hurt Ivy, you get nothing. Nothing!"

Cormel smiled. "Oh, I assure you that whatever I do, she'll enjoy it. And so will you. You shouldn't have toyed with me, Morgan. Kalamack can't help you anymore."

"I beg to differ," Trent said, and a new fear slid through me. Not him. I couldn't bear it if my mistakes got him hurt.

"Look," I said, and Cormel's eyes narrowed as he realized I was about to make a list of demands. "I just saw Felix with his soul, and it nearly killed him right there. I know I promised I'd find a way for you to keep them, but it totally freaked him out! Listen to him!"

Felix's wail rose up almost as if on cue, and I shivered at the lost sound of it. I wasn't the only one. Almost all the laypeople in the crowd were scared. It was only the heavies who maintained their "pound them" attitudes, and some of them were showing doubt.

"Perhaps if you'd been successful, he wouldn't be so distressed," Cormel said dryly.

"That *is* success you're listening to!" I said. "I've got his soul. Are you blind?"

Shock cascaded over Cormel. "You . . . have it?" The upright, polished master turned toward Felix's raw screams. It sounded as if someone was torturing him. "I thought . . ." His expression hardened. "You dangled his soul before him? Like a *toy*?"

"Easy," Trent whispered as I pulled my bag forward.

If that ugly thing touched me, I'd let Felix's soul out right here and now, regardless of how hard it had been to catch. "We have it," I said, and my fingers dipped into my bag to find the gritty, cool feel of the bumpy glass. I held it aloft, then jerked it back when Cormel began to shake. "It took all five of us, but we've got it."

"And you call us unfeeling animals," he rasped, eyes black. "No wonder he grieves!"

Swallowing hard, I held it tight to my middle. Cormel watched as if it was his own soul I held. "I can fix it to him," I said, but I wasn't sure he was listening anymore as he stared at the bottle. "But it will send him into the sun." *Please believe me. I don't want to have to do this.*

Felix's screams had become more insistent, and clearly upset, Cormel leaned to speak to one of his perfectly dressed aides, not a drop of blood on his coat or a scuff on his polished shoes. "Of course he is in pain!" he said when the man scuttled away. "Give him his soul, Rachel, or Ivy will suffer."

I had known it would be no other way, and as Trent stood behind me smelling of broken leaves and snapped twigs, I pulled myself straight. "Fine," I snapped, knowing my doubt over Ivy's condition was a more powerful goad than seeing her here before me tied up. "I'll do it!" I added, "But I want to see her first."

I jumped when Trent leaned close, whispering, "Close the deal. Make a sure end to it."

I almost cried at his words. He knew I had no choice, even if it meant the end of the undead, and he didn't think any less of me. *I had to trust*

Landon. Shoulders tense, I faced Cormel again. "I'll do it, but I want your word that this pays my and Ivy's debt in full. Everything. And when Felix walks into the sun, there'll be no retaliation and no more demands for your souls."

Felix's cries cut off with a strangled suddenness. Cormel's lips twitched, and I remembered the aide rushing off. Anger radiated from him as he pushed forward until I put up a hand and he stopped that same eight feet back. Pixy dust glittered in his hair, and I knew Jenks was hovering above us in the dark. I could see the lines of worry around Cormel's eyes, feel the tension in him, the overwhelming need he was trying to hide. Cormel wanted his soul. Nothing would stand in his way—not now that he might be so close. "There will be no tally of debt made until I have my soul," he said, and I shook my head.

Nina's shoe scraped the cement behind me, and Trent touched my elbow before dropping back to make sure that she woke as herself and not Felix.

Hands on my hips, I moved forward until Cormel could've reached out to throttle me. I was safe enough, seeing that he knew I was far more malleable when he hurt others than when he hurt me. And besides, Jenks was up there somewhere. "Your soul was never mentioned in the original agreement. I said I'd find a way for you to *keep* your soul. I've done that."

"And you refuse to implement it!" Cormel shouted.

"Because it's going to send you into the sun!" I said, hearing Trent shushing Nina and trying to get her to stand up. "Are you blind? I'm trying to help you!"

Cormel was silent. His eyes flicked to Trent and Nina, then deeper, to his people ringing us. Finally his eyes touched upon the Hollows, and then rose to the sky. I wondered if he was saying a curse to a God who had allowed this to happen—or just looking for Jenks.

"Cormel," I said, soft, so my voice wouldn't shake as my knees were. "I'll fix Felix's soul to him, but only because you're forcing me, and even then only if you agree that when it's over, we're done. That neither I nor Ivy owe you anything. No retaliation. *Nothing.*"

Cold and unyielding, he stood before me as those who trusted him listened. "Not until we all have the security of our souls will I call it done."

Frustrated, I backed up a step, wanting to look at Trent but not daring to take my eyes off Cormel. "Did you not hear Felix?" I said, looking from him to the scared vampires behind him. "Your own people have doubts, enough that an entire camarilla stood up to you to stop me from even trying. The elves think you can't survive with your souls either. That's why they taught me the charm to fix a soul to an unwilling body in the first place. They *want* you to kill yourselves so they can step into the vacuum of power you will leave behind."

Cormel's eyes flicked behind me, and I heard Trent sigh.

"It wasn't Trent who told me the charm, it was Landon," I griped. "Cormel, I know this isn't what you want to hear, but listen to me," I pleaded, but Cormel turned to look behind him at his people. "We can't always have what we want. Trust me, I've tried."

He sniffed, unable to believe I might know what I was talking about. "You gained this knowledge of fixing souls from the dewar?"

I hesitated, wondering if it had been a mistake bringing up the elves, but if Cormel had followed me here, then he knew who'd been going in and out of my church. I nodded, heart pounding. He was making a decision. I could tell. And I probably wasn't going to like it.

"Prove to me that a soul of the undead can again be fixed. Do that, and I will call the debt you and Ivy have accumulated null."

I shivered at his expression, both riven with a coming pain and hopeful that I might be lying. "It will send Felix into the sun," I breathed, and those in the front whispered my words in a rising wave to those in the back, gaining strength and fear as it went.

Cormel dropped his head. His eyes were a normal brown when they met mine again. "He's halfway there already," he said in regret. "We will do this at my house."

Trent scuffed forward with Nina, but I didn't move. I was *not* going to go under the ground with him. I might never come back up. "No," I said, and Cormel jerked to a halt.

"Are you suggesting we fix his soul here?" he said bitterly, indicating the cold darkness. "I won't do this here, nor at your church, nor at any elf holding," he finished, grimacing at Trent.

We needed a neutral place, and unfortunately one was staring at me just across the open grass. "Luke and Marsha's," I suggested, and I swear I heard Jenks dart off to check it out.

Cormel grimaced, but it was nearby, and I might even be able to sit down. "Neither one of them is my child."

"But you have enough pull with their masters or you wouldn't have used them in the first place to try to kill Ivy."

The master vampire thought about that for a moment, his lips twitching when Nina regained her balance and glared at him, her fear for Ivy overpowering her fear of him. "Clear the building," he said gruffly, gesturing. "Make sure the apartment in question is secure."

The vampires began to break up, some jogging to the apartments, but most simply vanishing into the night. Cormel waited, as still as, well, the undead, the wind moving the hem of his coat the only motion about him. Frowning and tucking the bottle back in my shoulder bag, I turned to Trent. Nina jerked away, snarling when I tried to take her other arm, and I backed off.

"You sure you don't have any other ideas?" I asked Trent as we started across the grass, Nina's aggressive stalking held in check by the vampires around and behind us.

"Not any you're going to like," he said. "You never know. It might work just fine."

Or it might kill Felix outright, I thought, but I didn't say it as we made our way to the road. But I'd do anything for Ivy. What happened after that was not going to be my problem.

Chapter 9

Felix sat on the couch not four feet from me, not breathing, not moving, creeping me out as he stared with red-rimmed, hungry eyes while I wiped the glass coffee table with a salt-soaked rag. The three heavies by the door weren't helping, even if the undead vampire was bound and gagged. I wished Cormel would get up here so we could get on with it.

I jumped at the thump from the bedroom, but Jenks gave me a thumbs-up before darting to the open kitchen. Trent, too, had started, and he turned from the vampire graffiti sprayed on the inside of the closed blinds. His eyes roved over the space, evaluating the lifestyle of the average living vampire, calculating the difficulty of getting out of here in a pinch, generally doing his warlord/businessman elf thing.

Apart from the ominous jagged and swirled vampire graffiti, the apartment looked the same as when I'd last seen it. I wondered if Marsha and Luke were still alive and running. It was possible, seeing that the real intent behind it all had been to get Ivy involved.

"Hey, Trent. Be a pal, would you?" Jenks called, and Trent went into the kitchen to take the top off a jar of peanut butter. It had been an exhausting night for everyone, but I thought it interesting that he'd asked Trent. He'd never asked me to help with anything remotely connected to his admittedly high caloric needs.

Must be a bro thing, I thought as I tossed the rag into the sink in the kitchen. Jenks rose up and down on a column of silver, peeved that I'd startled him. We were all on edge as we waited for Cormel's thugs to give him the all clear so he could come up, making me wonder if there was a charm or a spell I hadn't found the first time I was here.

My fingers were cold, and I knelt with the low table between me and Felix. I could feel him watching as I brought the bottle out of my shoulder bag and set it on the table. Felix's eyes turned a savage black, but he didn't move. My heart thudded, making things worse. This was so dumb. Where in the hell was Cormel?

My head snapped up when the man searching the bedroom ghosted out with a vampiric quickness, his nose wrinkling at the smell of burnt amber. Vampires didn't generally like burnt amber—thank God. My thoughts swung to Ivy, who'd never said much either way, something I appreciated. Nina was downstairs waiting for her—which didn't sit well with me.

I knew Ivy could take care of herself, but not when she was suffering from internal injuries and was weak. But Nina loved Ivy. That made her dangerous as she'd do anything to be with Ivy, up to and including killing her. Vampire logic didn't make sense to me.

The hiss of a match drew my attention as Trent lit a huge pale green candle. "Better?" he said as he waved the match out. He looked odd in someone else's kitchen. *I should stop being selfish and tell him to go save the world with Ellasbeth. He has a daughter with her, for God's sake. Why am I letting him endanger himself like this?*

But I needed his help, and I forced myself to smile even as Felix began a weird growling hiss. "Better, thanks," I said as the clean scent of sea foam overpowered both the scent of sulfur from the match and the reek of burnt amber rising from all three of us. Leave it to a female vampire to have a candle that could outstink the ever-after.

"You're doing the right thing," Trent said as he sat in the closest chair. His eyes were on Felix, but all I could think was, *This is a mistake.*

"I don't like being forced," I said softly, and he gave my shoulder a squeeze before picking up the bottle and giving it careful scrutiny. In front of us, Felix groaned.

"No one does," he said as the vampire began to pant through the gag, black eyes bulging in anger. "Don't blame yourself for what follows."

Maybe. Uneasy, I took the bottle from Trent and set it back on the table to get Felix to settle down. I prided myself on being able to find a way out of just about anything, but not this time. Cormel was going to get his way—to the letter of the law and no further. My eyes flicked to Felix, and my jaw clenched. *Ivy, I will not let this happen to you.*

My bag of scribing salt hit the glass table with a gentle hush and I dug deeper. Jenks's wings clattered, an instant of warning before voices rose in the hall. It was Cormel, and Trent stood when the unassuming-looking man came in without even a knock, flanked by three more of his heavies and an aide. I stifled a shiver as we made eye contact, but he was already frowning over Trent's presence. How many guys did Cormel need, anyway?

Conversation low to the point of inaudibility, Cormel toured the apartment, making me uneasy as he circled to finally settle at the most comfortable chair between the gas fireplace and the shuttered window. He wasn't exactly behind me, but I didn't like it, and the Möbius strip clinked loudly when I set it down. Felix was staring at me again, and Cormel steepled his fingers, smiling at me, making me shudder. *Do I stay where I am with Cormel just outside my easy sight, or turn and put Felix out of my sight?*

"He's good," Trent said as he shifted to a second chair so he could see both vampires.

"They don't let you run the United States if you're not." Stomach knotting, I reassured myself that I had everything. Salt, rod, little bowl for the egg, the egg itself . . . Nina hadn't known what color Felix's soul radiated originally, so the scarf was a neutral black.

"Technically, I was never sworn in, but thank you," Cormel said as he idly peeped through the blinds from where he sat.

Jenks rose up from the counter, his fingers buried in a torn piece of paper towel. "We doing this or not? I got plans tonight."

I knew his mood stemmed from worry for Ivy. Cormel let the slat fall and turned to me, black eyes showing his impatience. My heart thudded. Landon was a conniving, backstabbing elf focused on his own redemption. I was reasonably confident the charm before me was going to do exactly what he said—if only because its origins were so nasty—but it was still going to turn and bite me on the ass. I knew it down to my toes. It wasn't a question of *if*, but *how*, and I steadied myself. "Can we clear the room a little?"

Cormel waved impatiently, and his scar-covered aide headed for the door. It creaked open, and the aide jumping back with a cry when a scruffy white dog skittered in, followed by two vampires.

"Rache!" Jenks shouted, and I yanked my bag to me, digging for my original bulky but true strong-magic detection amulet.

"It's a dog!" I shouted as the two men chased him into the bedroom amid the hoots and derisive comments from the watching thugs.

"Hey!" someone yelped. "Watch it! No! That way!"

Buddy barked and ran back into the living room. His feet were leaving muddy prints on the carpet, and panicked by the reaching hands, he skittered under Trent's chair. The vampires slid to a stop, unwilling to reach under Trent, sitting with his ankle on a knee and his hands laced. Buddy growled, but it was a frightened noise.

"Relax, it's a dog," I said again, trying not to watch Bis crawling in along the ceiling. He'd been downstairs with Nina, and if he was here now, then everything was okay.

"I can tell it's a dog," Cormel said sourly as his men clustered around the one who'd been bitten, his hand cradled protectively close. Felix's eyes had dilated to a full, hungry black. I frowned, anger finally finding a toehold in my anxiety and shoving it down.

"I mean, it's Buddy, the dog that lives here, not Luke or Marsha under a transformation curse," I said, and Cormel's eyes narrowed even as he beckoned to one of his people.

"Remove him," Cormel said, pointing. "He belongs in the pound."

"Whoa, whoa, whoa, there, vamp boy." Jenks darted to the center of the room. "This is his turf, not yours. If someone got bitten, that's not the dog's fault."

Trent dropped his hand below the bottom of the chair, and Buddy stopped growling to sniff it. "He's probably just hungry," Trent said, and I watched, surprised when he stood and went into the kitchen. "You hungry, Buddy?" he called, voice high, and Buddy thumped his tail.

"Everyone leave him alone," I said when Buddy slinked out from under Trent's chair, skulking into the kitchen when Trent began opening cupboards, looking for his food.

"We don't have time for this," Cormel said dryly.

"You want him out, right?" Trent's expression was calm as he searched. "That's not going to happen until he trusts you. He's probably not eaten for days." His attention went down and he smiled. "You need a bath, Buddy. Where have you been?"

Jenks hovered over them, and I watched a camouflaged Bis inch into the kitchen, intrigued. "Dumpster, by the smell of it," Jenks said, fingers pinching his nose. "And the river. Cats are better, even if they do try to eat you. They at least keep themselves clean."

Trent found a bag of food and Buddy whined, nails clicking. "Good boy. Here you go."

The kibble clattered into a salad bowl, and Trent set it down with a disarming look of satisfaction. Jenks on his shoulder and Bis clinging to the ceiling beside the fan only added to the odd tableau. All three watched him eat, and then Trent bent to shake even more into the bowl.

Smiling, I turned away, shock a cold slap when I found Cormel had moved and was sitting in the chair right beside me, staring. *Holy shit!*

"Right," I said, smile gone, and Cormel nodded for me to get on with it. "Ah, he needs to be prone," I said, glancing at Felix, the undead vampire glaring malevolently at me, apparently not appreciating the kindness to stray dogs.

Two of the men by the door came to shift him, seeing that his hands and feet were bound.

"Soon, Felix," Cormel crooned when Felix began to struggle. "Soon. Give her a chance to work. I'll remove your gag if you promise not to howl."

Felix's eyes were entirely black, but when he nodded, Cormel patted his hands, taking a small jackknife from his pocket and cutting the gag himself. Jenks and Trent hastened back to the living room, leaving Buddy to growl at the vampire inching forward to grab him.

The gag fell away. "She stole it," Felix said, his voice crawling down my spine as he fixed his unblinking eyes on me. "Make her give it back. *It's mine!*"

Cormel patted his shoulder and stood, the knife tucked inside his overcoat along with the gag. "She didn't steal your soul. She captured it so she could fix it properly." He turned to me. "Isn't that right, Morgan?" he threatened.

I nodded, glad when Trent took the chair behind me again. "Keep him there," I said, not liking Cormel being this close. "If I'm interrupted, his soul will return to the ever-after."

"You might lose it?" Felix exclaimed, his alarm sparking my own fear. "Give it to me! Now!"

"I'll lose it if you interrupt me or take the scarf off your face before I tell you to."

Stark fear marred Felix's young face, giving me a glimpse of what he might have been. Cormel shot me a look to be more gentle before he leaned over Felix and patted him on the shoulder. "She won't lose it, Felix," he said, reminding me that for all their casual disregard for the lives of those they destroyed, they had a weird sense of protection for those they deemed worthy of it. That their children seldom entered that category was indecipherable vampire logic.

Trent leaned over me, the lingering scent of ever-after obvious. "I should do the charm. You're better at defense than I am," he said, almost breathing the words.

Jenks's wings were clattering in worry, and I wished he'd park it somewhere. "No," I said, thinking back to Trent's numb shock of capturing Felix's soul. I was the demon here. I could do it. "As long as no one interrupts me and he doesn't remove the cloth until I say, it should be fine." Chin rising, I looked over the room, not liking how many people were in here. "I need to anoint anyone who's staying in the room with spider silk so his freed soul isn't attracted to them. I've only got a few strands."

Jenks rose up, arms crossed. "I don't need any. No vampire soul will find me."

Cormel gestured at his thugs, and I breathed easier until I realized *all* of them were heading out, leaving just him to maintain control of Felix. And the bastard smiled at my unease. "Kalamack?" he said, almost taunting. "Are you staying?"

My pulse quickened. Rule number one: never be alone with a master vampire. Misunderstandings were often fatal. "He's my spotter in case I need help."

"You are unsure of the charm?" Cormel said, and I lifted my chin, thoughts of Landon's inexperience and hidden agenda warring in me. The man wanted me dead. What in *hell* was I doing trusting that his greed for recognition would keep me safe?

"I've never done it before," I said, my unease coming out as anger. "Trent is here in case there's a snag. Got a problem with that?"

"Can we get on with this?" Felix growled, and Trent pulled his spelling cap out, hastily arranging it on his head before pulling his ribbon from a pocket like a magician. Draping it around his neck he sat down, his ankle going to his knee and settling back to look confident and unmoving. Buddy trotted out from the kitchen, and no one said anything as he flopped down at Trent's feet with a happy sigh. Trent gave Cormel a mute look, daring him to protest.

"Begin," Cormel said sourly.

My fingers shook as I unfolded Ivy's borrowed black silk scarf, the strands of this morning's spiderweb in it. It had been hard to find this late in the year, impossible if not for Jenks. Still kneeling, I draped the first strand over Trent's shoulder. "Thank you for staying," I said, starting when he unexpectedly took my hand, eyes pleading.

"I should do this. It was my idea to trust Landon."

"Yeah, let him," Jenks said, and Buddy sneezed from the pixy dust.

But something in the feel of his hands about mine said he wasn't worried about Landon. It was something else. "And have Cormel say *I* didn't fulfill my agreement?" I said, and Cormel cleared his throat impatiently. "No." I slipped from Trent's hands, feeling a tingle pull all the way through me. "Jenks? Here."

The pixy's chin lifted, and I stared at him until he dropped down and tweaked a tiny piece from Trent's strand. "Happy now?" he barked at me, and I stood.

"Ecstatic." My mood worsened as I looked at Cormel. "Sir?" I said, holding out the scarf. I wasn't going to get any closer to him than I needed to.

Motions slow, he took a long strand and draped it across the buttonhole of his coat. He still hadn't taken off his coat, and his suit under it looked expensive and exquisite, the kind that Trent had once worn all the time.

There was one strand left, and I carefully plucked it free, intending to put it on my hair.

"What about the dog, Rache?"

Crap on toast, what about Bis still hiding at the ceiling? Lips pressed, I broke it in two, holding the larger strand out. "Here, you give it to him," I said, eyes going to Bis in the kitchen. "I don't think he likes me yet."

Jenks's gaze was crafty, dust sparkling as he dropped down. Wings clattering, he took it, darting first to Buddy and then the kitchen, pretending to get another dollop of peanut butter before rising up to give the last strand to Bis.

Cormel was frowning, and my stomach clenched. The world was going to change again. I should have worn nicer shoes.

I took a deep breath and reached out my awareness, laying a mental finger, as it were, upon the nearest ley line. My sour expression melted away as the energy flowed through me and back to the earth, connecting me to all things. It was akin to a warm bath, a shot of tequila, and an hour's massage, easing my tension and instilling in me the confidence of past spells. Feeling the first hints of a soothing numbness, I began to spill the salt into a pentagram.

As if pulled from the energy flow itself, the beating of drums seemed to rise in my memory, making my motions sure and steady as I felt as if I was drawing on the skill of all of those who had come before me. Landon hadn't said anything about the elven chant coming into play this soon, but it felt right, and I let it flow through my actions. *Ta na shay.* See me. See me recognize you.

A gentle warmth from the line tingled through me, my fingers no longer cold and slow. With a sudden shock, I recognized the faint feeling of lassitude slipping into me and I jerked from it. My smooth motion pouring salt bobbled. A tiny slip of sand marred my perfect pattern, and I froze. Felix jerked as my fear hit him. I didn't need the Goddess's help for this, and alarm that I might fall under her sway this easily was a shock.

"Rachel," Trent pleaded, and I shook my head.

"I'm fine," I said as I finished my pattern, not knowing why Jenks was hovering so close. He'd seen me spell worse charms than this. Besides, I was entirely hidden from the Goddess, even if I should stand on the highest tower and shout for her. I was alone, and it hurt after being a part of something so much bigger than myself.

Trent's hand found mine, and I gave it a quick squeeze to tell him I was okay. He always seemed to know when I thought of the mystics. They'd let me see around corners and almost through time. Giving them up had bought Newt's silence, so I knew they were real, my blackmail going both ways as my silence protected her as well.

I exhaled as the last of the salt went hissing down. The lines of the pentagram took on a faint glow in the glare of the overhead light. Satisfied, I reached for the aspen sap. The grinding feel of the glass stopper was familiar, and I didn't set the stopper down as I touched the stylus to it. The thin rod had cost almost as much as the sap itself and was guaranteed to be from the same Colorado field the sap had been taken from: a thousand trees, but one genetic organism. It was a potent symbol. Souls were as unique as trees, but they all sprang from the same source, the same beginning.

Trent whispered for Jenks to back off as I anointed the two feet of the pentagram. His dust burned, and I looked up at the jolt of connection to the rising spell, blinking at Felix's shiny dress shoes parked on the arm of the short couch.

"I'm sorry," I whispered, my spellbound voice coming out almost as a croak. "Can you take off his shoes and socks, please?"

Young face drawn up in affront, Felix wiggled until he sat up. "You forgot?" He looked at Cormel. "Cormel, her skills are inadequate. She failed to fix it to me in the ever-after, and she will fail now."

Cormel was already moving to Felix's feet since Trent was obviously not going to do it. "Dear Felix," he soothed. "Your soul was unable to bind to you because you were in Nina. Morgan will do this, or she and Ivy are forfeit. Lie back down."

The drums seemed to fade at Felix's voice, and I took a cleansing breath. The stylus in my hand glistened at the tip. "Shoes? Socks?"

Cormel was untying them even as Felix protested. "It's *my* soul. This demon witchery is unnecessary. Make her let it out of the bottle. It won't harm me. It won't harm anyone!"

One shoe was gently removed, but as Cormel slipped his sock from him, Felix's expression became nasty. "You stole it!" he shouted, erratic, as if Cormel were taking his defenses from him, not just his socks. "You took it from me. Give it back!"

"She found it for you, Felix." Cormel unlaced Felix's other shoe, keeping his ankles tied with knots made secure from long knowledge. "It would be Nina who would have your soul otherwise." His other sock was pulled from him, and Felix whimpered. "Remember?" Cormel said as he put a hand on his chest and forced him down. "You were in Nina in the everafter. Sit back. Don't take the scarf from your eyes when she puts it there."

Damn it, if Felix didn't cooperate, it wasn't going to work and I'd be left with nothing. My gaze went to the covered windows. Sunrise was eight hours off, too short a period of time to do much of anything if this should fail.

But Felix had gone still in waiting, his feet pale next to the stark blackness of the hem of his pants. They looked cold and too soft for all the people he'd trod upon. They reminded me of Al's hands outside his gloves, vulnerable and revealing, always hidden.

"Keep him still," I warned as I leaned across the space to touch the rod to the underside of his arches and made him jump. I wondered if he'd have any regret when his soul returned. I knew lots of people who felt no regret for the people they'd hurt, and they had souls.

Leaning back, I caught sight of Trent's tense worry. He regretted. He had guilt. I'd seen him more than once in the early hours of a sunless morning, sitting beside the bed, waiting for me to wake and tell him with a smile that he wasn't a bad person.

The choices we make, I thought as I cracked the hummingbird egg with my thumbnail before dropping it into a ceramic dish. Landon hadn't said what to use, and ceramic was as neutral as glass. Damn it, I didn't even know if I was doing this right. Jaw clenched, I used the sap-soiled stylus to dab the egg white of binding on the black scarf.

Immediately the line I was holding seemed to refine itself, the energy feeling more potent as it narrowed to my desires. I was doing it right, and that scared me even more. The phantom drums in my head pounded, and I shivered, wishing to remain hidden even as the chant called attention to me.

"Is it supposed to be glowing like that?" Jenks whispered, shushed by Trent.

"Show me your palms, please," I whispered, head down as the spell wavered over my skin as if looking for someone to soak into.

"Is that my soul?" Felix said, voice high as he wiggled.

"Soon," I breathed. The magic filled me, slowed my muscles. "Show me your hands."

He did, and I dabbed them, my heart pounding in time with the drums. *Ta na shay* rose through me, even as I desperately wanted to hide.

Blood, I thought, fear slicing through the drum-borne lethargy. I needed a drop of undead blood. My head snapped up, and Jenks darted back, shocked at my worried expression. "Ah, I need a drop of his blood," I said, flicking a look at Felix.

"My blood?" Felix snarled, and I drew back as Cormel moved to get between us.

"Felix," he coaxed, his thick fingers looking odd against Felix's young body as he forced him to stay down. "It's for your soul. Just a drop so it can find you. Let me. From your thumb," he suggested, and I nodded. I didn't want to risk contaminating the connection on his palms, but his thumb should be okay. I guess. *God help me do this right,* I thought as I rummaged in my bag for a finger stick. I didn't know what was on that knife Cormel had used to cut Felix's gag. One by one, Felix was losing his bonds.

I pushed the finger stick across the glass table to Cormel. He picked it up, clearly already knowing how it worked. The snap of it opening was familiar, and Felix held out his bound hands, never taking his mistrustful gaze from Cormel as he pricked his thumb. Felix hissed as the master vampire retreated, careful to not get any blood on himself.

Buddy began to snore, immune to everything now that he was home and his stomach was full. Bis was creeping down the wall beside the door, and Cormel frowned, noticing him when a nail scraped.

This is for Ivy, I thought as I got to my feet. Reaching across the distance, I touched the wand to Felix's thumb before pressing it to the top of the silk pentagram. My knees wobbled as the energy flow sharpened to a crystalline hum. The spell was ready. I only had to finish it.

But the beauty of the lines, clouded until I found this very moment, was hard to look past, and I blinked a tear away, shaken. I hadn't seen them like this since losing the mystics. The reminder hurt. I could see evidence of their passage all around me, but they couldn't see me. Perhaps the punishment was fitting.

"Trent, stop this," Jenks protested, and I bowed my head, shaky hand raised to tell Cormel I wasn't backing out of it. Breath held to hide the heartache of what I'd lost, I touched the rod to Felix's forehead.

"Close your eyes," I said, and Felix did. His lips closed over his fangs, and the blackness in his eyes was hidden. He looked normal, frightened, and hopeful to the point of pain. He exhaled and didn't breathe again, and I felt the magic beginning to rise in the room, prickling along my thumb until I rubbed it out. *By the prickling of my thumb . . .*

"Trent . . . ," Jenks whined, his wings making an odd sound.

"It's perfect," I said again, breathless and disoriented as I turned back to the charm, confident Felix wouldn't move for fear of losing his coming soul. "I'm fine," I echoed, breathing in time with the drums. *Why are my fingertips tingling?*

"Cormel?" Felix called, eyes opening and panicked. "Why am I bound!"

"Peace," Cormel said, and Felix dropped back with a whimper.

I shivered as Cormel whispered the word. I could feel Trent behind me as I rolled the black cloth into a cord and wove it through the Möbius strip. As each inch scraped through, it was as if another layer of dross peeled from the lines and my connection deepened. My head hung, and I dropped the metal band to clank against the table. Dizzy with knowing, I shook the salt out. I didn't think my eyes were open. I couldn't tell—sparkles blocked my vision.

"You okay, Rache?"

I blinked fast. It was Jenks. I could tell because his dust was a frightened black, and the rest of the sparkles were a white so pure they were painful.

"Fine," I said, blinking again, and suddenly the sparkles were gone. It had just been the spilled salt on the table that I'd been looking at. "I'm fine."

Oh God, everything was transparently sparkly, as if I was going to get a migraine. Black cloth in hand, I found Felix's expression, hopeful and longing. "It may make you walk into the sun," I warned, and Cormel stiffened.

"I don't care," he moaned. "Finish it!"

Someone was holding my elbow, and I shook as I covered the vampire with the shroud of finding. That same someone handed me a bottle, and I recognized Trent's slim fingers as I stood and peeled the wax cover off.

"Stay with me, Rachel," Trent said softly, drawing me back, and like a breath exhaled on a winter night, a haze pulled from the bottle as I wove it through the air over Felix, his soul remaining still as the bottle slipped away from around it.

"Cormel?" Felix whimpered, sounding like a lost child.

How can a spiderweb fend off an angry soul?

"I'm with you," Cormel said as he stood over him, envy and jealousy in the slant to his eyes as he gripped Felix's shoulder.

I'd be lucky to escape with this one task, I mused, hazy as the elven drums became my entire world. *Tislan, tislan. Ta na shay cooreen na da* wove through my mind, tingling over my skin, soaking in until it found my chi and sent my blood moving to its cadence. I watched in awe as the hazy presence slipping from the bottle grew, the last of it joining the rest like water. My eyes closed, and vertigo took me.

Tislan, tislan. Ta na shay cooreen na da wove through my breath, and the freed soul pulled strength from the salt, growing more substantial. Landon had been wrong. The Möbius strip hadn't balanced the spell. It had charged the salt, and I watched the soul pull it in, becoming stronger.

"It's close," Felix groaned, and Cormel pressed him into the couch, keeping him unmoving. "Cormel, I can feel it!"

"I can see it," Cormel said in awe, and Felix's bound hand rose to his face.

"Don't let him move!" I shouted, and the spirit recoiled at the echoes of my voice. "Hold him. It's searching!"

"Holy mother toad piss," Jenks swore, but the first feelings of doubt trickled through me. It wasn't going for Felix. It wasn't finding him. Why? I'd done it right. I knew it to be right!

Ta na shay. Ta na shay. The chant swirled through me, but I felt the soul lose interest and begin to fade as the power of the salt was spent. It was returning to the ever-after. I'd seen this with Kisten, and my panic flared, making Cormel's eyes flash to black. It wasn't the charm that was failing, it was me. I needed the Goddess, and though I was saying the words, my heart wished for the opposite.

Oh God, I was going to have to call on the Goddess.

"Cormel!" Felix screamed, and Cormel forced him down, his eyes fixed to mine.

"I will tear her apart, carefully held dream by carefully held dream," he threatened. "It will not be fast, and I will enjoy every minute of it."

Oh God, I had to do this.

Hear me! I screamed into the line, silver and pure as thought itself. *See what I do! Lend me your skill. Ta na shay cooreen na da!*

"Oh no," Trent breathed, and the humming of Jenks's wings dissolved in the thrum of the eternity bound in the cracks between worlds.

Tislan, tislan. Ta na shay cooreen na da, I begged, thinking of Ivy. I could not fail her. What happened to me didn't matter. *Ta na shay. Ta na shay,* I begged, letting the line take me as I looked for the bright sparkling thoughts of the mystics.

And I found them. Very close.

Jenks groaned as I shivered, feeling the touch of purple feathers in my mind. Whirling eyes not seeing me poured forth their strength all around but I couldn't touch it. Again I whispered, *Ta na shay. See me. Help me.*

One lazy eye hesitated, falling to me. My pulse thundered in my ears, and I lost myself to the line until that's all there was and I wasn't sure if I still stood in that tiny apartment at the edge of Al's ley line. The mystic didn't recognize me, and I wrapped my awareness around that single spot of light. *Please help me,* I begged as it began to lose interest, searching for something else. *Give your strength to me. It will make my life hell if you do.*

The mystic's attention darted back to me, drawn by my last thought. I cowered under its full strength, and another turned from the glory of the stars to look. *Who are you?* the mystic mused, more to itself than me. *I remember . . . before you.*

Ta na shay, I fumbled, trying to be seen but easily forgotten. *Help me.*

But it was too late, and my soul quailed as more feather-lidded eyes found me and opened wide.

I know you! one called in terror, but others grasped the thought raging through them like fire as if it was joy. *You are the becoming!*

Shit, this was not working. *I'm sorry,* I thought, then made a quick twist in the wave of energy flowing through me. Panic flared, but it wasn't mine, and that fast, I took the power of the Goddess and made it mine.

"Rache!" Jenks shouted, and my eyes flashed open.

Trent was not holding me upright. He was forcing Felix's feet to the couch. Cormel was sitting on the vampire, the cloth pressed against his face and snarling. Felix was screaming, out of control as he tried to be free.

"*Tislan, tislan. Ta na shay cooreen na da!*" I screamed, convulsing at the purity of the line arching through me. It exploded from me, lighting the room in a flash of purple and silver. Jenks flew end over end into the kitchen, his face aghast as Bis caught him inches from the wall. Trent and Cormel were flung from Felix. I couldn't see Jenks's tears, but I tasted them in my mind as the mystics brought the image to me, as gentle and easy as breathing. They scintillated within the room, power with direction, just needing to be tasked.

Oh God, what have I done?

"*Cooreen na da!*" I said again, and the energy filling the room collapsed into Felix, carrying the wandering soul with it.

Felix screamed, the sound finding the pit of my soul and squeezing. It was the cry all make when they first breathe, but behind it was a world of understanding, of pain, of knowing.

For an instant, no one moved, and then Felix screamed again.

Scared, I dropped the line. Blackness hit me, and I stiffened, afraid to move. It was gone, everything, and I froze. I could feel nothing.

"Rachel!" Jenks called, and the world rushed back. Trent took me in a crushing embrace, and I breathed. Numb, I felt his heart beat against me. It reminded mine of what it was supposed to do. It was dark, and I didn't know why.

"Breathe," Trent said, his hold never easing. "Stay with me, Rachel. This is where you belong."

"I know," I mumbled, but the words seemed hard to form.

Pain iced through me when Felix screamed a third time, and my eyes opened. Trent held me as I stood. Cormel struggled with a bound Felix on the couch. Beyond them, Bis stood on the kitchen counter with Jenks. The gargoyle's red eyes were round, and his skin was blacker than the line was white. "Am I okay?" I whispered, and he nodded.

"You broke the lights," he rasped.

Blinking, I realized I had. Only the glow from Jenks's dust and the candle Trent had started lit the room.

"My God," Jenks whispered, and my gaze shifted to him. "It worked! He's got an aura!"

The hunched shadow of Cormel let go as if stung. Shock—unusual and frightening in the undead—shone from him, a forgotten, unneeded emotion. He staggered back as a faint bluish-green haze, patchy and thin, began to rise from Felix. It was his soul, and it was struggling to escape even as Felix writhed, trying to contain it.

"Take the cloth!" I exclaimed. "Burn it! Now!"

Cormel reached out, hand drawing back as if afraid to touch him.

"Oh, for Tink's ever-humping loving," Jenks swore, darting down and snatching the silk off Felix.

"Burn it!" I cried out, struggling against Trent's arms as a thin ribbon of aura trailed from Felix, mixing with Jenks's dust as he flew to the candle.

"No!" Felix howled, back arched and searching, and then the cloth hit the flame. It went up in a flash. Jenks darted to safety. Felix collapsed, sobbing, but it was different this time, broken, relieved, full of pain. His soul was trapped in him. This wasn't going to be good.

I can do better than this, I thought, shaking as Ivy came to my mind. She wouldn't have such a hard time of it since she hadn't been dead for two centuries.

Cormel inched closer to Felix. "Is it done?" he asked, and I nodded, only now realizing that I was still in Trent's arms.

His hold was tight in fear, and I looked up at him, seeing the stress in the lines by his eyes. "I'm okay," I said, and he let go fast.

Jenks hovered close, eyeing me sharply. "You sure?"

My knees felt funny and my head was humming, but I nodded. Cormel dropped to his knees before Felix as the vampire sat up, hands shaking and tears of regret and guilt spilling down his cheeks. This was not going to end well. *Ivy would handle this better.*

"Rachel is okay," Bis said, but he was still black in fear as he jumped to my shoulder, his tail wrapping tightly around me. I couldn't feel the lines at all, and for the first time, I was glad of it. I shouldn't have wrested the Goddess's power from her, even if I gave it right back. She was going to start looking for me again, changed aura or not.

"Okay, Rache is all right, but what about him?" Jenks said, and we turned to Felix. My stomach hurt as Felix sobbed, sitting up and trying to wipe his eyes with his bound hands. His bare feet on the carpet looked odd with his business slacks and pressed shirt. It had worked. The real question was, would he survive its success?

"You can let him go," I said, my voice sounding ragged to my ears. I was suddenly fatigued, and I waved off Trent's help as I sat down. Buddy was gone. Smart dog. *Are my hands sparkling, or is it my imagination?* "He's got his soul," I added, though it was obvious. For better or worse, he had his soul, and it seemed to be working. *Ivy . . .*

"She is not okay!" Jenks snarled, and Trent leaned closer to the hovering pixy.

"Yes she is," he insisted. "Look at her."

"I am, cookie farts. She's not okay!"

Bis leaned to put his face next to mine. "You're okay, Rachel. I can tell."

But I wasn't sure how he knew. I started shaking, the entirety of the evening coming down hard. The Goddess had recognized me and my mystics had found me. She'd be on the lookout now. I'd be lucky if I could even use the lines.

"Where is Ivy?" I said, and Cormel looked up from where he still knelt with Felix. I didn't like the hunger in his eyes. It wasn't for blood, it was for his soul, and I held my breath, ready to move though every part of me was pained and sluggish.

Trent moved to get between us. "It's done," he said firmly, Jenks hovering beside him to create a united front. "She paid her and Ivy's debt. Give us a token that you free them."

Cormel turned to Felix, and my lips parted when Felix finally looked up. His eyes held sorrow, but there was hope, too. "I am me," he said, voice broken. "I am whole." Eyes shining with tears, he clung to Cormel. "I don't hunger! Rynn, it's gone! The ache is gone." His head dropped. "Let them go. If she can do this, any witch can."

Cormel stood. Trent shifted, becoming a threatening shadow in the flickering candlelight. "I want my soul. He's whole and undamaged. Do it now!"

"I did what I promised," I said, taking Trent's arm so I could stand up, awkward because of Bis's weight, slight as it was. "You know how to find your souls. I'm not going to do it."

"You refuse *me*?" Cormel shouted, and Felix looked up, blinking.

"Find someone else!" I said, tentatively tapping a line and breathing in relief when I felt no change, no recognition. "I'm not the only demon in existence. Talk to one of them," I said softly. "You can't afford me anymore."

Cormel's eyes narrowed, black in the shadow light. "Perhaps. Remember you said that."

What did he mean by that? I wondered as Cormel helped Felix to his feet. The once-powerful vampire was falling apart. Only time would tell if he could piece himself back together.

"I want a token that our agreement is fulfilled," I demanded, leaning heavily on Trent. "If you threaten Ivy or myself, you'll find out what it is to face a free demon, Cormel, and you'll lose."

He hardly even gave me a glance as he helped Felix to the door.

"Cormel!" I shouted, and he flung the door open. My anger evaporated. Ivy was there, Nina supporting her. Surrounding them were his men, all of them frustrated that they'd been commanded to stay out.

"Here is your token," Cormel said, his teeth clenched. "We are done, Morgan. You and Ivy owe me nothing, and I owe you the same."

Ivy hung in Nina's grip, eyes dark as she took in my ragged state and Felix's slumped weariness. The light of possibilities was in her eyes, and

Nina was flushed and breathless. Buddy came from the bedroom at the sound of the door opening, and he trotted to Trent.

"Don't come back to me," Cormel said, his expression empty as he looked at Ivy, Felix hanging on his arm. "I will not see you."

Ivy blinked fast, and Nina pulled her out of the way when Cormel gracefully carried Felix through the door. Immediately his aides descended upon them, and in a shockingly short time, they were down the stairs and gone.

"He has his soul?" Ivy finally asked, and I nodded, stiff as I forced myself to move. *Where's my bag?*

"I'm so tired," I breathed as I found it and shuffled to the door, not protesting when Trent scooped me up.

"I told you she shouldn't do that dumb charm," Jenks muttered, and I tried to focus. Bis. Where had Bis gone?

"She's just tired," Trent said, then more stridently, "No, we're not taking the dog."

"But he doesn't have anyone," Bis complained, then giggled as Buddy licked him.

My eyes are closed. How do I know Buddy is licking Bis?

"She's just tired," Trent said again. "Come on. We could all use a shower."

I nodded, my head falling onto Trent's chest. I was too tired to think, but a shower sounded good.

Chapter 10

I can't. Allergies," Nina shouted over the wind from the backseat of
my MINI Cooper. It had been closer than Trent's car at Eden Park, a
relief to get back even if I wasn't driving it.

Jenks's wings drooped as Bis leaned to see the dog, wiggling on Ivy's
lap. "You don't look allergic," the pixy said, and Nina made a prissy, fake
sneeze even as she rubbed Buddy's ears. The top was open, and the dog was
enjoying himself, tongue hanging out and his tail smacking into the back
of my seat with a regular rhythm that nearly matched the clicking of the
turn signal. We were almost to the church, thank God. Even with the top
open it smelled like vampire, burnt amber, and stinky dog. Reason two for
taking my car instead of Trent's.

Nina was in too good a mood for my liking: too good, and too in control. I didn't think Felix had the presence of mind to be dipping into her
thoughts right now, but it felt as if the worst was yet to come. In contrast,
Ivy was tense, her motions edging into that vamp quickness she always
took great pains to hide from me.

Trent had driven us to the church despite my protests. I'd counted six
yawns from him so far. Bis was on my lap, expression mournful as Jenks
continued to try to get someone to take the dog home. Jenks was right. We

had enough strays. Rex could take care of herself in a pinch, but Buddy was high maintenance.

"Carport?" Trent asked when we found our street, and he took the curve fast, shooting into the covered spot on momentum. The headlights flashed and bobbed as we careened to a stop, and I braced myself, startled when Bis jumped into the air. Trent wasn't angry, he simply liked driving my car to its fullest extent.

Ivy and Nina didn't wait, Nina swinging her legs up and over the side of my small car and to the cement before using her vampire strength to lift Ivy carefully to the walk. "This way, Buddy!" Bis called, and I heard the happy sound of clicking nails and jingling tags.

"This isn't going to end well," Jenks said sourly before he darted up and out. "Bis! Keep that dog in the garden until he pees on something! Tink loves a duck, you don't bring someone into the garden who doesn't know how to bury their own crap!"

I watched Ivy slowly manage the front steps with Nina's help. Seeing me with Trent, she smiled softly as Nina yanked the door open, the woman's chatter never stopping as they went in. Finally the door shut. We were home, but I was too tired to move. My smile faded.

The keys jingled as Trent handed them to me. "You want me to carry you in?"

His tone was amused, but the sad thing was, I was tempted. "Give me a minute. I'm just tired." Tired and not wanting to have to go in and deal with the mess.

"Me too." He yawned again. "I'll call a cab to get back to Eden Park. I don't want to leave you without a car."

"Thanks. Take Jenks with you, okay?"

His phone hummed, obvious in the midnight silence. Taking it from a pocket, he silently looked at it, sighed, and tucked it back. "Ellasbeth?" I guessed, and he nodded.

"If it's important, Quen will call. Huh. I think I left my briefcase in the ever-after."

He had, but I wasn't going to suggest we go back and get it. I knew I should be in a better mood, but I was just so tired. "Do you think Cormel will hold to his agreement?" I asked. Maybe that was what had Ivy uptight.

"To the letter. He won't go to the demons, though. He's going to talk to Landon."

"Let him. I'm done with it." Expression sour, I pulled my shoulder bag from the floor. Landon's charm had been perfect, but he'd known I'd have to make contact with the Goddess to finish it. That's why he'd given it to me. *Son of a bitch* . . . "Trent, the mystics recognized me."

Trent was silent for half a second, and then he moved, his motion fast as he got out. "I think I left my tablet inside. I should get it before I go."

"You saw them, didn't you?" I said, confused. He hadn't ignored me, but burn my cookies if he didn't look . . . scared. Our doors shut almost together, and I gathered my resolve. I wasn't going to let this go and possibly fester. "You and Jenks both," I said as I met him at the back of the car. "The mystics."

Eyes on the street, Trent looped his arm in mine. "Yes."

My pulse quickened. "Is it bad?" I asked, that same nauseous feeling clenching in my stomach as the memory of that black nothing I'd felt rose up. Jenks's call and Trent's arms had brought me back. It felt as if I had nearly fallen into shadow. "Trent . . ."

"They follow you like puppies," Trent said softly, our steps slowing. "Ever since we captured Felix's soul in the ever-after. Are . . . they speaking to you?"

He *was* afraid, and I shoved my own fear aside. I knew I'd seen Bis and Buddy with my eyes closed, both of them on the floor as Trent carried me out. It had been a compilation vision of at least a dozen mystics, cobbled together and presented to me in a way that my mind could interpret naturally—sophisticated and practiced. They weren't the Goddess's mystics, but the ones that Newt trapped in reality so they couldn't poison the Goddess. They were alone and unable to become, but the alternative was their complete obliteration. But had I heard them? No, the connection had not been that deep.

"No," I said softly, and Trent breathed a sigh of relief.

"Good," he said, his fingers finding mine in the dark as we walked to the church, lights flickering on inside to show where Ivy was. "I don't think you should do wild elf magic."

I gave him a sideways look as I opened the door. "You think?" The warmth and light spilled out, and I squinted as we went inside. Trent's hand was on the small of my back, and I listened for not-there voices telling me about the scatter pattern of the photons, but my thoughts were silent. *Safe?* I thought, then, with a touch of melancholy, a more certain *empty.*

"Oh, Rachel," Trent said, somehow knowing as he pulled me into a hug right there in the foyer. "I'm so sorry."

He wasn't talking about tonight, and I tucked my head against his shoulder, breathing in the spicy scent of wine and cinnamon under the reek of burnt amber. I refused to cry, even though I ached. It was stupid to cry over something that would hurt me if I had it. It hadn't been a choice between the mystics and Trent, though that's how Newt saw it. Keeping them would have destroyed the Goddess and changed me beyond what anyone could handle.

"I'd give them up again in a heartbeat," I said, and he tilted his head to give me a kiss. My eyes closed as our lips met. Tingles followed by a swath of warmth plinked through me, and I pressed into him as my arms went around his neck. Even if it *had* been a choice between them and Trent, I would've taken Trent. I didn't have to explain things to him, and he knew how tight to hold, when to go along with an idea, and when to slow me down so I could think.

The vibrating hum of his phone was almost unheard, but I dropped back to my heels. *Too bad I'll only drag him down from what he could be.*

Trent frowned, and from the hallway, Nina called to Ivy that she'd only be a few minutes. The bathroom door shut, and shrugging, I looked at his pocket and his humming phone. "You probably should take that. She's going to keep calling."

He said nothing, but his grip eased, and I found a smile. "You want some coffee? It's going to take at least thirty minutes to get a cab out here."

"Sure, thanks." Pulling his phone out, he looked at the screen and dropped it back again. "I need something to wake me up," he said, then yawned. "Sorry."

My hand found his fingers, and towing him almost, I headed for the back of the church and the scent of brewing coffee. The sound of the shower from my bathroom was obvious, and I winced, thinking I must stink with burnt amber and vampire fear.

Jenks, Bis, and Buddy blew into the hallway from the back living room, and I jerked into a hunched duck. "No!" Jenks said, his dust an irate red. "Someone tell Bis he can't have a dog!"

"We already have a cat," I said, and Bis's wings drooped as he hung upside down in the doorway to the kitchen. Buddy stood under him, tail waving and neck craned. "They won't get along."

"I'll take care of him," the little gargoyle pleaded, and Jenks made a harrumph, fists on his hips. "I'm fifty years old and I've never had a pet," Bis complained.

Shaking my head, I ducked under him and went into the kitchen. "He's awake in the day, and you're not." Ivy smiled at me from her usual chair before her computer. She liked normal, and we'd had precious little of it since most of Jenks's kids had left.

"He's up now! I can train him in the dark. He already knows how to use the cat door."

A soft smile curved the corners of Trent's lips up as he crouched to fondle the dog's ears. "I've never had a pet either, Bis. Inside pet, I mean."

"See?" Jenks crowed. "Even Trent knows it's not a good idea."

Trent eyed the pixy, his expression making it obvious that hadn't been what he was saying. Bis did a front flip from the top of the doorway to land right on Trent's shoulder, startling both him and the dog. "We can't take him to the pound."

Why am I the boss all of a sudden? I went for the coffee, hoping it'd all just go away, but Jenks's wings rose in pitch, making my teeth hurt. "Trent can take him," Jenks said suddenly.

"Ah, no." Trent rose, his hands up in protest. "I can't take care of a dog."

Bis lightened to his usual pebbly gray, and Jenks bobbed up and down like a yo-yo. Even Buddy seemed to like it as he waved his tail, responding to Jenks's excitement. "Tink's titties, you can so. You got a pack of them. What's one more?"

Again Trent's phone hummed, and I held out his coffee to him as he frowned. "He's a mutt, not a hound. He needs more attention than I can give him."

All true, but I'd go along with it just to get the dog out of my church.

Trent set his coffee on the table so he could look at his phone, and Jenks dropped down, sparkles floating on the black brew. "Ellasbeth will hate him," he enthused. "Come on. The girls will love him."

I leaned to see it was Ellasbeth. "She's just going to keep calling."

Trent sighed. "Do you mind?" he said, face twisted up unhappily, and when I shrugged, he answered the call. "Ellasbeth. Yes. Just finished. I'm getting a coffee while I wait for a cab." He hesitated. "Eden Park. We drove Rachel's car back. Are the girls okay?"

I took my coffee to my usual chair. Jenks, though, hot on a chance to get Buddy out of our church, remained by Trent. "You can take him for walks," the pixy prompted. "And he pees on your plants to mark your territory for you. What more could you want from a best friend?"

"It sounds like you've done your research," Trent said. "Will you excuse me?" Turning away, Trent headed out of the kitchen and to the back living room. "Ellasbeth? Yes, I'm here. Can I talk to Quen?"

Buddy, Bis, and Jenks trailed after him, and I smiled at Ivy in the new peace. She rolled her eyes and I pushed my untasted coffee to her. "Thanks," she said, her long, pale hands slipping around the porcelain. "Just as long as the dog doesn't end up here," she added, and I nodded, getting up to pour myself a new cup.

Hesitating, I took only half a cup, leaving the rest for Nina. Warm cup cradled in my hands, I leaned against the counter. "So . . . how does it feel?"

Ivy's eyes flicked to mine and held. "To be free of all of them? I don't know." Her focus eased and she smiled faintly. "I've never been alone like this. Scary, maybe?"

Scary? I set my coffee down and crossed the kitchen in three strides. Ivy looked up, startled, and then I dropped down right there so I could give her a hug. "You're not alone," I whispered, my arms around her and breathing her in. Slowly her hand touched my back, hesitant and light. The memory of her teeth sliding cleanly into me rose and fell, a flash and then nothing.

"That's not what I meant," she said, and I let go of her. "I'm scared," she said, eyes beginning to swim as she looked at the ceiling. "I'm scared, even as I've got this wonderful thing happening." Her eyes fell to mine. "I've always been untouchable, protected by someone so powerful he alone can abuse me and call it love. For the first time I'm my own person. What if something happens?"

I gave her a squeeze, smiling. "No one is going to touch you with me around."

She made a bark of laughter at that, wiping her eye. "That's funny. I remember saying the same exact thing to you when you moved in."

"And no one did, did they?" I glanced at Trent as he strode down the hall, phone to his ear. Bis, Buddy, and Jenks followed with noisy chatter.

"Don't be absurd," he said, voice faint from the sanctuary. "The girls were never in any danger. Vampires have a soft spot for children. They wouldn't have touched them."

It was true, and I looked back at Ivy to see her lost in a memory. "You okay?" I asked, and her focus sharpened on me. There was sorrow in her, even as she was glad to be free of them. She nodded, and I stood.

"He's going to walk into the sun, isn't he?" Ivy asked.

"Pretty sure," I said glumly. "How's Nina?" Meaning, was she strong enough to survive it?

Ivy's grip was white-knuckled tight on her coffee. "She hasn't gone a day without him in her mind to steady her," she said, eyes down. "I can't save her. She just can't stop. He's in there now, I can tell. Maybe I should just walk away."

He was in her now? My God, I would have bet my life that he wasn't. "Ivy . . ."

"I can't save her if she doesn't want to be saved, Rachel!"

There was a sudden sliding of dog nails in the hall, and we both turned when Trent poked his head into the kitchen, his phone pressed against his shoulder. "Rachel, can I use your room for a moment. I need a door."

"No door ever stopped me," Jenks boasted as he hovered behind him. "Trent, I'm telling you it's a great idea. She's going to hate it!"

I nodded, and Trent smiled a quick, terse thanks and vanished.

"Hey!" Jenks darted after him. "You're the one who wants her gone!"

Ivy looked depressed as she stared into her coffee. I hesitated, then called out, "Jenks? Will you and Bis check the walls?" Jenks hovered backward into the archway until I could see his utter disbelief. "I'll get him to take the dog. Just leave him alone, okay?"

Bis looked in, upside down and around the doorframe, both sad and happy. "Yeah?" Jenks said, and when I crossed my heart, he flew off. Bis dropped into the air, and followed.

"He doesn't want Buddy," the gargoyle complained. "I can take care of him. I promise!"

There was a scrabbling of claws and a squeak from the cat door as the three of them finally left. Sighing, I looked at Ivy, still despondent and lost in thought.

"It's going to be okay," I said, but my confidence was faltering. "You've been fighting them your entire life. She's only been doing it for six months."

Her shoulders were stiff, and she started to cry. Ivy, who could do anything, was crying silent tears, unable to move for fear of falling completely apart. "She doesn't have a lifetime to learn," she protested. "She's got days. He's going to walk. Cormel knows it, but he wants his soul so bad he's ignoring it. He's going to walk, and she's going to die with him!"

The shower went off, and she stood, mourning a future not even here yet. "Oh God, she's going to go mad."

"Ivy." She wasn't listening, and I squeezed her shoulder. "Ivy, look at me!" Finally she turned back, and I tried to smile, even as my heart thumped in fear. I'd do anything to save her, to see her happy, but never had I thought it might mean I risked my life for someone I didn't even like all that much. "I've been thinking about this," I said. "I think I can modify Trent's binding charm so that you can carry it around with you, like in your purse or something, and if she does die, you can catch her soul."

"But . . . ," she whispered, hope almost painful in her eyes.

Still, I smiled. "I know it's not exactly what you want, but if you have her soul, it won't be in the ever-after. I think if we fix a soul soon enough, there would be almost none of the trauma that Felix is showing. Maybe it's not that he has his soul back that's causing the trouble. Maybe it's the guilt for all the things he did that is sending him over the deep end. He was never that stable to begin with."

Tears fell freely, and she smiled, looking beautiful. "You think?"

Eyes welling, I pulled her into a hug. I had to do this, the Goddess be damned. "I know."

Ivy started at a soft scuffing of bare feet, and we jerked apart as Nina cleared her throat. I flushed though we'd done nothing wrong, and Ivy hurriedly wiped her eyes. Her chin lifted, not to hide that she'd been crying, but rather a clear statement that she wasn't going to talk about it.

"Sorry," Nina said, looking domestic with her hair up in a towel and Ivy's black robe tied around her. "Didn't mean to interrupt."

I backed up from Ivy. Jealousy was normal, expected, and I almost welcomed seeing it since it meant she loved her. "Did you leave me any hot water?"

Nina's smile was wide but clearly fake. "You bet."

"Thanks." My smile was honest, though, and I gave a nod to Ivy as I left. She looked a hundred times better. This was what she had been worried about, terrified she was going to lose Nina when Felix walked. I was going to make two bottles, not just one. I'd find a way around needing the Goddess's help.

"Don't be silly," Ivy said loudly as I reached the bathroom. "She's just glad I'm okay. I did get hit by a car yesterday."

Had it only been yesterday?

No way was I going to put my same clothes on, and I knocked softly on my door, then went in. Immediately my expression eased. Trent was stretched out on my bed, the stuffed animal he'd won for me at Six Flags shoved under his head, his feet all the way down to the folded-up afghan. His eyes were shut, and his phone was in his loose grip. I could hear Ellasbeth talking.

"Yes, I'm listening," he mumbled, eyes shut.

My heart went out to him, and I carefully slid the phone free, edging backward to the door and slipping out. He didn't even notice, seeming to settle in even deeper atop my covers.

Breath held, I eased the door shut and leaned against the wall. "I'm trying to understand, Trenton," Ellasbeth's perfectly reasonable voice said from the tiny speaker. "But you're ignoring the consequences of your actions."

I wanted to lash out, drive her away. I *loved* Trent, and she was going to ruin it! But what I did was clear my throat and pleasantly say, "Excuse me, Ellasbeth?"

There was a moment of shocked silence, then, "Rachel? I'm talking to Trent."

Jenks hummed into the hallway from the kitchen, and I waved at him to be quiet. "Actually, you're not," I said, and the pixy hovered close, grinning. "He fell asleep, and I'm asking you not to call again for at least four hours unless it's an emergency."

She was silent, but I could hear her anger as she breathed. A small part of me felt bad. I'd vacationed in Camp Dumped before, and it hurt. "Look," I said, holding the phone closer. "He's been up for forty-eight hours. Jumped realities twice, rescued a soul from hell, and adopted a dog," I said, and Jenks gave me a glittering thumbs-up. "He's doing the smart thing and catching some Zs before coming home, okay? And until he wakes up, I'm holding his phone in case there's an emergency. Is this an emergency?" I knew it wasn't, but I couldn't resist the tiny dig.

"You are not his wife," she said caustically.

"Neither are you," I said right back. Okay, maybe two digs.

"No, I'm just the mother of his child."

I warmed even as I waved Jenks back. "Right, I'm glad you brought that up," I said, doing my utmost to be reasonable, but wanting to impart a few things to her and the only way she listened to anyone was if they hit her with a stick. "God help me, but I'm the only one who thinks you spending time with the girls is a good idea, and I'm starting to have second thoughts. I'm your advocate for Lucy, so quit pissing me off."

Again she was silent, worrying me. A silent elf is a thinking elf, and Ellasbeth wasn't known for her kind thoughts.

"Ellasbeth, Trent is trying to do the right thing by the girls, but every time you force your way in, you're making demands that make him feel more threatened." My head hurt, and I took a breath, hating myself. "If you would back off a little, he'd be a whole lot more comfortable with the idea of sharing Lucy."

Why am I doing this? I thought. But for all the rightness between us, I couldn't help Trent, and Ellasbeth . . . Ellasbeth could. I might not like her, but I'd seen her with the girls, and she was a good mother. Trent loved me, but if I took away his choice, our love would be tainted with the thought that I'd selfishly ruined his shot at what he'd been striving for his entire life.

I'm not afraid to love someone.

"You said you weren't going to confuse him," Ellasbeth said. "He has responsibilities, demands, and now you're *sleeping* with him!"

I slumped against the wall, guilt warring in me. "Yeah. Sorry about that. It just kind of happened." She huffed with anger, and I forged ahead. "But I'll tell you what, Ellasbeth. Tell me that you love him—"

"I love him," she said hotly, and in some way, I think she did. She was too bitter not to.

"Then tell me you love him enough to support his decision to try to ease tensions between the elves and demons, and I'll drive him back to his estate myself." *Say no, please say no . . .*

"What does that have to do with anything?" she blurted out.

It wasn't a no, but it wasn't a yes either. "Everything," I said, even more conflicted. "You can talk to Trent in four hours, 'kay?"

The phone clicked off from her side of things, and I hit the end key. "That was fun," Jenks said, and I met his eyes, not sharing his enthusiasm.

"No, it wasn't." Crap on toast, I was shaking, and I tucked the phone into my back pocket, thinking it felt unfamiliar. "Excuse me. I have to leave Trent a note."

The pixy was grinning as I opened my door, warning him to stay out as I shut it. Trent's feet had shifted, and I pulled the afghan up over him, smiling at his face, relaxed in sleep. "Thank you for keeping Jenks safe tonight," I whispered as I reached for the notepad beside my clock.

"Don't go."

His whispered voice slid through me. Warm and content, I sat on the edge of the bed. "I talked to Ellasbeth," I said as I pulled the afghan up even more. "You can crash here. She's going to call in four hours."

His hand came out to find me, and the blanket fell away. "I heard," he said. "Don't go."

He slid to the far edge of the bed, afghan raised for me to join him. "I need a shower," I said, eyes on my closet, and he pulled me down, arm going over me as he gentled me to him.

"I like the way you smell."

A quiver shook me as he sighed and spooned closer. It was warm where he'd been, and the scent of him was everywhere, the hint of burnt amber almost not unpleasant. My shoes felt funny on the bed, and I felt him sigh. "I have stuff to do," I protested, not moving.

He tugged me closer. "I like that you care about Ellasbeth," he said, shocking me. "She's a hard woman to understand. Her heart is good, though."

"Um, yeah." He was falling asleep again. I could stay until he did.

"Promise you won't leave me," he whispered, my hair moving in the breath of his words.

"I already did that," I said, but I was looking into the future, and I saw myself alone. Why was I even pretending? But I knew why.

"No, you almost left me tonight." His words were slurring. He was drifting off, not really awake. "You almost became shadow. I saw it. Promise me you won't go. Don't leave me. I won't know what is right and what is wrong if you do, and I like doing the right thing."

Becoming shadow. I lay there unmoving, suddenly very much awake as I recalled the blackness of nothing. It had been real, and he and Jenks had pulled me out of it. "I'm here," I breathed, needing to feel him behind me.

"I've not done anything really wrong in a long time . . . ," Trent said, words trailing into nothing. "Thank you."

I couldn't move, the warmth between us comforting. Slowly Trent's grip eased as he fell asleep. I listened to him breathe as I wondered how it had gotten so complicated.

Falling in love was the easiest thing in the world to do. Why was it always so hard for me to survive it?

Chapter 11

Something had changed. I froze, even as my eyes opened and my fingers clenched on the top of my afghan. The warmth behind my back was gone. I could see little in the predawn gloom of my room. *I fell asleep,* I thought, not surprised. Trent had been spooned up behind me, and we'd both been tired, the stress of meeting Cormel's demands bringing me down long before I'd usually fall asleep.

The sound of breathing drew my attention. Trent was a dangerous shadow at my propped-open window. My pulse pounded. I'd done this before—waking up to an approaching threat—but Trent being with me was new. We'd both fallen asleep, still dressed and with our boots on— probably a good thing in hindsight. "What's going on?" I whispered.

Trent gestured me forward, his gaze fixed outside. "There're people among the stones."

Crap on toast. I pushed the afghan off and stood. He looked as scary as all hell hunched at my window, and I felt queasy from lack of sleep. "Where?" I tucked my hair behind an ear and leaned closer to find the scent of spoiled wine amid the lingering burnt amber. He wasn't happy. Neither was I.

There was nothing to see in the predawn murk, not even a pixy sparkle. "I don't see anyone," I whispered as I tucked my shirt in. I needed a shower in the worst way.

"Me either, but they're out there." Trent squinted out the window. "Hear the birds? I've been listening to them for the last half hour, and something is wrong."

Chilled, I held my arms around myself. He'd been tucked in behind me, wide awake as he held me and listened to me sleep. Otherwise, how would he have heard the change in the birds? A robin chirped an alarm call, answered by another. *There're people among the stones.*

"Cormel promised. He promised to leave us alone!" I protested as I drew back.

"He promised that you no longer look to him for protection." Trent took his hand from the window. "It might not be him."

My thoughts zinged back to the vampires at Eden Park. *Swell.* Not six hours ago I'd told Ivy that it would be okay. Damn it, how could I have just fallen asleep? Worried, I reached my awareness out and tapped the line out back. Energy slipped in, and my skin tingled where it touched Trent. He was already tapped into it, and feeling almost shy, I slipped my hand into his.

His grip was warm, his fingertips slightly rough. They'd raise goose bumps should he trace them over my skin. He took a slow breath as we both eased our respective holds on our energies, and with a swirling back-and-forth tide of tingles, our balances equalized.

"This is *not* what I wanted to do today," I said, hands still intertwined as we looked for the first hints of the intruders.

Trent's grip tightened at the sudden sound of pixy wings. Hands clasped, we turned as Jenks slipped in through the crack under the door. His dust was a dull silver, and he stopped in shock when he saw us looking at him.

"You're up!" he said, a thread of brighter gold slipping from him. "And dressed. Tink's titties, you were sleeping? Seriously?"

Trent's fingers left mine. "Who's in the garden?" he asked.

"Oh yeah." Humming closer, Jenks landed on the sill, hands on his hips in his best Peter Pan pose. "Jumoke and Izzy are doing a count, but it's vampires. None of them is Cormel's."

My teeth clenched. "Son of a bastard," I whispered as I reached for my phone, only to remember I'd left it in the kitchen. I had Trent's, though, and I handed it to him. "Where's Ivy?"

"Out," Jenks said, bringing both Trent and me up short. "She and Nina took Buddy to a vet-in-a-box to get him checked about an hour ago."

"She left?"

"Yeah. That's when the vampires showed up. I wasn't going to bother you unless they moved. Hell, if I'd known all you were doing was lying next to each other with your *clothes* on, I would've told you right off. Tink's diaphragm, you were *sleeping*?"

Ivy isn't here. My first flush of fear shifted to an ironic relief, and I sat on the edge of my bed so I could pull up my socks without taking off my boots. "They aren't after Ivy. Why?"

"I'm more concerned with who." The dim light from Trent's phone made his face severe. "No calls, not even a text," he muttered. "I suggest we leave the church, circle around back, pick off one at the outskirts, and find a quiet place to chat. Mark's is open, isn't it?"

My lips parted. "And let them have the run of the church? I just got it cleaned up!"

Jenks bristled. "We can take them, cookie bits."

Trent glanced up, a hard, I'm-down-to-salvage look to his face. "No doubt. We can stay and fight them off, but we'll leave significant damage to the church and we might never find out who sent them or why."

Allow them access to everything in the hope that they don't damage or steal it all? It hadn't worked in World War II, and I didn't expect any difference now. "I need my splat gun," I said breathily, and I walked out into the dark hallway.

Jenks's wings clattered behind me. "We can't sneak out, anyway. We're surrounded."

I wasn't sure what I was going to do, but I'd feel better with a little more to back my words up with than a smile and whatever magic I knew by rote. I strode into the kitchen, panic icing through me when a dark shadow swooped forward. Almost falling, I slid into a defensive duck. The ley line iced painfully through me as I recognized the sound of Bis's wings and drew a surge of power back.

"Bis!" I said, my exclamation barely above a whisper. "Give some warning, huh?" I hadn't been able to feel Bis's presence since Newt changed my aura, and I kind of missed it.

"Sorry." Black teeth catching the light, he landed on top of the fridge and gave Trent a bunny-eared kiss-kiss.

Bis didn't look sorry, and I glanced over the dark kitchen wondering what I could eat without opening the fridge. The light would tell them we were awake. I plucked at my shirt, wishing I'd taken a shower. I knew I stank of burnt amber, but my nose had gone deaf. Irate, I reached for my coffee, cold and untouched, at the table. "Where's Belle?" I asked, grimacing at the tepid bitterness. Rex could take care of herself, but I worried about the flightless fairy.

Bis ruffled his wings, red eyes seeming to glow as he glanced out the window. "With Rex. Real professionals. No high heels or noisy phones. They know how to sit still and not move."

Trent looked up from texting something to Quen, probably. "Your life is never boring, Rachel."

"I could do with a little boring." My reach to open the nuker hesitated. It had a light, too. Disgusted, I set the cold cup on the counter and warmed it up with a charm. Ceri had taught me this, and a stab of regret cooled my anger.

"Nice," Trent said. He'd seen me do this before, but probably not with such quickness. I was edgy, and I jerked again when Bis landed on my shoulder.

"You want to jump out?" Bis said eagerly. "Let them find an empty church? We need to go soon. The sun is almost up."

My eyes flicked to Trent. That was why they were waiting. Sunup would put Bis and an easy escape out of reach. I was starting to like robins a lot more.

"We are *not* abandoning the church," Jenks said, wings clattering.

Keeping silent and my options open, I scooped up my splat gun and checked the hopper. The charms were not old, but they weren't new either—and vampires were fast.

"Rache?"

Jenks hovered, waiting for me to agree with him, but all I did was tuck the cherry-red paintball gun at the small of my back. Going to a drawer, I got a couple of extra canisters of CO_2 to fire it. Someday I'd figure out a charm to propel them, but until then, it was good having a spell that would work without connection to a ley line.

"Ah, Rache?"

I leaned against the counter and sighed. I didn't want to flee. Why were they even after us? Cormel couldn't make me do anything. But then my heart thudded as I thought of Ivy.

"I need to call Ivy," I said as I pulled my shoulder bag off the table. Damn it, I'd told her she'd be okay. I'd told her there'd be no reprisal. I shouldn't have filled her head with such do-gooder tripe. I was going to get her killed.

We had about ten minutes until sunrise, and Trent sat casually against the table, ankles crossed and looking calm and even a little sexy. "Bis . . . ," he drawled, catching my attention. "Can you leave undetected, find a vampire at the outskirts, and jump him here?"

My finger scrolling through my numbers slowed and my eyebrows rose. Jenks began to chuckle. "Oh, I like that," he said as Bis nodded.

"We have time," Trent said, his smile shifting to an ugly hardness. "If we can find out who and why, I don't mind leaving. Especially if we can drop back and hit whoever planned this while their main force is still here."

My God, the man might be a business tycoon, but his heart was that of a warlord elf.

Jenks's dust pooling on the center counter turned silver. "Let me find Jumoke. He'll know who would be easiest to snag."

I kind of felt bad for whomever Bis was going to snatch. Then I caught a glimpse of movement between the tombstones and the guilt went away.

"Back in a sec." Bis gave me a poignant look before he took to the air, a draft sending my snarled hair back as he followed Jenks out of the kitchen and presumably into the garden.

We were down to kidnapping, and heart pounding, I texted G2G to tell Ivy to go to ground, then hit her number, wanting to give her more than a text could handle. "I've got zip strips in the top drawer there," I said, phone to my ear. *Please pick up. Please.*

"I've got something better." Motions holding a hard intent, Trent cleared off the center counter, piling everything on Ivy's stuff. I knew it would irritate her to no end. My skin tingled as he pulled more heavily on the line, and I hoped they didn't have a magic user out there with them. They might be able to feel it.

Finally Ivy answered her phone, and I pressed it to my ear. "Ivy, thank God."

"Rachel? Why are you up so early?" she said, following it immediately with "Shit, what happened? Is everyone okay?"

Clearly she hadn't gotten the text yet. She sounded fine, and my eyes closed in relief. I could hear dogs in the background. "We're okay," I said, and I heard her say something muted to someone else. Nina, probably. "The church is surrounded. Bis is going to jump us out as soon as we know who it is, so don't come back. You're okay, right?"

With a slight shock, I realized I *wanted* to run. It was something new to me, but perhaps I was only now realizing the fragile nature of life. I wasn't running away, I was running to find a stronger position. Whoever this was, they weren't going to get away with it.

"Cormel!" Ivy hissed, her vehemence taking me aback.

"I don't think so. I'll let you know who as soon as we find out. Are you being followed?"

"No." She was distracted, and I wondered what Trent was wanting to do with the overhead rack when he eyed it.

I jerked at the sudden displacement of air, reaching for my splat gun when Bis popped back into the kitchen. His claws were pinching the shoulder of a terrified vampire.

"What the hell?" the young, surprisingly muscled living vampire shouted, eyes pitch black and short fangs sheened with saliva. He took a breath to shout for help.

"*Ta na shay, sar novo,*" Trent said softly, every word seeming to have edges. My skin crawled, and the aura about his hand glowed a soft silver. I froze when he reached out and the glow vanished from his hand to blossom anew over the vampire—swamping him in a heartbeat. The vampire's exclamation choked off. He stiffened as the charm soaked in, and he went still.

"*Sar novo,*" Trent said again, shoving the vampire against the center counter where he slumped, eyes open, breathing, but clearly unable to move voluntarily.

The entire thing had taken maybe three seconds.

"Uh, Ivy, I have to go," I said, impressed and a little scared. "Please. Don't trust Nina," I said, ashamed, and the hum of Jenks's wings dropped in pitch.

Ivy was silent, then, "Okay," and the conversation ended with a click.

My eyes were on the terrified vampire as I put my phone in a back pocket. Bis had puffed himself up larger, managing to look menacing next to Trent. Jenks, though, didn't give a fig about impressing our captive, clearly more upset about abandoning the church as he wiped the soot off his wings. "Rache," he started, and I rubbed my forehead. It was the right thing to do, hard as it was.

The garden, my kitchen. But to stay and fight might get someone killed when we would be better off dropping back and attacking with more strength later. I was trying to make smarter decisions—I loved Trent, and realizing I'd abandon the church to get him out of this threat was . . . a gut-wrenching shock, both happy and sad.

"This won't take long." Trent didn't sound like himself, and I watched, chilled, as he reached up into the rack, his motions sure and steady, his eyes never leaving the vampire's. The vampire panted, small noises coming from him as he tried to break through the binding charm. Trent looked awful, showing a part of himself he wasn't proud of—and being with me had brought it forth again.

Spoon pressed right under the vampire's eye, Trent leaned in. Voice hardly audible, he whispered, "Who's organizing this?"

I felt Trent's pull on the line lessen, and the vampire wiggled, still caught but able to move now. "You're dead, Morgan! You lied to us, and your life is forfeit!"

"I didn't lie!" I exclaimed, then lowered my voice. This smacked of torture, even if Trent hadn't done anything but threaten him with a spoon. *A spoon right under his eye.*

"*Flagro,*" Trent intoned, and I stiffened. The tip of the ceramic spoon glowed with heat. Whimpering, the captive focused on it, and the scent of frightened vampire rolled into the air.

Jenks darted close, his irritation obvious. "That won't work. He'll make it feel good."

"Not if I scoop his eyeball out."

Horrified, I gasped. He had to be kidding. "My God. Trent!"

Ignoring my hand on his arm, Trent blew on the spoon to send the heat over the terrified vampire's face. I couldn't *believe* this was happening, and I gasped right along with the vampire when Trent pressed it to his skin, the word "*Caecus*" intoned with a terrible certainty.

"Trent, stop!" I shouted as the vampire arched in pain, horrified. Jenks simply hovered, clearly not caring. Seeing me ready to smack Trent, the pixy darted over. "Get a grip, Rache," Jenks whispered, perched at my ear. "It's not real."

My breath exploded out from me, and I hesitated. Sweat trickled down Trent's face where it had beaded. His grip was white knuckled on the vampire under him, pinned to the center counter with a savage force. There was a small crescent shape of red under the vampire's eye, hardly worth calling a burn. It was more of a pressure mark. It was all show. Everything.

The terror, though, was real.

"Who!" Trent shouted, the vampire moaning under him. "Why!"

Trent pressed the cooled spoon under his other eye, and the vampire screamed again. Lip between my teeth, I darted a glance at the window. They weren't going to wait for sunrise if they knew we had one of their own.

"My eye!" the vampire howled, struggles growing violent. "You took out my eye!"

His eye was fine, blind under that last spoken charm, but I didn't like this side of Trent.

"Tell me, or I'll take out the other!"

Jenks shivered, his wings making a cool spot on my neck. "Tink's a Disney whore, Rache. Your new boyfriend is kind of scary when he's pissed."

"Tell me," Trent threatened, pressing into him. "Now!"

"It's the elves!" the vampire screamed. "The elves."

My lips parted, and I met Trent's suddenly ashen gaze as he let up.

"Some elf called Landon. He said you're lying," the vampire gushed. "He said you know how to bring back all the undead souls and you lied that it would send them into the sun. He said he'd bring all the undead souls back from the ever-after, but we had to kill you first to keep you from reversing his magic. He said you want us to *die* without our *souls*! That you're a *demon*!"

"He's the one lying!" I exclaimed, and Jenks darted out. That scream had probably traveled. "Landon wants to wipe out the masters. He's the one who put them to sleep last July!"

Trent let go and the man dissolved into a sniveling whimper. I could see Trent's self-disgust, and I brought his hand to my lips, startling him. He hadn't hurt the man babbling before us. He'd tricked him, tricked him to save our lives.

"You lie," the would-be assassin said, his fingers feeling his face. "I saw Felix. He has his soul. He doesn't hunger. He's whole." Fear flashed over him, stark and ugly. "I don't want to lose my soul. You're a monster! You took my eye!"

Trent frowned. "Landon betrayed you," he said, making a decisive ending gesture.

The vampire gasped, hunching into himself as the spell broke. Slowly his hands fell and he looked straight at us, wonder in him. "I can see . . ."

Expression still holding that awful hardness, Trent turned to Bis. "If he moves, claw his eye out for real."

I knew Bis would never do such a thing, but after seeing Trent bluff his way to a confession, the gargoyle hissed, claws scraping lines in the stainless steel.

"I told you Landon was going to use us," I said, then softened as I saw Trent shaking. He'd waved off my concern, but I'd known something like this was going to happen. Cincinnati had gone to her knees when the masters had merely fallen asleep. That Landon would try to kill them again wasn't surprise. The surprise was that I kept thinking he was sane.

Trent splayed his fingers to gauge their shaking. "We'll be okay. There isn't a safe way to bring all the souls back," he said as he made fists of his hands. "Ellasbeth hasn't called me in over six hours. You told her to call back in four, yes?"

His voice had hardened, and I nodded. He thought Ellasbeth and Landon were working together? Maybe, but Ellasbeth wouldn't destroy an entire demographic to further herself. Would she? "But you told her if she ever did anything like this again . . ."

My words trailed off. I'd really thought she'd play nice if she had a shot at something normal with the girls. Logic said she was working with Landon, but my gut said different. I'd seen her with the girls. She was Lucy's mother and loved Ray as if she were her own. She wouldn't risk them like this. Not now. Not if there was another way.

"Maybe I should tell her killing me won't give her Lucy," Trent said.

My shoulders tensed. "Quen gets custody first? That's a great idea. No one can kill him."

Trent made an embarrassed sound. Glancing behind me to the cowed vampire, he winced. "Ah, not exactly. I made you Lucy's legal guardian if I died or was missing for more than six months. If we both go, Al gets her. Ellasbeth probably doesn't know about that clause."

Shocked, my head snapped up. "A-Al?" I stammered. "Why not Quen?" But what I really wanted to know was why Al?

Trent was swooping about the kitchen, jamming charms and Ivy's bottled water into my bag. "Making Quen Lucy's guardian would make him a target, and I won't risk Ray. Al being Lucy's guardian will create a custody battle long enough for Quen to run off with both Lucy and Ray. Besides, if Al has custody, no demon will dare touch her. Or Ray."

I dropped back a step as I looked for the logic. It made sense—sort of.

Trent handed me my bag. The sill was empty, and I looked in my bag to see Al's chrysalis among the rest. *Really?* "I'm sorry," Trent said, jaw tight. "We have to go."

Crap on toast, we were going to leave them the church. I started as Trent took me in a quick embrace, my arms pinned between us as he gave me a squeeze. The vampire was watching, but Bis gouging the counter with his nails kept him unmoving.

"I should have seen this coming," Trent whispered, his breath making tingles against my neck. He sighed, his grip beginning to loosen. "I thought that by bringing Landon in close, I could out-think him. You were right. Is Ivy okay?"

Jenks darted in, his dust telling me everything I needed to know. They were advancing. "She was when I called," I said as I reached behind me for my splat gun. The vampire's eyes widened when I smoothly pulled it out and shot him. He started to rise . . . then fell back, slumping all the way to the floor in a tangle of arms and legs.

"Jeez, Rache!" Jenks complained as he rose up and down. "Give a pixy some warning!"

If there hadn't been umpteen more coming our way, I would've shoved the window open to air the place out. Frustrated, I faced Trent. "We need to get the girls. Both Lucy and Ray."

Trent shook his head. "We need to play dead."

"Huh? Why?" I said, taking the tablet Trent was handing me and shoving it into my shoulder bag.

Frowning, Trent stepped over the vampire to look out the window. "If we play dead, Landon will have to admit he can't bring their souls back. Support for him will fall apart. All we have to do is wait."

"Let the vampires bring Landon down." *And Ellasbeth*, I added silently, knowing Trent was upset she'd taken this drastic step. God knew I was disappointed. He must be crushed.

"But the church . . . ," Jenks said, and Jumoke and Izzy flew in, each of them holding a bundle and looking tragic.

I swallowed hard. If we were going to play dead, something was going to get busted up really bad to sanction it. "It's just a pile of rock, right?" I said, voice breaking. "Is Rex outside? Belle?"

Jenks nodded, scared. "Belle won't leave. Rache, we shouldn't either."

Trent gestured to Bis, and the gargoyle jumped to my shoulder, his tail wrapping tightly around me to secure his hold. The kid could jump only one at a time on his own, but if I warped everyone's aura to look the same, we could all go together. *Probably.* "I'll try to contain the damage, but if worse comes to worst, Jumoke and Izzyanna can move into my gardens. You, too, Jenks," he added, and Jenks frowned, a black dust falling in the center of the golden sparkles. "Belle doesn't have out-of-season newlings to look after," he added, and Jenks stiffened.

"I'm wherever Ivy and Rache are."

Trent's arm slipped around my waist. "I don't want any of you hibernating. Can you get them there safely, Jenks? We can't go. It's the first place they'll look for us, and I can't take this to my girls."

Looking even more disgusted, Jenks nodded again, his expression softening as he saw Izzy holding her tiny middle. "Call me."

Trent's expression relaxed, making me love him all the more. "Thank you," he said, looking over the church as if it was his own. "Have Quen escort Ellasbeth out and close the grounds. He's to go into hiding if he has to, but Ellasbeth is *not* to leave with the girls."

My gut hurt at the thought of damaging the church. *It's just a pile of rocks,* I told myself, but it was *my* pile of rocks.

"It's going to be fine, Rachel," Trent said, but the pinch to his brow said differently. "Ellasbeth will be years contesting it in the courts. We'll be back long before that." I met his eyes, and he added, "The trick will be to die convincingly without doing too much damage."

"You think a modified heat charm?" I said, knowing there was a firewall between the old part of the church and the new.

Trent shook his head, his eyes on the vampire at our feet. He took a breath to say something, then froze. His eyes went to the hallway.

Jenks's wings clattered. Jumoke and Izzy darted out, wings silent. "See you in a few days," Jenks said as he circled me, his dust falling as if in protection. "Trent, if she dies, I'll cut your pointy ears off and eat them in front of you."

I wasn't sure if he was joking or not, but Bis had tightened his grip. "Where do you want me to jump you?" he asked, clearly worried and smelling of iron and pigeon.

The tunnels? I thought, but it was too late, and we ducked below the counter at the soft scrape of shoe in the living room. "Go!" I mouthed to Jenks, and he gave me a last disparaging look as he darted out. This was going to be tricky. We had to destroy the back of the church and get out before it took us with it, and do it all so whoever was attacking would think we were caught up in it.

"Victor?" a masculine voice hissed, and I glanced at the vampire, his legs still in view of the hallway. *Oh yeah. What about him?*

"Now!" Trent shouted, and we stood, my hand reaching for my splat gun.

What in hell am I supposed to do? I wondered, shooting at the vampire in black.

Apparently it was the right thing as the man snarled, showing me his teeth as he rolled in to make room for the rest. The window over the sink exploded inward, and I swung my gun, little puffs of air unnoticed in the howl of attack.

Someone touched me. It wasn't Trent, and I loosed a blast of energy through my body, sending the vampire screaming in pain to fall backward into two of his buddies.

"That's right!" I yelled, shooting at them, but they darted back and my spells broke harmlessly against the cupboards. "Run, you little chip-fanged wannabes!"

My heart thundered. Eyes wide, I found Trent. He looked magnificent, magic arching from hand to hand as he blasted anyone who got a foot inside the kitchen. There were six down already, and he took out the two I'd missed even as I watched. Breathless, I smiled as he shouted and blew a hole right through the wall and four more crashed backward into the fireplace. That was okay. Ivy had been talking about opening the two rooms up.

"Trent!" I shouted, realizing Bis was still on my shoulder, his wings open as he kept his balance. "I think we can do this!" I wouldn't have to leave my church. I wouldn't have to abandon the only place I'd ever felt was mine.

His expression was wild. He met my eyes, and something plinked through me. *He loves me,* I thought, knowing he'd do anything if it would keep me safe, even if that meant letting me do something stupid like try to save my church.

A head poked up behind the smoldering couch, visible past the broken wall. There was a sudden flurry of motion, and five bodies dove out of the open back door. The one remaining slowly stood. Smirking, he dropped something heavy. I watched it fall as if in slow motion.

Trent grabbed me, spinning me down and around. Bis's wings flapped madly as we hunched into a ball.

The last vampire launched himself at the door, fleeing.

I gasped, trying to figure out what was going on.

"Now, Bis!" Trent shouted, and the world exploded.

The roar of fire washed over us, eating away at the bubble Trent had thrown up.

And then it was gone, the pulse of heat vanishing into the hum of the lines and then evolving into the shush of water on a beach. Bis had jumped us, and I had no idea where we were.

My heart thudded as we slowly stood from our crouch. It was dark, hours before dawn. My feet sank into cool sand. We were on the West Coast? Behind us was the great blackness of the Pacific, before us the extravagant lines of a modern two-story home, wall-to-wall windows facing the beach. The wind lifted through my hair and pulled the heat from the bomb away.

My church, I thought, forcing the lump down. Everyone I loved was safe.

"Ah, where are we, Bis?" Trent said, and I let go of his hand.

Bis shifted his claws, and I winced, not wanting him to know he'd broken skin. "Uh, I hope you don't mind," the clever kid said, his wings arching up behind my head in his version of a shrug. "I had to pick somewhere the sun hadn't come up yet."

"It's not Lee's," Trent said, and a knot of worry eased as I heard a piano playing the same phrase over and over until something sounded right.

"Alice, what do you think about this?" a familiar voice called out, faint over the surf as the phrase was hammered out again, and I smiled.

"It's my mom's," I said, starting forward, eager and trying not to cry. Bis had taken me home. He'd taken me to my mom.

Chapter 12

I woke for the second time in the same day with a smile on my face. Eyes closed, I stretched a foot down to find Trent's, feeling his arm over me tighten as I nudged him awake. My mom was cool. The thought of offering us two rooms hadn't even occurred to her as she fussed and burbled over getting us settled, finding us toothbrushes and me a nightgown. The shower had been heaven, and the cool sheets better than death, as Ivy would have said.

My eyes opened. A deliciously masculine arm was resting on me. Beyond the expansive floor-to-ceiling windows, the sun was nearing noon by the slivers of light leaking in past the half-open blinds. Trent, too, was just waking up, having spent some of his morning talking to Takata before slipping in behind me for a couple of hours. Our usual sleep schedules weren't compatible at all, but that didn't seem to matter when you were fighting time-zone shifts and an all-nighter.

All I cared about was that I woke up with Trent beside me for the second time in less than twenty-four hours, and it felt . . . right.

Warm and content, I rolled to face him. The silk of my mom's nightgown was a soft hush, and when Trent pulled me close, I snuggled in, wishing I had more mornings like this.

"Hi," I said softly, and his eyes opened. They were brilliant green from behind his tousled hair, clear and rested even if his stubble was thick. It made me feel good to see him that close. His thumb traced tingles down my bare arm, and I tilted my head, finding the soft skin under his throat with my lips and giving a gentle pull.

Suddenly he was a lot more awake. The bed shifted as he found my mouth with his, the kiss lighting through me with a shocking pulse. His hand pressed my shoulder, and my fist tightened at the back of his neck. I was suddenly a lot more awake, too.

"Donald?" echoed in the hallway. "Do we have any more strawberries? They've *got* to come out of there eventually. It's after noon!"

Breathless, I pulled back. Our lips parted with a sharp smack, and I realized his leg had slipped between mine, almost pinning me—not that I minded. His smile was content as we listened to Takata's rumbling voice answer my mom, and I snuggled into him. I didn't particularly want to get up, but even as my mom might have bunked us together, she also wouldn't have any hesitation about knocking on our door.

My pulse slowed. I listened to Trent's heartbeat, breathing him in and reluctant to move. I liked waking up like this, but was it realistic to even hope it could last? As in a permanent situation? I knew better than to look for a happily ever after. My track record spoke for itself.

"Still can't see it?" Trent said.

My lips quirked. "How do you do that?" I asked softly, and his hand traced tingles on my shoulder as he slipped the thin strap down.

"It's inevitable," he said, as sensation raced from his touch. "We do well together. For example, what do you want to do today?"

My schedule was already full of handling the unknown, but I sat up, willing to play the game. "Oh, I don't know," I said, knowing Trent would be recognized anywhere the moment he set foot in public. "Have strawberries for breakfast, lay out on the beach, maybe do some bikini shopping. A little light dinner on a boat. Go to bed before the sun comes up. Wake around noon and do it again."

Propped up on an elbow, he smiled and tucked my snarled hair behind an ear. His stubble caught the light, and I wanted to feel its roughness. "See what I mean?" he said, the sheet slipping to show a new and very nice angle of him. "That's exactly what I want to do."

Smirking, I scooted down and tucked myself next to him. My real list was a lot different: check the news to see if our fake death gamble worked, make a soul bottle for Ivy, dodge uncomfortable questions from my mom.

Suddenly I realized Trent's hand was moving, ever moving, against me, running behind my ear with a comfortable security, as if he'd been doing it for years. "There's absolutely nothing I can do," he said around a sigh, gazing past me to the private beach. "And a hundred things I should."

He was worried about his girls, but I couldn't resist letting my fingers drift downward over his chest. His body tensed, and I smiled. "We should play dead more often. This is the nicest morning I've had in a long time."

"There's always room for improvement." Trent's weight shifted as he leaned over me. His hand made a delicious path of tingles as it slipped up under the hem of the short nightie, settling in a tight grip on my waist. I smiled and reached for him, pulling him down into another kiss.

My eyes closed as I breathed him in. The hint of my mom's soap made him even more familiar, and my hand made steady progress down his side and thigh before I drifted inward to find him. His breathing changed, and I lingered as his lips left mine, skating down my neck and to my breast.

"Alice, they're still asleep." Takata's voice jerked through me, and Trent jumped.

"They're three hours ahead of us," my mom protested. "We've got to go, and I'm not going to sneak out of here and leave them a note!"

"So *you* knock on their door," Takata grumbled. "Why are you making me do it?"

"Oh, for God's sake, I'll do it," she said, and the sound of her steps rang loudly on the tile. "Watch the waffles, will you? They need to get up."

Trent looked down at me, his interrupted passion shifting to amusement crinkling the corners of his eyes. "I am up. They need to go away."

"Sorry," I said with an apologetic wince, and he rolled to sit up, settling himself beside me with the blankets pulled across his lap.

"Good morning, Ms. Morgan!" Trent said loudly as he stared at the ceiling, and I gave him a backhanded smack.

"See, they're awake," I heard her admonish Takata. "Go check the waffles."

She barely knocked before pushing the door open, and I yanked the blanket up as she peeked in, bringing the scent of maple syrup and cooked batter with her. "Good morning!" she called happily, her hair pulled back and looking more like my sister than my mom in casual jeans and a classy sweater. "Breakfast is ready. You can eat it while it's hot or let it get cold, but I didn't want to leave without at least saying good morning."

"You're leaving?" I said, grabbing the blanket when Trent threatened to drag it off me.

My mom bustled forward, heels clicking as she went to open the blinds all the way. Sunshine poured in, and my eyes hurt. "We're catching a flight out this afternoon. Big day today!" She turned, beaming at us. "Damn, you look good together. Rachel, if you screw this up, I'm going to be pissed. Trent has—"

"Mom!" I shouted, and she blinked, turning a slight shade of red. Trent wasn't helping, and I gave him a pinch to keep quiet when he opened his mouth, presumably to ask what she thought he might have that I might be interested in.

"Sorry," she said, surprising me. "I just wanted to see you before we left."

"Where are you going?" I asked again. "I've got some spelling to do, and I thought you might be able to help. With the shopping if nothing else."

"A-A-A-Alice?" Takata shouted. "Where's the cinnamon?"

Her eyes lit up, and then she frowned, clearly torn. "Oh, I can't, sweetheart," she said as she scooped up my jeans from the floor and folded them. "Donald and I have a flight to Cincy in a few hours. I've got your funeral to plan."

"It worked!" Trent exclaimed, and I smiled as my mom's eyes glowed in anticipation.

"This is going to be fantastic!" she gushed as she fiddled with the fringe on the seventies lamp they had stuck in here. "If I can't plan your wedding, I can at least arrange your funeral. Donald has a song and everything. You're going to love it!"

Oh God, she was going to do the eulogy. "Ah, Mom?"

"Get yourself up," she said as she backed out of the room. "We leave in ten."

The door clicked shut, and I thumped my head back. I'd never be able to leave my church again. If I had a church to go back to.

Trent threw the covers back and swung his feet to the floor. "I don't know what you're talking about," he said as he stood, every yummy inch of him catching the light from the beach. "Your mom is . . ."

"Is what?" I looked at the slowly rising spot in the bed where he'd been and sighed. Just twenty minutes more. Was that too much to ask?

"Fun," he said, stretching.

"Uh-huh." I sat up and wrangled my hair back into a scrunchy. "Picture *fun* on prom night or a PTA meeting. My mom was an active parent."

Head down, I scuffed past Trent toward the attached bathroom. I'd told Ivy we were bugging out, and I hadn't called her since, not wanting to blow our story of being dead. But now, after a handful of hours, I probably should tell her we were okay. Even the six hours it would take for my mom to get there was too long to have her worry.

I gasped when Trent snagged me, pulling me, bouncing, back onto the bed. My breath came in fast as his weight pinned me, and I gazed up at him, feeling desired as the entire length of his body pressed into me. "I like you in the morning the best," he said, eyes on my hair as he tucked it away from my face.

I'd give just about anything to have this forever, and I smiled up at him, liking him the best when he was relaxed and happy, stubble and all. "Maybe we should just keep playing dead."

Silent, his worry slid back behind his eyes. "I'm sorry you saw that yesterday."

"Saw what?" My fingers played with the rims of his ears. I knew what he was talking about, but sometimes it was better to pretend.

Propped up on his elbow, he took my fingers in his and kissed them. "With the vampire."

My breath came in fast, and I tilted my head, trying to catch his eyes with mine. "It wasn't anything I didn't know was there."

"It . . . I promised myself—"

"Trent." I pulled him to me, finding his lips with mine, feeling a thrill coil down through me and rebound against his own desires. Slowly I eased back into the pillow, but his eyes were just as worried, just as furtive. "I know who you are. And I love you."

His eyes darted to mine, and the first hints of a smile eased his worry. "I don't deserve you," he said, sitting up and pulling me into a heartfelt embrace. "I love you, too," he whispered, his warmth tingling between us as he held me close.

"Waffles are out!" came faintly through the walls.

My throat was tight. I gave him a final squeeze and his arms eased their grip. I wanted this to last, but even now I knew better than to hope. Trent gallantly held my robe out for me to shrug into, tying it with a suggestive firmness before finding his own robe. Disheveled and feeling odd, I followed him out of our tiny space and into the world again, my hand loosely in his as if I was afraid that if I let go, I'd lose him right then.

I'd gotten the full tour last night, or this morning rather, but seeing Takata's home in the daylight only accentuated the clean lines, spacious rooms, and sparse but comfortable furnishings. It didn't look much like my mom's old house, but my mom didn't look much like herself either. She was wearing trendier clothes and had a far more relaxed smile. Losing the emotional baggage in Cincinnati suited her.

The kitchen was bigger than mine, with rich wood and gleaming metals. It opened up to a lower living room, three sides of which were glass looking out onto what had to be a private beach since I hadn't seen anyone on it yet. The ceilings were high, and the second story where the bedrooms were overlooked it. A piano took up one bright corner, and a small library the other. Between them, a TV was turned to the news, and as we entered, Takata muted it from behind the kitchen counter.

Takata smiled as he took off his apron, still shy over my finding out he was my birth father. Most of his more famous songs had their inspiration in what he'd lost by giving me and my brother to his best friend and the only woman he'd ever loved. Now my father was dead, and though my mother missed him, it was good to see her in love again.

"Morning," he said, pointing to the eat-at bar and two place settings.

"Thanks, Donald," I said as I slid up onto the seat, feeling both welcome and awkward. My mom was out of the room, and I leaned in across the bar. "Hey, try to keep her from making my funeral into a circus, okay?"

Trent snorted, turning it into a cough as he took the chair beside me. The waffles steamed, but he reached for the coffee instead. Takata smiled, his big teeth and wide lips almost a shock as I saw myself mirrored in him. "I'll try, but you know how she gets."

I sighed, my wandering gaze finding three bags and Takata's guitar sitting next to the door. "Enthusiastic," I muttered, then blinked when Trent took his fingertip out of his mouth, smiled, and poured a dollop of syrup into his coffee. Must be the real stuff.

"You get your drive from her," Takata said, and I met his eyes when he reached across the counter and gave my shoulder a squeeze. "It looks good on you."

"Thanks," I said dryly, not sure if it was enthusiasm or desperation that kept me going. I usually didn't put syrup on my waffles, but seeing Trent enjoying himself, I dribbled some on, needing to shove my robe sleeves back out of the way as I cut dough into pieces.

Takata hustled to take Mom's bag, and from the corner of my eye I saw the front of Trent's main building on the TV. The banner, KALAMACK PIE SLICING UP SOUR, ran below it before it went to commercial. It was official, then. We were dead.

I took a bite of waffle, leaning forward as the syrup dripped. If this was dead, then sign me up.

"About time you got out of bed, sweetheart!" my mom called cheerfully, then gave Takata's orange pants and striped shirt a disparaging look. A pang went through me as I saw the little clues we learned as children telling us that our mother was leaving to do grown-up stuff: her hair was brushed into a professional topknot, her heels clicked smartly on the tile, there was a blush of heavier makeup, and her jewelry was just shy of extravagant. Her expression was eager and her motions deliberate. I knew when I gave her a hug good-bye that she'd smell of her favorite perfume. Suddenly I wasn't hungry.

"What are your plans for today?" my mom said as she fixed her scarf, not oblivious to my mood but ignoring it like always. "Use the house as if it's yours," she said before I could even frame an answer. "There's a boat at the club, and the sweetest row of shops in town."

"Ah, I need to do some spelling," I said, giving Trent a thankful glance when he gave my fingers a supportive squeeze under the bar.

"Mmmm." My mom paused, then strode forward to take a key from a rack behind the pantry door. "I've got a studio upstairs. It's nice and sunny up there. Help yourself."

I took the smooth, small key thinking it looked like it would open a file cabinet, not a door. "You keep it locked?" I asked hesitantly, remembering my mom liked to experiment. She was quite good, and I'd been told on more than one occasion that if it hadn't been for Robbie and me, she could have been one of Ohio's premier spell spinners, the elite few who have the knack of creating new spells by modifying existing ones.

"Just the expensive stuff." My mom's eyes were on Takata as he came back in, this time wearing something a little more subdued but still clearly "retired rock star" with metallic socks and red shoes. "Thank you, dear," she said as she adjusted his wide collar, then turned to me. "Ah, ignore what's under the sink, okay? I've been meaning to take care of it."

"Sure . . ." I tucked the key in the robe's pocket, exchanging a questioning look with Trent before I spun on the stool to watch her getting ready to leave. My plate was on my lap, and I picked at a piece of waffle. "I'm working on something for Ivy. God knows when I'll have another day off again from saving the world."

I had meant it to be sarcastic, but my mom nodded, totally serious. A car had pulled up outside, and Takata headed for the bags. "Use what you need," my mom said as she checked inside her purse. "That woman needs a little goodness in her life. If you can't find what you want, I've got an account in town at Jack's Imagineering." She looked up, breathless and alive, and I set my plate down and went to give her a hug.

"You're the best, Mom," I said as my arms went around her, and I was a little girl again, watching her leave for a job interview or rare overnight trip. "Thank you."

She blinked fast, eyes bright as she pulled away. "Just looking after my little girl. Gotta go! See you later, sweetheart. Enjoy! Don't show up until after the funeral, okay? Oh, and I'll tell Robbie. Don't worry about it. He's going to be pissed." She hesitated. "That you played dead, not that you're really alive."

Good to have that clarified. I glanced at Takata. He was laughing. "Okay. I'll try."

Trent stumbled as my mom jerked him into a loud, noisy hug, and I edged sideways over to Takata. I'd hugged him only a couple of times, and he still felt tall and awkward to me, his arms holding me with a hesitant firmness before he rocked back, face having a touch of sadness for opportunities lost even as he stood in my life again. "You're doing good."

"So are you," I said, meaning it. "She's happy, and I'd love you for that if nothing else."

Head down, he smiled as he looked at my hands in his. "Don't wait too long to come out of the woods," he said, his gaze coming back to mine with a wise wariness. "Too many people depend on you to stand between them and the rest."

I knew what he was saying, and I nodded even as Trent reached between us and shook his hand. The two of them exchanged words that really didn't matter apart from the meaning behind them. It was weird and sort of uncomfortable as Trent and I stood in white robes and with sticky fingers in an extravagant house that wasn't ours and watched my parents leave.

The car drove slowly through the winding curves until it was lost behind skinny evergreens and boulders the size of my car. The silence of the house soaked in, and I heard the wash of the water for the first time. No one knew we were here except for Bis, and he was sleeping. It felt like Sunday, but no Sunday I'd ever had.

"Well?" I said as I turned, startled at the figure Trent cut before me. I saw him so rarely with such a thick stubble. He had the remote in his hand, and I wasn't surprised when he pointed it across the huge room and unmuted the TV. It was showing a mix of familiar and unfamiliar reporters in front of Trent's gatehouse. The big names were there this time along with the local, and I frowned. Even the *Washington Inderland Press.*

". . . the continuing investigation into Kalamack's supposed death," the woman was saying, and I followed Trent back to the sunken living room and the cushy white couches. I recognized some of Trent's security people, and I felt bad for their stricken expressions.

"Longtime associate Rachel Morgan has been called into question as the I.S.'s main suspect, despite claims that she perished along with Kalamack during an organized vampire hit."

"What!" I exclaimed, bouncing back up before my butt had even hit the cushions. "Me?"

Trent shushed me, upping the volume.

"But until a body can be found, or Rachel Morgan herself, this theory will remain a wishful thought by I.S. personnel."

My breath puffed out. The press knew it was bunk and that was half the battle.

"Oh, Rachel. I'm sorry," Trent whispered, and my head jerked up, my stomach clenching at the image of the church now on the TV. It had been taken from across the backyard and it showed the entire back end burnt and black. The original stone of the church was covered in soot. Ivy's grill still stood sadly under the big tree beside the picnic table.

"I think the original structure is okay," he said, and I realized he'd taken my hand and I was sliding into him as our weight pushed on the cushions. "I'm so sorry. You know we'll rebuild it. Before the first snowfall."

No one was in there, I thought, eyes closing as I remembered my spell books. Those would be hard to replace. And the picture of Jenks and me in front of the Mackinac Bridge. All my ley line stuff. Everything that Trent hadn't stuffed into my shoulder bag—gone.

"I'm okay," I said, though I felt like throwing up. At least I hadn't done it. It had been someone else. *Landon . . .*

"Though the I.S. denies allegations that Morgan and Kalamack were the victims of backroom deals and assassination, it's interesting to note that the deaths of Morgan and Kalamack fall closely alongside the elven dewar coming forth with a magical-based method to restore souls to the undead, something Morgan and Kalamack publicly touted as dangerous."

"We did?" Surprised, I glanced at Trent. He was flushing, his lips pressed in irritation.

"I issued a statement," he said, eyes riveted to the TV. "Your name came up, but I *never* said anything about you agreeing or disagreeing."

I was used to the press getting things wrong, either through carelessness or intentional bashing, and I turned back to the TV. A frown pinched my brow at Landon being interviewed before the FIB building. The banner ELF HIGH PRIEST, SA'HAN, LANDON ALEXANDER scrolled under it. The sky was bright and his hair was shifting wildly under that funny ceremonial hat. The sun in his face made him look older. My eyes narrowed. Now that I thought about it, that hat of his looked a lot like one that Newt favored. "Son of a bastard," I muttered, and Trent grimaced, trying to hear.

"The newly evolving elven community is pleased to offer a way for a long-suffering demographic to find peace and wholeness."

"Bull!" I shouted, and Trent pointed the remote again, upping the volume.

"I'm personally delighted that with a collective show of union and direction we can help another species find a permanent, healthy balance that we've only recently found ourselves, in great part due to Kalamack's efforts."

I tensed. "Did he just say the vampires killed us because we stabilized the elf population, and that he's trying to make up for us shifting the vampires down a rung on the power ladder?"

Trent nodded, his elbows on his knees, making his robe fall open. "Be careful, Landon."

Again I was reminded of David's threat, and I stifled a shiver. Landon had the backing of the dewar and enclave, but Trent . . . Trent had practice at doing the ugly thing.

The reporter had taken the center of the screen again, clearly wrapping up. "The sudden disappearance and probable death of Kalamack has left lawyers from many fronts scrambling for control of Kalamack's continually dwindling assets, a prospect that promises to be tied up in the courts for years as obscure contracts and entitlements suddenly emerge."

The rims of Trent's pointy ears turned red. "But ask for their silence, and you have to buy it. I don't want to do this anymore."

I glanced at him, knowing he loved the power plays, the intrigue. "Meanwhile," the announcer said as the TV went back to a shot of the newsroom, "daughter Lucy Kalamack will remain in the care of Ellasbeth Withon at the Kalamack estate."

"What!" we both shouted, and Trent reached for his phone, his hand slapping into his robe instead.

"Ellasbeth Withon has been fighting for legal custody of Lucy for nearly a year, since Kalamack secured custody of the then three-month-old. Ms. Withon is also a person of interest in Kalamack and Morgan's disappearance."

"She has the girls," Trent rushed, and I felt his fear slip through him, turning him tense.

"Trent, breathe," I said, pulling him back down when he tried to stand. "Look at me. It's okay." Panic rimmed his eyes as they finally met mine. "It sounds as if they haven't left the compound," I said, scrambling to keep him thinking, not reacting. He was safer to be around when he was thinking. "It might not even be true. Quen might have Ellasbeth locked in a closet for safekeeping and just be feeding that tripe to the press to explain why she's there."

"Ellasbeth Withon had this to say when she invited us onto the grounds," the newscaster said, and we both turned to the TV, our hands joined.

"Or maybe not," I breathed as I saw Ellasbeth sitting in the greenhouse, Lucy eating a cookie on her lap and Ray patting the table and the sparkle of pixy dust there. "I will not believe that Trenton is dead," she said, her chin raised and her professional speaking skills making her seem just scared enough and deserving of sympathy. "He was with Morgan at the time of the fire, and if anyone can keep him alive, she can. Until he comes back, I will keep our girls safe."

She was looking right at the camera, and I shivered. She was talking to Trent.

Trent was as pale as his robe, and he sat back, almost vanishing into the cushions. I knew he wanted to call Quen. It might destroy the illusion that we were dead. We'd never be able to flush Landon out. We had to wait.

"Maybe she had nothing to do with it," I suggested, remembering her silence when I told her not to call back for at least four hours. She hadn't called back at all. Had she been trying to give him the room I told her he needed, or had she been trying to keep him asleep until the sun rose and we couldn't jump out?

Trent silently fumed, and I gave his hand a squeeze. "You don't know she's working with Landon," I said, and his eyes finally came back to me.

"No, but she can play it very cool," he said. "She won't move until she's sure we're dead or her lawyers have a way to take Lucy."

I remembered Jenks telling me how Ellasbeth had tried to kill Trent when he had abducted Lucy. Part of me was outraged, but another part knew I'd do anything to stop someone from breaking into my house to steal my child, too. *Stopping is different from killing . . .*

People change, I mused, still wanting to believe Ellasbeth wasn't involved. "Maybe we should have left little pieces of our DNA on the ceiling."

"There was no time." Trent's response was so fast I knew he'd been thinking about it, too.

The TV was back to commercials. "I was kidding," I said. "At least she can't take Ray."

The mention of his adopted daughter seemed to bring him back, and Trent worked himself out of the cushions. "Quen would kill her if she tried," he said, clearly uncomfortable. He stood, turning the TV off and frowning at the newly black screen.

Sighing, I wiggled my way to the front of the couch and managed to get up. My God, the thing was a comfort trap. "Come on," I said as I took his hand and tried to lead him away.

"What? Where?" he demanded, following obediently.

I shrugged as I looked over my shoulder at him. "We can't do anything, and playing dead was the entire point. Let's go look at my mom's studio."

His fingers slipped from mine, and he set the remote down, reluctantly turning from the TV. "They aren't even at the airport yet, and you're in her spelling cabinet?"

Somehow I found a smile. "You never poked around in your mom's spelling cabinet when she was gone?"

My heart seemed to melt when Trent smiled. It was laced with worry, distracted, but it was real, and it meant a lot. I knew how hard it was to want to fix something and have to wait.

"I stole all my best revenge spells from my mom when I was in junior high," I said as I hiked up my robe and took the carpeted stairs. "I swear, I think she left some of them out for me to find. Like the one that gave you zits or made your voice break?"

"Clever."

"And hard to trace since hormones were already jumping around," I said, hesitating when we reached the top step. It was a huge, open corridor, windows letting in the light and the sound of surf. My mom was cool, and she believed in plausible deniability as a way to find justice in the dog-eat-dog world of teen angst.

Trent eased to a halt beside me. "Which way?"

I felt a light pull to the right. I couldn't even tell you what it was. The scent of ozone, maybe? The faint vibration of an uninvoked circle? "Here," I said, following my nose past open windows all the way to the end of the hall. The sound of surf became louder, and quite unexpectedly the outer side of the hallway opened up to a sun-drenched corner room.

"Wow," Trent said as we slowly crossed from the carpeted hallway back onto tile, the floor a beautiful mosaic of white, black, and teal laid out in spirals and circles. It would be my favorite room just for that, but it got better. Several benches, each having an overhead rack or fume hood, gave it the look of a lab. There were several built-in burners, a waste zone, and one corner devoted to live plants. One tinted-glass cabinet against the interior wall held herbs, and another books. I assumed the ley line stuff was in cupboards. An open, ultramodern-looking hearth took up a corner. From the hook hanging down from the high ceiling it was functional, but I think Takata used it as a place to sit more than my mom to stir spells at by the number of magazines piled up beside the pair of comfortable chairs between it and the wall. There was an empty coffee cup on the table between them, and a sheet of music half hidden under the rug.

"This is fantastic," I said, fingers running enviously over the magnetic chalk-ready slate counters as a smile of delight eased the tension from my forehead. I could tell there were no electrical lines, no pipes, no phone, no TV, nothing to break a circle. It was a fortress by way of lack, like an island.

"So, you think you can work here?" Trent said, beaming at my awe.

I nodded, eyes on the open notebooks with works in progress carefully detailed in my mom's handwriting. She was spelling again, and it made me feel good. "Absolutely."

Trent went to the spelling library, his fingers running over the spines with the fondness he reserved for the horses in his stable. "Rachel, your mom has been sandbagging. She has a fabulous collection."

I fingered the key in my robe pocket, knowing that anything I could ever want would be here. Trent knew the charm, and I could tweak it so Ivy could invoke it as needed. The rest would fall into place. Finally something was going our way.

"It's going to take some trial and error, though," Trent said, surprising me anew with his stubble and disheveled appearance.

Smiling, I leaned against the counter, hardly able to wait to get started. It was a beautiful room, a pleasure to work in. "Maybe we should get dressed first if we want to save the world."

Trent's grin was wide as he came back, tugging me to him. "And a shave, maybe. Sounds good to me. I love watching you work."

I swayed into him, my eyes on Takata's little piece of the room and wondering if Trent was going to claim it, but by the gleam in his eye, I thought not.

He was going to help, whether I wanted him to or not, and that was the best feeling in the world.

Chapter 13

The sound of the water through the open windows echoed my intent as I sat cross-legged atop the slate counter within a protective pentagram and carefully etched an ever-smaller spiral into the bottom of the tiny bottle. I barely breathed, my entire world cycled down to the golden glow of glass and the thin tracing of silver flowing from the stylus. The shushing of the waves was the heartbeat of the world, ever present, seldom noticed, and linking every moment together from before there was life to now.

To say it felt as if I was connected to the all, to everything, was an understatement.

I reached the center. The stylus lifted, but I didn't want to move. I was content, still, and I knew with an unshakable certainty what was important and what wasn't.

Ivy, I thought, and a stab of fear broke through my muzzy peace. A drop of silver quivered at the tip of the stylus, and I held my breath as I moved the pen from the bottle.

"I thought I lost you there," Trent said, startling me, and I looked up, smiling even as the silver dripped onto the counter.

"I should take a break," I said, handing him the bottle. Beside me were over a dozen rejects making me feel guilty about using my mom's silver ink. It wasn't exorbitantly expensive, but we couldn't melt the silver down and reuse it either. They had to be trashed, bottles and all.

Saying nothing, Trent put the bottle under the scope modified to look at odd-shaped things. I stretched for the ceiling. My back cracked and my legs protested as I slid to the edge of the counter and my feet hit the tile floor. The sun was past its zenith, not close to setting but still making a bright glare on the water that reflected in with a wavy, relaxing pattern. "Good?" I said around a yawn, and he pulled back from the scope. I rather liked his smile.

"Looks good on the scope," he said, taking the bottle out from under it. "Let's see if it resonates."

This was the real test, and I watched his focus become distant as he somehow put his consciousness into the spiral. He began to whisper the elven words to resonate along the silver, and I shivered as I felt a slight pull when my soul recognized the summons.

"Perfect." Exhaling in a puff, he came blinking back to me. "Take a look. The lines actually glow."

Flustered, I shook my head when he extended it. "Ah, no thanks," I said, then added when he gave me a questioning look, "I might attract more attention than I want."

"Mystics?" Green eyes expressive, he put the bottle in my hand. "Your aura lost most of its sparkle yesterday. I think you slipped them. They're probably halfway to St. Louis."

My lips parted, my relief surprising in its depth. "Seriously?"

He nodded, and I took the bottle, smiling at the thought of the mystics stymied and slowly crossing the same terrain that we had last year. Exhaling, I tried to put my awareness into the bottle. It was kind of like focusing on my navel, and I whispered the words of invocation. "*Tislan, tislan. Ta na shay cooreen na da.*"

The world became less important . . . and a remembered soothing numbness stole out from between the cracks of reality, rising up to envelop me, dissolving me in the words slowly spinning in the circle of sound and lassitude.

Until a sharp jerk pulled through me. My head snapped up, and I blinked as I stared at Trent. He was right in front of me, his hands on mine still wrapped around the bottle. Concern, quickly hidden, flashed over him.

"I take it back," he said, using more force than expected to yank the bottle away. "Don't do that again."

"So it works?" I was breathless, and I unkinked my hands and rubbed at their stiffness.

"I think you almost put yourself in there." Brow furrowed, he set the bottle on the opposite counter where there was no chance of mixing it up with the discards. "I think it works fine, but I'd still put a drop of blood in it as an attractant."

I nodded, not as pleased as I thought I would be. My intent was to help Ivy, but what if it worked on pulling healthy souls from healthy people, too? Crap on toast, had I just reinvented a demon curse from an elven one? "Maybe this isn't a good idea."

The clatter of flawed bottles shocked through me as Trent ran a hand over the counter to dump them into the same box we'd found them in. "I see what you're thinking," he said, the box going back on the counter. A faint smile on his face, he came close. "I didn't lose myself. I think it's only because you scribed it. Or maybe because you've been centering yourself all afternoon drawing spirals." He squeezed my shoulder to bring my eyes up to his. "It's not going to pull anyone in without an attractant."

"I suppose." My thoughts turned to the question of whose blood I should use. Ivy's was what her soul was used to, but mine might be what her soul longed for.

"You did good," he said confidently as he slid the unused bottles to the back of the counter. My mom had a most excellent spelling area. We'd used about a third of it, spreading out to help minimize possible contamination. It was getting late, and I squinted at the lowering sun as my stomach rumbled. We'd been here all day, not even breaking for a real meal, though Trent had raided the kitchen to bring up cider, sliced apples, and more strawberries. My eyes drifted to the empty plate by the fireplace. My mom had a little piece of heaven here. She deserved it.

"It's a great spell," Trent said, concern furrowing his brow at my continued silence. "I think you should register it before someone else copies it."

A flash of pride pushed my anxiety out. "We don't even know yet if it works." Flustered, I took a salt water–soaked rag and began to wipe down the counter. We had no real way to test it, but my thoughts turned to Ivy as I slowly cleaned the counter. If I didn't have two bottles, she'd only give hers to Nina.

My eyes went to the sun, still fairly high over the water. It was dark in Cincinnati. "I can make another one before the sun goes down," I said softly. I knew Trent wanted to get out on the beach, but I didn't know how long this interlude of peace would last.

"We've got time." Leaning in, he gave me a quick kiss before taking up the box of waste bottles and starting for the stairs. "I bet there's a grill somewhere. I can make kebabs and rice."

My cheek was tingling from where he'd kissed me, and I touched it. "Mmmm, sounds good. This shouldn't take long. I can chop veggies."

Nodding, he headed down the open hallway, box of bottles in his arms.

The sound of the ocean became obvious again, a heady warmth radiating from the sand coming in with it. My hands were damp with salt water, and I went to rinse them. I'd have to redraw the pentagram for the new charm. I knew the recitation words by heart now after having done this for each of the flawed bottles. It wasn't just the bottle that made this work, but the twenty minutes' prep work of intent and sympathetic magic that went along with it.

Hands dripping, I reached for a paper towel with Halloween bats and tomatoes on it. A quiver rippled through my chi, shocking me to stillness. From nowhere, malevolent intent spilled over me. The shush of waves slowed, ebbing as the sound of ancient drums pulsed within me, rising, ebbing, coming back even more insistently with thoughts of revenge and the intent to punish. Focus blurring, I reached for the counter. The sensation of hatred rose until it leaked through my aura to sheen like an evil sweat. It was an attack . . .

Dizzy, I stumbled into the counter, hand to my middle, a sparkling, breathless pull shifting through me as if searching, looking under the puddling black smut on my aura for something. My eyes widened as I felt the searching intent wrap around my chi . . . and take me with it.

Stop! I thought as I yanked myself back, panicking as the alien sensation redoubled its effort, assaulting my soul with more demand. The drums fell back to my core, and I gasped as ancient rhythms beat out a punishment and my fear opened cracks for it to delve deeper.

Let me go! I screamed when the curse fastened on a different part of me. It was an attack, looking for something in me to trigger its full strength.

Get out! I demanded, but I couldn't wrap my will around it. It was like smoke, evading me as if I wasn't even there. I reached for a ley line, shocked when it slipped my grasp. It was damaged from a thousand years of earthquakes, and I didn't have the knack of cradling it to me like those who lived on the coast did.

My pulse hammered. My knees gave way and I hit the floor as the curse dug in, using my own fear to protect it. The world tilted and jerked as it adjusted its grip like a shark on a fish. The drums thundered. My heart beat in time with it. I didn't have what it needed to invoke, but pulse by pulse, it swallowed me further.

Groaning, I felt my palms hit the tile floor. For one instant, the drums and the thundering beat of the curse were contrary. My breath came in with a gasp, and I caught a glimpse of sun and blue tile. With it came the realization that I was caught in a rhythm-based curse. If I could find one tiny bit of separation, I could wedge it off. I had to make my pulse erratic, out of sync with the drums.

Terrified, I held my breath and huddled on the tile. My knees pressed to my chest, and I closed my eyes. My pulse had matched the drums, and the curse grew stronger. Panic was a white-hot wash, and my lungs burned. I had to shift my pulse. It was my only chance.

Let . . . go, the curse demanded as sparkles flashed before me and my lungs burned. I. Would. Not. Breathe.

And then . . . my thudding heart stuttered again, missing a beat.

It was enough.

With a snap, the curse's hold on me broke. I gasped as if coming up from the ocean depths, sucking in the air as if it was heaven itself. My pulse raced. The drums were counter to my body rhythm—and they couldn't find it again. My hands pushed on the cold mosaic tile, weak as I lay there and breathed. My head hurt, and I wanted to throw up.

"Rachel!"

It was Trent, and I groaned as he sat me up. His hands were hot, burning almost. "Not so fast," I whispered, eyes still closed.

"My God," he said as he sat on the floor and held me. "You're ice cold. What happened? I felt it all the way downstairs!"

Shivering, I managed to crack my eyelids. "Nothing," I croaked. "I didn't do anything. I was cleaning the table. It felt like—" I was hyperventilating, and I stopped breathing to try to slow it down. "Something attacked me," I said, then took a deep breath. I couldn't help it, and I fell against him, cold and nauseated. "It was aimed at me. It was aimed at me, but not me."

He was silent, and realizing I wasn't making any sense, I forced my eyes open. *I'm on the floor,* I thought, then lifted a hand to touch his shoulder. It took a lot of effort.

"I'm okay," I said, but he wouldn't let me get up. "It was a curse. It never fully invoked. The invocation element was missing. I didn't have it."

Okay, that didn't make much sense either, but it was hard to explain. Who makes a curse that needs something from the victim to invoke? A highly complex, person-specific charm? But then why hadn't it found what it needed?

"The invocation element was missing?" he echoed, and I bobbed my head.

"It searched my mind, and when it didn't find it, it tried to invoke anyway. I managed to beat it off. I don't think I could have stopped it if it had found what it wanted."

Trent's brow furrowed. "Okay," he said, arms going all the way around me. "No more spelling today," he added, and my stomach lurched as he lifted me.

"Trent, I'm fine," I protested, but it was all I could do to put my arms around his neck and hold on. "I'm telling you, I didn't do anything."

"And you haven't had anything to eat today but half a waffle and a handful of chips."

I looked over his shoulder at the dishes by the fireplace. It hadn't been a real sit-down lunch, but there'd been a lot of calories in it, and it hadn't been that long ago. "I ate more than that!" I said, making a little wiggle. "If you felt it, then it wasn't anything I did."

"Right." Huffing, he started for the hallway. "We're done for today."

"Trent. I'm fine. Put me down." I stiffened. Feeling it, he hesitated at the top of the stairs, his jaw tightening before swinging me down.

My feet hit the floor, and I staggered, hand going behind my back to prop myself up on the rail without him seeing. I held my breath, pulse thundering as the world swam and steadied. *Maybe that curse had taken something from me after all.* But I knew it hadn't. I had just needed everything I had to fight it off. Trent looked mad, his hand ready to catch me. I thought of the dwindling daylight, then my queasy feeling. I couldn't spell like this and get any usable results.

"Maybe we should turn on the news," I said meekly.

Immediately Trent's irate expression eased, telling me how hard it had been for him to stand there and wait for me to come to the same conclusion he had. I couldn't help a tiny little smile. He cared, not only that I was okay, but that I made my own decisions even if he felt they were the wrong ones.

"Why are you smiling?" he grumbled as he followed me down the stairs, hovering almost.

"Because I love you, too," I said, and he chuckled, the last of his anger vanishing.

My balance shifted as I stepped down for the next step, and I froze, unable to move as a sudden uproar exploded in my mind. I cowered, hands over my head. It was the collective. Something had happened in the ever-after. Thoughts of revenge and joy were a slurry of contrasts. Trent's hand touched me, and like a knob twisting the focus, it swamped me.

I woke up at the bottom of the stairs. My elbow hurt, and I stared up at Trent as he held my head to his chest. He looked scared. I was too.

"Trent, what's going on?" I warbled, and his expression hardened.

"I don't know." His eyes looked deep into mine until he was sure I was okay. "I'm carrying you to the couch. Don't try to stop me."

Fear kept me silent. The memory of being helpless sifted to the topmost of my thoughts, scaring me even more as he lurched upright with me. I knew how to be passive. I knew how to be still to preserve my strength. That didn't mean I liked doing it. *This too will pass,* I thought, pinning my fraying calm to it. Something had happened. I was okay. *But it might happen again.*

Trent set me gently into the cushions. It felt different from this morning, and I pulled my knees to my chin, making room for him as he pointed the remote and turned on the TV.

A sitcom blared out, the laugh track sounding trite. Trent began flipping through the channels. My tension wound tighter, fear growing as I put distance between myself and both the attack and the outcry from the demon collective. I couldn't have been the only one who'd felt it.

Trent paused at a news station. The woman was professionally charming, and the man flirted harmlessly as they discussed the new school format being implemented. "Nothing on ICTV," he said, arm extended to change the channel.

"Try the weather channel," I said, eyes fixed on the screen.

"Are you serious?"

I nodded. "They don't have to check the validity of their stories like the national news."

Frowning, Trent looked at the back of the remote where Takata had taped a mini guide. "Okay. The weather channel." Arm pointed, he clicked again.

". . . strange phenomena in the sky observed over the Atlantic Ocean tonight," an uncomfortable-looking woman on the beach was saying, the wind shifting her jacket even as her eyes kept darting to the surf. "Experts at the local marine study outpost are trying to link it to the sudden crab migration you see about me."

She jerked, kicking at something outside of the camera's lens. "The beaches are covered with the rarely seen but not uncommon tomato crab. Most mass migrations are tied to full moons and high or low tides, and it has local and international animal behaviorists stumped."

And the woman standing there with them creeped out, I thought.

Trent's arm lowered. "That's . . . odd."

My lip curled. Revenge and thoughts of punishment had searched my soul, tried to take me. There was usually a reason for the myths and symbols that dogged some animal species like flies, snakes, and . . . crabs. Crabs were the worst.

"The crabs are steadily moving inland," the woman was saying, making an awkward jump as she almost stepped on something. "Apparently it's happening up and down the coast as far north as Maine and as far south as lower Georgia."

"Not Florida?" I wondered, stifling a shiver as Trent sat beside me.

"No one's lived in Florida since the Turn. They probably haven't checked yet."

The newscaster handed it off to the station, which had somehow gotten an interview with a local marine biologist. "See what Inderland Entertainment Tonight is saying," I asked, knowing their programming wouldn't have to be cleared or verified either.

Trent turned the remote over to find the channel number. "IET isn't on until six."

"It's six in Cincinnati," I said, and he grunted, hesitated in thought, frowned, and clicked the right number. Yeah, I didn't like that the sun was down on the East Coast either. Whatever was happening there would probably hit us in three hours.

"Inderland Entertainment Tonight," he said, eyes fixed forward. "What do you think they will know that CNN doesn't?"

"CNN is an hour late in breaking anything new," I said, listening to the trendy, size 1 woman in six-inch zebra heels interviewing a beatnik college kid with wide eyes and too many friends in the background trying to get on TV. "Ghosts?" I said, turning to Trent. "Are they talking about ghosts?"

"I think we should try CNN," he suggested.

"No, wait!" I said, grabbing for the remote, but he was too fast, jerking it away. "Go back!" I demanded, breathless until he did.

"He like came right at me!" the kid was saying. "Creepy as shit and ragged. I thought it was a joke until it grabbed me. I tried to get it off me, but I sort of went through it a little. My friends pulled it off me, and we got the hell out of there. I've never seen anything like it. It wasn't even real except where it grabbed me!"

"It was a surface demon," I said, pulse quickening.

Trent's wandering attention snapped back. "No."

But the skinny woman was talking, a still shot of an underground train platform behind her. "Reports of similar incidents have been coming in from all over Manhattan," she said, and I wondered if she was going to change to more sinister makeup before the night was over. Maybe put a bat in her hair. "The first indications that this is a belowground-only assault seem untrue as the wraiths are beginning to venture above on the streets, causing havoc."

"Yeah, it's kind of hard to grasp the concept of polite society when you've been out of it for a hundred years," I said, grimacing as a blurry, shaky shot clearly taken from a phone showed a surface demon hissing at a car before diving behind the stone wall at Central Park.

"Those *are* surface demons!" Trent blurted out, sounding almost betrayed.

Great. Just great. Depressed, I unkinked my hands from around my knees and put my feet on the floor. "Damn it, Trent," I complained. "I never would have played dead if I had thought they could actually do it!"

"But they can't!" Trent's gaze was fixed on the TV, his shock obvious.

Tired, I rubbed my forehead. "Maybe that's what I felt. What we both felt," I added, even though he hadn't said anything about an elf-born curse ripping through his soul.

He jerked straight, and I could almost see the thoughts aligning. "I didn't feel an attack. I felt a call to arms." Hand rubbing over his face, he leaned back into the cushions, his brow lowering and his expression getting darker.

Subdued, I took the remote and set it on the table before it fell between the cushions. Elven magic had attacked me. It had passed over him and struck me—even if it hadn't found what it needed to fully invoke. I had a bad feeling that whatever it had been, it had been aimed at the demons, not just the surface demons.

"You're a demon," Trent said softly, and I nodded, taking his hand in mine. "You're in the collective."

I'd felt an outcry, one so violent and explosive it had reached me even without a scrying mirror, knocking me flat on my ass. Depressed, I watched a group of people on a bus try to catch a surface demon only to have to beat it off a woman when it turned the tables on them.

"How did they manage it?" Trent said, distraught. "It can't be done."

But they did it. "Try the regular news now," I said, and Trent let go of my hand to stretch for the remote.

". . . new phenomena of what spellogists are calling a spontaneous release of surface demons from the ever-after. Elven Sa'hans are telling us these are actually the material manifestation of the souls of the undead and to leave them alone as they search for their bodies."

Trent grimaced. "They are not Sa'hans. They're frauds."

Frauds or not, they'd managed to get the surface demons into reality. I was starting to think again, and my shoulders scrunched up almost to my ears. Something had happened in the ever-after, something bad. Uneasy, I looked over my shoulder to my mom's unseen spelling room. I'd been through most of the cupboards, and there'd been no scrying mirror. I could probably summon Al without it, but he was pissed at me.

Unless he's trapped somewhere. He won't kill me if I rescue him, will he?

"The ghostly, frightening images with half substance are showing up in most major East Coast cities," the newscaster was saying, "the vampiric souls appearing in a steady progression west with the setting sun."

Trent crossed one ankle over his knee. I'd never seen him look so confused. "I don't get it," he said, gesturing. "There isn't a way to move them to reality."

I glanced at the clock on the cable box. It was very close to sunset in Cincinnati. Stretching, I took the remote and clicked over to CNN. Sure enough, an excited, somewhat nervous man was standing at Fountain Square, the sky still holding the pink from the sun. I had figured they'd be either there or in Detroit. It was too early for Chicago. Behind the reporter were clusters of living vampires. The atmosphere was one of breathless anxiety.

"Sunset . . . ," Trent whispered, and the newscaster spun, voice rising as he described the sudden appearance of nearly twenty surface demons. My expression twisted as the cameras zoomed in on them, their ragged auras and gaunt limbs standing out against the sunset-red sky, making it look like the ever-after. People squealed, and most of the surface demons ran for the street, looking for somewhere to hide.

Two, though, hesitated, hunched and furtive as they hissed at the vampires coaxing them closer. Trent said nothing, and I clicked back to New York. The undead there had probably figured it out and were likely in the streets looking for their souls.

"Mmmm," Trent grunted, easing closer to the TV as a news reporter tried to stay in the limited streetlight as she nervously explained what was going on behind her. The sun had been down for a while. It was dark enough for the undead.

My lips parted as the camera swung and steadied to show a surface demon melting into a rapturous vampire. He wasn't a master vampire. He was hardly a vampire at all, actually, one of New York's homeless vamps living under the streets and existing on addicts until someone bigger took him out. But he'd found his soul—and it was trying to bind to him.

"My God, Landon did it . . . ," Trent breathed, but I wasn't so sure this was going to have a happy ending. You couldn't see an aura through a TV, but it still didn't look like a repeat of what had happened up in Luke and Marsha's apartment, even if the vampire was sobbing, holding on to the corner of the building as the guilt and shame of his soulless existence crashed down upon him.

Spontaneous joining? I wasn't buying it. "What's to keep it from spontaneously leaving?" I asked. We'd had to burn the gateway through which Felix's soul had entered him to keep it from simply going back out.

Someone had stopped to help the vampire, now weeping inconsolably. The newscaster looked uncomfortable as she told people to stay off the streets and out of the way as the vampires found their souls.

"I guess they think we're dead," I said, not feeling at all good. I wanted to call Ivy and see how Felix was doing. "The surface demons will be showing up here in about three hours," I said as I looked at the bright golden light.

His eyes on the TV, Trent got to his feet. "They seem to be staying in the main population centers."

So far, I thought glumly. "You really think they're free? For good?" If they were, then that soul bottle I'd made was going to be more than useless.

Trent hesitated, watching the TV as if it might have the answers. "I've no idea. Maybe their release was what you felt on the stairs."

Or the attack in my mom's spell room, I mused, an ugly thought trickling through me. If it had almost taken me, then maybe it had hit the demons, too.

I jumped as he spun, almost running to the stairs. "Where are you going?"

"To get Bis!" he shouted.

Fidgety, I looked out the big windows at the bright sun. "Trent? He won't be awake," I called, then gestured as if to say "I told you so" when Trent came back with Bis perched on his arm like a huge sleeping owl. My bag was over his other arm, looking funny against him.

"We have to get to the ever-after. Find out what happened." Trent stumbled into the living room. He thrust my bag at me as he sat down on the edge of the couch. Motions tense, he tickled Bis's ear. "Bis, wake up."

The little guy scrunched up his eyes and pushed at him with one leathery wing. One red eye opened, saw me, and squinted closed in the sun. "It's kind of hard when he's in the sun like that," I said as I shifted to put him in my shadow. "Bis!" I shouted, pinching his wing.

That sort of worked as Bis flung his wings out to smack Trent in the face. "Bis, wake up!" I shouted again. Kind and gentle wouldn't work. We'd be lucky to get even an eye open again. "Bis, we need to get to the ever-after. Bis? Bis!"

But he didn't even stir.

Trent stared at me, and my teeth clenched. "I've got an idea. Trust me?" I said.

"Uhhh," Trent stammered, and I tugged my shoulder bag onto my lap and grabbed his arm.

"Bis!" I shouted, touching that awful ley line and shifting all our auras into it.

"Rachel!" Trent exclaimed, but I wasn't sure if it had reached my ears or was only in my head as we suddenly were in the line, broken and tasting of earth and sky all at the same time.

With a mental gasp, Bis was awake, startled as he suddenly found himself floundering.

Dalliance, I thought, and with a curious flip of awareness that I had yet to master, Bis tuned our auras. If I could get any answers at all, it would be at Dalliance.

Chapter 14

What is *wrong* with you!" the little gargoyle shouted, red eyes glaring, his voice echoing in the empty space as we materialized. "I was sleeping! I could've dropped you!" His voice came back again, all the louder. But then he turned, wings drooping as he saw where we were.

Dalliance was currently an Asian eatery, the low tables holding bowls of steaming rice and pots of tea, overlooking a courtyard complete with a koi-stocked pond, raked pads of sand and gravel, and tiny trees. A jukebox, out of place and time, stood as the only indication that everything was a solid illusion. Several cups of tea had spilled, and the place was empty.

"Where is everyone?" Trent said, his tension evolving into a cautious investigation as he lifted a lid and breathed in the steam. There was no damage, no evidence of threat apart from the spilled tea. They simply were not here. Anyone. Not even the staff.

The teapot clinked as Trent set the lid back in place. An elven spell had attacked me. I'd barely fought it off. But I wasn't a cursed demon. *Al* . . .

"Bis, take us to the mall," I said, scared. I could probably find someone at the mall who'd talk to me without charging me for it.

Subdued, the little gargoyle nodded. Trent stepped to us, and with hardly a breath of displaced air, the varnished wood and rice paper screens melted into loud eighties music and a steamy warmth.

My mouth dropped open. People were everywhere, howling, dancing, swinging from the banners the demons had hung to try to dampen the echo. Shocked, I fell back against the fountain. Foam spilled up behind me, and I jerked forward. There was a bubble charm in it, and blue-and-pink froth spilled over and onto the floor.

"What happened?" Trent gripped my elbow and pulled me off the jump-in circle.

Speechless, I shook my head as I tried to take it all in. People were everywhere. They were ecstatic, even the familiars in charge of the shops had left them to get slushies and ices from the abandoned pushcarts. It was as hot as always, but goose bumps rose when I realized that there were no demons here. *None.*

"Bis, take me to Al," I said, and both Bis and Trent turned to me, aghast. "Take me to Al!" I demanded, hiking my shoulder bag up higher. "The demons are gone! That's what I felt! Something attacked them!"

"How?" Trent whispered, but I was already pulling him back onto the jump-in circle.

The demons were gone. Every last one of them. Something had tried to kill me. Al had to be alive. He was stronger than I was.

But as Bis's field enveloped us, I realized what had happened. I was a witch-born demon, free of the original elven curse. Al wasn't. That's what the elven spell had been looking for to invoke on—and Al had it.

My heart pounded as the heat and noise of the mall vanished, echoing in my thoughts as the scent of woodsmoke filled my lungs and the stone floor of Al's spelling kitchen formed under my feet. If not for the accompanying glow from a nearly dead fire and the subliminal whisper of voices from that creepy tapestry, I'd never know we'd arrived. Bis was getting good at these short hops, and I touched his wide-spaced claws on my shoulder as I looked to the small hearth and then the shadowed ceiling. It was dark, but I could tell that Al wasn't here.

That doesn't mean he's dead, I thought, my shoulders nearly to my ears as I handed my bag to Trent and went to stir up some light from the fire.

There was a stack of actual wood logs instead of Al's usual peat-moss chunks that reeked of burnt amber, and I put the smallest on the coals. Orange sparks flew when I dropped it on, and I wiped my fingers free of the greasy bark, turning to take in the room as it brightened.

Mr. Fish sat on the bottom of his glass, gills pumping, and I frowned at the tall glass-fronted cabinets, all open and the books and ley line equipment gone. The small table between the two hearths was clean, not a notation or hint of script remaining. Anything smaller than a bread box was missing.

"Where's his stuff?" Trent said, and a muffled, surprised grunt came from the bedroom.

I spun to the archway as the thick wooden door engraved with spells and embedded with metallic symbols swung inward. Light spilled out, and I squinted at Al's trim silhouette, his gloved hands holding a mundane oil lamp. I backed up in relief, both happy to see him and unsure how he might react. He was okay, but that didn't translate into his being glad to see me.

"Newt?" he said cautiously, low voice utterly devoid of his usual British lord accent.

"It's me," I said. "Thank God you're all right. Wha—"

I gasped, backpedaling. My back hit the slate table, and then Al was on me, his hand across my neck. "Al!" I cried out, and then my voice gagged to nothing. I smacked his arm, digging at his fingers, and he let up enough for me to breathe.

"I said I'd kill you if you ever showed up in my rooms again!"

"Stop!" I cried out as Trent grabbed Al, and my air choked off again.

"*Detrudo!*" Al snarled.

I heard Trent and Bis slam into one of the cabinets, glass and wood shattering.

"I had to know if you were okay!" I said, and then his fist tightened again, choking off my air. Reaching up, I pinched his nose, and he jumped, fingers easing enough to let me breathe.

My air came in quick, thin pants as he lowered his face until inches separated us. "You came to steal my things!"

I fixed on one of his eyes, seeing myself in their red, goat-slitted pupil. "I came to see if you were alive," I said, and his grip tightened, his eyes narrowing as my breath gurgled to a stop.

"Let her go, you ass!" Trent shouted from the floor, and the sounds of sliding glass became obvious as he shook the shattered cabinet off. "She's here because she thought you might be *dead*."

"To steal what's left of my miserable life," he breathed. My hands ached and my arms began to shake as I kept trying to wedge him off me. If I used magic, he would, too, and he knew more than I did.

"She thought you were hurt!" Trent said, his voice between us and the fire. "She doesn't care about your things. She thought you needed help!"

Snarling, Al pressed into me, fingers tightening until black stars began to blot my vision.

"You are *killing* her!" Trent said, and I heard a dull thud as his fist met Al's face.

Al's fingers let go. My breath came in with a gasp, and I rolled to my front, the cool slate of the table soothing against my flushed cheek. Hand to my neck, I choked and gagged, eyes watering as I pushed myself up. Bis was on the mantel beside Mr. Fish, scared to death.

"*You* are going to kill *her*, you putrid little elf!" Al snarled, and Trent drew himself up, his face white and his expression hard. "There is *nothing* that will survive what's coming. And it's your fault."

"I'm okay," I croaked, trembling as I waved Bis off, and he landed on the back of Ceri's old chair, still in its accustomed place. Seeing me upright, Al scooped up a carpetbag and tried to shove the rolled-up tapestry into it. Trent was going to kill me? Nothing here was his fault. It was sort of mine. Trent stood between us, my bag spilling out over the floor behind him, and I don't think I appreciated him more than at that moment. "What's coming?" I whispered, voice raw.

"The end," Al muttered, his frustration growing as he fought to get the tapestry into the bag, clearly bigger on the inside than the out. "I see you washed the Goddess slime off you. Too bad it will keep coming back."

He was talking about the mystics, and I squared my shoulders. It was going better than I had thought it would. I was just glad he wasn't dead.

"An elven spell tried to kill me," I said, and Al turned the tapestry end over end to fit it in the bag, but it unrolled as if trying to stay out. "It wasn't the Goddess, it was the dewar and the enclave."

"Surprise, surprise," he muttered.

"It couldn't get a grip on me," I said, gently pushing Trent's hand off me when I edged past him. "But then I heard the collective cry out. I thought . . . it took you."

Shoulders hunched, Al threw the tapestry at the wall in frustration. It hit with a thud, the sliding fabric sounding like a muffled scream as it landed on the floor and slowly uncurled. "It was . . . ," he said, eyebrows lowered as he stared at me, ". . . a cry of joy, Rachel Mariana Morgan."

My chest hurt. "Please don't call me that. You left me. I didn't leave you."

Al flicked his eyes at Trent as he yanked his carpetbag up. I stepped closer, feet scuffing to a halt when Al growled, "Yes. You did."

"Because he's an elf?" I exclaimed, frustrated.

Al's expression twisted even more. "Exactly," he said, the words dripping scorn and hatred. "Love has made you into a tool, Rachel, and like a tool, you are oblivious and will be cast aside when your job is done."

"I am not," I whispered, cold, but the thought that Trent would soon remember his place among his people weighed heavily on me. Quen was right. I was a phase, a happy dalliance.

"You are blind, Rachel, even as you are a part of it." Al pointed at me, his anger stemming from a deep wound. "Elves ask too much. They bring only destruction. That is what they are. They've always been such, even when we tried to crush them from existence. And it will kill you."

"But you loved Ceri," I pleaded, and Trent grunted as if only now getting it.

Al's pointing finger slowly dropped, his depth of hatred chilling me.

"Just so," he said bitterly, looking at his empty room. "You begin to understand?"

"You can't blame this on Ceri," I said, a new fear slithering through me. He'd loved her, loved her enough to break the rules and free her from her servitude in such a way that I could save her life. From there the world changed as Trent used her to begin to pull his people back from extinction.

Love had turned my goals to his, and I found a pre-curse DNA sample so Ceri's baby would be free of the curse. And now, bolstered by the mere hint of success, the elves had begun to eliminate everyone more powerful than themselves. Perhaps Al was right.

Horrified, I watched him stuff the last of the things on the mantel into the bag like Santa in reverse. His thick fingers hesitated at Mr. Fish, and then he closed them, leaving the brandy snifter where it was. "Where has everyone gone?" I asked, scared.

Gaze flicking to Trent, then Bis, sitting wide-eyed on Ceri's chair, he hesitated. "Anywhere they want," he said, waving at Bis until he moved to Trent's shoulder.

Anywhere? My thoughts went back to the empty state of Dalliance, and then the celebration of familiars at the mall. He said it had been a cry of joy . . .

"Oh, your elven brethren have made a large mistake," Al said to Trent as Ceri's chair was wreathed in a haze of black and shrank down to the size of my hand. "One we will exploit to the fullest and wipe them from existence once and for all," he said, using both hands to shift the smaller but clearly just as heavy chair into the bag. "Revenge is a tricky beast. Her claws face both ways. I don't mind a few more scars. They'll be unnoticed among the rest."

Trent paled. "The curse that attacked you . . . ," he whispered, and then he reached for the slate table, his balance gone. "The Goddess help us," he whispered, expression haunted. "That's what I felt. It was a call to break the curse."

"What curse?" I said, feeling as if I was on the brink of a precipice.

Al snapped the bag shut and lifted it easily. "Not break exactly, but when they modified it to force the surface demons to reality, they created a loophole." He spun to his fire and took the iron, rapping the ash from it. "I'm leaving now. You can have the tapestry. I never liked that thing anyway."

My heart thudded. "Al, wait!" I called out, but with a tweak on my awareness, he vanished in a curl of black-tainted ever-after.

Bis shifted his wings, and the room abruptly seemed a lot colder. I turned to Trent at his soft scuffing of feet. He had sat down, sinking into

Al's simple three-legged stool, elbow on the table and head in his hand as his thumb ran over a tiny scratch in the surface. I'd seen Al like that more than once. The hatred between the elves and the demons went far deeper than I'd thought. "Trent? What happened?"

He looked up, a hint of the fear of the unknown in the back of his gaze. "It must have taken the dewar working in concert with a good portion of the enclave," he said, and then his focus sharpened on me. "That's what you felt in your mom's spelling room. The unbinding spell recognized you as a demon, and when it couldn't find the curse keeping you in the ever-after, it just kept trying to take something, anything. The demons figured out what was going on, and now they're free."

My lips parted. Free? As in reality?

Suddenly I got it—the entire mess. Landon had made a huge error. He'd freed the surface demons to get rid of the undead, but once they walked into the sun—which I was sure they would—it'd be the demons who'd replace them as the rule makers and breakers, not the elves.

Grimacing, I reached for Mr. Fish. I didn't think Al was coming back. "We should go," I said, bending to pick up my bag. There was nothing here. Everything that had meant anything had been taken, held in that little carpetbag.

"Cincinnati?" Bis spread his wings in anticipation. "But you're supposed to be dead."

Trent edged from the softly mewling tapestry. "It doesn't matter now."

No, it didn't matter. And I was *not* going to help Landon save the world. He'd made his choice, and it wasn't my responsibility.

But as I felt Bis's aura slip around us, I had a bad feeling I was going to have to anyway.

 Chapter 15

The steeple was a dark slash against the underside of the clouds, red with the reflected light of the Hollows. Stray gleams of streetlight eked through the unmoving trees, making lumps and shadows in the graveyard. There was no friendly glow from the back porch. There was no back porch at all, and I held Mr. Fish carefully as my steps through the damp, unmowed grass slowed and the extent of the damage became evident.

Trent steadied me as I stepped over the low stone wall separating the garden from the graveyard. His hand was warm on my elbow, and I leaned into him, trying to tell him with my touch that I didn't believe what Al had said. *He's not using me,* I thought, but the uglier part of me added, *This might not have happened if you'd walked away six months ago.* I slowed, pulling away from him as the heartache of my church fell on me.

The rank, acidic scent of things that shouldn't be burned was choking. The kitchen and back living room were gone; only the broken remains of what wouldn't burn were left to show there'd ever been anything there. What was probably the stove and the fridge poked through what was left of the roof, all of it well below the original floor and filling the crawl space. Gutter work, twisted from the heat, was the most recognizable thing.

The stones of the original church were black and glistening from the soot and heat. Plywood had already been fixed over the open hallway, and it looked oddly high up from the ground without a porch to ground it. It was worse than seeing it on TV—cold, dark, and sad with chunks of our lives out of place and hardly recognizable.

"I'm sorry," Bis said, and I touched his feet, ignoring the lump in my throat as I pushed forward. My pace faltered when the ground became squishy from the water used to put out the fire. My coffeemaker: gone. The mug with the rainbows on it: gone. My spelling books: gone.

"There's Jenks," Trent said in relief, and somehow I smiled at the bright trail of sparkles arrowing down from the belfry.

Bis's wings shushed against my head, and my smile became real as I continued my list of don't-haves: no funerals, no songs of blood and daisies, no feeling guilty for surviving because I had fled. "Jenks!" I called as he circled, his wings a slow hum of indecision as he tried to read my mood. "Wow, they made a mess. You okay?"

"Hell yes!" Clearly relieved, he dropped down to Trent's shoulder since Bis was on mine. "You're lucky I'm not human size or I'd give you a smack," he said, and Trent hid a grin. "Where've you been? Eww, the ever-after," the pixy said, answering his own question. "Is that where you ditched the mystics? Your aura looks great. The demons are here. In reality. Why by Tink's little pink dildo did you let them out?"

"I didn't," I said, and Jenks looked at Trent, the shock on his angular features lit from his own dust.

"It was Landon." Trent grimaced at his shoes, now three inches deep in the mud that had once been my backyard. "He made a mistake." He took my hand, and I gave it a squeeze. His eyes held a thread of heartache, a need to talk. This wasn't a mistake. Al was bitter and jealous, unable to look past his own hurt, and Trent loved me. But even I knew I wouldn't be able to help him reach his goal. *His goal of elf supremacy?* God, I wasn't going to do this right now.

Jenks's wings brightened to a hot silver. "Landon? Figures."

I shivered when a drop of water from the big tree landed on my back. The bark was singed, and I hoped the fire hadn't killed the tree outright. "Apparently, if you engineer a curse loophole big enough to allow shambling zombies/surface demons through, real demons can follow." I picked my way through the mud, both wanting and dreading to see what was left.

Jenks's wings clattered. "Ah, you have to go in around the front if you want to go in. I wouldn't. It's pretty bad. They hosed everything down."

Nice. How many times is my church going to be trashed this week?

Jenks winced, arms over his chest. "Cleaning crew comes Wednesday. I would've had them sooner, but the building inspector has to give it an all clear."

Again Trent's hand found mine, his touch easing my clenched jaw when a soft warmth stole into me, sparkling where our fingers twined. "I know it's uncomfortable with Ellasbeth there, but I could use your help with the girls," he said, his anger at Ellasbeth making ugly, half-heard shadows in his voice.

"Tink's panties, yes!" Jenks exclaimed, and Bis shifted his wings, clearly uneasy. "Your house. That's a great idea. Jumoke and Izzy are already there."

Jenks wants me to leave? Maybe it was worse inside than I imagined. My gut said Ellasbeth wasn't doing anything other than trying to roll with the punches, but logic said otherwise. The chance to look her in the eye might tell me more.

"Thanks," I said as I turned to the stone walk that led to the front. "I'll take you up on that." There were huge boot prints in the mud where there'd never been mud before. It made me feel violated in a way the missing kitchen didn't. "Ivy knows I'm not dead, right?"

Jenks's wings clattered as he left Trent. "Yep. She's at her folks with Nina."

"Everything okay?" I questioned.

"You think I'd be hanging out here waiting for you if she wasn't?"

True.

"Cormel knows you're not dead, too," Jenks added, and I jerked to a stop. Mr. Fish's water sloshed and Trent almost ran into me, his attention fixed on his phone. "Don't look at me!" Jenks shouted. "I didn't tell him! He came over about an hour ago. Told me to tell you not to interfere with the undead souls."

The unsaid "or else" was obvious. My frown deepened as Trent's phone went dark and he slid it away. "If you didn't tell Cormel I was alive, who did?" I muttered.

"Your mom?" Jenks hovered just a little in front of me as I headed for the tall gate, his eyes darting nervously to Trent and back again. "She's having too much fun arranging your funeral. The news has a wake watch going. Tink's tampons, she's a little scary, you know?"

Yeah, that sounded like my mom. Frustrated, I shoved the gate open with my foot. Bis left, making widening circles until he found the steeple. Jenks went with him, the pixy talking so high and fast I couldn't follow it.

"Landon isn't going to be happy you're still alive," Trent said softly.

"Too bad," I said, tired, and Mr. Fish shuddered at the bottom of his glass.

"One thing an elf hates more than giving something for nothing is when a plan falls apart—and it's falling apart. I doubt freeing the real demons from the ever-after was his intention. Cormel saw what we had to do to keep Felix's soul bound. He knows this spontaneous melding isn't going to stick." He hesitated as I dug my car keys out. "Rachel, you're not a tool."

I jerked to a stop, shocked at the quick topic shift. Trying to smile, I met his eyes. "I know." But my heart ached, and seeing it, he pulled me close, careful not to spill Mr. Fish.

His arms were warm, and he smelled of burnt amber. Tears threatened as his hand found the back of my head and he held me close, sighing heavily. "Al is trying to drive us apart," he whispered, and I nodded, needing this. "He's jealous that we made a stand and he didn't." He leaned back, smiling at the track of a tear on me. "I'm not going to walk away from you. I never wanted to see the elves destroy everyone, just not go extinct."

"I know," I said, voice wobbling. The "I'm not going to walk away from you" hit me hard. "But Landon does."

"What Landon wants doesn't mean anything. He's not the Sa'han."

I was starting to wonder if Trent was either, anymore. Maybe that was why he'd agreed to reopen relations with Ellasbeth. Damn it, he wasn't using me, but I wasn't going to come out of this where I wanted to be either. He couldn't be both.

Jenks rose up from the carport, his dust an impatient red. I swallowed down my heartache, disentangling us and starting back to the front walk. Trent's hand stole into mine immediately, and my chest hurt. "Thanks for coming back with me," he said. "I know it's going to be hard with Ellasbeth there, but I love you, Rachel, not her. This is for the girls, not me."

For the girls? Yes, I'd put up with Ellasbeth for the girls. Somehow I managed a smile.

"And don't worry," Trent said, his hand trailing deliciously along the small of my back as we passed the untouched trash cans, "I won't make you cook or anything."

"I can cook," I said, then louder, "I can so!," when he arched his eyebrows.

"I've never seen it," he muttered, and Jenks darted to us.

"Hey! You mind if I ride over with you?" he asked. "Jumoke, ah, he said I could bunk with him and Izzy. This is so weird."

He was leaving the garden unguarded? I turned to look behind me at the destruction. *Oh God, is it over?*

"Bis is going to watch the church along with Belle," he added, and my breath came rushing back. "He wants to talk to his dad if that's okay with you."

Squinting in the dark, I tried to find Bis, looking scary and solemn on the very top of the steeple, his red eyes glowing. "I think that's a great idea," I said, again wondering how much I'd messed the kid's life up by being in the wrong place at the right time. But Mr. Fish's water was showing little rings from my trembling hands. It wasn't over. We weren't going to live at Trent's. It was temporary until we sorted everything out. I didn't think any pixy or fairy would mess with the garden in the meantime. It was Jenks's by law, and even the pixies respected that, in awe that humanity recognized one of their own as having rights and responsibilities.

"Rachel, are you okay?" Trent asked, and I nodded, gazing at the church as if I'd never see it again. The streetlight was brighter here, and I could just make out our names over the door. The I.S. tape across the door moved, and an official-looking paper fluttered under the bell.

"Mind if I drive?"

"No, I got it."

Trent sighed as we headed for the carport, and my smile slowly faded.

He is not using me. I knew it to the grit in my soul. But the end result might be the same, especially if the elves continued to refuse to follow him—because of me, because I was a demon. Landon's fairy tale was one they could get behind, easy and satisfying. Learning to understand those you hate and fear is harder. I was pulling Trent down. Making his life impossible.

My boots were silent on the stone walk. Three streets over I could hear shouting. Sirens were coming from downtown. Maybe we should take the long way to Trent's. "Some things shouldn't be changed," I whispered, meaning the vampires but thinking it related to me, too.

Trent's hands dropped to my lower back, and I shivered. "Convincing Cormel of that won't be easy." Head tilting, he eyed me. "That's not my phone."

Starting, I pulled my bag open, surprised when I found my phone glowing. I hadn't even felt it ring. *Six calls?* I hadn't been in the ever-after and out of service that long. My eyes flicked to the DON'T CROSS tape as I read Edden's name.

"It's Edden," I said, setting Mr. Fish on the hood and flipping my phone open. "I gotta take it. It might be about the church."

"I'll drive," Trent said, his worry obvious, and I handed the keys over. "Edden!" I said as Trent went to open the passenger-side door for me and I hustled around the front of the car. "What are you doing calling a dead woman?"

"No," his preoccupied, muted voice said. "Yes. Yes!"

Settling into the seat, I held the phone closer. "Edden?"

"Rachel!" Edden's voice became stronger. "Don't you ever look at your messages?"

"Not when my answering machine is melted," I said, and Jenks snickered, the pixy having parked it on the rearview mirror where he could hear.

"I've been trying to reach you for an hour," the FIB captain complained. "Why did you let the demons out?"

"I didn't let them out, and I didn't take your calls because I'm supposed to be dead!" I said, echoing the irritation in his voice. My jaw clenched at the thought of Al running around Cincinnati. But if he was truly free, wouldn't he go somewhere sunny?

"If you didn't do it, who did?" Edden said, and I heard a door shut and a new silence.

Grimacing, I wrangled the phone as Trent handed me Mr. Fish. "Landon," I said, pleased when the brandy snifter fit perfectly into the cup holder.

"On purpose?" Edden barked, and then sighed, realizing how dumb that was. "You don't happen to know where he is, do you?"

Trent settled behind the wheel, and we exchanged a worried look. "No." Landon was AWOL? *Great.*

"I could really use your help," Edden said, and then muffled, "No! You want them to end up as toads? Set up blocks and keep people back. That's it." There was a brief silence. "Rachel?"

The car had started with a satisfying *brumm,* and I watched the open top fold out, settling over us with a whine and a thump. "Any leads on who blew up my kitchen?" I asked, and when Edden said nothing, I added, "Sorry, I'm retired."

Jenks made a burst of dust from the mirror, and Trent put up a finger for him to high-five.

"Rachel . . . ," Edden complained.

"No." Phone tucked between my shoulder and ear, I managed to lock my side of the top down. "Ask Landon to help you."

"Rachel, the I.S. is focused on policing the soul parties in the big parks. They're ignoring everything, demons included. We're trying to handle it, but you can guess how that's going."

Trent leaned close as he turned to look behind us to back up, and I swear my skin tingled as I breathed him in, burnt amber and all. "Demons are terrorizing Carew Tower," Edden was saying, but I was still enjoying Trent. "They let the big cats out of their enclosures at the zoo, and I've got multiple reports of them taking over the bus line. The demons, not the tigers. Sunrise is hours off, and I need your help!"

I pushed my fingers into my forehead, trying to decide if I wanted to tell Edden this might not go away with the sun, but my home had exploded and no one had admitted it had happened other than the building inspector. "And this is my problem why?" I asked as Trent backed up. Jenks clutching for the stem of the rearview mirror.

"It's your problem because you're the only one who can help!" Edden said. "With great power must also come great responsibility."

"That is *bull!*" I shouted, and Jenks's wings burst into a surprised red. "The only thing great power ever gave me was a dwindling bank account and a court order to stay out of San Francisco. Where was the FIB when my church was attacked, Edden? Where were you when you knew damn well the vampires were plotting to kill me? The I.S. I can understand, but what about you? Has anyone even been out to my church to investigate?"

Trent's grip on the wheel tightened, and I settled back in my seat and angled the vents to me. "Look, I gotta go make spaghetti for Trent. He doesn't think I can cook." *Little girls like spaghetti, don't they?*

Edden's sigh only made me angrier. "Making the vampires accountable will take more money than rebuilding the church," he muttered.

"So they get away with it?" I said bitterly as Trent took a turn too fast and Jenks swore at him to slow down.

"You're a demon, Rachel. What can we do that you can't?"

Pissed, I held the phone closer. "I'm not saying you should've tried to stop them, but you are ignoring the fact that it happened! If you don't say it's wrong, then you're telling them you agree. And now you want me to bail you out of trouble because I have the balls and skills and associates to make a fist of it?"

Make a fist of it? Crap on toast, where had that come from?

Jenks was looking kind of worried, and I resolved to ease up a little. Edden was way over his head and the I.S. wouldn't help. I was going to do what I could, such as it was, but I wanted to know I wasn't out there by myself. Edden, though, hadn't said anything, and not wanting him to hang up, I said, "Look. I agree that master vampires crying in their cups isn't a good thing and that demons laughing in theirs is even worse, but either I'm a part of this world or I'm not. Either you stand up and say something, or you ignore it and tell them it was acceptable to try to kill me."

I jumped when Trent's hand landed on mine and he gave it a squeeze.

"I see your point," Edden finally said, and I exhaled. "I should have lodged a formal protest, posted on the FIB news feed, gotten a team out there to make a report. We're too used to ignoring things out of our control."

"Thank you," I whispered.

"But the I.S. isn't functioning and demons are causing trouble." Edden's voice quickened. "Can you get them to back off? We've got laws on the books for demons now, but no way to administer them."

Laws on the books. If there was one thing demons understood, it was rules. The trick was to get them to go along with them because I wasn't going to spend the rest of my life enforcing them—even if I was the only one who could. *Damn it, how did I get here?* Fingers pushing into my forehead again, I hoped Ivy was okay. "Where are they?"

Jenks sighed, and Trent's grip tightened on the wheel once more. We'd stopped at a red light, and when it turned green, he sat there and waved at the car behind us to go around.

"I've got a group at a coffeehouse two blocks from the FIB," Edden said, and Trent flicked the turn signal on. "We've got it cordoned off but . . ."

"Junior's? I mean Mark's?" I asked, wincing. Sweet ever-loving pixy dust. What was it with that place?

"Ah, yes. I think that's the name of it."

I had my shoulder bag, but there wasn't anything in it that would be of use against uncooperative demons. *Damn it back to the Turn.* "Okay," I said around a sigh. "I'll talk to them. Keep your men back. Just having them there is enough of a statement. I don't want anyone turned into a toad."

"Rachel, I'm sorry," Edden said, his entire demeanor shifting now that I'd said yes. "I never thought of it that way. You seem so capable of anything."

"Don't worry about it," I said, not liking the empty streets as we sped over the bridge and into Cincinnati. No one was out here, and it was creepy. "I'm still going to send you a bill."

I could hear the smile in his voice, the relief, when he next spoke. "I've got a couple of tickets for the FIB picnic with your name on them. Oh, and don't get Trent killed, okay?"

Trent's teeth caught the gleam of the streetlight as he smiled, and I felt his hold on a ley line tingle through me. "Hey, tell the I.S. I could use a couple of vans designed for ley line witches, eh?"

A burst of dust lit the car. "Shit, Rache! You're going to arrest them?"

I didn't have time for this. "Maybe."

"You got it," Edden said, and I nodded as I hung up and closed my phone.

My stomach quivered, and I dropped my phone in my bag. *Splat gun, lethal detection charms, gum, key-chain flashlight, a pair of ankle socks I'd worn the last time Trent tried to teach me golf. Mr. Fish.*

Yeah, that ought to do it.

Chapter 16

You sure you want to do this with Jenks and me?" I said as we slowed at an FIB blockade.

Trent waved at the FIB guys, and recognizing us, they gestured us through. "Absolutely," he said distantly, and I felt warm, loved in a way. This sucked. It really sucked. It was so not fair to have Trent this close and finally understand what Al and Quen and Jonathan had known all along. What Trent and I wanted was never going to happen. I couldn't keep dragging him down like this. He could end all of this by taking control of the enclave. *But he couldn't do that with me at his side . . .*

What we wanted might not make any difference in a few minutes, though. The lights were up high at Mark's, and I could see figures at the tables even before we parked. My grimace deepened as Jenks checked his sword, and I pulled my shoulder bag onto my lap. Ivy would be fine at her folks' house, and she was in no state of health to help me.

"I swear, this place has got to be on an invisible ley line or something," Trent said as we pulled in. There were only a couple of cars, and my brow pinched seeing the people afraid to move as they sat between demons in suits. *Crap on toast, Mark is probably in there, too.*

"What's the plan, Rache?" Jenks asked, the snick of his sword catching my attention.

Plan? I looked up from Mr. Fish. "Ah, yeah. Right. Plan."

Trent put the car in park, and I got out. Hip cocked, I waited for Trent, knowing he probably had that cap and ribbon of his somewhere and needed a moment to get it in place, but he immediately joined me. The music was loud, and there was masculine, aggressive laughter.

"Plan?" Jenks said again, and I waved to the FIB guys at the end of the street. I felt good with them there, even knowing they couldn't do anything.

"Plan," I said, rocking into motion when Trent's shoes scuffed. "How about, let's go in."

Jenks's dust flashed an irate red. "Tink's titties, that's her plan? *Go in?*"

Trent shrugged, relaxed on the surface as he pulled the door open. "Works for me."

"Just like old times," Jenks said, cracking his knuckles as he darted in over my head.

"I'll take the ones on the right," Trent muttered as the door closed, chimes jingling.

The laughter stopped as they noticed us. Trent was pulling deeper on the ley lines, but I did little more than make a casual connection. I couldn't best one demon, much less eight. No, there were nine now, and they were shifting in their chairs to face us. If I couldn't do this without turning it into a magic slugfest, then it was over before it had begun. When you got right down to it, magic was an asset only if you were up against someone who didn't have any.

My heart thudded. Demons hated elves. Sure, they had ridden with Trent to bring down Ku'Sox, but bringing Trent in here had been either really stupid or really smart. He had some protection as a freed familiar, but "accidents" happened.

Al was in a corner booth with Dali and Newt. Six paper-and-wax cups of coffee in various stages of emptiness sat between them. Newt beamed at me, in contrast to Al's outright hostility. Most of the demons were at the long center table tormenting those two couples. The people were terrified, unable to leave with the demons draping their arms over their shoulders. Their relief when they saw me made me angrier still.

Plan. "We get them out first," I said, boldly striding to the counter.

Mark was there making something with crushed ice and hadn't heard us come in. He was holding up pretty well, but his relief when he saw me was astounding.

Trent moved behind a couple. "Go," he said, and they stood, chairs sliding and demons staring at Trent in uncertainty as the couple scrambled to leave. Seeing them headed for the door, the remaining two people stood, sinking back down when the demon beside them growled.

So far, so good. Let's push it a little more. "You really should reevaluate your life choices," I said as I leaned against the counter, thumbs in my pockets. The demon looked vaguely familiar, but I didn't think I'd ever done business with him. Like the rest of the demons here, he was in a business suit, jewelry flashing and hair slicked back. Only Newt and Al maintained their usual attire, Newt in her androgynous robes and elven dewar hat, and Al in his green crushed-velvet finery. His anger that Trent was still with me was almost palpable.

My skin tingled as someone pulled heavily on a line. I didn't think it was Trent, and my knees went wobbly when two more demons did the same. "Why are you here? With that *elf*?" the demon said, voice oily with domination.

His barest hint of doubt was like a spark on a dark night, and I pulled it to me, fanning it higher with a confident smile. He was unsure, not about his skills but that this might end when the sun came up. I could use that, give them a fairy tale to think about so they'd go away and ponder the truth of it for a few hours until they knew for sure.

Smiling, I leaned over the table between him and the couple, showing him some cleavage in exchange for their freedom. "You remember Trent. He's my boyfriend," I said, and the couple rose at Jenks's urging, racing for the door. "He's taking me to his place and I'm making spaghetti, but the FIB asked me to stop on the way and give you a little welcome-to-reality message." The door chimes jingled, and I straightened. "Seeing as you might be here for good and need to start being . . . what's the word . . . accountable?"

He laughed at that, ugly and mean. Pulse racing, I backed up, glad Trent had put himself at the door. Past the windows, a car's engine revved and the small Pinto drove right over the sidewalk, taking the curb hard enough to leave sparks as it found the street and drove away. If he had really wanted them, my cleavage, such as it was, wouldn't have stopped him. "Mark, my usual!" I called out, making a finger motion for Jenks to join Trent in a doomed attempt to keep my way open.

"S-s-sure, Rachel. Double espresso grande latte, no fat, no foam, with a pump of raspberry in it. Extra hot."

I felt better. Mark had been through this before. He had the emotional skills and a circle behind the counter to hide in. "With cinnamon on top," I added, and the demon I'd just flashed snorted. "You got a problem with my drink order?" I said, and he raised a hand, his expression mocking. I gave him a long look before turning my back on him to go to the pickup window. The speakers blew with a pop, and chuckles rose when I jumped.

Shaking my hair out, I leaned against the counter. More demons were jumping in, and I was getting nervous. Well, more nervous than I had been. Even with Trent at the door, I'd never make it out of here unless they let me. I thought it interesting that no one had gone to the other side of the globe and to the sun. They *were* afraid it wouldn't last.

"I know you're having a good time on a Sunday night, being freed from the ever-after and all, but if you're going to stay, we have some rules," I said, smile wide.

Al clenched his jaw, but Newt was delighted even as that demon, Mica, I think, brought his cold stare from Trent to me. "We weren't freed, we fought our way out," Mica said.

"You're Mica, right?" I said, and he nodded. "Sure, you fought your way out," I agreed, "but tomorrow is a weekday and you should be thinking about finding somewhere to work and a place to live because you're not bunking with me." They were laughing, Mica's face holding the most amusement of all. "You don't want to exchange one prison for another, do you? I won't say Alcatraz is inescapable, but they plugged the hole I used."

"My God, is she serious?" Mica turned his back on me, but I thought it telling that he was looking for support among the rest. It was a new world despite their boasting and power, and they didn't know if they were going to see the sun. Such a small thing, but it would chart their every thought until they knew.

Trent's hold on the line strengthened, and my gaze flicked to his. *Not yet, Trent. Not yet.*

"This is our world now," Mica bragged, but more than one set of eyes was pinched in concern. I had a scant few hours to convince them that condescending to play in our rule set was better than them playing out of it.

"The elves will fall first," he said, and those who'd just popped in agreed with him. "Vampire society will falter if they lose their souls again. It will fall if they retain them. The witches will align with us as our poor cousins, and the Weres will heel or be leashed. The world will change."

"Why even bother shifting realities if you're going to make it just like the ever-after in your new war?" I said, and more than one demon furrowed his brow in thought.

"Coffee up!" Mark said, and I took it, eyes closing in bliss as the first sip hit my tongue, warm, sweet, and bitter, all at the same time.

"Oh God, that's good," I said, and Mark backed into his uninvoked circle with a nervous smile. Trent was still at the door, and I told Jenks to stay with him with a twitch of my finger. Dali noticed, putting a hand on Newt's arm to keep her silent when she took a breath to say something.

"The world will change," I said, echoing Mica, setting my coffee down even as that first swallow buzzed through me. "See, I think that's funny. It already has, and you missed it."

Al's scowl hesitated. Emboldened, I pushed from the counter to claim a spiral circle inlaid on the floor as my own.

"Why are you here?" Mica said, but he wasn't moving. "You think the elves mean anything?" he added, goat-slitted eyes flicking to Trent. "They have no Sa'han. It's the only reason you've been allowed your game of pretend. You're doing us a big favor."

Guilt was a quick stab, and I refused to look at Trent, knowing my feelings would give me away. "I'm not here for the elves, I'm here for the FIB," I said flippantly. "Before you get yourself into more trouble, you need to know there are laws on the books now concerning demons, demon magic, and demon activity."

They laughed, but there were more than twenty of them in here now, all but the original eight or so standing at the windows, listening. "We don't recognize any law but our own," Mica said, turning his back on me.

"It's your choice. You sure it's a good one?"

It wasn't me who made him turn back around, it was the questioning faces at the window. At the corner booth, Dali squinted at me in warning. Warning me to be careful? To be quiet?

"I'm serious," I said lightly, moving to keep their eyes on me. "You've been stuck in that stinky hole of forced existence for too long, and the world has changed. Al might be able to adapt, but most of you need help. I can do that."

"You think we need *help*?"

It had been Dali, and my pace bobbled at the flash of fear that lit through me and died. *Damn it, they noticed.*

"I don't think you see what's going on here," the round, powerful demon said.

I could actually hear the soft hush of sliding fabric as everyone turned from him to me. Swallowing, I lifted my chin. "I see demons having coffee in a coffee shop. What do you see?"

Dali hesitated, looking at the deeper meaning past my simple statement. I'd gotten to know them pretty well in the last year or so, and I knew that this was what they wanted. They wanted acceptance. They wanted to be part of something alive again, something where their voices and actions meant more than a stale circle of parties and distractions. But their pride, I knew, would get in the way. They were all-friggin' powerful. Blah, blah, blah. What did it really mean when all was said and done? Nothing. Nothing they did meant anything.

Feeling them waver, I shook my head. "It's not the same world it was two thousand years ago. Hell, it's changed in the last six months to *make room for you*," I said, words almost tripping over themselves as I tried to get it out before someone opened his mouth and ruined it. "They knew you were coming, and they made room for you." Someone snickered, and I spun. "Hey!" I shouted, and Trent jumped, his hold on the line zinging through me. "They made room for you. Don't you get it? They didn't make weapons, or spells, or traps. *They made room!*"

Arms crossed over his chest, Mica stared at me. "They're scared and stupid."

"It means you belong, damn it!" I shouted as a rumble of discussion rose. "Are they scared? Hell yes. Are there going to be people who will try to ruin it for you? Goad you into making decisions so that fear overflows and starts a war? Absolutely. They wouldn't be people if they didn't, but that doesn't rub out the fact that *they made room for you!*"

"We thrive on war!" Mica exclaimed as the demons closest to him inched away.

I gave him a disparaging look until his eyes narrowed. "Right," I scoffed. "And that's why you can't live on the ever-after's surface anymore."

Mica stood. Trent stiffened, and I moved. Arms swinging, I got in Mica's face. The demon hesitated for the smallest instant as I stared up at him, expression cross. "Trent just spent almost a year getting legislation on the books for you. Lost his fortune doing it," I barked at the demon. It seemed to be the right approach, as the tension defused with a soft chuckle from Dali.

"Ah, not all of it," Trent said from the door.

"Ruined his reputation," I continued, hands on my hips.

"Er . . . ," Trent muttered.

"An *elf* did this," I said loudly. "Not just any elf, but the same one whose father found a way for me to survive being a demon. He broke the curse, you idiot! What more do you want? I want this to work. I want all of you here with me in the sun. Don't screw this up for my kids, Mica, or I swear I'll take care of your family planning for you the hard way. Permanently and painfully," I added just for the hell of it.

Oh God, I couldn't back up without looking scared, so I stood there, praying someone would say something.

"Work in *their* system?" Al said, and I spun, both relieved and petrified at his next words. Of all the demons here, I feared his voice the most. "Settle down? Get a job? Pay taxes?"

I warmed at the titter, and I lifted my chin. Mica backed up, and I inched away from him as well. "Why not?" I said. "It's better than starting a war that you'll eventually die from. And that's another thing. No more stealing people into slavery. It would be a nice gesture of goodwill if you freed your familiars."

Trent winced, probably thinking I'd gone too far, but if I didn't ask for more, they'd give me nothing. Sure enough, most laughed. I was losing them. Al knew it. They all did.

"Not going to happen, Rachel," Al said, the thread of genuine sorrow sparking my hope. "We will not be taken again by elven trickery." He looked at Dali and elegantly sipped from his paper cup. "A job," he scoffed.

I stifled a shudder as Jenks hummed closer. "They're not going for it," he whispered.

My jaw clenched. This was my only chance, and I'd be damned if I let Al ruin it with his "poor me" attitude. "Hey!" I shouted, making Jenks ink a bright dust. "You *will* keep your mischief and misdeeds within the confines of the laws of this society, or I'll sling each and every one of your asses back into the ever-after and Trent will curse you to remain there forever."

"Ah, Rache?" Jenks whispered as Trent paled.

"You know we can do it," I said, warming at the dubious looks. "We beat Ku'Sox."

"Rachel!" Trent cried in fear, but I'd already felt the pull on the line and had spun, my word of invocation filling the circles I'd asked Mark to paint the floor with last year.

Demons cackled and guffawed as Mica's shot was deflected into the ceiling by Trent's cast charm before coming close to hitting my protection circle. Scared, I looked first at Trent, remembering to breathe when I saw him wreathed in his own protection, Jenks at his side.

My hand glowed with my power held in check, and I slowly spun to Mica. Fine. We could get the hard part over with first.

"That is enough!" Newt said as she stood, and the laughter slowly ebbed.

Trent came forward to join me, and I dropped my circle, loving his grace and bound anger—and that he was strong enough to stand beside me when my life got ugly. My God, he looked good, his feet barely seeming to touch the floor, and the tips of his hair floated, waving before his brilliant green eyes.

"That could have been a mistake," he warned Mica as he stood a little in front of me, his voice having a singsong cadence and holding an unsaid threat. "Don't do that again."

Adrenaline seemed to rake over my skin as Al stood as well. "You had my help bringing Ku'Sox down," he growled. "I don't stand with you anymore."

I edged past Trent, trying to get to Al before he jumped out. I knew him, and I knew the signs. He was leaving. Running away again.

"Fine," I snapped, and someone from the back laughed. "Run off so they can kill me without you watching. But put a playroom in your new mansion, Al, because if Trent and I die, you get Lucy."

Dali's head jerked up, and I swear I heard Jenks's dust sizzle, on fire. "He what?" Jenks shouted, but I was staring at Al, reading his shock. He wasn't going to jump out now, and that's all that mattered.

"Mother pus bucket . . . ," the demon said, his blocky face pale as he looked from me to Trent and back again. His cheeks flashed red at a laugh. "I will *not* be responsible for elf brats!"

Trent's presence edged in beside mine again, and it was all I could do to not take his hand, but big bad-ass runners facing down a coffee shop full of demons do not hold hands. "I had the papers drawn up six months ago," Trent said, and Jenks hit the table, his wings unmoving. "If Rachel and I die, Lucy goes to you. You'll hold the elven future, Al."

"Oh my God," Newt breathed, and Jenks made it back into the air, his bright silver dust falling from him like stardust.

"I will *not!*" Al bellowed as he spun and fussed, but I could tell he was flattered. The demon was dying inside that someone—anyone—trusted their children to him. I blinked fast, wanting to give him a hug, but bad-ass runners didn't do that either.

"It'd be easier just to let both of us live," I said, but only Al, Dali, and Newt heard me over the caterwauling of laughter. "And if you kill just one of us, you won't survive the revenge of the other. I promise you that."

Al was speechless, a hand on the table as he tried to understand.

Newt gave a long, meaningful stare to Dali, and when he shrugged, she slipped out from the booth. "Gentlemen?" she said softly, then shouted it, "Gentlemen!"

Slowly they quieted. Trent and I backed to the middle of the room.

There had to be at least fifty demons in here, and I heard the cooling click on. It didn't smell as bad as I thought it would.

"Gentlemen," Newt said a third time as she smoothed her robes. "I propose we take the time until sunrise to weigh Rachel's proposal."

"I do not make deals with elves!" Mica protested. "They're chattel! Slaves!"

No one moved, either away from him or toward him. They were balanced, and I forced myself to breathe.

"Perhaps," Newt said, voice as silky as a slinking cat. "But they haven't spent the last two thousand years trapped in a bubble of reality kept alive by tenuous threads of energy as we have been. Rachel is a demon. She's also the elven Tal Sa'han, the one who sways the actions of the putrid, stinking chattel of an elf. You can strike a deal with her—can you not?"

My mouth went dry, and I edged back until I could feel Trent's warmth. Tal Sa'han. Quen had called me that once in bitter sarcasm, and while Mal Sa'han held romantic overtones, Tal Sa'han did not. It wasn't exactly an adviser, but rather the person the Sa'han thought of when he made decisions. *I ask myself: Will this decision take me closer or farther from you? And then it's so clear. Even if it doesn't make sense at the time,* resonated in me, and my pulse quickened. But he wasn't the Sa'han. It was a title awarded by fealty, and no elf looked to him anymore. *Because of me.*

"I will *not* bind myself to human law!" Mica said, jerking me back to the present. "We're free, and we take our rightful place!"

"You don't know that!" another demon exclaimed. "What happens if we're pulled back when the sun comes up?"

Mica's hand glowed with black smut. "What if we aren't?" he proposed.

Trent inched up to stand beside me, his eyes darting as he took in the demons with a professional eye. "They're divided," he said, breath tickling my neck. "Interesting."

I suppose, but I'd be more excited if they were all for behaving themselves. Did it matter if Trent wasn't the Sa'han if the demons thought he was? It wasn't as if they'd ever come to an agreement with Landon.

Newt cleared her throat, putting me on edge as she came to stand beside me in a clear show of support or perhaps protection. "Where do you want to be next week, Mica?" she said, and I shivered at the certainty in her voice.

"Alone in some godforsaken island cathedral playing god with people terrified of you? I've done that. It gets boring fast. I've looked at these human laws, and they're more complex and devious with loopholes and clauses than Dali can structure in a thousand years. Their court system alone boggles the mind with the red tape that can be used to twist ends. If we can't work our will within them, then we don't deserve the name demon."

They were listening, but only a fraction were happy, and none was convinced.

"We have a chance to be a part of something again," she said, stockstill. "All in favor of playing by the rules and making Rachel our liaison with reality-based law?"

I jerked, and beside me, Trent grunted. "Hey, wait a moment," I said, but Dali had stood with a resounding "Aye!"

He was the only one.

"Opposed?" Newt said cheerfully.

"Nay!" I said, panicking. "I never agreed to this!"

"Never!" most of the demons had shouted, but a few were silent, and I panicked some more as I shook Trent's hand off my elbow.

"I suggest you leave, Mica," Newt growled, and I swear the air sparkled around her. "Go away so we can get on with it."

But only Dali had agreed, and I pulled on the line, my knees wobbling as I yanked what I could from the rest to try to prevent a bloodbath.

"Bravo, Rachel," Newt praised, a small smile hovering over her face. Her eyes darted past me, and her hand flashed out in threat. I spun, doing the same. *Mica.* Our thrown energy smacked into the demon before he could loose his magic, bowling him over the table and into the far wall. Demons scattered to avoid him, and the black flickering in his fist went out as he groaned.

"Maybe you should leave," I said, voice quavering. They wouldn't make a decision until they knew if the sun would sling them back to the everafter or not.

In pairs and groups they left, their expressions varying from worry to outright anger as they winked out. I didn't care where they went, only that they were gone. Mica was the last, his murderous look chilling me as he vanished.

She'd called me the Tal Sa'han... My pulse quickened, and I met Trent's eyes, finding him just as thoughtful as I.

"Damn woman!" Jenks shrilled, and I shivered as his dust seemed to burn my aura. "Where did you learn that?"

"Al," I said, seeing him still with us. The demon was sweating, and I wondered if he'd been as scared as I'd been. I took a breath to try to mend the rift between us, but he vanished, the black curl of ever-after magic swirling up as if to smother him before it fell in on itself with a soft pop. My stomach hurt, and I blinked fast. At least he hadn't tried to kill me this time.

"That went rather well." Newt's words were precise and holding zero sarcasm.

"Well, you say?" Trent said, shaky as he almost fell into a chair.

"That was good?" Jenks echoed, dust sparkling as he flew to Trent. "Did you really give him your kid if you and Rachel kick off? Damn! That's either really stupid or really smart."

Trent eyed him sourly. "It'll ensure both girls' safety if Rachel or I aren't here to see to it."

Dali snickered, easing back into the booth to take up most of the seat. His opinion that it was really stupid was obvious.

"They left," Newt said saucily. "I'm here drinking mar-r-r-r-rvelous coffee. Therefore, it went well. Mark, love. Another if you will? Put it on my tab."

Tab? I slowly sank into the nearest chair. Mark wobbled to the door and turned the closed sign around. Good idea.

Elbow on the table, Dali dropped his chin into his hand. I caught a hint of worry as he looked at the clock. "Three against all the rest? Not good odds, Newt."

He had included me. Interesting.

"Four." Trent's attention rose from his hands, having been gauging their shaking.

"Five," Jenks added, and Newt eyed him until the pixy flipped her off.

Shrugging, Newt sipped her cooling coffee. "They'll come around as soon as they know they won't be pulled back to that hole come sunup. They're just worried, poor dears. It's not as if we have to *trust* the elves. Just not let them kill us."

Poor dears, my ass. Tired, I looked for and found my bag, still on the pickup counter.

Newt's eyes shifted to the window. A big black car was pulling up in disregard to the parking lines. It wasn't the I.S. vans I had asked for, and Newt laughed at my fast inhalation when burly vampires began getting out. Shit, it was Cormel. But then I grew angry. *Ivy.* She'd better be okay. He promised, damn it!

Jenks hovered before Trent and nodded to the window. Trent sighed when he turned to look, and I could almost see him begin to pull himself together, his professional mask slipping over him to hide his fatigue. I thought it interesting that he'd let it drop in front of Dali and Newt. "I'm never getting home tonight. Ellasbeth is going to flay me alive," he grumbled as he tucked his shirt back into his pants.

"I know the feeling." I could think of a few reasons Cormel might be here, none of them good.

Newt wrinkled her nose. "Vampires," she scoffed as Cormel emerged from the car, tugging his coat's sleeves down as his people jogged around to the back of the store to look for possible trouble. "They remind me of surface demons in suits. Trenton, thank you for your offer to stay with you until I can arrange for the legal purchase of an estate."

Trent jerked, clearly surprised, as Jenks hovered backward, mouth curling up in a laugh. "Ah, I would be honored . . . ," Trent said, and Dali chuckled as well, seeming to gather himself to leave. Seeing it, Trent paled even more.

"Hey, that's not a bad idea, Trent," Jenks said as he yo-yoed up and down. "If that dog doesn't get Ellasbeth to leave, the demons sure as hell will."

Licking his lips, Trent stood, all professional polish gone. "Ahhhhh."

"Dog?" Newt stood, and I froze when she leaned over to give me a professional cheek-to-cheek press. "Trent, I'll fetch my horse and stable her. Dali, you know where the elf lives, yes?"

"It's my bloody line running through his office," the demon muttered.

"Ah, as much as I'd like . . . ," Trent was saying, but it was too late, and Newt pressed her cheek against his as well, her lips smacking to make a kiss sound.

"I'll make you spaghetti. Rachel will be too busy tonight," the demon said primly. "Little girls *love* spaghetti."

"N-Newt . . . ," I stammered, but she vanished along with Dali as one of the vampire thugs jimmied the locked door open. Behind the counter, Mark made a sad, tired groan, and I gave him my best "sorry" look.

"Ellasbeth is going to kill me," Trent said as the lock snapped and they opened the door.

"Nah," Jenks said as he took to the air and hovered between us. "She's got lousy aim. Remember?"

Tired, I turned as the first of Cormel's thugs sauntered in. The spicy scent of confident vampire pricked my nose, diving deep and fanning the small flame of fear higher. The suave, pretty man in his bad-boy leather reminded me of Kisten, and I quashed it. They were all afraid if you looked deep enough.

He stopped in the middle of the room, his nose wrinkling as he took in the faint scent of burnt amber and rich coffee, and smiling, he gestured for us to stay where we were.

Like I had a choice?

Chapter 17

The thumps of car doors closing pulled my attention to Cormel. "Ivy . . . ," I whispered, and Trent tersely shook his head. His brow was pinched in thought, as calm and collected as ever. I wished I had his trust in vampiric deals and agreements.

"If he wanted Ivy, he'd have her already," Trent said as he tucked his phone away. "My guess is he wants to talk to us about the surface demons."

Jenks *had* said he'd warned us off them, but we hadn't done anything. Yet. And I sent Jenks to assess the situation since Cormel seemed to be content to chat with his thugs while his people checked out the back. *Paranoid much?*

FIB officers watched a safe two blocks down since getting a coffee wasn't illegal. I didn't expect them to help. Didn't want them to. They'd only get themselves killed. What had I been thinking telling Edden to make a stand?

"Ivy had better be okay," I muttered as Mark sighed from behind the counter and Cormel entered the shop, his motions graceful with the ease and inevitableness of death. The man had run the country during the Turn, and his confidence was absolute. Handing his felt hat to the man coming in behind him, he stood just inside and breathed in the air, nose wrinkling as he scented demons under the rich coffee and tang of spent magic.

"Demons," the man said, his Bronx accent obvious. "Have you gotten rid of them, then?"

"No. Why?" I said, and Cormel nodded to Trent as he shrugged out of his coat and carefully set it on the chair by the door.

"You're a hard man to find lately, Kalamack."

"Cormel," Trent said in greeting, the thinnest trace of magic flowing through him making my skin tingle.

Blinking, I turned to Trent when Jenks whistled appreciatively. Not only was Trent's hair slicked back and clean, but he was clean shaven. "H-how . . . ," I stammered, then, "When did you learn that?"

A hint of red about his ears, Trent adjusted his collar. "It came with the, ah, circumcision curse. Kind of an all-encompassing trim-and-neat . . . spell."

Do tell . . . I gave him an askance, approving look. Cormel was eight feet away, and all I wanted to do was run my hand over Trent's smooth face. My eyes lost their focus, and when Cormel cleared his throat, I flushed.

"If Ivy is not okay, I'm going to slice your chest open with a plastic spork and rip your wrinkly heart out."

"Charming . . . ," Cormel drawled, and my eyes narrowed as he shifted one foot to stand directly on a painted line, in effect preventing Trent or me from circling him with the patterns in the floor. "I'm glad the rumors of your demise were premature."

Premature? I thought dryly. Was that a threat?

Making a show of breathing in my rising anger, Cormel smiled. "Get me a small black coffee," he said to the tidy man with him. "No cream. And whatever anyone else wants?" he asked pleasantly.

Okay, he was being nice, but that only made me more suspicious.

Jenks came in from the back smelling of fresh air. "I'll have a butter-cream latte if you're buying," the pixy said, and Cormel blinked before waving his hand at his aide to get one.

"You're not afraid of me anymore," Cormel said, and I shrugged, my attention on the parking lot behind him. The FIB had moved in and they were talking amicably with Cormel's men. I felt a twinge of guilt. It wasn't safe. Why had Edden listened to me?

Cormel cleared his throat, and my focus shifted to him. "Oh, sorry," I said, and Trent hid a smile behind a cough. "Ah, no. No, I'm not."

"You've no idea what that does to the undead," Cormel said, his voice a mix of velvet and smoke. Behind him was the mundane sound of coffee being prepared, a study in contrasts.

Tired, I leaned against a table. It began to slide, and I jerked up again. "Yes I do. That's why I apologized. Would it help if I shivered a little?" I said sarcastically. "Pressed up against the wall, maybe?"

"Shame what happened to your property," Cormel said lightly. "Exploded boiler, was it?"

Jenks's wings hummed louder, hands on his hips and near his sword as he hovered between Cormel and us. "It was my property, blood bag, and it's going to take a lot more than a coffee to make up for it."

Not a flicker of shame showed itself as Cormel settled his feet firmly on the floor, put his hands behind his back, and rocked forward and back. "You will return the demons to the ever-after."

Is that what this is about? My shoulders eased. Ivy was okay—so far. "I'm not the one who freed them. Talk to Landon."

Still as death and unmoving, I watched his thoughts realigning themselves in a pattern I couldn't guess at. "He's missing. You will send them back," he insisted, a hint of a threat behind the professional cajoling. His lackey had come back with his coffee, and Cormel took it—never shifting his eyes from mine.

My skin was itching, humming almost where it was closest to Trent. It was kind of uncomfortable, and I edged away from him. "No. I like them where they are."

Trent tensed at the flicker of anger crossing Cormel's face as the vampire sipped his drink. "Landon claims you are able to reverse the spell and send our souls back to purgatory. That would be a mistake—Rachel."

He had said my name, but he was looking at both of us. "How's Felix?" I asked, knowing I'd hit a nerve when Cormel ignored my question, taking the top off his cup and going to the condiments bar. "When the sun comes up he's going to walk."

"Ah, Rachel?" Trent said, feet scuffing as his eyes flicked from me to the FIB guys outside. "The intent is to avoid conflict. Not incite it."

"I like poking at dead things," I said, and Cormel gave me a disparaging glance as he tore open two of the salt packets they had out for the breakfast sandwiches. "Felix is going to walk, and he knows it!" I protested. "Cormel, this can't work. Admit it!"

Cormel calmly poured the salt into his coffee like sugar. "He's doing much better."

"It doesn't matter how many sunrises you chain him in the basement for, he's going to walk. I'm sorry, but the entire idea of the undead having their souls is wrong."

"You. Out," Cormel said tersely, and his aide left, head down and stinking of fear. Cormel was silent as the door chimes jingled, motions sharp as he stirred the salt into his coffee with one of those lame little sticks. "I'm here for two reasons," he said, his gaze flicking to the FIB men among his own, making me wonder if he was as eager to avoid an interspecies confrontation as I was. "I will have my soul, and you will remove the demons from reality. I will *not* have them here mucking up the current power structure."

Trent's small sound of agreement was as significant as a gasp. That's why he was here. Cormel was rightly worried about the demons, and Landon was missing. *Damn it, Landon. If you're going to break the world, you need to stay around to put it back together.*

Jenks's wings hummed a warning, and I strengthened my hold on the nearest ley line. It was more dangerous now that Cormel was alone. "You knew Landon was using you to try to topple the vampire power structure."

"Obviously." Cormel sipped his salted coffee. "And you will finish what he began."

"Cormel, I can't!" Frustrated, I pushed into motion. Jenks darted into the air, and I resolved to calm down when both Trent and Cormel jerked. "I can't," I said again, voice softer. "Undead souls running around, spontaneously merging? You're going to lose your entire population of the old undead. Why do you think Landon gave you your souls to begin with?"

Trent looked pained, but I knew he believed as I did.

"As I said before, this is why you're alive, Morgan," Cormel said, and a thread of fear slid through me at his anger. "Fix it."

Fix it. He made it sound so simple. "I swear, Cormel, if you go after Ivy I will hunt you down myself."

Cormel's expression was stoic. "Ivy is safe. Fix it."

"Order up!" Mark called loudly, but Jenks hung where he was, over my shoulder. Cormel said Ivy was safe, but I didn't believe him. Neither did Jenks. I thought of her at her parents' house, knowing there was probably a crack team of efficient assassins within three minutes of her driveway. I never should have made a deal with him. Vampires and five-year-olds played by the same rules, and both threw tantrums when they lost.

Frustrated, I sat down. My cooled coffee was before me, and I reached for it, warming it up with a quick thought. "Why should I? You tried to kill us so Landon would bring back your souls."

Trent made a pained noise, but honestly, everyone in the room already knew it.

"Your lives were reasonably safe." With a sound of sliding linen and wool, Cormel sat down across from me, and surprised, I searched the vampire's expression. He was a hard man to read. I didn't know. Seeing me staring, Cormel saluted me with his salted coffee. "If I wanted you dead, you'd be dead. The destruction of your church was a warning. A reminder of what everyone's place is." His eyes were pupil black when he looked up. "You will do what Landon cannot. You will send the demons back."

I exchanged a quick look with Trent. I'd give just about anything to be able to read Trent's mind right now, but I had a pretty good idea of what he wanted. Too bad it wasn't what I wanted. "Yeah?" I said, leaning back in my chair. "I like them here."

"Rache!" Jenks protested.

"Well, I do!" I said, embarrassed. "They've been stuck in that hole for three thousand years. Maybe if they saw the sun once in a while they wouldn't be so crabby."

"Crabby?" Jenks darted over, and I covered my cup so his dust wouldn't get in it. "That's not crabby. That's a two-year-old on a sugar high after missing his nap!"

I frowned at him and his Peter Pan pose on the wilted flowers. "They aren't that bad. You just need to get to know them." Trent sighed. I found his hand under the table and gave it a squeeze. He didn't like my decisions, but he'd back them up.

"You have a week," Cormel said, and I shifted my focus past an angry Jenks to Cormel fitting a lid back on his cup. It was the universal signal that this meeting was over.

An entire week. Wow. "Or what?" I said snottily. "You gonna kill everyone important to me?" *Shut up, Rachel. Your mom is in town.* My eyes narrowed and I stood, knees shaking. There were at least eight vampires outside, a dozen FIB officers. I didn't want to risk them. I didn't want to risk Trent either. "You need me," I said, pointing my finger at him as Trent stood as well, his calm beginning to crack. "You need me because as soon as the sun rises, every single vampire who gained his soul tonight will commit suncide, and you know it!"

"You will fix this," he said, hammering each word into me.

Trent's presence was a whisper beside me. "Ah, Rachel? You're making some rather large policy statements."

"Yeah?" I wasn't going to do it. I'd fight them to get them to behave themselves, but I wasn't going to force them back in that pit. But there were FIB guys in the parking lot, and I tried to calm down. "I'm not the one busting in here with ultimatums," I muttered. "And I'm not going to make the demons go anywhere but to driver's ed, maybe."

Cormel sat across from me, his chest not moving as his pupils widened and the air seemed to shimmer between us. I couldn't tell if he was pissed or trying to bespell me. "Remove them," he demanded, the hunger in his gaze breaking the illusion of a kindly political leader and laying bare his true intent. "Or Kalamack will be your whipping boy."

Pissed, I reached across the table, fear making me stupid. Cormel was faster. His fingers encircled my wrist, as cold as steel and twice as unbreakable.

"Rache!" Jenks shouted as he darted forward, sword bared. Cormel's eyes flicked to the pixy, and my breath came in a single, unhurried draw as I felt Trent pull on the line. I felt it flow into him, saw it almost as a bright silver ribbon that sang. A familiar tingle raked over my skin with the rustle of feathers. Purple eyes flashed open in my mind, rejoicing echoed between my thought and reason as somnolent mystics awoke, eager to dole out mischief in a splashing banquet of overindulgent intent.

Stop! I demanded, and they washed up against my will, cheerfully jumbled and riding the wave as I realized I was gripping Cormel's neck while he pinched my other wrist. Purple eyes spun madly, wanting me to give them direction. Between one heartbeat and the next I saw the FIB arranged outside, heard the tense decisions being made beyond the constructed calm within the chilly parking lot. I felt the indecision within Cormel, the unending agony pushing him to believe what he knew to be untrue. I saw a flicker of pain, real and new in him as his thoughts, spinning in unchanging circles, widened into the possible understanding that he could not have what he most wished for.

And then my heart thudded and I realized I'd somehow crawled up onto the table, kneeling to put myself inches from Cormel's face. His canines were bared and sheened with a slick saliva, and his breath held still within him. His fingers gripped my wrist, and my free hand remained around his neck, thumb poised and stiff to jab into his larynx. He didn't have to breathe, but it would still hurt—not to mention impede his ability to talk for a while. Mystics wreathed us so thickly I could almost see them. They played in my hair, making it float. I wasn't afraid. Cormel was a small thought, one already dead and spinning in circles.

Damn it, how had they found me? I thought, only now recognizing that the mystics had been in the room for a while, making Trent's aura tingle against mine.

But Cormel's black eyes had scummed over with a long-dead fear. Jaw trembling, he stared at me, remembering the feel of the mystics on him, knowing they could hold his death if I wished it. He'd been a master vampire for a long time, but he started out as all of them do, as someone's toy. And he remembered being small. I'd made him feel it again. *Oh God, I was deep in it now.*

"You will leave Kalamack alone," I said simply, never letting go of his eyes as more people came in, halting when Cormel waved them off. It had been my fear that had brought the mystics back, fear for Trent—and now I was really up shit creek.

Slowly I let go of him, edging backward off the table as Cormel's thugs clustered in small knots. My wrist was tingling where Cormel was still holding it, and he let go in the sudden realization that it, too, was a conduit for the mystics. "I may be a pawn," I said as I locked my shaking knees. "But I've been to the other side and survived the trip back and can move like a queen." Pixy dust sifted over us, and my skin burned. "Don't piss me off."

Behind me were people stinking of fear and nylon. I could feel the give of rubber tread from heavy boots, and the chill being lifted off from skin too long in the cold. None of them was my sensation. The mystics had brought them to me, eager to become a part of something again. I'd gambled and lost. The demons would never listen to me now.

But he had threatened Trent . . .

Swallowing hard, I sank back into my chair to try to hide my shaking hands. Damn it, I loved Trent. I'd risk everything and all to keep him alive. It made me strong but vulnerable to manipulation at the same time. *Love sucked.*

"You okay?" Trent's voice was low, and my chest hurt at the new fear in him, one born from the heart. He knew the mystics had found me again. Blinking fast, I reached to touch Trent's hand on my shoulder. He was still holding on to the line, and he started when the pure energy from the mystics washed through him as they used his connection as a way to get back to the line and ride it like an ocean current. The power in me lessened, and I breathed easier.

"Ask me tomorrow," I whispered, and his grip tightened in understanding. I didn't feel good. People in suits and smelling of vampire surrounded Cormel. Our eye contact had been broken, and I wanted to leave.

"Tink's a Disney whore, Rache!" Jenks exclaimed as Cormel began to slowly distance himself. "He's as scared as a tick under the bed."

Yeah. Me too. I'd been ready to kill Cormel to keep Trent safe. And though Cormel had been shocked to find my hand around his throat, I couldn't shake the growing feeling that he'd almost been expecting it. Even as he bent his will to survival, a part of him wanted to die. Looked for it. Ached for it. Maybe that's why he was so adamant about getting his soul?

"Rache?" Jenks called, his excitement faltering as he dropped down to search my face. "You're okay, right?"

My head came up as I recognized Ivy's voice. Jenks spun where he hovered, darting to the door as she elbowed her way in. "Get out of my way!" she exclaimed as she fought her way through the growing crowd, and Trent's hand tightened on my shoulder when I smiled at her. Thank God she was okay.

Nina was hot on Ivy's heels, the jealous little vampire scowling. I watched her visibly catch herself as the scent of frightened vampire hit her. Eyes lowered, she concentrated on the floor. Ivy, though, pushed through it as if it wasn't there.

"Rachel," she all but breathed as she reached me, and I rose to give her a hug. "I-I . . . ," she stammered, and then, "Are you okay?"

I almost missed the flash of guilt that crossed her. It wasn't reflected in Nina, as much as sanctioned by the crafty woman's smug expression. "I'm okay," I said, my suspicions tightening. *Something had happened* . . .

Feeling it, Ivy let go. "Trent texted me that you might need some help."

"Trent?" I hadn't seen him on the phone. Surprised, I turned to Trent, stifling a shudder at the sensation of mystics peeling off me to dance in the pheromones and guilt she was giving off. "When did you have the time?"

Trent shrugged, the rims of his ears reddening as he watched Cormel's thugs begin to leave. "I type fast."

"Like a fourteen-year-old girl!" Jenks exclaimed, a happy ball of dust at his shoulder.

Cormel was putting his coat on with a formal stiffness, clearly not liking being watched by the admittedly proud but helpless FIB. We weren't done yet, but I'd given him something to think about as he sulked in his hole in the ground.

"Too many people in here," Nina muttered. She was doing really well despite the fading stink of frightened vampire. And then it struck me how good Ivy looked, a flush to her cheeks and moving better than she should for having been in intensive care less than two days ago. My eyes jerked to hers, and a flash of self-loathing and guilt crossed her before she turned away. Even having access to Trent's full-strength Brimstone shouldn't have her looking like this.

"Ivy?" I questioned, and Jenks rose up, clearly pleased when Edden walked in, glancing at us as he shook Cormel's hand and held the door for him.

"Don't let the door hit your ass on the way out," the pixy smart-mouthed. "Trent, you call him, too?"

"Yes," Trent said from behind me. Fingers trailing reluctantly from me, he went to Edden, the stocky FIB captain making his slow way to us. The gray looked a little heavier, the worry wrinkles a little deeper, but his eyes were just as sharp and his smile inviting when he saw me.

But even as I met his smile with my own, I ached for Ivy's guilt. I wasn't seeing the effect of Brimstone alone. She'd satisfied her hunger for blood, and not just the little sips she'd been allowing herself while making love, but a huge grasping amount that was selfish and demanding. Nina had goaded her into it, and she had succumbed. It would account for Nina's increased stability as well, which might be reason enough to ignore it but for the little fact that it meant Nina was only exchanging one master for another.

"Ivy," I tried again, and she turned away.

"Rachel!" Edden boomed, the force behind it honed by years of arguing with thickheaded FIB officers. "How did I do?"

He was grinning, and I couldn't help but smile back. Catcalls and hoots rose up as I gave him a hug, rocking back and seeing his pleasure in the embarrassed flush on his round face. "I owe you, Edden," I said, and he smiled all the wider. "Big-time. Don't ever do it again, okay?"

"It was a calculated risk." Edden looked out the plate-glass windows, a flicker of spent worry saying he was lying. "Cormel doesn't want any bad press right now. We just need to travel in packs more often."

"Or pair your men up with a demon," I said flippantly.

Edden's feet scuffed on the painted floor. "Ah, yes. About that."

Jenks's wings clattered in the new chill flowing in with the outgoing officers. "Can we go now?"

I nodded, spent adrenaline laying like a heavy coil in my middle as I waved my thanks to Mark. He was behind the counter stoically handing out drink coupons as he refused to make anything despite his being open twenty-four hours a day. Mr. Fish was probably dead from the cold in my cup holder, and I wondered if I dared a warming charm lest I cook him.

"Your folks okay, Ivy?" I asked as Nina all but bolted to the door. I really wanted to talk to her, tell her that one night of hunger was not a failure, but she wouldn't look at me. Jenks shrugged, his shifting dust telling me he'd figured it out as well. What a pair we were; Ivy had fallen off the wagon and I was harboring mystics again.

"Ah, Rachel . . ." Edden pulled me to walk beside him, and I winced as Ivy strode out the door, her head high and jaw clenched. "Rachel, you talked to the demons," Edden prompted.

"I'm working on it," I said as I hesitated before going out. "You should be okay tonight unless someone gets a wild hair up their, ah, yeah." My voice faltered as Trent breezed past. "It won't get bad until they know if the sun is going to force them back," I finished, voice softer.

Edden seemed pleased as he stuck his thick hand out for me to shake. It was rough, with just the right amount of strength, and I felt a moment of connection, of being needed, part of something. "That's all I can ask for," he said, making a "wrap it up" motion to get his men out. "Thank you. I'll have someone get right on your arson case."

"Thanks." The welcoming feeling grew as I left and took a deep breath of the good Cincy air not stained with vampire or demon, but smelling of deep river and chill. Cormel's car wheels crackled and popped over the loose stones on the pavement as they found the street and drove away. The taillights blinked red at a stop sign, and then they were gone.

I shivered, not moving as Trent handed me my bag. My stomach rumbled, and I looked at my hands. They weren't shaking anymore. *The mystics were back.* "Ivy?"

Trent was right next to me, and I turned to him. "Trent . . ."

A shiver took me as he tucked a strand of hair behind my ear. "We have time. All the time in the world."

"Thanks." Feeling breathless, I spun. "Ivy!"

She hesitated at her mom's car, the door already open. Nina grimaced from the other side, and I paced forward, head down as I rummaged in my bag. "Here," I said, feeling unsure and nervous as I stopped before her. "I, ah, made this for you."

Behind her, Mark was pushing out the last of the FIB guys, locking up and bolting the door before shutting off the lights. Fingers shaking, I found the cool shape of the tiny bottle. Nina pressed jealously close as I put it in Ivy's hand, and they both looked at it, the faceted shape catching the buzzing streetlight. "What is it?" Ivy asked, her usual hesitancy where my magic was concerned blunted.

"It's something to catch your soul in," I said, curling her cold fingers around it. "Keep it in your pocket."

Ivy's head snapped up, and I could have cried at the hope in her eyes.

"Until Felix laughs and means it, I'm not calling this a good thing, but if you have your soul in a bottle, then it's not in the hell of the ever-after," I said. "You don't have to do anything, just keep it within your aura. And don't open the top once your soul is in there."

"You did it?" Ivy said, looking at the stop sign where we'd seen Cormel last.

"Well, we've not tested it," I offered, but she pulled me into a hug, her hand fisted at my back pressing into me hard. "I can't imagine that if you get your soul back right away there would be that much trauma." It was a hope only, but one I clung to with the same fervent wish that Cormel clung to his lies.

She was nodding as she pulled back, her eyes dark with unshed tears, anxious to be away. Behind her, Trent leaned against the car, thoughts pinching his brow as he waited with Jenks on his shoulder.

"I'll be at my dad's." She hesitated. "Unless you need me?"

Nina was smiling, but it was a thinly disguised grimace. "Cormel is going to be too busy tomorrow to worry about us," I said, looking for my keys until I remembered Trent had them. "Dali and Newt are terrorizing Trent's house, so I'm going over there to run interference."

"Okay." Her eyes came back to me, and she hesitated, looking for words.

"So it's the younger who find their souls first?" I blurted out, not wanting her to go until I could tell her she was a good person, and she shook her head even as Nina clenched her jaw, clearly wanting to leave.

"No, it's how close you are to your death place."

"Cormel died in Washington," I said, thinking he'd have a long wait if his soul had to travel only by night. Unless he went to find it.

"Only those within twenty miles of their death are reuniting, but he expects it to make it here in a week." She hesitated. "If nothing changes."

"That's the same time frame he gave me to get rid of the demons," I said, glancing at Trent when he started my car. It wasn't a silent rebuke to get me to hurry up, but a way to get Jenks out of the cold.

Eyes holding guilt, Ivy gave me a last hug before turning away. Grim, Nina hustled to the other side of the car and got in. I backed up, reluctant to leave Ivy alone, though I knew she needed to be with her dad. Her mom would be distraught but safe. I'd found out last year that she'd died in New Orleans. It would be weeks until her soul found her.

But what made my steps slow as I walked back to my car was knowing that Cormel knew I was right, otherwise he would've gone to find his soul. He knew I was right, but he wanted me to be wrong so badly that he was ignoring it.

Tomorrow was going to be one hell of a day.

Chapter 18

It was anguished and alone, even as others of its ilk hovered supportively nearby—forgotten and abandoned, curled into a tight ball in the center of my presence like a lion cub seeking comfort from a dead lioness—unresponsive even as everything about her screamed memories of comfort and warmth.

I saw myself through it, my dream cycling down to this tiny spot of torment until its heartache became mine. Confusion and betrayal soaked into me until I wept, not understanding. I'd searched for so long, and now there was nothing. I'd been forgotten, like a dream finding the window shut against it.

She doesn't see, the mystic moaned to the others, and they clustered about it, trying to make it feel better, that it would become. But it wouldn't.

I took a breath in my dream to shout that I saw them, that I was here, that I was. But a soft gong distracted me, blurring my intent. It came again, and my dream broke apart as the waves of sound moved through my unconsciousness and pushed me awake.

That's Trent's alarm, I thought groggily as a chill slipped under the covers. The bed moved and my weight shifted as Trent pulled from me, stretching to reach his phone.

I sighed, eyes closed as he rolled back, his warmth up against me now dulled with a sheet between us. The weight of a hand pressed into the bed at my left shoulder as he propped himself up over me and leaned to try to see my face. "Rachel, did you want to get up?" he whispered. "I can tell you what happens."

A fuzzy-feeling smile came over me, and I rolled onto my back. Eyes opening, I tucked his hair behind one of his pointy ears as he hung over me. The light was dim with the coming sunrise since the drapes at the French doors to the garden were open, and it made his eyes dark. He was himself but different. "I like you best this way," I said, seeing him rested and still soft with sleep, smelling of soap from his shower before he'd come to bed.

The bed shifted as he found my fingers and kissed the tips. "The sun doesn't wait for lovers or villains. Up or not?"

I groaned, gaze on the elaborately painted ceiling of horses and the hunt. The sun had risen on the East Coast almost half an hour ago, and we both wanted to know if the demons and vampire souls had been pulled back to the ever-after. "Up," I said, and his smile widened at the pained sound in my voice. This was insane, getting up at dawn, but I was starting to become used to it even if my stomach hurt and my thoughts were slow. Horrors, as my mother would say.

Trent kissed my fingertips again. "I'll see if the coffee is going," he said as he rolled to the edge of the bed, and I watched him, listless and unwilling to move yet. The faint light outlined his skin, accenting his abs and thighs defined by his horsemanship. I sat up and shoved my tangled mess of hair back and tried to imagine his gorgeous body tamed by the years, more mature but no less attractive. Yes, I wanted to be there, but as I looked at the shadowed opulent room with its heavy furniture and extravagant lushness and attention to detail, I had a hard time seeing myself here longer than a weekend. On the few occasions I'd been here without Trent, I'd felt lost, as if I was curling in around something that didn't recognize or have a need for me. Sort of like my dream.

Propped up against the headboard, I watched him hike his slacks up. My God, the man had a nice stomach. "I'm going to miss you today," I whispered.

Trent's smile vanished briefly as he put his shirt on. Head down over the buttons, he said, "Believe me, I'd rather be spending it with you. Just because I have the right to speak before the dewar doesn't mean they have to listen." He worked the last button and tossed the hair from his eyes, making my heart stop with his smile. "You want to try to meet up around noon?"

I fumbled for my own phone, squinting at it and seeing that I'd gotten a call from Edden last night. It wasn't tagged as urgent and I set it back down. I'd been planning on spending the day with Jenks and probably Ivy at the church to find out what we'd lost and what could be salvaged. "Only if you're really available," I said as I scrunched back down into the warm blankets. "You know you're not going to have time for a coffee, much less lunch."

The bed shifted as he sat next to me to put on his socks. "I'm only going to be across the river. There might be more support among the dewar than at first glance. It's easy to stand by and do nothing, even when you know it's wrong, harder when someone calls you out on it. If we have a wave of suncides this morning, it will be easier." My smile froze, and he looked up, one sock in hand. "That's not what I meant."

"I know," I said, touching his hand.

Expression grim, he put his ankle on a knee. I'd seen him do it a hundred times before, but never to put his sock on. "That doesn't make me feel any better or this any easier."

I was silent, my hand tracing along his back as he leaned over his foot. "Trent," I said softly, remembering my dream. "Are the mystics still with me?"

His fingers fumbled, and alarm brought me still. "Ah, why do you ask?"

"I had a weird dream."

His smile wasn't exactly fake when he stood up, but he was hiding concern, which only fueled my own. "Not unusual when you're woken up early," he said, words a bit breathy as he dragged a shoe out from under the dresser. "You scared me last night."

"Really? What part?" I scooted farther back, against the headboard. "When I tried to throttle Cincy's head vampire, or when I stood up to Mica?"

His expression caught at me when he sat back down beside me. "When the mystics found you. Rachel—"

"Oh God. It's bad, isn't it?" I said.

Smiling, he cupped my face, but there was sorrow in his eyes. "You might be sparkling just because you're glad to see me."

Crap on toast, it was bad. My hands clenched themselves, and I looked at them, twisted about themselves into a knot in my lap.

"Rachel," he breathed, pulling me to him. My arms went around him and I held my breath, trying not to cry. I hadn't called them to me even if I'd missed them. I'd done everything right, and I was exactly where I'd started. The elves hated Trent because of me, and with the mystics, I'd probably lost the demon support, too. It was falling apart, and I couldn't stop it!

"You're not hearing anything, are you?" His words shifted my hair, and I shook my head. What happened in a dream was *not* reality. And there were no voices showing me visions around corners. His grip on me shifted, and I looked up to see his relief. "Then you're okay," he said, making my heart almost break that he cared that much. "Promise me you'll tell me if you do."

"Promise." My foot twisted under me was falling asleep, and my other, hanging out over the edge of the bed behind him, was getting cold. I wasn't going to move, though, not with Trent holding me, telling me he loved me without even a word. "What time is your appointment?"

His breathing shifted, his shoulders tensing. "Nine forty-five."

It was only a few hours away. "I'm sorry," I said as he let go. "If it wasn't for me, the enclave would be listening to you and you could have stopped this before it started."

Trent's eyes widened. "Is that what you think? Rachel, if not for you, then I'd probably have been the one to start it in the first place. I like who I am. Do you know how long it's been since I did? Listen to me." He took my shoulders, leaning over to find my eyes. "You and I are an excuse for the dewar to try and wrestle control away. This would've happened regardless."

"But not to this extent," I said, and he collapsed in on himself, holding my hands between us as he chose his next words. "You can't be the Sa'han if you're with me," I said miserably. "They won't let you."

"It's just a title," he said, but even I could hear the lie.

"One that gives you a voice, one that people follow."

His lips pressed into a resolute line. "I'm not letting you go, so stop it. We'll get through this. Besides, if the demons call me the Sa'han, then maybe that's enough," he said, a hint of worry tugging at the corners of his eyes.

"Maybe," I said miserably. *I will not cry. I won't!*

"The demons won't listen to Landon, but they might me. I've ridden the hunt with them. Fought beside them to eliminate a threat. If that's not being the Sa'han, then what is?"

The depth of his commitment shivered through me in the predawn gloom. "But how . . ."

"This isn't your fault," he said, bringing me to him again, and the tingles his whisper started racing through me. "We can do this together. I can't do it alone. I don't want to."

My eyes closed as I soaked in his warmth, his hands firm without binding, their slow motion against me suddenly taking on a new meaning. I took another breath, and that fast, my desires flipped to another direction. I licked my lips and Trent's breath quickened.

"You know, we've got a good ten minutes until sunup," he said, his fingers tracing over me and the flimsy nightie I had over here. "They won't have any real information about Cincinnati for at least twenty."

I pulled back to see the heat in his eyes, the desire. "We can't," I whispered, smiling.

"Why not?"

He wasn't confused per se, but clearly wary at my smile, and I pulled him closer, turning our embrace less amorous and more friendly. "Because someone is pinching my toes," I said. Trent hesitated, and I almost laughed. "Really. Someone is pinching my toes."

Realizing I was serious, he leaned to see around me. "Ray!" he exclaimed, and I held my arms out for the little girl. She was about eighteen months now, sweet with her blanket in her grip, her dark hair carefully combed and her even darker eyes solemn as she pinched my toes for our attention. She couldn't have been there very long, and her expression was troubled.

"Daddy?" she said, her high voice clear. "Oucy no. No!" she demanded, pointing to the door, now open a crack. I hadn't even heard her open it, but she was a quiet little thing.

Trent pulled the toddler up, bringing the scent of baby powder and snickerdoodles with her. Dressed and ready for the day, she pointed again at the door, her features tight in distress. I could hear Lucy, her sister, shrilling something in the background as I fixed Ray's collar.

"What is Lucy doing that she's not supposed to?" Trent said patiently, and Ray scrunched her face up, clearly wanting to spill the beans but not having the vocabulary yet. "Lucy?" Trent called, loudly, and the little girl's enthusiastic shouts became closer.

"Daddy!" the toddler cried, shoving the door open so hard that it bounced against the wall and nearly closed again. But the blond, excited girl was already in here, a strip of toilet paper in her grip as she danced in a circle, somehow not breaking it. "Happy birthday!" she shouted, throwing it up into the air and silently watching it drift down.

"Oh my gosh, that's so sweet," I whispered, and I swear Ray rolled her eyes.

Lucy clapped her hands and ran for the bed. "Hi, Aunt Achel!" she shouted, flopping against Trent's knees, making Ray shove Lucy's hands off him.

I pulled Lucy to me, glad that Trent hadn't started dressing them alike. Lucy was only three months older than Ray, but their personalities made the difference seem larger. Squishy and wiggly, Lucy bounced in my lap until I penned her in with my arms, bringing the wonderful smell of innocence to me.

"Hi, Lucy," I said, careful to not talk to her like she was a baby but a real person. "Is that toilet paper? Shouldn't it be on the roll?"

She slid from me, running to where it lay on the floor and throwing it back into the air with a jubilant "Surprise!"

Trent looked up from playing a finger game with Ray. "There were streamers at a party, and now she won't leave the toilet paper alone." Ray held her arms out to me, and I took her willingly. "Ellasbeth is supposed to be watching them," Trent said, his eyes on the door. "Though to be honest, Quen is keeping an eye on them as well. And Jon. Everyone."

"You think she's okay?"

Standing, Trent ran a hand over his chin, mildly concerned. "She's still fighting jet lag. Maybe she fell asleep reading to them again. Unless she left. That'd be nice."

"She wouldn't do that," I said as I arranged Ray's very dark hair. I knew that Trent believed Ellasbeth agreed with the elven dewar's opinion that the world would be better if we weren't part of it, but I wasn't so sure. "Maybe you should check on her," I said, because I sure as hell wasn't going to. Not in my nightgown.

Trent nodded and held out his hand to Ray. "Ray, where is Ellasbeth?"

Blinking her dark eyes, Ray slid from me. Her hand looked small as it fit into Trent's. Wobbling only slightly, she looked at the door. "Shhh. Nap," the little girl said, and I swung my feet to the floor.

"That can mean anything," I said as I stood and glanced at my phone. It was almost sunup. No time for a shower now. I could do it after the news.

Trent's frown took on a shade of concern. "I'll be right back," he said, starting for the door. "Lucy? Where's your mommy?"

"A-a-a-a-asleep!" Lucy crowed, throwing her toilet paper banner again and watching it drift down. "Surprise!"

Trent held out his other hand. "Show me?" he asked, and she jumped over to him, her dress flying up to show her tights.

"Come on, Daddy!" she said, dragging him off.

Ray turned before they left, and I made an open-and-closed hand wave to match hers. Ducking her head shyly, she trailed along behind Trent, leaving the door open. I didn't mind, but I did put on a borrowed robe before I scuffed into my slippers. I could hear Quen talking to Trent, and I wasn't quite up to more people yet. The morning garden beckoned, a gray patch of solitude and calm after Lucy's exuberance, and after a look at my phone and the time, I shuffled to the big French doors. I wasn't going out into the living area until Ellasbeth knew I was here.

Besides, if there was a real problem, Quen or Jon would be on it. It might look as if the girls had been wandering the upper floor unattended, but both Jon and Quen were big on letting the girls explore freely within sharply defined boundaries. Either one wouldn't have a problem letting them walk in on me and Trent—each for different reasons.

Lucy's shrill voice was punctuated by masculine rumbles as I hit the code at the box by the door and opened it. The first breath of morning damp cooled my flush as I recalled the pandemonium the first time I'd opened it without the code. Birdsong and what might be the clatter of pixy wings drew me out onto the sheltered patio. There was a small koi pond with steam rising from it, and tidy flower beds carefully raked and put to bed for the coming winter.

I wrapped my arms around myself as the coolness slipped up my legs. A soft scuff yanked my attention to the small patio table for two, and I jerked to a halt. "Al?" I said, fear for being coated in mystics flashing through me. I froze, unbelieving, as he stood, clearly having been waiting for me out of sight of the door. At least I hope he'd been out of sight. "What are you doing here?" I warily shuffled closer in my slippers and robe, having to trust that he wouldn't come here, out of his way, to choke me to death. "And in a suit?" I added, thinking he looked dashing, though very different. *He wasn't trying to kill me. That was good, right?*

He looked up from the hat in his hands. "I didn't change for you," he said, his proper British accent only a hint, and I nodded, more nervous yet. The tight pin-striped suit gave him almost a forties look. He'd trimmed his physique as well with a narrower waist and shoulders not as thick. It made him appear younger, less mature, more hoodlum, but not quite a thug—the hairstyle shifted it to professional? *Professional what, though?* I wondered as my eyes slid from the hat he placed on the table to his shiny shoes. The demon did like his shiny shoes, stylish hats, and glasses that he really didn't need.

"It's a different look for you," I said, and he sniffed.

"Not everything I do revolves around you," he said quickly, as if I might think he was softening to me. "I have my reasons."

"It looks great, but I thought you looked good before," I said, and he hesitated as if never having considered that. Remembering where I was, I glanced back at the open door and inched closer. "What are you doing here?" *And how long have you been here? Did you look in the window? Did you see me happy with Trent and his children beside me?*

Al's gaze was on the door when I turned back around, and my eyes narrowed in mistrust. "I want to ask you a few questions," he said. "Is now a good time?"

It wasn't, but I went back and shut the door. "You put Ellasbeth to sleep, didn't you."

He smiled, and I knew it was the same old Al despite his new look. "Was it you who destroyed the back end of your church?"

"No." *What is his game?* I wondered, arms over my middle again.

"Was it . . . Trenton Aloysius Kalamack?"

"No," I said again, coming closer until only feet separated us.

"Tell me about it in your own words."

Tell me about it in your own words? I stood before him, head cocked. "Why?" The scent of burnt amber was almost nonexistent, and I wondered how he could lose it so fast when it always took me a week of showers.

"I want to know." Nose wrinkling, Al flicked something away from me. "Disgusting creatures," he muttered, and I backed up, thinking he was talking about the mystics.

"I can't hear them," I rushed to say. "And I didn't call them to me." I shut my mouth, thinking that to tell him they'd showed up when Cormel had threatened Trent was a bad idea.

Al's jaw tightened, and I felt a pang at his disgust. "Ah, it was one of the vampire camarillas," I said to distract him. "Cormel made a deal with the elf dewar that if they got rid of Trent and me, the elves would bring their souls back from the ever-after."

"So it was Cormel's men?" he said.

I licked my lips, remembering Al had seen Cormel last night outside Junior's. "No."

Al sighed and clasped his hands before him. "No proof. That should be your middle name, Rachel Mariana Morgan."

Why is he even interested in this? "Look," I said, thinking this was a lame excuse to check on me, but it was better than choking me to death. "They were vampires," I added, and he made talking motions with his hands. "Bis snagged one and Trent got a confession."

"A forced confession means nothing," he said, and I wondered if the demons were working on some point-of-law thing they wanted to use somehow.

"Why are you badgering me?" I asked, and he casually sat, tugging at his sleeves before remembering the lace was gone.

"You're very defensive," he said. "I'm simply ascertaining what happened that morning."

Yes, but why? He waited silently, and I finally said, "There was a mix of vampires from a lot of camarillas. No one took responsibility, but last night Cormel said the attack was his effort to remind Trent and me of our place in life."

Goat-slitted eyes unfocused in thought, Al steepled his fingers. "This was last night?"

Someone has been watching old Godfather *flicks,* I thought as I nodded, and then I said, "Yes," when it became obvious I needed to actually say it. "I didn't blow up my church, but I did take advantage of it to pretend to be dead." I leaned one palm against the table, shivering as the cold from the iron seeped into me. "Why are you here?"

His lip curled, and I forced myself to stay unmoving as he flicked nothing off me, his finger just missing my robe. "I thought you might be interested in seeing what happens to the surface demons when the sun rises."

I glanced at the house, imagining Ellasbeth's reaction if I came in with him. It might be worth the fallout. "That's why I'm up at this godforsaken hour. You want to come in and watch the news with us? Quen makes a good cup of coffee."

Al blinked, quickly regaining his aplomb. "No, thank you," he said, the barest shifting of his feet giving away his surprise. "I thought we could do this out here."

"Sure," I said softly, then stiffened when Al spoke a word of Latin, gesturing with his usual flair. It lacked a little something without the lace and velvet, but his eyes still glowed with the pleasure of doing something no one else could, and I tightened my hold on the ley lines as a sheet of black-tinted ever-after coalesced into a hunched shape right there on the patio.

Crap on toast, it was a surface demon, and I reached out to circle it.

Al was faster, and a second sheet of power snapped shut around the surface demon with a solid thump I felt in my soul. "Nasty little bugger," he said, both feet on the floor as he scooted to the edge of the metal chair and peered at it, elbows on his knees and head tilted.

Uneasy, I inched closer. The surface demon hissed wildly, pounding against the wall even as smoke curled up from his fists. Or maybe it was a her. This one had hair snarled down to her waist, and a decidedly delicate cut to her jaw—even if spittle was dangling from her chin.

"Who is that?" I whispered, and I stopped short, not having realized I had moved to stand right next to Al as if wanting his protection.

Al's expression was closed. "I've no idea. Newt gave it to me." His gaze lifted to the sky lightening in the east. The tops of the trees were already glowing, and it wouldn't be long before we had our answer.

"Look, the sun," Al said as if it wasn't obvious. "Let's see how well the elves have fucked this up."

I was holding my breath, and as the sun touched the top of Al's containment bubble, the surface demon hissed, hunched as if afraid. Eyes wide, it went silent for three heartbeats, and then without fanfare, it vanished.

"Hot damn!" I exclaimed, spinning to Al. My lips parted. His eyes were closed, and his jaw was clenched as if expecting to be whipped. "Al?" I whispered, and they opened. Slowly his tension eased, and he exhaled, fingers shaking as he hid his hands behind his back.

"There, you see?" he said confidently, but what I'd seen was his fear. "Typical elven sloppiness. Rachel, if you are *ever* that careless, I'll strangle you with your own charm."

"Al . . ." I touched his shoulder and he jerked away. This was why he was here, not to show me the flaw in the elven curse. He'd been afraid, and I was the one he'd come to. "You weren't sure if you could stay," I said, and his eyes flicked to mine.

"What? Nonsense," he grumbled, taking his circle down with an unnecessary wave of his hand. "The elves haven't crafted a decent curse in three thousand years. Pull up your second sight," he said, grimacing at empty space. "What a nasty piece of work. I was never for their creation in the first place, but you do have to admire the pure savagery of it all."

He'd once told me demons had created vampires, which would in turn mean they'd created surface demons, and feeling uneasy, I pulled up my second sight. It wasn't hard to do, but I didn't do it often, not liking the red-smeared, gritty vision overlaid on the green of reality.

Sure enough, the surface demon was there among the sparse grass and sunbaked dirt that existed this far out from the city center. It howled soundlessly at the sun, clearly not happy to have been forced back. Hissing, it turned to Al and myself, and I dropped my second sight to become invisible to it. "Holy crap on Velveeta toast," I whispered, shaken as I imagined this happening everywhere as the sun slowly crept across the surface of the world.

"Just so," Al said, a hint of what might be sympathy in his voice. Shaking, I felt my way around the table to settle in the second wire chair. There were going to be lots of unhappy vampires. I had a feeling that I wasn't going to get to muck out the church with Jenks and Ivy today. This was bad. If the vampires had been ticked at me before, they'd be doubly so now, blaming me for the elven failure since Landon had set me up to take it.

"That is what happens when you try to tweak a well-crafted curse," Al said, flipping his hat. "It's always better to start from scratch than mend flaws created by a modification."

"What about the vampires who found their souls last night?" I asked.

"They are soulless again," he said, attention distant as he flipped his hat to land squarely on his head. "The long undead will be most unhappy that their headlong rush to their demise has been interrupted. I predict that by noon, the elves will be spelling to bring their souls back again. They want the old undead gone, and this is the easiest way to do it." He set his hat on the table between us. "But you already knew that," he said, voice low. "Killing them with a kindness. Perhaps elves are more like us than they wish to admit . . ."

I rubbed my forehead. The sun was barely up and I was tired already. I needed to call Ivy. "This isn't my problem."

"Of course not." Al stood and brushed at his coat, watching the way the sun hit the fibers. "There's a way to save them, the undead I mean."

I looked up, hesitating when I realized some of the threads in his suit sparkled. "How?"

He twirled his hat, running it down his arm, across his back, and down to his free hand where he caught it and jauntily placed it on his head. "If you break the path between the two worlds—"

"I'm not going to destroy the ever-after. It will be the end of all magic," I interrupted.

"Why not?" He eyed me speculatively. "You've seen Cincinnati without her undead. You can end it all right here. Break the lines and no one goes in or out. You might learn to like living without magic. It may be the only way to survive us coming home."

He meant the demons, and my arm dropped, chilled against the cold metal. "Why are you concerned about Cincinnati or the vampires?"

"I'm not. I simply don't want to go back." He turned to me. "*Ever.*"

If he was proposing an end to magic, it was a good bet he had a way to fix it. "Then maybe you should try playing by our rules."

"Maybe we already are," he shot back.

"Right." Mistrusting this, I leaned back in my chair, tugging my robe closed when it threatened to fall open. "So I break the lines to keep surface demons out and you here. Everyone is mad at me." I hesitated as he beamed at me. "Except the demons, who set themselves up as king."

"That's about it."

"You do it. I don't have time to learn a new life skill," I said, and he put a hand atop the table, leaning over me with his breath smelling of Brimstone.

"You are the only one with mystics in her." He took a breath. "Rachel."

I put a finger on his chest and backed him up. "So now mystics are a good thing?"

"Does it feel like a good thing?"

The birds were getting noisy, and I shook my head. It didn't feel good. Not at all. "I didn't ask for this," I said, and Al looked toward the house.

"Be careful what you wish for," he said, and I watched as a sheet of ever-after fell over him, clothing him back in his usual green crushed-velvet coat and top hat. His shoulders broadened, and his middle became thicker, more muscular.

"Because you might get it," I finished, wondering why he'd changed until Ellasbeth's voice rose in distress. Great, they were coming out here, and I tugged my robe closer. "Be nice," I warned Al, and he gave me an innocent look.

Oh God, it wasn't just Trent, but Ellasbeth and the girls, too. Lucy made a shrill demand when she spotted Al, thumping her fists into the door to be let out.

"Rachel didn't charm you," Trent said as the door opened and Lucy darted out before he saw Al and me waiting. "You simply fell asleep."

"Trenton!" Ellasbeth shrieked, panicking as Lucy ran to Al.

"Allie, Allie, Allie!" the little girl cried, flinging herself at the demon's knees. Al winced, hastily covering his crotch as she flung her doll around. Ray was no less captivated, watching Al from Trent's hip, her evaluating eyes never looking away.

"Get her away from him!" Ellasbeth demanded, frozen at the door as she wanted to both fly at him and run back in the house.

"Good morning, Ellasbeth," I said, and she looked at me, horrified and hyperventilating as I calmly sat at the table.

"Ellasbeth," Al purred, delighting in the fear he'd instilled as he sat down and took Lucy onto his lap. "How nice to see you."

"Trent! Get her!" she screamed again, and Trent sighed, waving Quen and Jon back from the window. "Get him out of here!"

I stood, uncomfortable in my robe all of a sudden. "He wanted to show me what happened to unbound souls when the sun came up."

Trent's eyes lit up. "And?" he prompted. Ray was beginning to wiggle to get down and get a closer look at the pink and purple flying horses that Al was making, each one coming from his cupped hands to Lucy's delight.

I couldn't stop my grimace. "We're both going to have a very busy day."

Ellasbeth was clinging to Trent's elbow, her face red and her fear obvious. "Surprise!" Lucy shouted as Al opened his hands and another horse neighed and leapt into the air. Giving me a tired look, Trent set Ray down, and the little girl toddled forward. I gentled her to me so Ellasbeth wouldn't pass out, and Ray leaned against my legs, watching Al and her sister.

"Get them away from him!" Ellasbeth demanded, and Trent took her elbow.

"The girls are safe. It's you I can't vouch for," he said, and Ellasbeth jerked her eyes from the children, her face red.

Al straightened as he let three horses go and Lucy ran after them, giggling. "I no longer steal people," he said as if insulted. "Haven't you heard?"

"Seriously?" I said, and he raised his hand, tilting it back and forth to say more or less.

Ellasbeth glared at Trent, refusing to go in even as his hand on her back began to look forceful. "You aren't believing this, are you?" she said.

I was having a hard time believing it, too, but I wasn't worried when Ray stood wobbling before Al, captivated by the horse charm. Her little hand went to his knee for balance, and Al froze, emotion cascading through him so fast I couldn't recognize anything but its depth.

"Why are you even here?" Ellasbeth exclaimed.

"Many reasons." Al was staring at Ray's hand, and I held my breath as he wiggled a finger under her palm and she gripped it, smiling up at him with her one-toothed smile.

Emotion hit me as Ray's carefully given but ultimate trust smacked Al like a ton of bricks. That fast it happened, and I knew he'd move heaven and earth for her now. Ray may have saved us all.

Lump in my throat, I turned. I didn't want him to know I'd seen, and if I stayed, I'd start to cry. "Ah, I'm sorry," I said, looking around as if my purse and coat were out here. "I have to go take a shower. Al, thank you for the information."

He looked up, and when he saw my damp eyes, he took Ray's hand off his finger with a frown. "I'm being gotten rid of."

Trent inched forward to take Ray, and I lifted her from Al. "You're welcome to stay for breakfast," Trent said as I settled Ray in his arms.

"I have already breakfasted, thank you," Al said stiffly. He was trying to be flip, but I could tell he was shaken. He hadn't expected Ray's trust, and it couldn't be taken away.

"Lucy, come here," Ellasbeth demanded, crouched with her hand held out, ignored.

"What time was your appointment with the dewar?" I asked, having forgotten already.

Trent jiggled Ray. "Nine forty-five."

"You, ah, think I could come with you?" I said, and Ellasbeth jerked, her attention on Lucy momentarily eclipsed. "I need to persuade them to leave the surface demons in the ever-after and the real demons in reality," I added, wincing. I wasn't going to be the demons' liaison, but someone had to say something, and I did have a reputation for saving large demographics—even if the collateral damage was high.

Ellasbeth finally got hold of Lucy, and she backed up to the door with her as the little girl protested. "You're joking," she said, voice distracted. "You want them here?"

"Absolutely," I said. My feet were freezing, and I wanted to go in.

Trent shrugged. "Sure. I'll pick you up at eight. You'll be at the church?"

Ellasbeth was struggling with Lucy. Exasperated, she exclaimed, "Yes, you both go. I can watch the girls."

My eyes darted to Trent, and then Al.

"*You* will watch the girls?" Al drawled, popping little blue horses into existence as fast as Lucy could pop them out of existence between her two hands. "I heard it was your idea to kill Trent and Rachel so you'd have the girls as your own."

It was out, and Ellasbeth's cheeks reddened. "That was not my idea!" she protested, and Lucy slipped from her.

Frustrated, Trent checked his watch. "Quen and Jon can watch them."

"I am *not* trying to steal the girls," Ellasbeth said hotly, and Trent absently took a horse out of Ray's mouth.

"I'm sorry, Ellasbeth," he said frankly. "Rachel seems to think the best of everyone, but I'm not that . . ." He hesitated.

"Naive, I believe is the word you're looking for," Al said, and I frowned, almost smacking him with the back of my hand.

"Lucy is my child!" Ellasbeth said, one hand gripping the wildly twisting little girl. "I can watch her."

Trent lifted his chin and started for the door. "I don't want you to."

I needed to get dressed, and I hesitated, wanting to say good-bye to Al before going in, but not wanting to do it in front of everyone.

"I can watch the girls until six," Al said suddenly, and I blinked. Face red, Al jerked his watch out of its little pocket. "Ah, that'd be six P.M., eastern standard time. I'm busy after that."

"You?" I said, and his complexion darkened. "You don't know anything about babies."

"Absolutely not!" Ellasbeth pushed her way into the courtyard, a mix of terror and anger.

Al seemed unperturbed. "They're not babies, they're toddlers. Besides, I'm third on the list, I believe?"

Trent was smiling, small but honest. "No, thank you. Jon can do it."

Ellasbeth struggled with Lucy, the little girl wailing about the dead horse in her tight grip. "What does he mean, third on the list?"

Trent and I exchanged a look, but Quen poked his head out the door, saving us from having to answer. "Sa'han? Ms. Morgan? Ivy has phoned. She's fine, but she's trying to reach Rachel. Felix committed suncide this morning and she'd like Rachel's help with Nina."

Fear slid through my soul, and I took a fast breath. The dewar would have to wait. "I have to go." I hesitated, wanting to touch Al to say good-bye but not daring to.

"Of course he committed suncide," Al said distantly. "That's why we had to separate their souls from their bodies to begin with."

"Go." Trent jiggled a fussy Ray. "I'll bring up your concerns to the dewar."

I looked at Al one last time before I started for the door. "Thank you," I said, trying to remember where I'd left my boots. "I'll do what I can."

"You're going to need all the voices you can get in the dewar, Kalamack," Al said loudly. "Poor use of resources to waste Quen and Jon tending your girls, especially when you claim to want this closer tie. Let me watch the little darlings."

I turned, half in the house, half out. Ellasbeth waited, her lilac perfume strong on the still air. Trent was frowning, but it was in thought, not concern.

"I'm not worried about the girls," he said, making Ellasbeth gasp. "I'm worried about you rummaging in my things. No. I'll take them with me. It will be a good reminder to the dewar."

Al pulled himself up, a hand elegantly behind his back. "I will be the perfect example of correctness."

Ellasbeth's hand went to the house for balance. "I swear, Trent, if you give our children to that demon to watch them, I'll never forgive you."

Trent looked at me, and I shrugged. "He won't keep them permanently," I said, and Al grinned to show his blocky teeth.

Trent set Ray down, and the little girl wobbled to Al, beaming as if he was a new toy.

"Trenton!" Ellasbeth shrieked, and Lucy finally slipped from her. Ellasbeth made a lunge after her, and Quen jerked the woman back, his expression stoic as she slapped his face.

"You get my standard sitting rate," Trent said, almost shouting over Ellasbeth's hysterics as Al picked Lucy up. "You stay on the top floor and out of my room. And my spelling hut. And everything else. No phone, no scrying, no showing them off to anyone. I want them here in my apartments at all times."

"De-e-e-elighted," the demon said, then vanished with both girls.

"Trent!" Ellasbeth screamed.

Giving her a sidelong glance, I sidled up to Trent. "You forgot to tell him no visitors."

Trent's breath hissed in between his teeth. "Oooh, I did, didn't I."

"Trenton Aloysius Kalamack!" Ellasbeth exclaimed as she pushed between us, her face red. "Where are my girls?"

He pointed inside when Lucy's laughing giggle echoed into the patio. Hand to her mouth, Ellasbeth bolted inside. "You're welcome to stay," Trent said loudly, but she was already inside. Only now did a faint worry line wrinkle his forehead. "Tell me this isn't a mistake."

Smiling, I gave him a hug. "This isn't a mistake," I said, feeling his arms take me in and make me strong. "He's the only one who might agree to play by our rules. The rest need to be shamed into it. Thank you."

I dropped back to see a lingering worry in him. "I'm going to miss you today, too."

He was tucking a strand of hair behind my ear, and I felt loved. "Maybe we can have dinner or something."

But I knew that I'd be lucky to end today still standing. If Felix had committed suncide, Nina was going to be out of control and Cincinnati's old vampires would be a conflicted terror of want, desire, and fear. What tore at me though was that Ivy's hope of ever saving her soul was now tied to a maybe.

And as I gave Trent a kiss and felt his grasp slip from me, I vowed that Ivy was going to get her happy ending. Even if it killed me.

Chapter 19

My breath caught and I stomped on the brake when the car ahead of me squealed to a stop. Head swinging, I flicked my eyes to the rearview mirror, wincing until the car behind me stopped as well. I was trying to get to Fountain Square. Ivy and I were having lunch before digging through the mess at the church. Yes, I should be in some library looking for how to close the lines, but Ivy needed me, needed me to tell her that one blood orgy wasn't the end. Besides, I had to do something normal for a few hours before I started saving the world again.

"What the Turn?" I said to myself, trying to see past the cars lined up before me. Traffic was at a standstill, and when I rolled the window down, I could hear a crowd and a bullhorn a few blocks up. I was nearly at the square. Something was wrong. *Ivy was there.*

Pulse fast, I jerked the wheel, driving in the wrong lane for a few car lengths to pull into a tiny—and illegal—parking spot for the meter police. I waved at the guy blowing his horn at me as I popped my FIB sign in the front window and grabbed my shoulder bag. Thanks to my weekend sleepovers at Trent's I was in a clean pair of jeans and a casual sweater, but I felt anything but professional as I locked the car and strode off, boots clunking.

Nina? I wondered, shocked as her voice came through the bullhorn, her aggressive urgency mixing with the rising roar of unseen people. Crap on toast, Felix had committed suncide this morning. A handful of other masters had gone from soul-induced depression to out-of-control raging when their souls were ripped from them. That they were forced underground was a blessing and a breathing space. Cops were everywhere, both the FIB and the I.S., and I strode up to the nearest. "Excuse me. What's going on?"

"That way, miss," he directed, and I jerked back before he could touch me. His expression hardened, and he actually looked at me. "There's an illegal demonstration at the square," he said, clearly not recognizing me. "Please go home."

They were almost lining the streets now, and everyone was being turned away. "Ah, I'm trying to reach someone," I said, thinking if Nina was in there, so was Ivy. "I mean, I was called in to work," I said, flashing my old I.S. badge with my spell-burned hair and dopey look. "Who do I talk to?"

"Hell if I know," the cop muttered as he looked at my street clothes. "Go on."

He didn't have to say it twice, and I slipped behind the forming human wall and hustled to the square, waving my outdated ID at everyone with a badge who looked my way. My pulse pounded, and the brief respite of people vanished. It wasn't a demonstration, it was a mob, and I stood in the middle of the blocked-off road trying to make sense of it.

Nina was on the stage with a bullhorn, trying to outshout the man with a mic. The crowd was split and ugly, yelling at the stage, hands in fists raised in protest. The huge TV was showing a national news station, but it was all bad, with excited newscasters standing, as I was, at the outskirts of similar protests in other cities. High above, people pressed against the windows of the surrounding buildings taking pictures. I.S. and FIB officers were everywhere, but apart from the ring of them keeping new people out, I couldn't tell what they were doing.

"I'm with the I.S.," I said, flashing my ID when a cop came close, and he went the other way. News crews were setting up on the corner, and I began to inch away before I was recognized. *Ivy, where are you?*

The sound of pixy wings jerked my attention, and I looked up, getting an eye full of pixy dust as Jenks dropped down. "Damn it, Jenks!" I exclaimed, eyes watering.

"Tink's a Disney whore, Rache, what are you doing here?" he exclaimed, his voice shrill as he struggled to be heard over the rising noise.

"Yeah, I'm glad to see you, too," I said sourly, hand up for him to land on. "I'm trying to find Ivy. What is Nina doing?"

He went to land, then darted back as someone jostled me forward. My hand hit a lamppost, and I stepped up onto the footing for a few extra inches as Nina's voice rose clear and strong, a hard surety in her voice that she'd learned from Felix. She sounded like a master, and it was chilling.

"The peace is false!" she cried, the vampiric pull in it bringing a good part of the crowd to silence. "Peace is death to the undead. It breaks them. Your masters are weeping. It's our duty to protect them as they protect us! They keep us safe, and now it's our turn. Even if they rage and threaten, we must withstand the anger knowing they love us! Their souls will kill them!"

"How long has she been up there?" I asked, one arm looped around the post for balance.

"Long enough." Jenks's wings were shading blue from the cold, and he vibrated them for warmth. "She's, ah, rallying the living vampires to protect the undead. Not everyone is happy about it. I don't know what's going to happen if the elves bring their souls back."

Concerned, I climbed farther up the pole. The crowd was ugly, and my brow furrowed when I heard a few "Let them die!" rise up. This was so not good. Had they forgotten already the chaos of Cincinnati not three months ago when the master vampires were sleeping?

"You can't deny them their souls!" the man with the mic shouted with the professional outrage of someone comfortable with the pulpit. "It's their God-given right!"

"Is it not our right to protect them?" Nina said, eyes black with threat. "We've always given them what they needed to survive. We can't give them their death! They've been tricked by the elves and their own desires!"

Nervous, I looked toward the river. Trent was only a few blocks away at the arena and the closed dewar meeting. It was too easy to imagine the mob storming the place. No one could stop it with the I.S. and FIB concentrated here.

"My master found his soul," Nina said, and the crowd stilled at the power in her voice. Felix had changed her, almost into a master herself with his thoughts running through hers for so long, and I shivered at the command. "It was fixed to him," she intoned, and even the zealot on the stage was silenced. "It tormented him day and night until he walked into the sun. Be glad the souls have fled. Hide your masters if they should return. They bring only pain."

"He was weeping in joy!" the man with the mic proclaimed, but beside Nina's impassioned presence, he looked cheap. "Who are you to deny him?"

"*He was in pain!*" Nina shouted, and the crowd began to stir. "The grace of the undead is that they feel no pain, and he was in pain. He was broken! Tell your masters the elves lie. Tell your masters they seek to kill them! Tell them even if they should beat you and send you from their sight. You must protect them because they love you!"

The voice of the crowd rolled between the buildings, drowning out both Nina and the man onstage. Worried, I got down from the pole. I had to find Ivy and call Trent. Get him out of there. Warn him.

"Your master died because God brought his sins home!" the man was saying.

"The elves sit in conference right now to bring their souls back. We can't let them do it!" Nina thundered. "They're trying to kill our masters! He walked into the sun!" she cried in pain. "He walked into the sun and now I am alone!"

Her anguish raged out, connecting with every living vampire there. They knew what it was to be alone. They feared it. The urge to rise up was almost unbearable. Felix had given her the strength of the undead and the passion of the living. No wonder Ivy loved her.

"My God," I whispered, jolted from her charisma when someone bumped me. "Jenks, is Edden here?" We had to get Nina to shut up, even if I agreed with her. The vampires were going to storm the dewar if this continued.

"Yeah." Jenks landed on my shoulder. "He's over by the curb. Where the horses are?"

I looked over the heads to where the mounted police usually hung out. Sure enough, there were two very unhappy horses, an FIB van, and a bunch of FIB guys clustered around something. A plan to get the people out of here, maybe.

"How am I going to get over there?" I muttered, gaze roving over the square. The huge vid screen was now showing the Cincy arena. The wind down there was intense, blowing the newscaster's hair everywhere as the dewar began to break up and people began to leave. My breath came easier. Maybe they were evacuating before the crowd decided elves were on a par with biogeneticists and lynched them all. *Maybe the vampires were trying to get rid of the elves . . .* So far, only Felix had died, and he'd been on his way out already.

"It's God's will they die!" the zealot was screaming, a harsh contrast to Nina's powerful anguish. "It's penance for the atrocities they have perpetrated! Let them be judged!"

Jenks's dust was a beacon as he hovered over me, looking for the easiest path to the curb. "Ah, Rache? Is that your mom?"

Oh God. I shoved someone, trying to see. My fear redoubled as I spotted her standing on a planter, hand in a fist as she shouted and gestured, calling someone a prejudiced prick and religious hypocrite zealot all in one breath. She looked fantastic in her outrage, and I almost lost sight of her when the crowd shifted. "Mom!" I shouted, then grunted when I got an elbow in the gut from some faceless woman. "Mom!"

She heard me. Somehow she heard me over the noise and confusion. She turned, her face still alight with the fire of battling injustice. Clearly this was where I'd gotten it from, and without even a glance at the stage, she fought her way off the planter and to me.

"Mom, what are you doing here?" I said when she finally got close.

"Oh, you ruined your funeral!" she moaned, giving me a quick hug.

She was okay, and I hugged her back. "Mom. We have to get out of here," I said, not believing she was worried about my funeral.

"No matter," she said, beaming as she shoved someone to get a smidgen more room. "The band crapped out on me anyway. Isn't it a marvelous day for a protest?"

Wincing, I held her shoulder so no one would force us apart. *Marvel-*

ous wasn't exactly the word I'd use. Nina was on the bullhorn again. Some were listening raptly, others—mostly human by the look of it—were booing. I could tell who were the living vampires not only because of the way they reacted to Nina but because they looked terrified. It was starting to slide from a mob to a riot. "Jenks? Find Ivy. My car is on Vine."

He darted off, making me envy his wings. My heart pounded. "Mom, we have to go."

But she was watching the stage as Nina exclaimed, "If there's one thing the living have learned, it's that what you want most will kill you. It's our time to protect them. We can't allow the elves to bring back their souls!"

My mom wiped an eye. "It reminds me of the Turn," she said, smiling. "But it smells a hell of a lot better. No one decaying in the alleys."

I elbowed someone out of the way so we could start for the street. "Mom, where's Donald?"

"He went to get me a coffee. It takes him a while. People recognize him, and he always stops and talks. It's a pain in the ass sometimes."

Visions of tomorrow's headlines began swimming before me. Stomach tight, I began to inch her to the curb. She jerked me to a stop with a hug. "I'm so proud of you, sweetheart. I've been watching Nina, and I think she's perfect for Ivy. It wouldn't take much to change your funeral into a wedding for them."

"Mom!" I said as I disentangled myself. "We have to get out of here!"

"I'm just saying she's smart, attractive, and has more determination than you. Look at her. Magnificent! She's so entrenched in her belief. It makes me want to protect the beastly things myself."

"We have to go," I said again, then jumped when my phone vibrated.

"Go!" she exclaimed, face flushed and eager. "It's just getting started!"

She turned to the stage, arm pumping in the air as I let go of her to fish my phone out. It was Trent, but I'd never be able to hear him. Just glad he was alive, I flipped the phone open. "Trent? You okay?" I shouted, hand over one ear as the zealot with the mic pointed at the TV and proclaimed that now they would know the true purity of the soul.

Clearly something had shifted at the dewar, and I turned to the TV, showing the riverfront with lots of blond men and women coming out of the stadium now instead of one or two as before.

"Rachel?" Trent's voice came, tiny and small. "I'm fine. Where are you?"

"I'm looking for Ivy. I'm at the square with my mom and Jenks!" I shouted. On the screen, a reporter I recognized elbowed a CNN reporter out of the way to get in front of Landon. "Nina's rallying the vampires to stop the elves from returning the undead souls. Trent, you have to get out of there."

"I'm going right now," Trent said, but I never would've understood it if I hadn't heard him whisper in my ear before. "You have to leave the square. Now!"

But the reporter had gotten Landon to stop, and the crowd quieted enough to hear her say, "Sa'han Landon, Sa'han Landon, can you comment on the sudden disappearance of the undead souls with the rising sun? Have the elves agreed on a course of action to bring them back?"

Her voice was echoing between the buildings, and the sound of the crowd diminished even more, punctuated by the occasional shout.

"Rache?"

I dropped my head, trying to hear Trent. "I can't leave without Ivy. Trent, I'm looking at Landon on TV. He's going to make a statement."

"Damn it, Rachel, get out of there!" he shouted. "It's about to get ugly!"

I tugged at my mom with my free hand, but no one was moving anymore, all eyes fixed on the screen as Landon raised his hands at the mics shoved at him. Behind him, people were leaving the arena with the quickness of rats fleeing a foundering ship. "Wait, I want to hear this," my mom said.

"It has been determined that the sudden absence of souls this morning was caused by the demons, not a failure in our original spell," Landon said, his benign young smile both practiced and convincing.

"You liar!" I shouted up at the screen. "It was your lame-ass spell that failed!"

People turned to me, and I scowled as Jenks's dust suddenly wreathed me.

"Rachel?" came Trent's voice, tiny from the phone in my hand. "Listen. To. Me. Get out of there! For God's sake, get out now!"

Jenks landed on my shoulder, his wings cold against me. "Ivy's coming. Don't move."

But moving was the last thing on my mind as Landon spoke. "We've decided on a course of action, one that not only will bring the souls of the undead back and lock them to this reality, but one that will also facilitate a smoother reunion with their original bodies and rid us of the demons now among us."

"You son of a bastard," I whispered. I stared up at the screen, almost oblivious to the new space around me and that the nearest people were whispering. "He's lying!" I shouted, and from the stage I could hear more voices raised in anger. "The demons didn't do it! It's the dewar elves with their sloppy spell casting. They're *trying* to kill the undead!"

"Ah, Rache?" Jenks said from my shoulder, too cold to fly well, but I stood there and fumed. Had they forgotten the chaos of when the masters were sleeping just three months ago? Their fear of the night?

"I would implore everyone," Landon was saying, "especially the living vampires, to find it in themselves to not take their anger out on the demons. We will resolve the issue in due course in a safe and efficient manner."

My jaw clenched. "You're saying that because it's only demon magic that can fix the souls permanently, and you need them! You *want* the vampires dead!"

"Rache!" Jenks shouted, and I jumped when he pinched my ear. Blinking, I saw the new eight feet of space between me and everyone else. My mom stood at my shoulder, and I could hear Ivy fighting her way to get to me. My phone dangled in my hand, and Trent's voice desperately shouted at me to leave, to get out.

I didn't think it was going to be that easy anymore.

"You see the lies!" the zealot on the stage shouted, and I spun to see he had the stage all to himself. "She is a demon!"

Oh God, he was pointing at me. Sure, I could do some magic and blast everyone, but that'd only get me in jail, if I was lucky. "Ah, Trent. I gotta go," I muttered, then closed the phone in the middle of his outcry.

Shaking, I tucked the phone away. The ring of people stared at me, more joining them every second. My mother took my elbow protectively. "Let's go," she said, but no one moved to let us through. Instead, they inched closer, expressions determined.

"Stop them! Make them answer to us!" the man on the stage shouted, and I gasped as hands reached out.

Instinct kicked in. I pulled heavily on the line. Someone cried out a warning, and I sent it through them, the power of the line arching from one to the other.

"Rachel!" Jenks shouted as it had no effect and I went down under a wash of arms and hands. There were too many of them, and my strength was diluted. Hands grasped and tugged, and I couldn't breathe. Someone pulled my hair, and I hit the pavement. I couldn't set a circle—there were too many bodies crossing the line and it couldn't form.

"No!" I shrieked as a hand clamped over my wrist, and then I cowered as I felt the snap of lavender strike through me as if in protection.

"*Corrumpo!*" my mother shouted, and I cowered again as a wave of energy pulsed forward, ripping the grasping hands away so the sun could beat down on me again.

Stunned, I looked at the one hand still on me. "Mom?" I questioned, and she yanked me up as if I was still fourteen and couldn't walk a block without panting. "Where did you learn that?"

"Get your hands off my *daughter*!" she shouted, her color high and her hair wild.

Jenks dropped down, and my mom let go of my wrist. "Jeez, Rache. Your mom kicks ass."

I took a breath. We weren't out of it yet. They were wary, but that guy on the stage was still yelling at them to attack us. "She needed to be to keep me alive," I said, edging forward and seeing people grudgingly begin to part. "She once took an orderly out with a bedpan so I could go home for the solstice."

"Move!" Ivy's voice came, and I turned. "Get out of my way!"

The man on the stage pointed, distance making him brave. "Stop them! She's a demon! She took their souls! If you act together, she can't stop you!"

"The hell I can't," my mother muttered, and hearing her, the people pressed back to make a path.

Ivy finally broke through. Her head snapped up at the harsh claxon that suddenly rang out. "Son of a bitch," my mother muttered, staring at the sky. "They're going to seal the circle. Run!"

I had no idea what she was talking about, but after seeing her blow a lynch mob off me, I wasn't going to question her. "Come on!" I shouted, grabbing Ivy's hand and running at the people circling us.

They screamed, parting in panic as we came at them, and we plowed through. Elbows hit me, and the scent of fear. My grip on Ivy never faltered as I followed my mom and Jenks's dust. Adrenaline was cold fire as I felt the prickling of a rising field. It was just before me, and I lunged, dragging Ivy behind me as I dove for the rising shimmer.

"No!" I cried as it licked over me, hesitating a heartbeat as it decided what side of me it would form on, and then I was through, Ivy in tow. We hit the ground together, and she spun to her feet with unreal grace.

Shocked, I sat on the pavement and stared at the purple-and-green shimmering field behind me. It was so thick, I couldn't see past it. My palm was scraped, and I rubbed at it as I tried to decide what hurt and what didn't. I hadn't known they could close the square like that.

My urge to rise vanished at the new pain in my shoulder. Hissing, I took my weight off my hand, then yelped when some guy smelling like vampire hoisted me up. "Hey! Let go," I shouted, then looked for my mom, even as the man got a tighter grip.

"It's a containment field," she said, smiling as an I.S. officer wrenched her arms behind her and zip-stripped her. "Donald and I got stuck in it once during a protest and they let us sit there for five hours before dropping it." She looked up at the man trying to haul her off. "Hey! I've a right to assemble!"

Jenks was grinning, darting back and forth to avoid a man with a net. "Your mom could write a book, Rache."

They were arresting us? "Dude, I'm on your side!" I exclaimed, then gasped when the guy who'd picked me up off the sidewalk shoved me at a car and wrenched my arms back. "Ow! Watch the shoulder!"

"Nina is still in there!" Ivy was screaming, and I heard the familiar thumps and pained grunts that happened when you told Ivy no. The man let go of me, and I spun, wrists bound as I leaned against the car to watch.

I kind of worked for the FIB. We'd get this sorted out as soon as we found Edden.

"Ohhh, that's going to hurt for a week," Jenks said in admiration as he hovered beside me, and I winced.

"Jenks, go find Edden, will you?"

"You got it!" he said cheerfully, and darted away.

Ivy was backed up to the shimmering barrier, keeping everyone a good eight feet away with her attitude. They knew who she was, and I thought it dumb they persisted. She was magnificent with her streaming hair and dark eyes, motions clean and sharp as she beat off two more agents who dared to try her.

I.S. officers in specialized vests were going in and out of the barrier as if it didn't exist. I hadn't even know they had this kind of thing. Ivy spun when Nina's voice carried as she was brought through, subdued in a straitjacket as they bundled her to an I.S. van. The zealot was right behind her, and I hoped they put them in separate vehicles. *What is taking Edden so long? This strip is too tight.*

"Nina!" Ivy called, and then I gasped as a man in a vest came through the barrier right behind Ivy and took her down.

Ivy struggled wildly, and my mom inched to stand beside me, eyes wide in admiration as my roommate wiggled, twisted, and finally succumbed to a martial arts grip that would snap her wrist if she continued, her free hand slapping her thigh in a show of submission.

"Good girl, Tamwood," the vampire who had downed her snarled. "Get me a restraining harness!" he shouted, louder.

"Hey!" I exclaimed, pissed. He was the same guy who'd zip-stripped me, clearly pleased with himself as Ivy was bundled up by his buddies. "I'm Rachel Morgan, and that's Ivy Tamwood. What are you doing? We're here to help!"

The vampire's smile chilled me, but his charms fell flat as I lifted my chin and stared him down. "Rachel Morgan," he drawled as he took his field harness off and handed it to a subordinate. "Resisting arrest? You're going to be locked up for a long time."

"I did not!" I said indignantly. "I did not do one thing to resist arrest.

If I had, I wouldn't have been arrested! Where's Captain Edden?" But as the vampire continued to smile at me, I was starting to have doubts. I hadn't done anything wrong except fudge a little on why I was down here, but once you went into I.S. custody, they could make you sit in a room for over a day before they had to charge or release you.

And here I stood, my magic gone because I played by the rules. I could almost hear Al laughing at me, telling me I deserved to be locked up if I expected a demon to get a fair shake.

"Cormel wants to talk to you," the vampire whispered.

"Back up, fang breath," I said, and his nasty smile faltered because he hadn't scared me. The reality, though, was a little different. Cormel? Great. He wouldn't accept that this was madness. I couldn't help him, and even if I could, I wouldn't.

"You're making a mistake," I said softly, gaze flicking to Ivy being hauled up from the pavement, sullen and angry.

The vampire looked back at her. I didn't like the way his lips curled in satisfaction. "Cormel wants you to fix this. Give him his soul."

"And be blamed for it when he commits suncide?" I snarled. It was starting to thin out this side of the barrier, though it would probably be at least an hour before traffic would be allowed to resume.

"That way," the vampire said, shoving me into motion. My mother was behind me, and Ivy in front. The I.S. van was dead ahead, and I wasn't going to get into it. Once you went into the I.S. tower, the law didn't seem to matter anymore. *And they are afraid of demons?* I asked myself, heart pounding. What did they know that I didn't?

"He wants his soul," the vampire said, pinching my shoulder as he pushed me along. "You either get it for him, or Ivy dies."

My pulse raced. I looked at Ivy, then the van. I tensed to do something, spinning when Edden's voice echoed out, "Whoa, whoa, whoa, what are you doing, Uric? These are my people!"

My knees almost gave way, and the vampire, Uric apparently, stopped, hands scrabbling to catch me as he suddenly had my entire weight to hold. "Edden," I breathed. "Thank God."

Uric hauled me back up, and the entire group of us came to a halt, mere steps from the I.S. van. "Since when?" he said boldly, and I jerked when he twisted the band around my wrist to make it hurt. "She can't work for you. She's Inderland."

Edden bulled his way forward, six uneasy but big officers behind him. "She's a demon," Edden said, gesturing. "There are no restrictive labor laws for demons. She's mine. Let her go."

The scent of angry vampire grew, and the man holding Ivy grunted as she jabbed an elbow into him. "She was resisting arrest," Uric muttered.

"I was not!" I went slack in his grip to keep him from hauling me off, then stood up when he tried to scoop me into a carry hold. "Edden, I made no move to resist arrest, or I wouldn't be here now and you know it! This is an abduction. Cormel wants me, and if I go in, I'm not coming out." I hesitated as Edden chewed his lip, making his mustache bunch. "Edden!"

Edden's eyes narrowed. He reached for me and Uric pulled me back. "Do the paperwork," Uric said, and Edden's eyes narrowed. Jenks hovered, unsure and uneasy.

"Hit me," Edden said, and Uric's hold on me tightened.

"E-excuse me," I stammered, then exclaimed, "Ow!," when Uric yanked me back a step.

"Hit him, Rache!" Jenks shrilled.

Uric gestured, and the men holding Ivy began wrestling her to the van.

"Rache!" Jenks shouted, and my mom pursed her lips.

"Hell, I'll do it," she said, and flung out her foot, kicking Edden square in the balls.

Clutching himself, he groaned as my mother muttered that she hadn't hit him that hard.

Everyone was looking at him, and it suddenly dawned on me what he was trying to do. "Let go!" I shouted, wiggling out of Uric's grip and doing a soft, barely there crescent kick at Edden's jaw as he froze, clutching his privates.

"Get her down!" someone screamed, and my eyes widened. They were all coming at me. Both sides.

"Look out!" Jenks shrilled, and I was suddenly trying to breathe as three men pretended I was a loose football and fell on me. The pavement hit hard, and I think I blacked out for a second. Oh God, I couldn't breathe, but it was Edden who hauled me up, a little rougher than he needed to as he shoved me at his men. I fell into them, gasping for air. Shit, I'd broken something, and his nose was bleeding. From the outskirts I heard a wolf howl rise, and a shiver ran up my spine.

"She's mine!" Edden yelled at Uric, inches in front of him and angry as Edden had to peer up at him around his watering eyes and bleeding nose. "She hit me, and she's mine! You hit an FIB officer, you go to the FIB. You can have her when I'm done with her. Got it?"

Breath fast, I looked for Ivy, not seeing her. She'd used the distraction and gotten free. From behind the crowd I heard a bang and the van holding Nina shook. Another howl rose. *David?* I hadn't seen any Weres in the crowd, but that didn't mean they hadn't been there.

My mom was grinning as she landed next to me against the cop car. "God, I love protest rallies." Her gaze went past me to the crowd. "Yoo-hoo! Donald! Come bail me and Rachel out, will you, sweetheart?"

Oh God, the news crews were here, and I hung my head as my birth father grinned and waved his checkbook. He had a couple of groupies with him, and I figured he'd get a ride to the FIB building with no problem.

"They're Inderland. They're to be in my custody!" Uric was shouting, eyes black and face red, and Edden shoved his chest right back at him.

"That woman assaulted me," Edden said, pointing at me. "She's mine unless she assaulted you first. Did she assault you?"

Uric's lips curled back, and I thought I saw the fear of self-preservation in him. "No, but Tamwood did," he snarled, and then his expression became even uglier when he saw the bleeding faces and cradled arms of the men who had been holding her. "Find Tamwood!" he shouted, and everyone scrambled into motion, even the one with the bad limp. My good feeling died as Uric focused on me for a long moment before turning on a heel and striding away.

"There's got to be an easier way to do this," Edden said, dabbing at his bleeding nose.

"Crap on toast, Edden. I'm sorry," I said, heart pounding. "I owe you big."

He put a hand on my shoulder and led me away with a quickness that told me he wasn't quite sure he had the legal authority on his side. "Don't think I won't call this in someday," he said, leaning so close I could smell the coffee on his breath. "Ivy just better keep that girlfriend of hers quiet." He glanced back over his shoulder, then dropped his head. "Damn, Rachel, don't you know how to pull your punches?" Edden dabbed at his lip. "I bit right through my lip."

"Sorry," I said, then gestured for Jenks to see if he could find Ivy. Knowing her, she was probably safe already. Humming his approval, he darted off.

"How is the investigation on my church going?" I asked, hands still tied behind my back. There was an FIB car up ahead, and I guessed that's where we were headed.

"I've assigned someone to it, but we've been kind of busy lately. What are you doing out here? It's not safe."

I looked back at the mess. People were being pulled out from behind the hazy field in ones and twos, the most cooperative coming first, apparently. "Yep, I figured that out. How about getting this zip strip off me?" I asked as he unlocked the back door and opened it. Takata was watching this, and I was embarrassed.

"Next time pull your punches," Edden said as he put a hand on my head and sort of scooted me into the backseat. "Watch your head."

"Edden!" I complained, and he hesitated, pointing for me to stay but not shutting the door. It was awkward with my hands behind me like that, and I sat sideways with my feet on the pavement. It smelled like stale man sweat, and my nose wrinkled in disgust. My mom was already free, talking to the officers and waving to Trent as his car slowly pulled under the DON'T CROSS tape. I jumped when my phone rang, frustrated when I couldn't reach it. Damn it, it was probably Ivy.

"*I* didn't do anything *wrong*!" I grumbled, pulling at the plastic-coated silver strip. Trent had gotten out, and my heart thumped as he talked to Edden. He shook Edden's hand before turning to me, his hands in his pockets and steps slow as he wove through the thinning crowd of officers.

"I told you to leave," he said when he got close enough, and my frustration vanished at his smile, both glad to see me and worried.

"I tried," I said, gaze shifting to my mom and then the I.S. van. "It got complicated." I scooted out of the car, awkward until he took my shoulder to balance me. *Turn-blasted zip strip,* I thought, and suddenly the wrist-band gave way with a little pop. Surprised, I rubbed at my wrists. "Thanks," I said as I sighed in relief.

"For coming down here? It was a calculated risk."

"No, for taking the zip strip off." Trent hesitated, and a cold feeling slipped into me. "Ah, didn't you just snap it?" I hadn't felt anything, but if he'd been quick about it, I wouldn't, seeing as the strip blocked you from all line contact.

"No."

Worried, I turned back to the car to find it. Uric must have put it on too tight and it just broke. But a cold feeling slipped into me when the backseat and pavement were bare. "It's got to be here," I said as I dropped to my knee and looked under the car.

"What?"

"The zip strip," I said, not seeing it. "One of the I.S. guys zipped me, and it just snapped." Worried, I dug down between the seat and the back to find an old pen and a plastic cup lid, but no zip strip. "You sure you didn't break it?"

Trent shook his head, and my heart seemed to stop. The strip hadn't broken. I had destroyed it. I had destroyed it with a wish, with a want, and I'd done it without access to the ley lines. There was only one way to do magic without access to a ley line, and my jaw clenched.

I had mystics in me. I might not be able to hear them, but they could hear me. And I think Al knew it. Was counting on it, maybe. He wanted me to close the lines, and it would take magic to open them back up again.

"Trent—" I started, then scrambled to grab my phone when it began humming again. It was Ivy, and I thumbed the answer tab, fingers shaking. "Ivy! Where are you?"

A velvety, angry voice flowed out, chilling me. "Don't wait too long," Uric said, and the phone clicked off.

Chapter 20

Trent's tiny car was plush, the fan pushing a warm breeze over me, making my hair tickle against my neck. My hands were on the wheel, but we were parked in one of the few spots on the street right outside the I.S. building. It had been a good hour since leaving the square, and Ivy was probably in there by now, settled in whatever cell they'd picked out for her.

Fidgeting, I tapped my nails on the wheel. I'd chipped one somewhere, and I ran my thumb over the rough edge as I looked at Trent drowsing, slumped against the window on the passenger side. Jenks was in the back window doing the same. I didn't want to wake either of them, but if I waited much longer, Cormel would start tormenting Ivy. I had one shot at getting her out, and I was lucky Trent was with me, sleepy or not. His bangs shifted as he breathed, and I stifled my urge to arrange them.

He shouldn't be here. He's too important, I thought, but Trent had flatly refused to leave. And I could use his help—a lot—so I sat here in his car hoping something would happen and I wouldn't have to risk Trent's life in order to save Ivy's.

Love stinks.

My attention flicked behind me to a car beeping as someone locked it. Trent stirred, quickly placing himself and straightening with a soft sound and a stretch. From the back, I heard the hum of wings. "How long have we been sitting here?" Trent asked, fuzzy with sleep.

"About five minutes," I lied, then shot a look at Jenks to shut up when the pixy darted into the front, his dust a tattletale orange. "You were tired. I was thinking."

Trent frowned as he looked at his watch and then to a smug Jenks. "About what?"

About the mystics in me, I thought, then decided to keep lying. "How good that island you offered me three years ago sounds."

"Yeah, Rache, but think of all the stuff you would have missed lounging on a beach with an umbrella drink." Jenks parked it on the dash and ran a hand over a wing, looking for tears.

Trent's smile took on a touch of longing. "Mmmm, yes." He began gathering his things to get out, and I just sat there, not moving. We had a plan, but I didn't like it. He hesitated, glancing at Jenks before settling back. Taking my hand, he pulled me to him across the small space. Eyes inches apart, he earnestly said, "We either go in under our terms, or they come get us when the sun goes down."

"I know," I said, thinking of how little I had in my shoulder bag. I needed his help, but I didn't want to risk his getting hurt—or worse.

Trent's grip on me tightened. "Ivy is down there," he said, and I almost pulled away. "Fighting our way in and out is chancy. This gets us halfway there."

"I know." Damn it, I'd worked hard to stay out of Cormel's grip.

"That is where we need to be," Trent said, and I blinked fast. He'd said *us*. He'd said *we*.

"This isn't your fight," I whispered.

"Rachel . . ." Trent squeezed my hand, bringing my eyes to him. "It is. This is more than Ivy, and even if that's all it was, I'm not about to let you walk into Cormel's office alone. Cormel knows Landon is lying about giving him his soul. He needs you alive to give him what he wants."

Jenks was watching us solemnly. "How does that make this your problem?" I asked, and Trent's eye twitched.

"He needs me, too. He just doesn't know it yet. I have to make him aware of it before he tries to kill me again," he said, and Jenks frowned.

Sighing, I looked past Trent and to the lobby door wishing I knew how to play this political game better. I'd spent two of the last three years of my life hating Trent and the last six months realizing it hadn't been hate at all. "I fail to share your optimism about our intrinsic worth to a master vampire," I said dryly, and Trent ran a hand over his stubbled cheeks, a flicker of surprise crossing him at the rough feel.

"Landon is trying to find enough support to close the lines," he said. "It's the only way to keep the surface demons in reality. If the lines close, magic ends . . ." He hesitated, unable to look at me. ". . . for the most part. If it happens, we need to be in a position to open them back up again."

My lips pressed in disbelief. "And we get that seven stories down in the earth?"

Trent nodded, shrugging helplessly. "If that's where you are, then yes."

He wasn't going to let me out of his sight. The soft snick of Jenks sharpening his sword seemed loud. "I still say that's a bunch of hooey, so I'll let you come with me," I said, and Trent smiled, leaning across the space to give me a kiss. His lips met mine, warm and tasting of cinnamon and wine. My eyes closed, and my heart gave a thump, almost an ache for how much he loved me—I loved him.

"There's that, too," he whispered as he pulled back, his fingers leaving tingles. "Ready?"

I was going straight into the devil's lair, but at least I had company. "Okay, you can come," I said as I looked behind the car for traffic and reached for the door handle.

Trent's touch pulled me to a stop, and I turned to see his worried smile. "Thanks," he said, and I choked back a bitter laugh before I got out, scared for Ivy, scared for me, scared for Jenks and Trent.

But I did get out, breathing in the good Cincy air as I sent my eyes up the imposing facade. Trent and Jenks were waiting for me at the curb, and I hustled forward. "Thanks for driving," he said as I came even and I hooked my arm in his. "The nap did me good."

"Me too, Rache," Jenks chimed in, and I tossed my hair so he could land on my shoulder.

"No problem," I said, playing along with the idea that we could actually do this. I wasn't leaving without Ivy and Nina, and my fingertips tingled as I strengthened my hold on the lines and filled my chi, then spindled even more in my head.

Trent held the door for me, and the wind blew my hair back as I went in. The first floor of the lobby was almost empty, and noise from the second- and third-floor offices filtered down the huge stairway. I looked up at the glass railings and desks, feeling my stomach knot. Head down, we angled toward the bank of elevators. There were at least seven levels downstairs, maybe more. I'd never been there, but Ivy had told me about them one night when she'd had too much to drink.

"The treasurer is on the third floor," Trent said, eyes flicking from the information sign.

"You think they'd let us post bail and leave with her?" I said, and Jenks snorted.

Trent's arm slipped from mine. "It will get their attention."

It would at that, but I figured we already had their attention. I'd sat outside their building for almost an hour. "I say we go down as far as we can," I said as I pushed the button for the elevator.

"Excuse me!" a somewhat feminine voice called out. "Yes, at the elevator?"

We turned to the tall man coming down the stairway. He was in a trendy suit, a living vampire by the way he moved, having confidence and fear mixed in all together. "Jenks, don't go too far but see what you can find out," I muttered, and he tweaked my ear before flying away, his dust matching the color of the marble floor exactly.

Trent sighed as he pulled himself upright and found a professional expression. The sharp taps of dress shoes on the stairs echoed as the man jogged down, his hands free and arms swinging. "Ms. Morgan?" he said as he got close, clearly nervous and more than a little excited. "Could you accompany me downstairs?"

"Maybe." Damn it, this felt wrong.

The clerk moved as if to put a hand to my back, and I jumped to avoid him. Flustered, the man tried to find his aplomb. "Mr. Cormel would like to speak with you," he said, all civilized, but there were two big guys at the lobby doors now, and people lined the glass railings, watching.

Trent scratched the side of his nose, not being ignored as such, but clearly not the focus of the man's interest. "I want to pay Ivy's bond," I said, though it was actually Trent's money that would do it.

Nodding, the clerk pushed the down button on a different panel. "He can arrange that."

"I bet he can," I said as the door opened and Trent and the clerk got in. Eyes wide, the clerk gestured for me to join them, and sullen, I stomped into the lift. "This is not a good idea," I grumbled as the doors closed and the clerk ran a card. Jenks hadn't made it, but elevators had never stopped him before.

"It's better than having them come at us over dinner," Trent said softly, and the clerk caught back a snort.

My eyes went to the panel. Sixth floor? Way out of reach of a ley line.

"Cormel is a reasonable man," Trent said, more for the aide than me. "He's not going to shove us in a hole." Trent's voice had been confident, but the tension in his fingers against my back gave him away. He was wire tight, and my own alarm ratcheted higher.

"Yeah, well, if he tries, I'm going to burn his office down to his red stapler." I could talk to the aide, too, and Trent's hand fell from my back as the doors opened to show a wide, brightly lit carpeted hallway. Two more pretty men and one sexy woman waited by the narrow table against the wall. Orchids and cut flowers made it less six stories under and more thirty stories up. The silk, linen, and jewelry they wore made no attempt to hide the scars.

The clerk with us hit a button to freeze the lift, clearing his throat and holding his hand out. "Your purse, Ms. Morgan. And your cap and ribbon, Mr. Kalamack."

My grip on it tightened. I'd lost contact with the ley lines at about level three. There wasn't much in the bag to begin with, but I was loath to let it go. One by one, I was being stripped of my defenses.

"And your phones?" he added smugly.

Sighing, Trent dug in his pocket. Expression amused, he handed the clerk his phone, cap, and ribbon.

I hesitated, but when Trent glanced at his watch, I shoved my bag at the clerk and stomped out of the elevator. *Was I a demon, or was I a demon?*

I swear, Trent was smiling when he caught up, slipping an arm in mine and slowing me down. Ivy was here somewhere. If they didn't give her to me, I was going to tear the place apart. "I hope your chess game is better than mine," I said softly.

"Me too," he breathed, and I wondered where Jenks was.

"This way, please," one of the men said, and I stifled a shiver at the two guards following. The walls were bright, and with the artwork from multiple periods and schools on the walls and pedestals, it felt as if we were in a museum. The air stank of vampire. No wonder Ivy had worked so hard to get out of here. Damn, my scar was tingling.

"You okay?"

"Ask me tomorrow," I said as the escort stopped before a glass-and-wood door and gestured for us to enter. Heart pounding, I went first, thinking it looked like any other corner office apart from the no-window thing. "It's better than an interrogation room," I said, then spun when Cormel bustled in right behind us, his motions vampire quick.

"I don't like it much either," he said as he moved behind the opulent, but largely bare, desk. "This is my office. Please, sit down. We have time to chat before everyone arrives."

"You mean Ivy, right?" I said, and he laughed, gesturing at the chairs. "Sit down, Rachel."

That made me feel oh so fuzzy and warm, and I eased into the leather chair closest to the door. Trent hesitated, then took the other. "I wasn't aware that you worked for the I.S.," Trent said.

Cormel laced his fingers atop his desk, clearly pleased. "I don't. The office came with Piscary's title. I do enough business here to warrant keeping it, but not enough to have a secretary. Thank you for saving me the effort to find you. Can I get you anything?"

My eyes narrowed. "Ivy," I stated, and he smiled. It was the smile that had saved the free world during the Turn, but it fell flat against me.

"Pleasure before business," he said, chuckling.

Lifting the chair under me, I scooted it forward until my knees were almost touching the desk. Sitting back, I put my ankles up on it. It was meant to bother him, and it did, but instead of pushing back, Cormel leaned forward until I could see he wasn't breathing. "Would you like something to drink?" he said, the words precise and clear.

I took my feet off his desk and leaned over it, the flat of my arms stretched out until my fists were right under his face and I could watch his eyes dilate to a full, angry black. "Where's Ivy?"

Trent cleared his throat. "I'd like a black coffee," he said pleasantly. "I don't know what Rachel wants. Second-guessing her is a mistake."

He'd given me a way to back off, and I took it, settling into the leather chair and trying to keep my breathing shallow and avoid taking in so much vampire pheromones. My God, they were thick down here. "Coffee," I said, and the man eased out of the room, shutting the door behind him. "Cormel, this is stupid. Felix walked into the sun. How much proof do you need?"

"Right to the point," Cormel said, sighing. "But wrong nevertheless."

"It will kill you," I continued, wanting to get out of here. "Don't ask me why, but I don't want to see you dead."

"Dead?" Cormel's pupils shrank, and I breathed easier. "No, you simply don't want to see us progress out of the trap we're in. Felix was not sane. I am."

"You think you're sane?" I said, almost laughing. "The longer you've been sucking people dry, the harder it is to survive the trauma of your soul. Give me Ivy and I'll see what I can do for the newly undead, but you having your soul will cause you to suicide. Landon knows it. He's counting on it. Why are you listening to him?"

Trent dryly cleared his throat, but I fixed my eyes on Cormel, daring him to look away. His lip had curled up to show a little more fang, making me wonder if I should back off.

"Landon is doing exactly what I want," the vampire said. "We will not perish but be stronger for our souls after we . . . adapt. Can you imagine it?" he said, eyes alight. "The power of the undead with the strength of the living?"

I thought of Nina, swaying the crowd with just that. "It's a dream, Cormel."

A flicker of unease crossed him. He knew, and yet he still persisted. Why? Steepling his fingers, he said, "Indications show that with enough time the emotions will fade."

"Guilt takes forever to fade."

"We have forever," he shot back, and agitated, I turned to the man bringing in three cups of coffee. It smelled wonderful, and no one said anything as he gave Cormel his first, then Trent, and finally me. The man practically backed out, and my eyes narrowed at his fear.

"To live forever will elevate us, make us strong," Cormel said, his attention on the tiny spoon as he sifted what was probably salt into his coffee. I'd be willing to bet it shifted the flavor more to a mug of warm, salty blood.

"Ask the demons how great forever is," I said, deciding to skip the coffee.

"Yet you've given Ivy hope," Cormel said. "You must believe it's possible for the undead to survive with their souls if you gave Ivy a magic to capture hers."

Shit, he'd found the soul bottle. "If you took it from her," I threatened, wishing I hadn't pushed my chair up so close. It was Ivy's, damn it! He had no right.

"I didn't take her magic," Cormel said. Expression blank, he sipped his coffee. "You've failed to convince me of the danger. I'll trust Landon a little longer."

"Then you're going to die!" I exclaimed, frustrated as he gestured for someone outside the office. "The longer you're dead, the more wrong things you do to stay alive, and the harder it is to survive the guilt in your soul. It's only the newly undead that might make it."

"There is no wrong!" Cormel shouted, suddenly standing. "I've done nothing wrong!"

I said nothing, not having even seen him move. Trent, too, was a little disconcerted, and I grimaced, not wanting to have Cormel at my throat but needing to make him understand.

Cormel edged from his desk, a hint of confusion marring his confidence. "They gift me with their blood, their aura, their soul. How can it be wrong?"

"It is," I said softly. "That's why you weep when you get your soul back. You can't have everything you want."

"Remember that," Cormel said as the door to the hall opened and Landon was shoved in. He looked disheveled, in the same robes I'd seen him wearing on TV. I figured he was about as happy as we were to be here, but the shimmer of satisfaction in the tilt to his head gave me pause. Slowly I stood, not wanting to be at a disadvantage. Trent remained seated, his fingers steepled and his ankle across one knee. *You shouldn't be here*, I thought, worried.

Landon pulled himself straight, seeming official in his purple and green robes and that hat that Newt favored. "Rachel," he said, giving me a nod. "Trent," he added sarcastically before turning to Cormel. "I told you it wouldn't last if they're alive. Kill them or the surface demons remain in the ever-after."

My gaze flicked to the two thugs just inside the door and back again. "We didn't send them back. Your spell fell apart."

"Rachel tells me you're lying," Cormel said, and Landon's expression blanked. "And I believe the actual wording of our agreement was that I'd remove them from power." He gestured to Trent. "I sent them fleeing to the West Coast. They returned and I isolated them. They have no power," he said, smiling pleasantly. "Bring back our souls. Now."

"The dewar is split because he lives," Landon said, but he was sweating. If I could see it, every vampire on the floor could smell it. "I won't bring your souls back until I have control."

"Won't, or can't?" Cormel sat down, leaving Landon and me standing.

"You'll not survive this, Landon," Trent intoned, and Cormel turned to him in speculation. "You'll die by your own hand. I'll have no regrets."

It sounded poetic, and I hid my shiver by moving to stand behind his chair. It was a good eight feet away from the desk, and I breathed easier. I didn't like his being here. Despite everything he'd said, I'd never forgive myself if he suffered because of me.

"It's business," Landon said dismissively and turned to Cormel. "Well?"

The vampire leaned back into his chair, making it creak. "The living are fascinating," he mused aloud. "You both seem to think you have leverage. You don't." He licked his lips to show his teeth. "I don't trust you, Landon."

"You *didn't kill* them!" Landon shouted, and I shrank back when Cormel stood.

"*You* are *lying!*" he thundered, and the guards outside in the hall came in. "I'm not *going* to kill them. I don't have to. All you need is control of the dewar, yes?"

Cormel wasn't going to kill us. Great. Somehow that didn't thrill me. Trent paled, and I put a hand on his shoulder. The stored energy in his chi tingled through me, and I felt our balances equalize. Neither of us could make a circle, but we had at least one good spell each.

"You will *stop* lying to me," the vampire said, motions smooth and controlled as he ghosted out from behind the desk.

Landon backed up, jerking when one of Cormel's thugs shoved him forward. Cormel closed the gap. "I know you lost control of our souls," the vampire said, reaching to arrange Landon's collar. "You didn't force them back because Rachel and Trent still live. You let them slip away. Blaming them to cover your error is disturbing."

I barely breathed as Cormel leaned in toward Landon. "If you have control of the dewar, can you bring them back?" Cormel asked. "The truth."

"Y-yes," he stammered, and Cormel smiled, giving his face a little pat. "But the dewar won't side with me while he lives."

Cormel turned his back on us to retrieve his coffee. "And the demons?" Smiling, still smiling, he leaned against his desk, looking at me over the rim of his coffee cup.

Landon's attention shifted between Cormel and Trent, clearly nervous. "I can force all of them except Rachel back to the ever-after," he said. "I can then close the lines so the ever-after will collapse, taking the demons with it."

He wants to kill the demons, too? I shook my head in disbelief. "You'd end all magic?" I said softly. "What in hell are you afraid of, Landon?"

Trent was the only one still sitting, and it made him look like he was in control—when he clearly wasn't. Or was he?

Landon sneered, telling me he was afraid. "Don't be stupid. I wouldn't end magic forever. With the entire dewar and enclave backing me, we can reinstate the Arizona lines."

Jaw dropping, I followed that through. He'd hold the entirety of Inderland hostage with the threat of destroying the lines if he didn't get what he wanted, when he wanted, whenever he wanted. Beside me, Trent made a small noise of appreciation, and I tightened my grip on his shoulder. Okay, it was a great idea, but not for us.

"The lines are dead. You can't reinstate them," I said quickly, wondering if Cormel had us down here to affirm or deny Landon's claim. "Why are you listening? He wants you dead."

Expression ugly, Landon took a step away from the thugs. "Nothing is impossible." He turned to Cormel. "And nothing happens until I control the dewar."

Cold, I gripped the back of Trent's chair. Cormel's eyes traveled over all of us, and with a little sigh, he pushed into motion. "We can take care of that right now," he said as he pulled open a drawer and brought out a folder. "Kalamack, where are your daughters?"

"My daughters?" Trent echoed, and my first fear that Cormel was threatening them vanished. They were with Al. Nothing could harm them.

"With a demonic babysitter, I believe?" Cormel drawled. Landon looked awfully smug all of a sudden, and I tensed.

"As a matter of fact, yes," Trent said, and I snatched the papers that Cormel was extending. Trent reached up and took them from me before I could read them, but then my jaw clenched as I saw the first few lines.

"Child abuse?" I spat. "Are you kidding?"

Cormel leaned back in his chair. "No. Mr. Kalamack is accused of child abuse for putting the girls in the care of a demon."

"You can't do that!" I exclaimed, but by Trent's pale face, I thought they not only could, they had.

"Criminal neglect and endangerment," Cormel was saying. "He may as well have dangled them from the top of the I.S. tower. Not a good choice, Morgan. Your idea, wasn't it?"

No, it had been Trent's, but I'd thought it was a good one. "They aren't in any danger! Al isn't going to hurt them!" Trent let the papers fall, and I scooped them up, hands shaking.

"Kalamack's actions are being seen as a political stunt to show demons in an uncharacteristic and false light. Of course, we can avoid all this . . . if you return our souls yourself?"

I froze, my stomach knotting. *Son of a bitch.* Ellasbeth was going to have the girls within the hour.

"This is for both girls." The scent of spoiled wine pushed out the vampiric pheromones. My pulse pounded as Trent stood and took the papers from me. "Ellasbeth can't claim Ray," he said, dropping them on the desk. "She's not her child."

Landon edged forward as Cormel spun the paperwork to him. "Lucy was the firstborn, was she not?" he said, peering over his glasses as he sat down and fumbled for a pen. "There should be sufficient dewar support with just the one girl."

"This isn't about power!" Trent exclaimed, and Cormel looked up from crossing Ray's name off the paperwork. "Lucy is my child!"

"Not anymore." Cormel lightly flipped through the pages and initialized the changes.

Horrified, I stood by the chair. This was my fault. They were doing this because of my association with Trent. He was trying to find a way to live with demons because of me, and it was costing him everything. *Damn you, Ellasbeth. Do you even know what you're doing?*

Cormel slid the pages back in the folder and closed it, an ageless hand resting atop it protectively. "Produce Lucy, or you will not leave this room."

My God, he was going to give Lucy to Landon. The girl was a living symbol of the elven future, and whoever raised her held her power until she was old enough to hold it herself. Scared, I sized up the thugs by the door. I'd had worse odds and fewer assets, but one of them was Trent—and I recognized an odd panic. There'd be no ley line this deep underground. I had only one spell's worth of power spindled, but when Trent reached up and put a hand on mine, I felt a jolting tingle. Lips pressed, he pushed more energy into me, and shocked, I remembered Trent had a familiar. He had access to a line, and through him, I did, too. *Not so helpless then . . .*

But my fear for him remained. "You're holding us on what grounds?"

Cormel looked at the ceiling and pushed back from the desk. "Kalamack for refusing a court order, and you . . . I don't know, but we'll come up with something."

I moved back from the chair, pissed as three of his people approached. "This is why you weep when you get your soul, Cormel. I'm almost ready to force it down your throat."

A flicker of unease passed over Cormel, but it was gone quickly. "Satisfied?" Cormel asked Landon, handing him the folder.

"Your souls will return at sundown," Landon said shortly, and Cormel's smile faded. "We have to wait until the lines are flowing in the proper direction," he added, then paled at Cormel's sudden snarl. "I will personally fix your soul to your body myself," he said quickly. "You can't force the tides, and we must wait until the flow of energy is conducive for the magic required."

Suspicious, Cormel looked at me, reading the truth of it in my grimace.

"And I need time to sway the dewar," Landon said with a relieved exhale.

I'd had just about enough. "You mean parade Lucy about like a trophy," I said as Trent got to his feet, shaking out his coat and stopping the vampires with one hard look. "You haven't earned your voice, Landon. You've not done one thing to prove you're fit to lead a school outing, much less an entire people."

"He can't force the demons into the ever-after," Trent told Cormel.

"Watch me." Landon's face was red as he held his papers like a shield.

"He can't reinstate the Arizona lines once he destroys the ever-after, either," Trent continued. "Cormel, you will be known as the man who allowed an elf to kill all magic."

There were too many people in here, and my back was almost to the wall. My heart pounded. This was easier when I didn't love anyone.

"The risk is worth it," Cormel said, motioning to the two guys still standing by the door. Crap on toast, they had guns. "Landon, if it's not done at sunset, you will die an hour afterward because I will wring the life from you personally. Take your stolen power and go."

Landon looked frightened as he edged to the door. Damn it, if he left with that folder, Lucy was gone. Frustrated and angry, I paced to Cormel. "He can't save you!"

The vampire's eyes were black when they met mine. "And you won't." He eyed the short distance between us and waved his men closer. "Take them away."

Frustrated, energy swirled to my fingertips. I wasn't going to get Ivy or Nina, and coming here had only lost Lucy.

By the door, Landon hesitated. "You strapped them, didn't you?" he asked, and I smiled at Cormel. It was wicked and promising pain, but he wasn't looking at me.

"No," he said, and I was jerked back as someone pulled me away from the desk. "We're seven stories down. They can't reach a ley line from here."

"Trent can!" Landon exclaimed.

I flung my head back. The sudden crunch of cartilage and the cry of pain raced through me, fueled by adrenaline. My grin widened at the cry, and I yanked my arm free, spinning and jamming my palm into the man's jaw for good measure. He fell back, but I was already turning. "You will not take Lucy from him . . . ," I panted, almost crawling over the desk to get at Cormel.

"Down!" someone yelled, and I heard Trent's voice raised loud in elven chanting.

Ta na shay swirled in my thoughts, making my heart pound and my lips pull back from my teeth. "You!" I snarled, and Cormel dodged out of the way, his eyes black in fear as he saw my desperate confidence.

I feinted, then scrabbled the other way, ducking his reach for me and spinning to slam my foot behind his knee.

He dropped. I could hear crashes behind me and Landon shouting spells. Someone shot one of those stupid guns. "Trent!" I shouted, turning.

Cormel's fist slammed into my head. Dazed, I did nothing when his meaty hand fastened on my neck, yanking me up with the strength of a wolf with a kitten. "You think you can best me?" he snarled, and I screamed under the pressure. Tears born in pain pricked, and I hung there, seeing Trent struggling under two vampires. I could smell ozone and gunpowder. A woman screamed for help in the hallway.

"Let go!" I exclaimed, the last of the energy in my chi sparking between us.

Cormel jerked, his hold coming back all the stronger. With a sudden tug, he yanked me to him, an arm wrapping around my neck. "God help me, how does that vampire bitch resist you?" Cormel murmured, his breath in my hair. "Do you know how long it has been since anyone has been able to hurt me?"

From somewhere, ever-after energy burst from me, and with an angry cry Cormel flung me away. I hit the wall, sliding down and rolling to stay out of his reach.

"*Corrumpo!*" Trent raged as I tried to find my feet, failing. Just as well, as a pulse of force exploded from Trent, knocking everyone down. The windows shattered into the hall with a loud pop, and frightened cries filtered in. Cormel was on his hands and knees. His men were disoriented.

I ran for Cormel, scooping up a gun as I went. Energy zinged down my pathways from an unending spool in my head. Trent must have given me more than I realized.

"*Cohibere!*" Landon bellowed from the floor, and I ducked even as Trent set a circle and the magic was harmlessly deflected.

I skidded to a halt behind Cormel, dropping down and wrapping an arm around his neck and shoving the gun to his head. "Give me Ivy. Now!"

Cormel moved, and I stung him with a pulse of ever-after. "You want to live forever?" I shouted, gun pressed against his head. "You need your brain intact! Tell them to back off! *Now!*"

It had gone silent. Landon was flat on the floor, a haze of energy in his hand. Trent was standing over the two vampires he had downed. He had a red mark on his forehead, and his eyes were angry. Whispers came from the hall, and I tightened my grip when six capable-looking vampires edged through the glass in the hallway. Each one of them had a gun pointed at me.

Cormel began to laugh, pissing me off. "Shoot her," he said to his men. "Try not to hit me this time."

My eyes widened. Shit, he had called my bluff.

"Rachel!" Trent cried out, and he went down under two vampires.

My breath came in. I could see everything. Landon on the floor, the court papers strewn before him, a scrap of Trent's pants showing from under the pile of guards, the scent of excited vampire stinging my nose.

The bang of the handgun seemed too small, and I knew before the bullet left the muzzle that it was going to be true. I had no time. My eyes closed and I wished it had happened some other way. Energy tingled, but I couldn't set a circle. Not without being connected to a line. He'd won. The bastard had won.

With a familiar *furp-ping,* the bullet glanced off a bubble and buried itself in the wall.

I tensed, feeling nothing but the sensation of tingles over my skin. My heart thudded in the new silence, and I opened my eyes. Someone had saved me. *Trent?*

But it hadn't been him. My lips parted. Cormel tried to move and I instinctively tightened my grip, shoving the handgun into him harder. A faint haze hung before me like a bubble, but it wasn't the expected red-tinted ever-after with shades of an aura, but a milky white.

Shit. The mystics.

Panicked, I looked at Trent. His face was pale as he struggled in the grip of two vampires.

"How . . . !" Landon sputtered, the papers scattered before him forgotten. "You don't have a familiar!"

I swallowed hard, my grip on Cormel tightening. "Yeah, how about that." Everything I'd been working for to get the demons to survive was gone. Even they wouldn't listen to me now. Not with mystics swarming through me.

"She must have taken a familiar," Cormel said. He had me on weight, but the gun beside his eye kept him still.

"That's right," I lied, and Trent shook off the goons on him. "You there. Put the paperwork on the desk."

"This won't change anything," Landon said. He was right, but I wasn't leaving without Ivy.

"Get Ivy in here!" I shouted. "Now!"

No one moved. "You're just going to have to kill me, Morgan," Cormel said, and it was starting to look like a good option.

Trent tensed as my finger tightened. It wouldn't take much. The world would be a better place. "Rachel! Don't!" Trent called out, and I looked at him, unbelieving.

"Why not?" I asked, watching Cormel's eyes dilate in fear.

"This isn't who you are," Trent said, shaking off the hands holding him.

"How do you know?" I shouted, and the whispers from the hall grew loud. "I already let one sniveling excuse for a person live because you asked me to. Maybe this is who I am! Huh? Maybe I'm just a murdering bastard and you don't know it! Why should I be any different from you? Why!"

I swear I saw a drop of sweat trickle down Cormel's neck. He wasn't breathing, terrified.

For three long seconds Trent thought about that. Head dropping for an instant, his eyes rose to find mine. The enormity of the past two days was on him, heavy and thick. "You're right," he said softly. "Do what you want."

Cormel's eyes closed to hide the fear and hope that I might shoot him dead and end it all.

Son of a bitch, this isn't who I am. Crying out in frustration, I shoved Cormel away from me. I never saw him hit the floor as someone flew at me, tackling me around the waist and sending me down.

"It's yours, it's yours!" I shouted as one sat on me and spun my arm around behind my back and another wrenched my wrist until I let go of the handgun.

"Get her off the floor!" Cormel bellowed, and I was yanked to my feet again. Like a huge cat, the master vampire paced before the desk, his fear just under the surface. Landon was a hunched shadow gathering his precious paperwork as if it was diamonds in a mine. But I couldn't look away from Trent, strapped and standing with a defiant gleam in his eye and a cut under his cheekbone. His suit was rumpled but the only fear in him was directed at me. He knew the mystics were working in me. I was a loaded gun.

"You going to kill me now?" I said. "And you wonder why you walk into the sun when you find your soul." The soft sound of Landon shuffling papers almost made me sick, and I stared at Cormel defiantly when he jerked to a stop.

"Don't harm her," he said, pointing, and my arm was wrenched back until I saw stars. "Put her in a box. One that has holes so she can breathe. Kalamack . . ."

His voice whispered to nothing, and my breath caught when I realized Trent didn't have the same value I did. My lip curled and I pulled the mystic energy together enough to make my hair begin to float. If he made one move to hurt Trent, it was going to start back up, and this time I wasn't going to hold back.

Cormel's lips were pressed tight as he looked from me to Trent and back again. "Put them both in a box," he said. "Kill his horse, though."

Trent didn't move as two vampires literally lifted his feet from the floor.

"Which one is his?" one of them asked, and Cormel looked at me in disgust.

"I don't know. Kill them all."

"Cormel—" Trent said, his voice cutting off when one of the vampires hit him.

Cormel turned his spilled coffee cup upright. "I'll get my soul, Morgan. One way or another."

"Yeah?" I managed before we were pushed into the hallway, my boots and Trent's dress shoes clinking among the shards of safety glass. We had two vampires each holding us, and though I could do magic, Trent would suffer if I did.

"Hey, Trent," I said as we were shoved past the onlookers and to the elevators again. "Was this about what you wanted?"

"Apart from his killing my horses, yes. Cormel now realizes he needs me."

We were at the elevators, and I looked at him, wondering how big this box was going to be. "Needs you? For what?"

His eye was beginning to swell, and he smiled as the doors opened and they muscled us in. "To keep you from killing him, of course."

Chapter 21

As cells went, it was one of the more spacious lockups that I'd been in. I didn't think it was one of the usual I.S. cells, though I could be wrong—it would be a mistake to lock the undead in a standard bar-and-cot five-by-eight. The fifteen-by-fifteen room had a toilet behind an opaque screen and a pedestal sink. There was even a mirror over it, cemented into the flat gray walls. I hadn't decided yet if it was a two-way or not, and by now, I didn't care.

There was one cot, which Trent was stretched out on with his hands behind his head, staring at the ceiling. One gray blanket and a thin, sad excuse for a pillow was all they had given us. I didn't mind sharing such a tight space with Trent, but I was beginning to have issues with us being down here at all, even if it was nicer than that damp HAPA cell under the museum, or the soft gray nothing of the demon lockup, or even the rat cage Trent had kept me in for a few days.

Frustrated, I looked at him, his green eyes fixed on nothing as he took slow, careful breaths. He was irritatingly relaxed, with his shoes neatly arranged under the cot and his slim feet in their gray socks just begging for me to come over and run my finger up the arch of his foot to make him jump.

His jaw tightened when I sighed impatiently, and I put my ear to the door, listening. It was soundproof, but I tapped it anyway. I still hadn't seen Jenks. Ivy was down here somewhere, too, and I hit a knuckle again, straining to hear an answering knock.

"What are you doing?"

I couldn't tell if the irritation in his voice was real or me projecting. "If we're in a cell block, then maybe Ivy's next door."

"Well, could you do it a little quieter?"

Not believing what had just come out of his mouth, I spun slowly on a heel. He was right where I'd left him, eyes closed and his neck muscles tight. "You want me to be quiet?" I said, and he cracked a single eye. "We're locked in a box and you want me to be *quiet*?"

Trent's eyes opened all the way, and he looked at his watch. "Not bad. Most people would be at my throat in forty minutes. It's been almost three hours."

"Well, I'm glad you're impressed!" Hands on my hips, I watched him swing his feet to the floor and stretch. "Landon not only gets control of the dewar but he also gets Lucy. Because of me. Because if not for me, none of this would be happening! Forgive me for being a little upset."

He eyed me as he finished his stretch, elbows on his knees. "Why do you think everything is your fault?"

"Because it usually is." Ticked, I gestured wildly. "If not for me you wouldn't be in danger of losing the girls, the dewar would listen to you, and you wouldn't be broke. And Tulpa." My face scrunched up in sudden worry and my anger fell flat. "Trent, what if they kill him?"

"Tulpa will be fine." He shook his wrist to spin the zip strip to a more comfortable spot. "I've had rival stables try to break into the grounds, and you were the only ones to make it."

"Still, with one Uzi and a parachute—" I started, and he held up a hand.

"Second, I'm not broke." Trent reached for his shoes, wiggling one on, then the other. "Third, Landon doesn't understand what makes Lucy important. Having her doesn't ensure a following. Stealing her does. Landon didn't steal Lucy, he used the law, and it won't bring him as much political power as he thinks." He hesitated, bringing a foot up to retie a shoe. "And last, if it wasn't for you and Jenks, I never would've had Lucy in the first place."

"Even so." Somewhat calmer, I came closer, wishing they had a chair in here. "They'd listen to you if it wasn't for me. Because of who I am and who I protect." Glum, I sat beside him as he laced up his shoe. Smiling, he put a hand on my knee. *Crap on toast, how does he make everything seem so easy?*

"Demons?" Trent patted my knee. "It's admirable. The vampires are simply afraid."

My breath came faster as I flexed my hand. That hadn't been ley line energy that had spooled from me to make that circle in Cormel's office, it had been straight from the mystics I had stolen from the Goddess. "They're right to be afraid," I whispered, uneasy. "I don't know why the demons haven't started turning the people in front of them at the grocery store inside out. Where do you think they are?"

Head cocked, Trent gazed about our small cell. "I think they're sitting on a beach terrorizing sand crabs. That's where I'd be if I'd just escaped from prison." Rising, he stretched again. His dress shirt had come untucked, and it pegged my attraction meter.

Wrong time, wrong place, I thought glumly. "How long do you think they're going to make us sit down here?"

Trent's eyes met mine through the mirror as he finger-combed some continuity into his hair. "Oh, sunrise tomorrow, I think, when every vampire who gets his soul tonight suicides." He arched his eyebrows at whoever was behind the glass before he turned to me.

"Then you think Landon will get enough support to bring the undead souls back?"

"Fear will push them into it." He was tucking his shirt in. It looked like he was getting ready for something. "It won't be long now," he added as he looked at his watch. "I'd probably feel the charm down here if I wasn't strapped."

Frustrated, I got up. "I flinched. I was so worried about you being hurt that I wasn't paying attention. And then, when I get Cormel where I want him, I chicken out."

Eyes serious, Trent held both my arms to my sides, making me look at him. "I like you when you're good."

I pulled away and flopped down on the bed. "Great, that's great," I said sourly.

Trent hesitated for a moment, and then, with an odd, determined pace, he went to the sink. "Why don't you take a nap. Just lie there and be quiet for a minute."

My head turned and I stared at him. "Quiet?" I almost snarled. "You want me to take a nap? Ivy is somewhere down here . . ." My words faltered as he ran his fingers across the tiny lip over the mirror. "And you want me to take a nap," I finished. "What are you doing?"

Trent's shoulders stiffened. As I watched, he turned the water on full force, and steam billowed up, misting the mirror so I couldn't see his face. "Washing up. Why don't you just shut up? Your bitching isn't helping any-thing."

I'm bitching? "Excuse me?" I exclaimed as I sat up. "I seem to remem-ber you in Cormel's office, too. This was one of the dumbest ideas—" He wasn't even listening to me, and my eyes narrowed, not in anger, but un-derstanding. He was looking for bugs, the mirror eclipsed by steam. "One of the dumbest ideas I've ever let you talk me into!"

He smiled as he shook the water from his hands. "Will you shut up and go to sleep?"

I hesitated, and he made a motion for me to say something. "Go to hell, Trent," I said, then kind of pushed on the bed to make the springs squeak as if I was rolling over.

Trent gave me a thumbs-up, and I carefully sat on the edge of the bed, not moving when he waved for me to stay. Crouching, he reached under the open sink, wedging out a tiny buttonlike object. Saying nothing, he carefully set it on the sink, next to the running water. There was no stop-per, and the water continued to flow, filling it halfway up.

Immediately he crossed the room, fingers on his lips as he went right to the back-left corner of the bed and found another stuck to the frame. This one went next to the sink as well, his eyes full of satisfaction. "That's the last of them," he said, his voice hushed.

"How did you know where they were?"

His shoulders rose and fell. "That's what I've been doing for the last three hours."

I pressed my lips. "You've just been lying on the cot for three hours."

"I've been listening, trying to find them."

I shifted down a smidgen when he came to sit beside me. "You can hear the circuitry? Damn, you've got good ears." I knew that Jenks could hear circuitry, but elves?

"Given enough time." He looked at his watch, grimacing. "It's more like feeling the waves coming off them, like reverse sonar. I didn't want to move until I found them all. Thanks for being so quiet. You really are something, you know? I was serious when I said most people would react badly. Thanks for that."

"Well, it's not the first time I've been in a cage," I said saucily. "Got any carrots?"

He chuckled at the reminder of his once keeping me in a ferret cage. "God, I was stupid," he said, shaking his head, and I touched his face, liking the feel of his bristles.

"We both were." Grinning, I leaned in for a kiss, jerking back when the lights went out. "Was that you?" I said, my flush of good feeling gone.

"No." His fingers found mine, and we didn't move. "I guess they figured it out." He sighed, and I gave his hand a squeeze.

"They wouldn't turn off the lights unless they wanted to get back at us, right?"

Trent made a small noise that wasn't agreement or disagreement, and a thin sliver of doubt wedged itself under my short-lived satisfaction. Maybe they turned the lights off not to disorient us, but so they could burst in and do something nasty.

"Ah, can you make a light?" Trent asked, his voice eerie coming out of the dark.

I froze, my thoughts zinging back to the mystics. He knew I had no contact with the lines down here. It was impossible for me to make a light. "No," I said quickly, my fear finding a closer home than vampires possibly attacking us.

"Rachel, please," he said, his arm slipping around my back as we sat on the edge of the bed in the dark. "I saw what happened upstairs. I know you're not happy about it, but this isn't a bad thing, especially if Landon breaks the lines."

"No, I can't!" I exclaimed, but he knew I was lying, and he pulled me into him.

"Can you hear them?" he whispered.

"No."

He was silent, then, "Are you lying to me?"

"Can't you tell?" I said bitterly.

"Not in the dark," he said, a hint of a laugh in his voice. "Make a light, and I'll let you know." His arm slowly fell from me, and I felt a moment of loss until he found my hands and cupped them in his. I felt our balance equalize, and then my breath caught when a faint glimmer within our cupped hands grew and blossomed.

"*Ta na shay, su meera,*" Trent whispered, and I shivered as I felt him siphon energy from me to him, and then into the charm, using me like a ley line.

"How . . . ?," I whispered, and the light became brighter, bright enough to see his expression pinched with worry and pride.

Damn it, I didn't have time to be fighting the Goddess, the demons, *and* the vampires, not to mention the court battle convincing twelve prejudiced elves that leaving your children in the care of a demon was not child abuse. But what pained me the most was that this—the mystics making our hands glow—was why Al wouldn't talk to me.

"Don't let go," Trent said, his fingers tightening on me so the charm wouldn't break. "Oh, Rachel, it's going to be okay," he said, pulling me into a one-armed hug. "I promise."

My eyes closed. The energy flowing through us somehow felt transparent without the usual taint of ever-after. It occurred to me that if we just left and went to that island in the Pacific no one would care if I had mystics in me or not.

"Are they speaking to you?" Trent asked, the thread of fear he tried to hide sparking through me, crushing the want for sand and sun and solitude.

I pulled back, feeling his absence keenly. My fear was reflected in his eyes, strengthened by love. "No, but they can hear me."

He blinked fast, his hold on my hands tightening. "It's okay," he started, and all the fear and anger I'd shoved down boiled up.

"It's not okay!" I shouted, and the light redoubled, making shadows in the small room. "Did you see Al's face when he saw me? Saw the mystics?" I took my hands from his, and the light continued to glow within them. I didn't know what spell it was since it wasn't aura based. I guess when you're line energy, it doesn't matter. "They're going to kill me."

"No one is going to kill you," he insisted. "Besides, I like the way your aura looks." I tried to smile as he gave me a kiss, his lips finding mine with determination. "And the way you smell with them in your hair," he whispered, fingers firmly at the back of my neck. "Why do you even care what they think about you anyway?"

My eyes closed, and I breathed him in, wondering how it could be so good and so bad at the same time. "Because they're the only group of people who aren't afraid of me."

"I wouldn't be so sure of that," a low voice growled.

My eyes shot to the closed door, then the sink. "Al!" *Shit, how long had he been there?* I panicked, the light glowing like a neon sign of guilt.

Trent stood, tension pulling him ramrod straight. "Where are my girls?"

Al's features creased as he scowled at Trent. "You are late. I told you I had to leave at six P.M. exactly, and it's after that now."

Trent took a step forward. "Where are Lucy and Ray?" he asked again, and Al finally took his eyes off me.

"In their beds," he said, thumbnail running under the nail of his index finger.

"You left them alone?" I blurted out, and Al rolled his eyes.

"Nothing will happen in the time it takes to tell you to find someone else to watch them."

I stood, setting the ball of light on the bed. "It's not like you went to the bathroom, Al, you're across the city. You can't leave them like that! Even if they are sleeping!"

Al's face was ugly when he pulled his eyes from the ball of light. "I'm three seconds away from them," he said with a sneer. "It would take me longer to take a piss than to jump back to them. My God, you're covered with elf shit. How can you stand yourself?"

I dropped back, ashamed and embarrassed. Trent stood beside me, a protective gleam in his eye. "We're a little busy. You think you could watch them for a bit longer?"

Al ran his eyes up and down me again in disgust before turning to the sink and the still-running water. "I see how busy you are. No. I have to go to work."

"Work?" I echoed, surprised. *Seriously?* Then I pulled my thoughts back from how much damage a working demon could do. "We're stuck here," I said, gesturing. "You can't leave them until we get back. It's the babysitter's creed. You have to wait until the parents come home, even if they're late."

Al picked up one of the bugs between two careful fingers. "Ellasbeth is there," he said, as if the bug was a mic. "She's a parent."

"Ellasbeth!" Trent's hand fell from me. "Go back! Stop them! Al, she filed for custody on the basis that leaving them with you is child abuse!"

Al spun, the bug in his fingers crushed to nothing as the sting of that soaked in. "Just. So," he said succinctly, the pain of betrayal simmering in the back of his goat-slitted eyes.

"Al!" I begged him. "You can't leave them with her!"

"I don't fucking care, Rachel!" he shouted, and I stumbled back. "I am a *demon*!"

I lifted my chin, frustration making me reckless. "Liar."

Al's eyes almost glowed in the light from my mystic-powered globe. "Excuse me?"

"You heard me." Trent was edging toward me as Al came forward, and I stood firm. "Now either get your butt back there until we can get ourselves out of here, or *get us out of here yourself*!"

"Ah, Rachel . . ." Trent was wincing, and I stiffened.

Al was toe to toe with me, and my knees shook. I stared up at him, not willing to kowtow to him anymore. So I had mystics in me. I didn't ask for them, and they were coming in handy.

"Get out of here yourself," he said, and I stifled a jerk when he flicked a strand of my hair. "You are disgusting," he said with a sneer. "Slimy with elf shit. Covered in them. How do you stand yourself?"

It wasn't really a question, but at least he wasn't throttling me anymore.

"And you should be glad of it," Trent said.

Al spun to him, and I took a grateful breath of air when his eyes left me. "Glad?" the demon spat, and I swear the hem of his trousers shook with his anger.

"Yes, glad," Trent said. "Landon is trying to shove the lot of you back into the ever-after and break the lines."

A low growl of disbelief and dismissal came from Al. "Never happen."

Trent eased forward to come between me and Al. "What if it did? The only magic will be Goddess based. You'd have to learn wild magic or stay helpless."

Al's eyes flicked to me, and I shrank back. Yep, I could do elven magic. So could they, but they'd have to admit that it was stronger than theirs, or at least more versatile. The chances of that were on a par with, say . . . us making it out of here alive. That is, possible, but only after a lot of hurt and effort. "You've made me late," he said darkly.

"Hey! Al!" I shouted as he grabbed both of us by the shoulder, but he was only jumping us out, and I felt nothing from the mystics even as the shadowed darkness of the room seemed to fold in on itself, replaced with the brighter warm glow of Trent's upstairs living room.

"Thank you," I breathed, and then my jaw dropped. "What did you let them do?" I said as I looked over the mess the living room now was.

"Ah . . . ," the demon said, clearly surprised as well.

Trent shoved Al's grip off him. "Lucy? Ray!" he shouted as he darted into the nursery.

"Three seconds?" I said tightly, striding after Trent.

"Well, ah . . . ," Al stammered.

"Rachel!" Trent shouted from the nursery, chilling me. "Call the switchboard. Tell them we need a med team."

Shit. I shoved past Al to look into the once-cheerful room. Fear made my pulse fast, but the room looked normal apart from Trent kneeling beside Quen, prone on the floor beside one of the toddler beds. Memories of seeing Quen dying in a field after trying to protect the woman he loved flashed through me.

But Quen was still conscious, and a hand reached up to grip Trent's shoulder. "We found them alone," he said, pain-filled eyes touching on Al briefly. "Ellasbeth had a court order and eight magic users. Jon . . . followed them. He wasn't hurt. Better than me, I suppose."

Better? No. But he was more savage.

"Where?" Trent demanded as he helped Quen sit.

"He's very upset, Sa'han," Quen choked out, then touched his mouth to have his fingers come away red with blood. "That's not good."

"Where!" Trent asked again, and Quen eyed him with a hot, fervent gaze.

"If we knew that, he wouldn't have to follow." Quen winced as he got his legs straight and tried to get up. "Ahhhhh, that's going to hurt tomorrow."

Trent's exhalation was loud as he stood, arm down to help Quen stand as he looked at me. "Did you call them?" he asked me.

"No." I turned to leave, needing to dodge around Al. "Don't you have to go to work or something?" I said bitterly. The girls weren't in any danger, but it still pissed me off.

"Uh . . ." Al held up a finger in thought, but his confusion was coated with guilt.

"Whatever." *Was it zero for the switchboard, or one?* I thought, not remembering in my panic.

I reached for the phone. Pain ripped through me, hard and fast. Gasping, I fell, the shallow stairs cutting into me as I landed. My breath came out of me in a pained groan. Eyes wide in agony, I could do nothing as my hand shook on the upper tile floor, outstretched for the phone and cramping as fire burned along my long muscles.

It was a curse, the same smothering black that had found me on the West Coast, now rolling over me with the unstoppable strength of waves against a cliff. A bright red seeped from a cut on my hand, the sharp throb hardly noticed over the spike driving through my head with each panicked pulse of my heart. The curse dove deep, the way easy for having been in me before. It was stronger, more focused, and I took a gasping breath, feeling it tear me.

"Rachel?" I heard Trent call, and my eyes found Al.

He was down as well, eyes open and glazed as he fought the same thing. Synchronized to the beat of ancient drums, we both clenched as the curse dug into our souls and began to pull.

"Trent . . . ," I tried to shout, but it came out in a whisper. My eyes opened, finding the clock in the kitchen. Sundown. This was the elves.

My teeth clenched. "No," I gasped, pulling my knees forward and inching toward Al. I might be able to fight this off, but Al . . . Al had no escape. "Not. Al!" I groaned, trying to get up the two stairs between us. My hand shook as it stretched out. Grasping. Reaching. I could not . . . breathe!

"No!" I said again, dragging myself forward until I finally touched his hand.

My breath came in cleanly, and I dove into his mind, finding the toe-hold the elves' curse had. *Not him!* I said once more, wedging the curse out of him with the clear, pure energy from the mystics.

With a resounding crack, Al's presence snapped from the elven curse. The how of it flew on wings of thought to the rest of the demon collective, and I felt them all break from it.

For an instant I hung in the demon collective, seeing them all as individuals, their fears, their pain, the tiny slip of hope they allowed themselves. Smothering them like a fog was the elves' plan of how they were going to imprison them and break the lines, committing the entire demon collective to a slow, terrifying death as the ever-after shrank to nothing and finally vanished.

And then they realized that they'd escaped once more.

Rage filled me, not mine but no less potent. With one thought, the demon collective bounced the curse back into the elves.

No! I demanded, overwhelmed as the elves spinning the curse were struck by the demonic anger, swamping them and turning their magic against them, snuffing it out to send their intent coiling up like a plume of smoke from an extinguished candle.

No! Stop! I demanded as the demons gleefully rolled the elves about, disorienting them so they could affix the curse to them and shove them into the lines and oblivion.

I reached for a frightened presence, trying to save just one . . . But the elf fought me, thinking I was trying to harm him. Claws raked through my aura, and I had to let go. *Stop! Stop this now!* I demanded, and it was as if someone backhanded me, sending me flying into nothing.

"Rachel!"

My eyes flashed open as Trent touched me. Mystics swarmed over us, blanketing the fire in my thoughts. I couldn't hear them, but they could hear me. *Stop this!* I screamed into my thoughts, and with the clean stroke of a knife-sharp thought, the mystics severed the demon collective from the dewar.

Beside me on the floor, Al gasped.

"Oh God, that hurt," I breathed, then groaned when Trent yanked me to him, almost crushing me as he sat on the highest step and held me in his arms.

"Are you okay?" he said, fingers splayed behind my head as he held me. "They burned you! Look at me! Rachel, are you okay?"

He let go just enough to see me, and groggy, I peered up at him, wondering why my skin wasn't red. It felt like I'd been burned. "'S okay," I lisped. "I'm here." I started to shake, cold though my skin burned. The mystics were thick. Everything hurt. "I'm fine. I'm okay. Look. I can tap a line and everything."

I didn't tap a line, but my hair floated as if I was, and the burn ebbed to a familiar tingle. "Where are the girls?" I said as I ran a thumb under his eye. For crying out loud, he was worried about me.

"With Ellasbeth, I presume," he said, and my gaze flicked over his shoulder to Quen staggering out from the nursery.

Al picked himself up, stiffly tugging at his lace cuffs and brushing cookie crumbs off his crushed velvet. He was avoiding me even as he stood there, listing slightly. He had to see the mystics on me, making my skin tingle. *Had the collective seen them?* But how could they not?

"Thank God you're okay," Trent said, crushing me to him again.

"The girls," I protested.

His breath came fast, and he held me tighter, so close I couldn't see Al. "Ellasbeth has them, not a terrorist. We'll get them back."

Quen coughed, and I pulled back to see him leaning heavily against Ceri's old high-backed chair. He held his ribs, and his nose was bleeding. "You are a poor babysitter, Al."

Al opened his mouth to say something, and Trent gave me a little shake.

"How am I supposed to let you go off and do things when you might be pulled out of my reality like that?" he said, and I winced as his aura seemed to tingle through mine.

"I don't feel very good," I said, the sensation of being overly full making me ill.

Trent tensed when Al leaned over to peer into my eyes, his hands on his knees as his back hunched. "I'm not surprised," he said dryly, giving me a final grimace before he slowly, almost painfully, walked down into the living room. "May I use your phone?"

Surprised, Trent's grip on me eased. "Sure," he said cautiously, and I took the tissue that Quen handed me.

"What does a demon need with a phone?" I said as I eased myself out of Trent's lap and just sat there on the stair, heart pounding and wishing the mystics would go check on something. Anything. Would just leave me alone.

Al gave me an askance look, hesitated as he peered over his glasses at the phone as if never having used one before, and then began punching buttons. My nose was bleeding, and I dabbed at it. "Al?"

"What," he said flatly, turning to stand sideways to me.

I cautiously brought up my second sight, relieved that it didn't hurt. His aura was patchy but enough of it was there that he could do magic. Trent's glowed with agitation, and Quen's was dark with regret and guilt. "I'm glad you weren't pulled back."

He frowned at me, then turned his back on us. "Good evening. This is Al." He hesitated. "Then why did you give me this number? You'd rather I just pop in?" he drawled suggestively.

Trent sat on the step with me. Leaning over, he whispered, "Who?," and I shrugged.

"E-e-e-exactly." Al looked back at us with an uncomfortable expression. "I'm informing you that circumstances require that I will not be able to clock in this evening at the required time." I froze as Al's eyes met mine for a moment. "As a matter of fact, I am, so I would appreciate it if my restitution would reflect that fact."

Restitution? As in paycheck?

"Not long," Al said, again looking at his nails. "Fifteen minutes ought to do it." He smiled wickedly. "Thank you. You too."

You could almost hear the silence crash down as he hung up the phone. "Where did you learn your phone etiquette?" I asked. My long muscles ached, and I rubbed at my calves.

Al fluffed the lace at his throat. "I had a craving for secretaries in the eighties until the hairspray began to catch in my teeth. Excuse me."

Quen pulled himself upright, the tissue wadded up in his fist. "Take me with you."

"Take you?" I said, becoming alarmed. "Where are you going?"

Al made a face at me, then looked at Quen. "Why should I?"

"Because you lost them," Quen barked, and my heart leapt. Al was going to retrieve the girls? Why? Why did he care?

"You're going to get them?" I tried to stand, but by the time I managed it, Al and Quen were gone.

I spun, reaching for Trent when my balance left me. "You think?" I said.

"I don't know." Trent steadied me. "He did lose them."

My pulse hammered. "And they expect us to just sit here and wait?"

"Well, he did say fifteen minutes."

"I can't sit here for fifteen minutes not knowing. I have to—" I wavered on my feet, breathless. Trent's hand on mine gripped harder, and a hand cupped under my elbow.

"You're as cold as ice. You need a bath."

"Trent . . . ," I protested as he helped me up the last stair and aimed me to his bedroom. His tub was bigger than the one in the guest bedroom. "I can't take a bath. The girls . . ."

But he just kept pushing me. "A demon, Quen, and Jon have gone to get them. I'm more worried about Ellasbeth and Landon. You need to learn the art of delegation."

I snorted, scuffing slowly across the carpet. Actually, a bath sounded great, and I winced when I thought of everything that had happened between now and my last shower. "Hey, I'm sorry about Lucy and Ray. I never thought he'd leave them like that."

Trent pushed the door open with his foot. The room was dark, the vid screen on one wall showing a live feed of the orchard, dim with sunset. "He was in a hard place," he said softly.

"Hard place!"

"He knew you were in trouble, and he loves you, Rachel."

I stopped dead in my tracks, pulling out of Trent's grip and putting a hand on the wall beside the bathroom door. "He does not!"

Trent's smile was easy and gentle as he reached a hand past me to flick on the light. "He does," he said as he slipped an arm behind my back and breezily ushered me in. "Not romantically, or even that of a father for a daughter, but he does. I think he sees something in you that he lost a long time ago and still mourns. He knew what would happen if he left the girls, and he went to rescue you instead."

Rescue me instead? I thought, feeling colder yet.

"That we were late in getting back was just an excuse to hide his fear for you. I would've done the same. The girls aren't in any real danger, even if Ellasbeth has them. Not like you."

Trent turned on the water, jiggling the taps until he was satisfied. "You think . . . ," I murmured, and he straightened, shaking the water from his hand.

"I know."

My expression must have shown my panic because he took my shoulders. "Don't read too much into it. It could have been coincidence."

"Right." I couldn't meet his eyes as a sharp hail came from the living room and Ray's crying suddenly pulled at my heart.

"I'll be right back," he said, almost jogging out of the bathroom.

"Be right back," I muttered as I turned the taps off. Glancing in the mirror, I shifted a strand of hair out of my eyes and sighed at my reflection before I pulled my shoulders up and tried to walk as if I didn't hurt everywhere.

It was a frightening thing to have the love of someone so determined, resolute, and unafraid of committing a great wrong for his personal right. The love of two men so determined, actually. I hoped I survived it.

Chapter 22

Bare feet scuffing the carpet, I halted just outside Trent's room. Trent was in the kitchen, taking Ray from Quen. The little girl was crying softly, clearly distressed. Al stood stoically beside the small breakfast nook, looking awkward in that suit from the forties. Quen was beside him, his weight on one foot and nursing a new bruise. Jon was with them, and a knot eased even if the tall, sour-looking man was red faced and furious.

But it was on Al that my attention lingered. I wondered at the shift of clothes and if what Trent had said about his making decisions based on a deeper feeling—his loss of something he now saw in me. Had he come to save me knowing he could get Lucy and Ray at his leisure?

And then it hit me. Lucy wasn't here.

I crossed the sunken living room, stomach light and uneasy. "Where's Lucy?"

Jon tensed, his long face becoming ugly in hatred. "He left her!" he snarled, and I reached for Ceri's high-backed chair, my skin prickling from a heavy draw from the line bisecting Trent's grounds.

Trent backpedaled toward the stairs, his hand protectively over Ray's head. Quen moved forward, first blocking Jon's outthrust, glowing hand, and then grabbing his wrist, wrenching Jon to kneel with his arm pulled behind him, almost snapping his elbow. Al stood there, suspiciously quiet, his belligerent expression hiding what I thought was guilt.

"He left her there!" Jon exclaimed, his short graying hair hiding his face, turned toward the floor. Ray's voice rose up in distress, higher than I'd ever heard it. "He left her there with that monster of a woman!" Pain making his eyes stand out, he looked up past his bangs to Al. "Demon or no, I will kill you for that."

My eyebrows rose as I remembered the savagery with which Jon had attacked Ellasbeth's people when they'd threatened the girls. Perhaps I was lucky to have gotten only pencils poked into me when I'd been a mink in a cage.

Trent's lips were a thin angry line. Ray was miserable in his arms as she clung to him. He wasn't saying anything, so I stomped over to Al, keeping clear of Quen and Jon from a faint sense of prudence. "Hey! You lost both of them. Why did you only bring one back?"

Al's gaze came back from Ray, his eyes flicking from me to Trent. "I have to go. My compensation, please."

My jaw dropped. "For babysitting?" I said, glancing back to Quen wrestling Jon back into submission. "Where's Lucy?"

Trent tried to be calm as he jiggled Ray, but his red ears gave him away. "I want to know if it's because you're angry with Rachel, or if you're actually trying to work within the law. Al?"

I jerked upright, spinning to them. "Law?" I blurted out, remembering that ridiculous claim Ellasbeth was filing. "You mean that lousy scrap of paper? Al! Are you nuts? That is full of crap and you know it!"

Al's shoulders stiffened as if taking on a burden. "She had a legal right," he said softly, and Jon grunted in pain, almost on the floor under Quen's nerve hold. "A legal paper and a scary woman from social services. Even a babysitter has to honor that. I have to leave. I'm late."

I reached out, jerking my hand back when he spun at my faint pull on his sleeve. "Not yet," I said, backing up. "You still have three minutes before you have to be at work. What do you do, Al? Are you Mickey D's newest fry cook?"

Okay, that may have been a little bitter, but how could he honor a stupid scrap of paper that was bull to begin with?

Trent patted Ray, the little girl finally having stopped crying. "If I'm not mistaken, he works for . . . the I.S.?" Trent guessed.

"The FIB, actually," Al said, and I sank down into a chair at the break-fast nook. "I chose the FIB over the I.S. because the I.S. currently functions on decisions from old white vampires who have lost touch with the ever-changing social structure and are slowly losing power. Progress and all."

Thunderstruck, I blinked. "You work for the FIB?"

Al tugged his suit coat straight. "I accepted a request to investigate the damage to your church initially, but I like it and I needed a job on the rental agreement other than former emperor of China." Trent was chuck-ling, but I failed to see anything funny.

"I get to push people around, poke my nose where I want, and no one stops me. At least not more than once," Al finished with a familiar evil smile.

Tired, I rubbed my forehead. "Did they give you a bright shiny badge?"

Al flushed, but I figured they had when he touched a breast pocket. That explained the weird questions he'd asked me earlier. Maybe he'd tell me how my case was going if I asked.

"I think that's commendable," Trent said, and Al's face twitched. "Quen, I left my wallet at Cormel's."

My God, he was going to pay the demon.

With a final pinch to tell Jon to behave himself, Quen let go of Jon. The taller man rocked into a sitting position, rubbing his shoulder as he slowly got up. Quen reached for his wallet, reminding me that my shoulder bag with my phone, keys, and splat gun were still at Cormel's as well.

"Commendable," I grumped. "Like me trying to get the world to ac-cept demons."

Trent took the cash that Quen handed him, easily jiggling Ray on his hip to have two hands free. "Who else will keep them in line?" he said as he handed most of it to Al. "You?"

Elbow on the table, I shook my head. "Heck no. Al, you can have the job."

Trent faced the demon. "Thank you for the return of Ray," he said calmly, but I could tell he was annoyed, not at Al, but himself.

"I can't believe you're paying him for that," I grumped.

"Rachel . . . ," Trent admonished, and I stood. Ray was reaching for me, and I went to get her. She looked miserable, far too aware of what was going on for her age.

Al looked at the folded money in his grip, never opening it to count it. "This is the damnedest way to run an economy."

I rocked Ray, the little girl snuffling pitifully, her grip on me tight and endearing. "Better than blackening your soul."

Al's expression became blank. "I fail to see the difference."

Trent gave Jon a sharp look to be quiet. "I know what you did. Thank you. I would have done the same. I'll get Lucy back on my own."

The demon's face twitched. "It was an accident," he said flatly. "If you get the paperwork that returns Lucy to you, ah, just summon me."

Had he just acknowledged that he cared? And what was with the request to summon him? My anger faltered. Perhaps the situation was bothering him more than I realized. And besides, it was impossible to be angry when holding Ray.

"It would be an honor to work with you again." Trent held out his hand, and Al took it, leaning in over their clasped fingers and jerking Trent off balance and into him.

"Don't think this means anything," Al said, then shoved Trent back. Al nodded to me, glanced at Ray, and vanished in an inward-falling haze of ever-after. A scuff behind me pulled my attention to Jon and Quen. I couldn't tell what had happened, but both men were angry, Quen still favoring that one foot.

"Huh," Trent said introspectively as he flexed his hand. "How about that." His gaze clearing, he smiled at Ray, still on my hip. "It's okay, sweet pea. We'll get your sister back."

I frowned as I realized the little girl had a silver flower in her grip that she hadn't had before Al left. There was no way I was leaving Lucy where she was, court order or not. "I don't have a problem breaking the law," I muttered. "Quen, you want to ride shotgun?"

Quen jolted into motion, and Trent raised his hand. "Stop," Trent said, his voice tired. "Please stop."

I scowled and Trent reached for Ray. "Jon, will you put Ray to bed for us?"

He was still waiting for me to hand him Ray, and the little girl gave me a big sloppy kiss, her tiny arms clinging around my neck with a feeling of trust I was loath to let go of. She smelled like lemon and sea grass, and her cheek was cool when I kissed it. I gave her to Jon, and the tall man made no move to take her to the nursery.

Seeing our determination, Trent shifted his weight and rubbed his forehead. "No one is going after Lucy right now," he said, and Quen dryly cleared his throat. "She isn't in any immediate danger. As ugly as Ellasbeth is in her efforts to gain her, she isn't going to harm Lucy. I'm more concerned about the immediate threat of the dewar."

"Exactly," I said. "With Lucy, they can do whatever they want. We need to get her back."

Ray was reaching for Trent, and Jon passed her to him so she could give him a good-night kiss. I watched his face, seeing the pain flash over it even as he held the little girl. Hand against her back, he looked at us in turn. "After having their own curse bounced back at them, I don't think they'll ever get the support to destroy the demons, Lucy or no."

"Maybe," I admitted grudgingly. But their fear would eventually turn to anger, and then action.

"It's late," Trent said as he gave Ray to Quen, the little girl reaching to go to her other daddy. "I'm going to have a quick shower and catch up on my sleep. I want to be up an hour before sunrise tomorrow. Quen?"

"Yes, Sa'han," the dark elf said, his manner subdued as Ray gave him a little-girl kiss.

I eyed him and Jon suspiciously. I wouldn't have put it past them to sneak out of here on their own, direct request or not. "That's it, then?" I said sourly.

Trent smiled, but I could tell he was dead tired. "Delegation, Rachel. It's how things get done." He hesitated, frowning. "Or forgotten. Which reminds me. Quen, could you move the horses in? Cormel threatened them."

I could tell by Quen's expression he was thinking the same thing I was. Busywork to keep him occupied until morning? "Credible?" he asked, craggy voice catching as he handed Ray back to Jon, putting her full circle.

"He's going after Tulpa to cut off my access to the lines while underground, but he'll take out the entire herd to get him. Chances are Cormel is going to be busy with the returning souls, but I don't want to risk it."

Quen was scowling, his midnight plans probably foiled. "Yes, Sa'han. I'll forward all your calls to your secondary phone." He turned to me, inclining his head with an unknown emotion darkening his mood. "Rachel," he said flatly, and then he turned to the stairs, moving slowly to hide his limp.

I wished *I* had a secondary phone. Trent was standing a little too close, and I looked up. "Your bath?" he prompted.

"I can't believe you're going to take a nap," I said as I glanced at the clock. "The only reason the dewar failed was because the sun was down and the lines were flowing contrary to shoving someone into the ever-after. Soon as it comes up, they'll try again. And what about all the undead? We've got surface demons running around again. I can feel it!"

Trent's hand went behind my back. I would've protested as he escorted me forward except I liked his hand there. "They didn't fail because of the flow of the lines. They failed because of you," he said, almost whispering it.

The nursery door shut with a soft and certain snick that Jon somehow made sound accusing. My steps into the lower living room slowed. Trent had asked Jon to put the little girl to bed to try to bring him down from his anger and rage. Suddenly I felt a lot more worried.

"Ahh," I hedged, not wanting to call it a night quite yet. "Can I use your phone to call my mom before she storms the I.S.?"

Trent's hand made tingles as it slipped from me. "Sure. Good idea."

"Thanks. I'll be right in."

He gave me a faint smile, hesitating at the door to his rooms. "Take your time. I'll be in the shower."

The couch pillows were on the floor, and I picked them up, replacing them before I sat down with the phone. The memory of being attacked washed over me, and I quashed the surge of anxiety. Trent had left the door open, unusual for the privacy-loving man. It was a clear indication that he was on edge and didn't want anything closed between us. The shower went on as I punched in my mom's cell number, and the faint soft sounds of running water were soothing.

My eyes roved over Trent's living room as I waited. It wasn't that bad, especially compared to the ruination of my church, and as the call connected, I stood to fix one of the pictures. I took a breath as the line clicked open, but my mom was faster.

"Trent?" her voice came, worried and fast. "Where are you? Is Rachel with you?"

I smiled, feeling good all of a sudden. "It's me, Mom. We're good. Al helped us."

"Your demon?" she blurted out, and my heart leapt as Jenks's wings became obvious in the background.

"Mom? Is that Jenks? Can I talk to him?" Thank all that was holy. Something was going right for once.

"I thought the demons were pissed at you," my mom was saying, but I hardly heard her. Ivy. I could hear Ivy! She was okay? She was with my mom!

"Thank God you called," my mom was saying. "Ivy's made an unholy mess of my front sitting room. Sweet Jesus, that woman has a temper when planning things. I don't know how Nina puts up with her, the sweet dear."

"Mom! Let me talk to Ivy," I said, then lowered my voice before I woke Ray up. "Mom!"

But she wasn't listening, hand over the phone with a muffled, irritated "What? No," and then an indignant "Hey!"

"Rachel?" Ivy's soft gray voice filtered through the phone, and I closed my eyes, holding the warm plastic to my ear and almost rocking in relief. Jenks was there, too, swearing at Tink, the sun, and her unmentionables.

"I'm fine. I'm at Trent's," I said, choking up. "I thought Cormel had you. They called on your phone."

"I lost it at the square. David got us away. Why did you go to the tower? Rachel, you could have been killed."

Tears warmed my eyes, and I wiped them away before they could fall. She was okay. I wouldn't have to live with the guilt of her languishing in a cell because of me. "I thought they had you . . . ," I said, sounding weepy. "Jenks couldn't find you. We thought—" My words choked off, and I just smiled. *Her phone. All they had had was her phone.* Jenks's wing clatter sounded like static over the line as he hovered by the receiver, and all I could do was grip the phone and smile.

"So you were going to rescue us? Of all the unplanned, thoughtless—" Ivy started, but I could hear the relief in her voice, and I picked up a vase of flowers, setting it upright.

"Yeah, I love you, too." They were okay. All of them. Slowly my shoulders relaxed.

"Rache, we were coming for you," Jenks said, guilt thick in his voice.

"You did good," I said, reluctant to tell them why Al had gotten me out. "Ah, I'm going to stay here tonight if that's okay."

"Back off!" I heard Ivy admonish Jenks, and I knelt to pick up the scattered stack of children's books. "At Trent's?" she said, her irritation clearly not directed at me. "Good. Don't come back into Cincy or the Hollows yet. It's crazy here, and you can't do anything. Now that I know you're okay, I'm going to head back to my folks' with Nina."

My motion to collect the crayons hesitated. "Maybe I should come in."

"Tink's little candy ass, Ivy, I told you not to tell her that!"

"I said back off! I can't hear when your dust hits the receiver!" Ivy said off the phone, and then to me, "We're fine. Nina crashed, but I think she's going to be okay now. There's no reason to come back until it's safe."

When was it ever safe? I sat down on the edge of the couch, guilt bringing my shoulders to my ears. "I'm so sorry, but you can't let your mom find her soul. Every vampire who does is going to commit suncide in the morning."

"She . . ." Ivy hesitated, and I tensed.

"Ivy?" Crap on toast, how did Ivy's mom find her soul that fast? It was just after sundown!

"She's okay," Ivy rushed on, but I could hear the heartache in her. "She's never wanted her soul before, but after seeing others find them . . ." Ivy's words trailed off, and I pressed the phone to my ear, heart aching. "Rachel, she wants her soul so badly. She knows it will kill her, but she wants it. She's hurting. I've never seen her in pain like this before."

"I'm so sorry," I whispered. Lucy's doll was half under the couch, and I pulled it out, propping it carefully in the crook of the couch. "Maybe . . ."

But there was no maybe. If she got her soul, she would suffer until she brought her soul, body, and mind back in balance—that is, until she committed suncide and died for good.

Ivy was silent, thinking. "It should settle down in the morning, right?"

Or turn really, really bad. I clicked off the table lamp, wanting the muffling gray of shadow. "I, ah, don't have my phone anymore either," I said, reluctant to hang up but having nothing more to say. "Just call Trent to get hold of me." Unnoticed until now, the faint glow of the downstairs bounced against the ceiling to light everything in a soothing haze.

"Trent's number. Got it. Call me before you get on the roads. I'll let you know where it's safe to meet."

This was bad. "Ivy . . ."

"Stay there," she said, voice hard. "I mean it. We're fine."

She was down to three-word sentences. Great.

"Yeah, we're fine, Rache," Jenks said, almost shouting into the phone. "Take a night off from saving the world for once, huh? We got this!"

My fingers were cramping, they were so tight on the phone. "Tell my mom bye for me. I'll be up before sunrise if you need me."

"Me too," Ivy said softly. "Bye."

"Talk to you then." I didn't hang up, and there was a telling hesitation as both of us sat there saying nothing, just . . . silent.

"Well, hang up already!" Jenks said, and I sighed when the phone clicked off. Guilt tugged at me as I set the phone down. Guilt, but what could I do? I had a lot of things I was capable of, but until I had a direction, a place to aim my frustration at, it would be for naught. I wasn't good at waiting, and now I had nothing to do until sunrise.

The doll looked lonely, and I pulled her onto my lap, holding her to my middle as if she were real. The undead with their souls were going to suncide. Every last one of them. I couldn't stop it. As soon as enough of the vampire masters were dead, the real battle between the elves and the demons would begin.

The soft sounds of Jon singing to Ray filtered out into the soothing gray, and the occasional clatter from downstairs gave evidence of Quen's business. The shower had been off awhile, and I wondered how much Trent had heard. Hugging the doll, I looked over the familiar shapes and shadows of Trent's life and wondered if I could fit in here—if I dared to try to belong to something not of my making. Or if I would just blow it all to hell.

Trent's silhouette eased into the doorway, backlit by the soft glow of a bedside lamp. The sight of him drying his hair almost made me cry. I wanted to belong to this so badly, but I was afraid I'd bring only more heartache. Look what I'd done to Ivy. To Jenks.

"I overheard you talking to Ivy. She's okay?"

I nodded. "She was with David all this time. Cormel only had her phone." He had lied, twisted me into coming to him, played upon my emotions because he didn't have any.

Trent was silent, then, "You want to go home?"

My head dropped to my fingers, clenched around the doll. His voice was low, holding emotion for me—about me—because of me. "No," I whispered as I set the doll in her corner.

He didn't move, looking lost as he stood there in his robe. "I wasn't thinking about anything other than preparing for tomorrow," he said, his voice moving up and down like music. "I can take you home. You have other people who need you. Jenks, Ivy, Bis."

My shoulders hunched as I felt as if I'd been punched in the gut. I wanted to be here. I wanted to be there. Fear threatened to swamp me just thinking about what I'd do if something happened to Trent. He always seemed so in control, so capable. Unfortunately his confident past was starting to get him in trouble in his shaky present. A mere six months ago, Cormel would never have dared to restrain Trent.

Trent tossed the towel to a chair. "Rachel?"

My head snapped up as the door to the nursery softly opened. Jon came out, moving like a shadow or a thought soon forgotten. His long face held no expression as he took in me sitting on the couch and Trent in the doorway. "Excuse me, Sa'han," he said as the door shut behind him. "I'll help Quen oversee the horses being brought in."

Trent scrubbed his scalp with his fingers, looking so much like I wanted him to be that it hurt. "Thank you."

A lump had formed in my throat, and I swallowed hard as Jon gave me a last evil look before he went downstairs. I'd never seen Trent's underground stables, but apparently he had an entire arena to practice his horsemanship in at a pleasant sixty-five degrees even in the winter.

"I'll get dressed." Motions abrupt, Trent turned away.

"Trent," I called, and he stopped short at the guilt in my voice. I said nothing when he came to join me when I gestured helplessly. He sighed when he sat down on the couch, smelling of soap and meadow and spiced wine.

He was tired, and I looked at our hands twined together. "I don't know how you do it," I said. "Going to sleep whenever you get the chance."

Trent smiled, his thumb rubbing my palm both rough and gentle. "It comes from trying to live with a human clock for most of my life." His arm went around me in a sideways hug. "I'm sorry. I was selfish to try to keep you here. Much of this feels like my doing."

"You haven't done anything," I said, leaning into him as his grip on me eased.

"That's just it. I feel as if I've been more of a hindrance than anything. I really thought we could walk in there and still get back out."

I gave his fingers a squeeze. "And you got caught. I know the feeling. Don't worry about it. How were you to know that Cormel . . ." I stopped and bit my lip. *That your clout was so damaged by me that it couldn't keep you safe anymore.*

"My selfish desires screwed up the alliance that would have united the dewar and the enclave under one voice." His head was down and his words were soft as he gave voice to long-held guilt.

Dropping my head onto his shoulder, I stared at nothing. "The dewar would have divided anyway, and you'd be married to Ellasbeth," I said, and I actually felt him shudder.

"No. You're right," he said quickly. "But no one is *listening* to me anymore."

I smiled in the dark, my fingers tracing the lines of his hand in mine. I'd never seen anyone who had two life lines before. He wasn't used to having his words ignored, and I understood his frustration.

"Three years wasted." He sighed. "Not to mention most of my business ventures."

"I'm sorry. Maybe we shouldn't have—"

Trent's hand slipped from mine, reaching to cup my cheek. "Don't even think it," he said earnestly. "The past few months have been the best in my life."

He was looking at my lips, and my pulse quickened. "Tell me it's going to be okay," I whispered.

His fingers ran a tingling path down my jawline as his hand dropped from me. "It's going to be okay. You want to go home?"

To a soggy church with no kitchen or electricity? Or Ivy's parents' place where the tension was so tight that it almost sang? Even better, a hotel room where I'd dodge my mom's pointed questions while the news inescapably blared? "No," I said, reaching up to feel his new lack of stubble under my fingertips, and I froze when he took my hand, kissing my fingertips.

"Damn it, Rachel," he said, the pain in his voice startling me. "When I saw you on the floor, I thought I'd lost you again."

He was holding my hand close to his chest, and I felt a pang of guilt for his fear. "I'm hard to get rid of."

"Yes and no."

The silence stretched and neither of us moved. It had gone quiet downstairs, and the world felt empty. "Do you think the undead who find their souls tonight will suncide?"

Trent nodded, a shadow in the dim room. "If the curse holds and they aren't pulled back," he said, then gave my hand, still in his, a slight squeeze. "At least Cormel can't blame you."

"He'll find a way," I grumped, and Trent seemed to pull himself together as if turning a page in his weekly calendar.

"There is a meeting tomorrow with a few key people. If you're not busy, I think your presence would be helpful."

Apart, no one listened to us, but together they might. "Let me guess," I said, bringing a knee up onto the couch and turning sideways so I could arrange his still-damp hair. "Whoever is in charge of the I.S. during this mess, the head of the FIB. Ms. Sarong and/or Mr. Ray." I hesitated, smiling. "Mark, maybe."

Trent laughed, the sound of it seeming to ease some of the ugly uncertainty away. "I'd really like you to be there, not necessarily as a demon representative, but as, ah . . ." He winced.

"As someone who might be able to fix this mess?" I said, and he exhaled in relief.

"Something like that."

His hand was on my foot, and I couldn't help a soft moan when his thumb ran right up the side of the arch and pushed on the nerve that ran to my back. "You know, I'm starting to see some benefits from dating a man who has weekly massages," I said, and he began to squeeze my foot in earnest.

"Actually, I'd like Dali there as well," Trent said, but I was hardly listening. "I wonder if he'd come if I asked? Etude, if he could stay awake. The elves are behaving badly, and I'm wondering if there's enough worry to gain letters of intent from them that would outline their concern and their policy against further elf-to-vampire aggression."

He let go of my foot and motioned for me to turn around. "Your shoulders look like rocks," he said. "All the way down to your feet. Five minutes, and that bath of yours will be a hundred times better."

I gathered my hair and turned as he swung one leg up onto the couch, tossing the back cushion to the floor to make more room as he settled me before him. "Sort of like a species intervention?" I said, then stifled a moan when his hands, strong from reining in impossible horses, began working my shoulders. "That's old school."

"What works never goes out of style."

His voice was preoccupied, and my head dropped forward. Trent's leg was beside me, bare where his robe fell away. "I'll see if I can work it into my schedule," I said, imagining there were better ways to use a couch. Unable to resist, I leaned back, ruining my shoulder rub but not caring when I tilted my head into him and found a freshly shaven patch of his neck. His arms shifted to go around my middle, and I smiled when my lips found him.

Trent's hands never stopped moving, becoming gentler as he touched my stomach and made a tingling path higher.

I turned my kiss into a soft, awkward bite. *Oh, this isn't going to work at all.*

Shifting, I turned to face him, settling almost into his lap with my legs wrapped around him. Arms about his neck, I found his ear and nibbled on it as my one foot kicked off another back cushion. *More room. Much better.*

Trent's hands held my waist, his thumb moving, pressing as he began to work his way inward to pull my shirt from my pants. My heart thudded as he slipped behind it, fingers both rough and smooth making a scintillating path up to find the curve of my breast.

His breath against my neck was delicious, and I made tiny hop kisses from his ear to his lips. Trent's touch became aggressive, and breathless, I pulled him to me, very aware that his robe wasn't covering much between us. His mouth against mine sent tingles over me, our passions rising, building upon each other.

Shock jolted through me when his teeth fastened on my lip. My eyes flashed open to find him looking at me, and my pulse hammered even harder at the heated desire in them.

"You're wearing too much," he whispered, and I groaned when his hands eased to my back, motions firm with intent as he reached the top of my pants. His lips found my neck, and I took a long, slow breath as his fingers worked to undo them. My knees were to either side of him, and the sudden give of the button was electrifying—the sound of the zipper bringing me back from the rising ecstasy.

I met his eyes to see his desire mirroring my own. I wanted everything, I wanted this. The silence was profound. I thought about Ray safe in her bed, then Jon and Quen at the stables. My hands were behind his neck, my fingers playing in the damp ends of his hair. "Is it worth it?" I said. "Everything you gave up?"

He couldn't take my pants off with my knees to either side of him like that. There was only one foot on the floor, and it was his. I smiled, knowing he was stymied. "You tell me."

I leaned to find his ear. I felt him tremble, his hands on me hesitate and move against me even more strongly as I nibbled on his ear. "I'll let you know tomorrow," I whispered.

"Mmmm." His grip on me shifted, finding my center of gravity. "I work best under pressure."

"Me too." I barely breathed the words, my hand trailing down his chest to wiggle the last tie closing his robe open. I tensed, knowing he was going to have to do something drastic if he wanted my pants off. His balance shifted, and I countered it, wanting to prolong this. He saw my wicked grin, and he smiled, changing his attack.

He went for my shirt, and I shivered as he pulled it and my chemise over my head in one smooth motion. They fell to the floor beside the couch in a soft hush. The cooler air gave me goose bumps, but they vanished in a wash of heat, driven away as his eyes traveled over me an instant ahead of his hands.

His robe was open, and I eased closer to him, my hands tracing an ever-circling path inward to find him. Trent's breath quickened as I dipped to his inner thighs, and then I gasped when he unexpectedly found my breast and gently bit me. "You wicked elf . . . ," I whispered, reaching for him, then almost lost it when he pulled a trace of energy from me.

My eyes widened at the scintillating feeling icing through me. We'd played with the lines before, and my pulse quickened. It was going to be like that, then.

I felt our auras begin to shift to find a middle ground, and I almost lost it when he suddenly dropped the line and everything he collected washed back into me, balancing in a wave of sparkles along my spine. "Ooh," I groaned, and in that instant of bemused sensation, he shifted his weight, pushing me back into the couch and pinning me there.

His robe fell open around us, and I blinked up at him, reaching to play with the hair behind his ears, letting little spills of energy trace a path where my lips had been.

"Hold still for just a bloody second," he said, and I shivered as he pulled my pants off, dropping them inside out next to my shirt. I arched my back, reaching for him as he returned, his hands tracing my lines from my foot to my hip, and rising higher until he found my mouth with his lips.

We kissed, breath coming fast as waves of energy swung back and forth between us. My hand ran over his tightening muscles, delighting me in how he tensed as I moved from his neck to his arms to his back and down to his buttocks, where I traced little circles.

His hands clenched in my hair as he nuzzled my neck, finding the old scar hidden under my new skin and nibbling it to life.

I could feel him pressing against me, and unable to deny myself and him any longer, I reached to find him. His breath quickened, and we began to move with each other, tiny sparks of energy shifting between us. His head dipped and he found my breast again as I eased my touch inward, muting the energy in my hands until it was a soft, gentle hum.

He gasped as I found his smooth skin. I slid my touch upward, tightening my grip, enjoying his smoothness and wanting him inside me.

"Not yet," he panted, and he shifted out of my easy reach.

I wiggled, and he pinned my arms next to my head.

A jolt of desire shook me, and I lunged for his mouth, his neck, anything as his weight settled on me, pinning me where I was. I found his lips, and he met my fervent need with his own, adding to my desire until I moaned.

I pulled one hand free, traveling down his back and circling in to find him again. His weight lifted, and I guided him in, exhaling as he entered, arching up to find him, letting him fill me.

Exhaling, he pushed against me, and my eyes opened. He looked wonderful over me in the dim light. A rising feeling of sparkles widened my eyes, and I gasped as he slowly pulled energy from me, almost like a slow climax. I could hardly breathe, letting him draw it forth until I couldn't stand it anymore and I pulled it back, making him start as our energies mingled.

I felt him there in my chi, his masculine taste on my lips, my skin, the line now being slowly pulled back into him again.

I let him take it, his warm masculinity slipping away, leaving me wanting, needing. "Oh God," I moaned, balancing, on edge as I pulled it back to me with the sharpness of a cracked whip.

His grip shifted, and I gasped when he took back, his lips drawing on my breast, his need filling me. Sensation slipped from me in a scintillating wave, tripping over every neuron where we touched. I felt my desire building, and with a ping of emotion, I tipped our energies over the edge in one quick wash.

"Oh God, Rachel," Trent gasped.

The unexpected jolt shook me. I reached for him, straining, and with a glorious release, my body shook.

Trent's hands on me clenched, and he groaned, climaxing right as I did.

I couldn't breathe. We hung in a joined sensation of ecstasy as our energy, shared and mixed, pooled and settled, perfectly balanced between us.

My heart pounded. Slowly I opened my eyes, seeing him above me in the dim light. He was smiling.

"Hi," he whispered, propping himself up on an elbow so he could shift the hair from my eyes.

I could still feel him inside me, still feel little jolts of sensation when either of us moved. Smiling, I reached up and tucked a stray strand of hair behind his ear. How could I be this lucky? "Hi," I breathed, my hand moving to feel the slick sheen of sweat on his shoulder. "I've ruined your shower."

"I can take another."

He didn't move, knowing better, and I winced. "Sorry about that."

He knew I wasn't talking about the shower, and he leaned down to kiss me, our lips parting with a sound so familiar, so right, that it made me ache. "Have I ever complained?"

"No, but—"

"Shut up, Rachel," he said, then kissed me some more. I couldn't very well talk with his lips moving against mine like that, and I gave up, giving in to the moment until I had to breathe again.

"We probably should have found a better place than this," I said, and he gave me several more kisses to shut me up.

"It's my house."

He was down to short sentences, which meant he was relaxed and feeling good. I smiled up at him, playing with the hair at the nape of his neck. Why in hell had it taken me so long to realize I loved him? "Okay, but you share it with two other men and two toddlers."

Trent's eyebrows rose, and he glanced over the top of the couch to the stairway. "You live with a vampire and a family of pixies."

Content, I sighed. "And yet we keep finding ourselves in this position." I watched his eyes lose their focus as my inner muscles released. Exhaling in relief, he shifted to lie beside me. There was just enough room on the couch, and I felt happy when he tried to cover us both with the free fold of his robe.

"I'll have to remember that one," he said, arm draped over me. "Get you to think about pixies and vampires to get you to let go of me."

Embarrassed, I ran my fingers over him, following the line of his muscles. "I'm worried. They don't have three miles of forest and a gatehouse between them and the crazy people."

I sat up and he sighed, shifting to sit beside me. "I know," he said shortly as he stood, gathering up my clothes before he pulled me up into his arms. "I'll get you back into Cincy before the sun comes up. Promise."

I gave up, the feeling of being loved pushing all else away as he carried me through his rooms to the warm bath he had drawn for me. And as he used his foot to open and close the doors, I found myself looking over his simple yet complex world, wondering how I fit in. Maybe I should give up on the thinking and just do it.

That had always served me well in the past.

Chapter 23

I couldn't see the sun apart from the glow on Cincy's towers, the blood red slowly shifting to a more familiar gold as it crept down the sides of the buildings as the sun rose. Mark's was busy, the music muted and the conversations tense with fear. It would've been impossible for Trent and me to have found a seat when we'd arrived a mere five minutes ago, but Ivy had been here for hours, rightly worried that the streets would be closed off when the suncides began. We clustered at her table to watch the news on her charging laptop.

Trent fidgeted as we waited for both our drinks and David, the Were currently at Cormel's emergency city meeting. They'd started about an hour before sunrise, continuing as the expected suncides became reality. Trent hadn't been invited, but I'd convinced the shocked man that crashing the meeting was a bad idea. David could bring back the real dirt, and Cormel wouldn't dare stuff the alpha Were in a hole to be forgotten—not as he would Trent. And whereas yesterday I might have gotten mopey about how Trent had been kicked out of his own meeting, now it only made me mad. I loved him, damn it. And everyone else, demons included, would have to get over it.

But the insecurity remained.

Grimacing, Ivy waved Jenks off as his dust blanked the screen, and I leaned forward to hear. Most of the people here were watching something similar on their various devices, and the unending circle of the same bad news of suncides and interviews was making me nauseated.

"... are asked to keep 911 calls to life-threatening emergencies," the professional woman said as she stood outside Cincinnati's main city building. "Suncides will receive faster responses using the number at the bottom of the screen." She took a breath, eyes flicking past the camera to track the sound of a passing siren. "Impromptu meetings across the U.S. in major population centers continue to search for ways to cope and hopefully stem the unprecedented numbers of vampiric suncides linked to soul reunions."

I winced as the woman was replaced by a shot of Edden, David, and Mrs. Sarong going into the very same building, their heads down to avoid the press. It was dark, clearly before sunrise, and I gave Trent's hand a squeeze under the table.

"But it's here in our own Cincinnati that all are watching, as former U.S. president Rynn Cormel meets with various members of the scientific and religious community who flew in earlier today from all points with the intent of developing an end solution to this tragedy."

My hand slipped from Trent's as he stood. "Excuse me," he said, eyes down. "I think our drinks are up. Rachel, you sure you don't want a muffin or something?"

I shook my head. It was too early to eat.

"Living vampires are demanding a removal of the free-roaming undead souls that some are beginning to refer to as surface demons in the wake of the destruction they cause. Experts are advising the living to check on their undead and protect them from unnecessary surface travel. If a loved one does find their soul, they're advised not to leave them unattended."

Jenks's wings clattered, and I followed his gaze to Trent weaving his way to the pickup counter. The coffee wasn't up. He just didn't want to hear any more, depressed that his voice was being ignored and that he was forced to work from secondhand information.

Jenks silently flew after him, startling the man when he landed on his shoulder. Ivy sighed and closed her laptop. Eyes red-rimmed from fatigue, she leaned back into her chair and nursed her sweet coffee. "The news is circling now," she said softly. "Nothing new."

Circling like the thoughts of the undead, I mused, brow furrowed when I remembered that's how mystics saw them—little lights in the dark that never changed. "You look tired," I said, and her eyes flicked to me.

"Didn't get much sleep. Did you stop at the church on your way in?"

My gaze dropped. "No, I'm afraid to." I wanted to know if she still had her soul bottle. I hadn't seen it, but it was small enough to easily fit in a pocket. "How's Nina?"

"Good." Her eyes looked up, and a tiny thrill of emotion spilled through me at the love in her eyes for Nina, the relief. "She's good. She . . . helped me yesterday when I thought Cormel had you. Grounded me. She's with my folks right now. I'm really worried about my mom."

Helped? I thought, imagining Ivy freaking out, her frantic terror disguised as planning a foolhardy rescue. Nina had probably had to take charge to keep Ivy from doing something stupid, such as confronting Cormel in person. *Oh, wait. That's just what I'd done.* But it had probably proved to Nina that her love for Ivy was stronger than her need for Felix, and I smiled because something good had come of it. Things would be better now.

"My mother is terrified," Ivy whispered, her hands laced about her cup. "Torn. She wants her soul. Wants a way out even if it kills her."

"I'm sorry."

Jaw clenched, Ivy swung her hair from her eyes and looked out the plate-glass windows at nothing. "This is hell, you know? An entire people cursed. What did we do to deserve this?"

I knew the demons had begun the vampires, probably as a cruel answer to a wish made in fear that grew like a disease, taking the guilty and the innocent alike. I didn't say anything, and the silence stretched. It felt like it was ending—not just because of the sirens and quiet desperation going on outside the security of the coffeehouse. Just . . . everything. "Ivy . . ."

"I know." She took a sip of cooling coffee, not looking at me. "I feel it, too. I wanted it to last forever, but things change. People change."

She was fingering the bracelet that Nina had given her, and I felt proud of her. "Not everything," I said, reluctant to let her think that after one night at Trent's I was abandoning her, the church, Jenks . . . *One night? Try a couple dozen.*

Smiling faintly she shrugged, barely shifting her shoulders. "How we react to things has. Are you happy when you're with Trent?"

I nodded, not surprised by her question.

"I would have called you a liar if you had said anything else." Sighing, she shifted her cup out of Jenks's dust when the pixy came back with a tiny mug. Trent was still at the counter, sprinkling cinnamon into an open cup.

"I should've come back last night," I said.

Jenks slurped his hot coffee. "There was no reason to. Besides, Ivy and Nina—"

"Shut up, Jenks," Ivy said, a faint blush on her cheeks, but her eyes were earnest as she waved the giggling pixy out from between us. "Sometimes I think Jenks and I stuck with this as long as we did because we were afraid you wouldn't find someone else who could survive you."

Swearing at his spilled coffee, Jenks stopped his gyrating and dropped down. Depressed, I put my head on the table, forehead on my crossed arms. *Someone who could survive me.* Maybe if I didn't keep putting him in life-threatening places.

"You know what I'd like to do once the church is fixed?" Jenks said. "Travel."

"To the Arizona desert?" I said, breath coming back warm and stale from the tabletop.

Ivy chuckled. "In your red boots and hat?" she teased, and I pulled my head up to see Jenks hovering, his dust red in embarrassment.

"It's not that," he protested, almost belligerent. "I could travel, you know."

I picked at a small dent in the table. "I think you should."

"Who'd watch your back?" The pixy snorted, turning to Trent coming back with three steaming cups. "Cookie bits over there? Just 'cause you're not in the church doesn't mean you're not out there doing dumb things."

"Thanks, Jenks," I said, smiling at Trent as he carefully set the hot coffee down.

"Here you go, Rachel," he said, pushing the one with the cinnamon to me before sitting down with his own straight black. "What did I miss?"

His voice was heavy with uncertainty, and I eagerly took a sip, hoping someone else would answer him. Jenks was on the edge of Ivy's laptop, his ankle crossing one knee to mimic Trent. Lips smacking, he took a long draft of his own brew. "I was just telling Rache how we should all move out to Arizona."

Trent relaxed, eyeing Ivy as she succinctly sipped her coffee with deliberate slowness. "Arizona, eh? Too hot for horses. I could go for somewhere else, though."

Surprised, I swallowed the bitter, nutty brew. "You'd move? Seriously?"

Uncomfortable, Trent eased back in his chair. "Sure, why not?" His eyes roved over nothing. "It might be nice to start again without my father's legacy hanging over me." He carefully sipped. "Anywhere else looks real good to me right now."

Jenks rose up, ankle still on his knee. "Meeting must be over. Al is here."

I leaned past Trent to see the back of the store. Al was indeed there in his forties suit, shaking off the last of the ley line as he stood in an elaborately painted circle next to the door to the back. My eyebrows rose as I realized it was a jump-in/-out circle, not so much having any magical power on its own, but simply a designated space to keep clear of boxes and merchandise for demons to come and go as they would.

My eyes flicked to Mark as Al strode to the order counter. *Mark, what have you gotten yourself into, inviting demons into your coffeehouse?*

Trent stood. "I'll get a chair," he said, eyeing the nearly full establishment. Al's presence had been noted, and people were gathering their things and making a beeline for the door.

"Demon grande, extra hot!" the barista sang out, and Mark snagged it before it got to the pickup window, handing it to Al himself with a smile that was too relaxed for my liking.

Demon grande? The barista had put a pump of raspberry in it and a sprinkle of cinnamon.

Ivy didn't move from her slouch as Al came to our table, standing over it and looking at me in disgust. His red goat-slitted eyes shifted to Trent as the man set a chair at the open end of the table, and I stiffened as Al walked behind me. But it wasn't the new chair he wanted, and he shoved the chair away with his foot, turning to the nearest table and glaring at the patrons until they took their things and scattered. Still silent, he moved the new table into ours so hard that Jenks rose up, swearing and shaking hot coffee from his wing.

Motions expansive, Al swung a chair to sit at the head of the now-longer table. I was starting to wonder why he was here. He didn't look happy.

Trent sat back down across from me and moved his coffee closer. "How did the meeting go?" he asked pleasantly.

"As expected," Al growled.

"I didn't know you were there." I stretched my foot out to find Trent's. I knew he hated getting this secondhand, and from Al no less. Feeling it, Trent smiled, but it was tense and vanished fast.

Al wiped his mouth, exhaling long as he came up from his first gulp of coffee. "I was the representative from the demon faction," he said, unable to hide his pleasure at being important and included. "Landon is devious . . . as are most elves. The vampires should be allowed to die; they're idiots, believing in fairy tales and dreams when they know they're damned forever."

I curled my hand around my cup to warm my fingers. "I take it that it didn't go well."

Al looked away as if peeved. "Landon's solution is to unbalance the lines—"

"What!" I exclaimed. "Does he have any idea what that can do? I spent an entire night balancing them and I am *not* doing it again!"

"Wait for the rest," Al grumbled, and I sat back down, not even realizing I'd stood. Jenks was laughing at me and Ivy was clearly amused, but I was pissed. I wasn't going to fix them again!

"His plan is to unbalance the lines, drain the ever-after to nothing, and use the energy of the ever-after's collapse to reinstate the Arizona lines."

I almost stood up again, jerking back into my seat when Ivy grabbed my arm. "Is he crazy?" I contented myself with that.

"Rachel," Ivy murmured. "You're scaring people."

Al hunched at the table, looking depressed, not outraged. "So of course the demons should be happy, happy and go along with it and help, seeing that if there is no ever-after, there's no way to banish us again," he said sarcastically. "Just because the vampires are lobbying for the Darwin award doesn't mean we are."

Trent's finger tapped the table in thought. "Setting aside the obvious downside to the end of magic, how would ending the ever-after solve the problem of the undead souls? Wouldn't destroying the ever-after ensure they remain in reality?"

"Not necessarily." Al laced his hands around his coffee. "The undead souls are still tied to the ever-after through the original curse. If the ever-after falls, they cease to exist. Problem solved, according to the elves. They're not admitting the possibility that demons will fail to exist as well. Apart from you, Rachel." His mood became introspective. "And all those Rosewood babies," he drawled. "How are they doing, the little tykes?"

I figured he knew they weren't dead, but I wasn't going to tell him. Ivy's eyes looked haunted as Al tugged the sleeves of his coat, frowning as if missing his usual lace. "Leave it to the elves to muck up a perfectly balanced curse," he said. "I never liked the cruel savagery of extending some sucker's life by separating the soul from the consciousness. To make that separation last from this existence to the next was too cruel for a demon, hence storing them in the ever-after, but an elf has no problem with it." Sneering at Trent over his cup, he took a sip. "Your race is monstrous."

Trent took a breath to protest, but I waved my hands for attention. "Wait, wait, wait," I said. "Next existence? You mean like heaven? Reincarnation? Seriously?" I looked over everyone. "You want to share with the class?"

Al sucked on his teeth, the sharp sound like a knife from a sheath. "How the hell should I know what comes next, if anything? I wasn't the one pioneering the technology. But I *do* know that if the undead souls have nowhere to shelter until the body truly dies and frees the consciousness, their souls will move on to the next plane, or whatever, without their consciousness. Even Newt doesn't know what happens after that line is crossed, but until now everyone went with a soul and consciousness together." He took a sip of coffee. "Cursed or no."

I sat back, stunned. I had no idea that the demons believed in anything after death, but Al seemed genuinely appalled that Landon would destroy the vampires' souls.

Lips curling, Al sneered at Trent. "Any wonder we tried to kill you foul things?"

"Hey, that's enough," I said as Jenks rose up in agitation. "Trent is on our side."

The door chimes jingled and Jenks darted to the door as David came in with two women, the first professionally dressed and having a sour expression, the second shorter, dressed in softer, flowing fabric that was no less professional. Both women moved with a grace born of responsibility, and I smiled when I recognized Vivian, the same woman from the witch coven who'd traveled with Trent and me to the witch conference last summer. "Vivian!" I called, and she smiled, touching David's shoulder as she pointed to us, then to the order window.

"Give me a sec," she called out. "Vampires can't make coffee to save their souls."

Jenks snickered. "Dr. Anders," he added, and I jerked to a halt halfway to a stand. Crap, the woman was right beside me.

My old ley line instructor pulled her attention from the order line, her narrow face taking in Jenks hovering protectively close. "It's professor now," she said to me as she took Trent's hand as he extended it over the table. "Kalamack," she said, adding, "I'll be right back. Rachel, good to see you looking so well."

Somehow it sounded sarcastic. "I'll, ah, get you a chair," I said, shifting to get out from beside her, grabbing one and setting it right next to Al and across from me. Jeez, the woman hadn't changed at all. Apart from the professor thing. No wonder Trent was so bummed about missing the meeting. This was big stuff and he'd been sidelined.

Heels clacking, *Professor* Anders got in line behind Vivian. Trent and David were gathering more chairs, and Al slowly stood. "Excuse me," he said softly, his eyes on Vivian.

"Leave her alone," I warned him, remembering the demon's liking for high-magic users. Al tugged his suit straight, smiling wickedly as he came up behind the two women. I took a breath to protest, distracted when David swung a chair around between mine and Al's and plunked himself down.

"Rachel," he said, squinting up at me with a decidedly attractive alpha-wolf stubble and confidence. "You're up early. How you doing?"

I sat back down, enjoying the scent of good earth and spicy pine that came from him. I could see the power of the focus shimmering in the back of his eyes, and I figured he was channeling the demon curse strongly today, seeing that he was acting as a mouthpiece for Weres everywhere. "Better than I thought I might," I said, glancing out the front window. "Is someone getting you a drink?"

"Vivian." He twisted awkwardly to retrieve his phone from a back pocket. "I hate meetings," he said as he set it on the table.

I totally understood, and I resettled myself. "Hey, thanks again for helping get Ivy and Nina out of the square yesterday," I said, and Jenks snickered.

"How is your jaw?" Ivy asked, pulling my attention from Vivian's giving Al the brush-off. *His jaw? Why? What had happened?*

Expression rueful, David felt his jaw, his eyes flicking to Ivy with more than a little respect. "Fine, thanks," he grumbled, making Trent smile. "Cormel is still trying to figure out how you two escaped."

Trent leaned forward over the table, eyes dancing. "Her magic carpet, of course."

"I am *not* a *rug*," Al said, and Trent jumped, unaware that the demon had been right behind him. Scowling, Al sat, pushing his chair so far back that he almost wasn't at the table.

Vivian and Professor Anders slowly made their way over, Vivian making a beeline for the free chair at the other end of the table to force Anders to take the chair between Trent and Al. Al smiled lasciviously at the older, uptight woman, surprise coloring his expression when the woman did nothing but give him a dry look and settle squarely in the space.

"Ah, David," I said to distract the demon. "Al brought up an interesting point; if Landon manages to destroy the undead souls, then it might negatively impact the undead, as their souls and consciousnesses might be forever divided. Is Cormel still buying into Landon's lies, or is he just stringing Landon along hoping I'll come bail him out when it doesn't work?"

David took the cup of straight black coffee that Vivian pushed to him. "That would've been good to bring up. Why didn't you?"

He was looking at Al, and from his distant inclusion at the end of the table, Al sipped his drink. "I'm not going to bandy about a questionable demon belief before six factions of Inderland society. And besides, I wasn't involved in the theoretical ramifications of the curse in question. I don't know how true it is."

Professor Anders's thin lips pressed into a line. "Demon?" she said in disbelief. "Why weren't you introduced as such?"

Smiling wickedly, Al inclined his head. "So as not to panic the leprechaun, my dear."

"Who was?" I asked, and then had to repeat the entire thing since no on was listening, captured by the emotions crossing through the tall woman. "Who was involved in the theoretical studies?"

Al pulled his gaze from Professor Anders. "Newt. Don't ask her. She doesn't remember."

Professor Anders leaned distrustfully toward Al. "You don't smell like a demon."

"He's a demon," Vivian said. "Why do you think I'm sitting way over here?"

Lips parted, Professor Anders flushed, her gaze alternating between Al and me. "You're her instructor," she almost breathed. "The one who taught her the curse to make a human a familiar."

Al grinned, taking her limp hand up and kissing the top of it. "I am. Would you like to know it?"

Oh God. He was doing it again. "He used to be," I said loudly, leaning across the table to pull Professor Anders's hand from Al and making the woman start. "He disowned me recently for dabbling in elven magic."

"Dabbling?" Al growled. "You're covered in it."

Professor Anders's eyes widened as she pulled up her second sight. "Holy seraph spit," she said, blinking fast. "Is that safe?"

David sat up, gaze flicking from Trent's proudly defiant expression and Al's disgusted one. "What? What's wrong with Rachel?"

Vivian's whistle made me flush. "Ah, that can't be healthy," the woman said, and Jenks went to sit on David's shoulder and fill him in.

"Can we get back to the topic, please?" I said, flushing.

"You look sparkly, Rache," Jenks said, wings clattering. "You must have gotten some last night, eh? Matalina used to glow for hours after we—"

"Shut up!" I exclaimed, and even Mark, behind the counter, chuckled.

"Fascinating," Professor Anders said, making me jerk back when she tried to touch my aura, apparently glowing from the mystics. "You practice elf magic, too? This is what happens without formal instruction. Why don't elves glow?"

Jenks rose up, clearly enjoying being the center of attention. "Because elves don't have bits of the Goddess bonded to them like Rachel does."

I scrunched down when the narrow-faced woman pinned me under her stare. "How does this impact your ability to do magic? Can you tap a line?"

The rest of the table was beginning to stir uncomfortably, and I winced.

"I'm sorry, Professor," Trent said, interrupting. "I'm more than happy to take you and Rachel out to lunch to discuss this in further detail, but we need to come up with a course of action and I still don't know what was decided."

I touched his foot with mine in thanks, but I thought it was his desire to get on with this more than anything else. It had been awful watching him fidget this morning, excluded from what was once his domain. I think he missed this more than the money or the notoriety.

Jenks dipped a cup of coffee out of my own cup. "Yeah, we have to save the world first before you can work on your next paper—Professor."

"Okay." Trent scooted his chair up, hand touching his breast pocket as if looking for a pen. "Landon is using the situation to try and kill the vampires through their lack of a soul. His method will further remove the source of magic so as to eliminate the threat of demons and witches—all to ensure elf survival. I simply fail to understand how Cormel can still believe Landon has his best interests in mind."

David pulled himself straight, his smile at my expense gone. "I think everyone is more scared of a world without master vampires than one without magic."

Clearly used to running meetings, Vivian began taking notes. "With the combined support of the coven and the enclave, the dewar can reinstate the Arizona lines with the energy from the shrinking ever-after."

Al lolled his head to the ceiling. "Lie . . . ," he drawled, and Vivian bristled.

"It is not."

Al's head dropped, and he found her eyes. "You wish."

"I agree," Professor Anders said, the sureness in her voice garnered from decades of arguing with know-it-all peers. "The Arizona lines are dead. You can't reinstate them. Once gone, they're gone. It's impossible to reverse a physical reaction like this; therefore, you can't reinstate lines. I don't care how big a collective, dewar, enclave, coven, or energy source you have."

Al's attention slowly slid to her, taking in her stark lines, her pigheaded confidence, and her utter refusal to be afraid of him. My eyes narrowed as he stuck a finger into her aura.

"It would be far safer to find a way to shove the undead souls back into the ever-after," the woman finished, shooting a withering look at Al.

"The ever-after is a hell," Ivy spoke up, her voice ragged almost.

"It wasn't when we made it," Al grumbled.

Professor Anders laced her hands before her as if there was nothing more to be said. "I'm sorry, Ms. Tamwood, but your kin is cursed. If it's a choice between them or us living in hell, I pick them."

Jenks's wings clattered as Ivy's eyes slowly blossomed into black. "What did my mother do to deserve to be cursed?" she said. "What did I do? How many generations need to suffer for one man frightened of death!"

Al shrugged, nonchalantly signaling Mark to make him another coffee. "You could always end the curse by letting them die. It's what they want to do, apparently."

Jenks's wings drooped. "And the world goes with them."

"So what do we do?" I said, keeping a tight watch on Ivy. "We can't allow an end to the ever-after, even to prevent the undead souls from killing their, ah, own. I can't live in a world with no magic."

David tapped the table with a thick knuckle. His hands were looking rougher these days, and I wondered if he was embracing his wilder side more. "Yes, I don't get that part. Why would Landon want an end to magic?"

Wincing, Trent rubbed his forehead. "Because elven magic isn't entirely dependent upon ley lines. We have an open forum through prayer and might be the only major magic users left if the lines go."

Might. He said might. As in demons *might* be able to use elf magic as well? Or might as in elves *might* not have magic either? The distinction was important.

"What about Weres?" David asked, understandably concerned.

"I think you'll be fine," Trent said, but David didn't look convinced. "Weres and leprechauns also use the Goddess's energy to shift and perform magic. I'd expect a slight reduction, but still functioning."

Not pleased, David slumped back. "It's hard enough to shift already."

"What about pixies?" Jenks asked.

"I think you'll be okay," I said, but worry that he wouldn't made the coffee sit ill in me. Landon wouldn't care if the pixies died out in his bid for elven superiority. Hadn't he learned anything from the history texts?

"There's always the chance that if he can't reinvoke the Arizona lines—"

"He can't," Professor Anders interrupted.

". . . that the Goddess will also lose her access to reality." Trent's lips pressed together in thought. "She won't be happy about that," he said, and Professor Anders drummed her fingers, clearly not believing in the Goddess at all.

Vivian set her pen down with a sharp snap. "I was going to advise the coven to support Landon, but this changes things."

"You believe in the Goddess?" Professor Anders scoffed, and Trent bristled.

Vivian simply smiled. "No. I was referring to the elves' ability to draw on a separate band of energy not collected in a ley line to perform their magic, one that might still be available if the lines were dead. Calling it a deity is no skin off my nose, and I don't want any religious entity holding the rest of Inderland hostage. Once the lines end, everyone will panic. They'll give the dewar anything and everything to reinstate them."

"Eat that, Ms. Professor," Jenks said, darting to make the woman wave a hand at him.

Trent seemed mollified, but I knew it was only recently that he'd begun believing in the Goddess himself. "I know nothing for certain," he said, "but Landon wouldn't risk losing the lines if he wasn't confident that he'd be able to continue to perform magic."

"A truer word has not been spoken," Al said, reaching over his shoulder to take the new cup Mark was handing him.

"Look," I said, and Al choked on his coffee.

"Oh God. She's got a list," the demon gasped, still coughing, and Jenks grinned, cup raised in a salute.

"We can't allow the undead masters to die!" I said, undeterred. "It was crazy last spring. Vivian, the news you got on the West Coast was sugar-coated. Cincinnati almost collapsed under mob rule. All services were cut. People went hungry because they were afraid to go outside, and for good reason. They're still trying to repair the damage, and I'm not talking about just the buildings."

Nodding, David ruefully rubbed his wrist, broken when he'd tried to stop Nina from crashing the van she was driving into a train.

"Rachel," Professor Anders said, making me jump. "Can the demons do anything? Perhaps they have a charm to banish the undead souls again. Permanently."

I twirled my almost full cup of coffee around. "Don't ask me. Ask the demon."

The woman leaned in across the table, reminding me of why I didn't like her. "Apparently, I am," she said, and I gave her a fake smile.

Al could hardly stand being ignored by her, and with a loud harrumph, he broke the woman's icy gaze on me. "No. And whereas ending the ever-after would forever eliminate the possibility of us being trapped there again, the risk is too great that we might find our own existence ending with it. The demons vote no. We are going to do nothing."

"Big surprise," I grumped, still watching my cup go around and around.

"Doing nothing *is* a decision," Al said tightly. "The old undead will die. The new undead will replace them, perhaps with souls, perhaps not. I can't *wait* to find out."

"Sadist," Ivy snarled, and Jenks rose up, concerned that she might lose it. It's hard enough watching your mother slowly become insane, but to sit at a table with someone who'd been around when the original curse had been woven was harder.

"Okay, okay," I soothed, and Jenks quietly flew over to whisper calming things into Ivy's ear. "No one is going to advocate letting this run its course," I said, watching Ivy. "Except the demons, who are a small but powerful and likely uncooperative faction."

Al inclined his head graciously, and Professor Anders sniffed at him.

"So where do we stand?" Trent looked at Vivian's notes in envy as she collected them together and tapped the ends on the table.

"I have yet to make my report to the coven," the woman said resolutely. "I'll give a vote of no confidence in Landon's plan, but they're scared." Her attention shifted to Al. "Scared of demons in reality, scared of vampires out of control, scared that humans will rise up against all of us when the vampires lose it again. I can almost guarantee they will vote to reinstate the Arizona lines and destroy the undead souls to save what they can of society."

"That is not fair!" Ivy exclaimed, and David nodded his agreement. I could see him already going over his resources, the worry pinching his brow.

Al, too, was glowering, but it was Professor Anders who said, "The academic society will not go along with this. The lines cannot be reinstated. Don't expect any help from us."

Vivian smiled cattily. "We never do."

The tension had risen, and I suddenly realized that Mark had quietly been getting people out the door over the last five minutes. Smart man.

"David?" Trent asked. "What can we expect from the streets?"

David started from his thoughts. "Ah, I'm not really a representative. I was there because they couldn't find anyone else on short notice."

The reality was that the Weres didn't *have* an overseeing board of individuals that governed the rest of their species, but if there was one, David was it, given the focus, and I touched his hand and motioned for him to be out with it.

"Um, I'll talk to the packs I can reach," he said, "but I can tell you right now, we'd rather have the vampires freak out as they reorganize under fewer masters than risk not being able to shift. We've hidden before, we can do it again." He glanced at Ivy. "I'm sorry."

But no one was sorry for Al, and he was under the same risk of extermination if the lines were destroyed.

Professor Anders let her clasped hands hit the table, clearly miffed. "The vampires have been scared into following a voice promising salvation. If we give them an alternative, I think they'll take it. I say our focus should be on finding a way to capture and fix individual undead souls before they have a chance to rejoin their original bodies. If nothing else, it might calm the vampires enough to realize Landon is playing them for fools. They don't want a world without magic any more than we do. I would like to head that up if I may."

Trent and I had already figured out how to capture an undead soul, but before I could say anything, Ivy drummed her fingers, clearly ticked. "Cormel won't go for individual collection. In fact, it's worse knowing that your soul is on the shelf, able to complete you but will end your life if you join with it."

I'm so sorry, Ivy. I keep trying to help you, and I only keep making things worse.

"Rachel has already pioneered and patented the white curse needed to capture an undead soul," Al said, his expression almost beatific as he gazed at the uptight professor. "I'd be delighted to explain it to you. How are you at making coffee?"

Professor Anders looked him over. "I make excellent coffee, but you're making your own." She hesitated, shifting away from him for the very first time. "I don't trust you."

Unperturbed, Al stood and extended a hand for her. "That is what makes it interesting," he almost crooned. "Shall we go to your lab? Or mine?"

"Al and Anders, sitting in a tree—" Jenks sang out, then yelped at the twin pops of magic exploding under him, one from Anders, one from Al.

Eyes squinted in mistrust, Professor Anders stood and placed her hand in Al's. The demon beamed, and she gasped as they just . . . vanished. Both their coffees went with them.

Trent shook his head in disbelief. "Okay, that was something I hadn't expected. Vivian, where are you staying?"

It sounded like things were wrapping up, and there'd been no decisions, just ideas that weren't going to work. "What about Landon?" I asked.

"I'm staying downtown at the Cincinnatian," Vivian said, tucking her notes away in a tiny purse that had to be bigger on the inside than the out. "Give me until noon." She hesitated as she stood. "Ah, make that three. They might not be up yet. I'll have a better idea of what the coven will do."

But I already knew they'd back Landon, and I slumped.

"Good." Trent leaned his chair back on two legs with his hands clasped behind his head, looking pleased with what we'd learned. "I've found a few pieces of support in the dewar. Perhaps we can pool our resources if you find enough dissent."

"I'll see what I can do." Vivian gave me a nod. "See you when it's done, Rachel. Try not to destroy Cincinnati like you did San Francisco."

"That was Ku'Sox!" I said as she nodded to Jenks and Ivy, both of whom looked as happy as I felt—that is, not at all.

"David, you want a ride somewhere?" Vivian asked, and David pulled himself out of his thoughts with a grunt and reached for his phone.

"Sure. Thanks."

Trent's chair came back down onto all fours. "Actually, David, I'd like to talk to you about something."

David perked up, hiding a sly smile that had Vivian putting a hand on her hip. "What are you planning?" she accused.

"Ah, just the local distribution of the packs to minimize disruption to services," Trent lied, and Ivy sent Jenks to get a croissant. We might be here awhile. "The same thing the packs did the last time the vampires panicked."

"Yeah, okay," the smart woman said, and then seeing that no one was going to say anything more while she was standing there, she stomped out to the rental car she'd driven them all here in. "I don't want to know, anyway, do I!" she called back over her shoulder before the door shut.

Excited, I sat up. All the busybodies were gone, leaving those who had the guts to actually do something. "What are we going to do?"

Trent smiled at my enthusiasm, then sobered at Ivy's calm, deadly anticipation and David's expectation. Outside, Vivian raced the car's engine and left. "Vivian will try, but the coven is going to side with Landon to banish the undead souls and drain the ever-after for the energy to reinstate the lines," Trent said.

"It's unethical," Ivy said bitterly, and I thought of the demons, facing their own maybe demise. It hurt that no one seemed to care.

"I agree," Trent said in placation, "but fear will convince the coven *and* the dewar to follow him. Our number one priority is to find Landon." Trent smiled at me, and finally my shoulders started to ease. "We have until tomorrow at sunset."

Jenks made a burst of dust in worry. "What's to stop him from doing it tonight?"

"It's the equinox," I said, only now remembering it. "Tomorrow, about an hour before sunset. If he's going to break the lines, that's when he's going to do it. All things will be equal."

Trent was nodding, and Ivy exhaled as she slumped back. "At least we have some time to plan this one," she said sarcastically. "Tomorrow?"

Hell, I didn't need a plan, just a direction.

"The thing about a collective curse is that it can be broken if the person orchestrating it is, ah . . ." Trent's voice trailed off as he searched for a word.

"Killed?" Jenks suggested, striking a pose and stabbing the sugar packets.

"I was going to say distracted," Trent said, and Jenks held his cup under the tiny stream of sugar spilling out.

"*Killed* works for me," David said. "I'm all for live and let live, but this guy is knowingly hurting too many people."

"Take Landon out and they'll just find someone else to do it," Ivy said glumly.

"Perhaps, but they will have to wait an entire six months. And if we can't convince Landon to cease, we might be able to work a clause into the curse that will shift it to our liking, but we have to find him first."

My eyebrows rose. "You can do that?"

Trent shifted uncomfortably. "With some planning. It's how the elves originally turned the curse around and trapped the demons in the everafter instead of us. Landon won't be looking for such subterfuge, but we have to physically be involved in the casting of the curse to break the lines, and for that, we need to find him."

"Ivy, I can use your help with that," David said, and the despairing look Ivy had been wearing since I walked in finally eased.

"Jenks can keep us clean," Trent said, and the pixy's sparkles turned a bright silver. "Which will leave you and me, Rachel, to twist the curse to our liking."

"And maybe Mark to make us a couple more coffees while we figure out how to do all that," Jenks said.

I couldn't help my smile. That totally worked for me.

Chapter 24

T his tastes like moldy mulch," I whispered as I set the tiny potion vial down and stifled a shudder at the gritty feel of it as I swallowed. The recipe made seven portions, and as I reached for another, I decided that I'd leave the last four for Trent. Elves had an affinity for blending into shadows, but the spelled ability to become virtually invisible seemed prudent. I didn't know if elves could store potions like demons could, but we figured it was worth a try. I was finding out they were more alike than different, which was about par for the course. The more I knew, the more I realized everything I'd been told was probably wrong.

Trent's breathing was slow and even as he napped on the cot, the light blanket pulled up almost over his head. He'd once told me that he envied the way most people could stay awake through the entire day, but I'd always thought it more effective to never need to sleep more than four hours at a go instead of an interminably long eight hours at a time. The world could end in eight hours and you'd never know until it was too late.

I hadn't been surprised when Trent had suggested coming out here to spell. The hut was hard to find notwithstanding its being mere steps from his back office, even with the fire going and giving off a telltale thread of smoke. There was no running water or electricity, which made it a very secure place to spell, if a little small. The table I was working at was actually a fold-up job, slipped out from under the cot.

And I liked it here, away from the polished simplicity of most of Trent's rooms. It was only here that I felt comfortable among the softer, earthy parts of Trent's nature carefully hidden away from casual bruising. Here he kept his favorite books—the ones that had helped shaped his ideas of right and wrong. A small shrine to his mother glowed with candlelight next to the summoning circle set within the ley line that nicked the inside corner of the building. Mementos from camp and college were cheek by jowl with scientific awards, the layer of dust an accurate determination of when he'd won them. Thank-you letters and pictures from people he and his father had saved with illegal genetic medicines were shoved in drawers along with brochures of places he'd never have time to go. The hut held everything that was dear to him, everything too precious to have where people could see it. That the mantel now held Mr. Fish and that black chrysalis from Al made me feel more than good; it made me feel like I belonged.

My coffee, instant prepared from water warmed up over the open fire, was cold. I'd make more but I was afraid the scent might wake Trent, and I'd just as soon have him asleep while I finished up the prep for crashing Landon's spelling party tomorrow. Not everything was legal, but nothing was immoral, and that was my guide these days.

I was tired of trying to overcome the bad guys with a few simple spells and throwing raw energy at them—as effective as it was. Earlier today Trent and I had made and imbibed potions to make ourselves almost invisible, to temporarily hold our breath for five minutes without stress, to make our hands sticky enough to climb walls, and to coat an attacker in a spiderweblike net. But after a morning of prepping spells and curses, I was beginning to have second thoughts. They all tasted like crap. I didn't know how Al stood being his own spelling cupboard. I felt ill, as if I'd eaten bad yogurt. And what if I forgot the word of invocation?

But if Trent would stay asleep for ten more minutes, I had one more spell to craft, one I'd rather finish before he woke.

The soft hum of pixy wings pulled my attention to the tiny window over the bowl currently being used as a sink. Dust glittered in the sun as Jenks landed on the narrow sill. I slammed down a third potion as Jenks leaned over his knees, a stick of yew as tall as he was in his grip.

"Is this long enough?" he asked, panting as he glanced at the sleeping Trent in envy.

I nodded, carefully setting the four remaining potions aside and clearing the table. My pulse quickened. It wasn't as if Trent would be mad, but he'd made it clear that he wasn't going to count on the demons to help. I disagreed. I was sure I could get them to help us stave off the elven trickery. I mean, they knew Landon was lying. Why wouldn't they help expose him? But to talk to the collective meant I needed another scrying mirror—something smaller this time, say small enough to fit in my shoulder bag.

"Thanks, Jenks," I said as I took the plates with their crumbs of cheese and crackers to the makeshift sink. The pixy propped the stick against the side of the open window frame. It still sported bits of green and peeling bark, and I smiled, seeing where he'd wedged it off the plant.

Jenks followed me to the table, coming to rest on my cold coffee cup as I swabbed the teak down with a salt water–soaked rag. Apparently teak was spell resistant. I hadn't known, and it felt really weird to be spelling on it. "Can I help?" he asked, and then a draft sent his dust into the fireplace to flame up with a hiss.

"Ah, sure." Brow furrowed, I shifted a footstool out of the path of a protection circle. It was inlaid right into the floor, making me wonder about Trent's mom. This had been her spelling hut, and it was a fairly large circle for most casual users. "Keep an eye on Trent's aura and let me know if he's waking up."

Jenks snorted, and I shot him a look to behave as I settled myself at the table with the hand mirror, bottle of wine, salt from Trent's stash, and the rest. The charm would temporarily strip me of my aura, which was the reason for the circle. Closing my eyes, I reached out and strengthened my hold on the ley line.

Energy was a jolt instead of the usual calm flow, and my eyes started open. The line was only six feet away, but there was a raw, serrated feel to it that I'd never felt before. I had a bad feeling that it was the mystics and that I'd gotten used to the smooth silk of power that they naturally gave off like a living ley line.

"Okay, let's get this started," I muttered, glancing at Trent as I set the protective circle. Jenks was inside it with me, and his wings shifted in agitation as the molecule-thin sheet rose up and around us.

I was reaching for the knife to pare down the yew stick to a proper stylus when the silver bell over the fireplace made a single, beautiful peal of sound.

My heart seemed to stop. I looked to Trent, then Jenks, his dust shifting to an alarmed silver as he turned to that tiny slip of ley line that crossed the hut's corner.

I spun to a stand. Al! The demon materialized in his green crushed velvet, his nose wrinkled and disdainfully brushing at his coat. "Al!" I almost hissed, still in my circle. *Crap on toast, not again!* At least he wasn't drunk this time. "Get out!" I exclaimed softly.

Jenks took to the air when Al seemed to shake his foot free of the line and stepped closer to the fire. His sleeve brushed the edge of my circle and it fell with the sensation of winter snow, our auras being identical thanks to Newt. "I should have guessed you'd be here," he said, a white-gloved hand reaching for the chrysalis he'd once given me. "Here, collected among that elf's favorite things," he finished bitterly.

"I'm not collected," I whispered. "And put that down. It's mine!"

Eyes mocking, Al succinctly put the black chrysalis into his front pocket, daring me.

Springs squeaked as Trent shifted on the cot, and my pulse quickened. Damn it, I'd wanted to talk to Al, but not in person, and not here! "Outside," I demanded, grabbing his coat and tugging him to the door. "Now, before he wakes up."

"Like I care," he muttered, but he was moving, and I got behind him and pushed.

"I want to talk to you," I said, again noticing he didn't smell like burnt amber. "Alone," I added, making Jenks bristle.

Al let himself be shoved out, but I think it was only because Jenks was having a personal issue with the "alone" comment. "Rache . . . ," the pixy protested once we were outside.

"Stay here," I demanded, tugging Al down the path. "I mean it. Just . . . keep Trent safe."

"Trent!" the pixy yelped, releasing a burst of gold dust rivaling the sun.

"Do this for me!" I exclaimed, voice hardly above a whisper. "Al, walk with me."

The demon snorted. "Walk with me . . . ," he drawled. "How poetic. You're turning into the little kingmaker, aren't you?"

"Sweet ever-loving pixy piss," Jenks griped. "I hope he turns your underwear to slugs!"

Jenks wouldn't follow me right away, and tension brought my shoulders up to my ears when I realized I was shoving a demon through Trent's private gardens. "How did you know I wanted to talk to you?" I said, pulse fast as I slowed down.

"I didn't." Al's voice was low, distant almost as he touched a coiled fern frond and it gracefully unrolled with the sound of green. "I came to stop you from making a mistake."

He came to stop me. My heart jumped at the thought that he might have forgiven me. I mean, he wasn't throttling me or threatening me. But then my brief elation died. "It's not a mistake. We could use your help in twisting Landon's curse to dust."

Al's steady pace faltered, and I stopped in the middle of a tangled cricket-filled clearing.

"Rachel, you can't shift the elven curse. The best you can hope for is to survive it. But it doesn't matter. You must come now as we prepare."

"Prepare for what? I'm not leaving Trent to do this alone. We could do this if the rest of you would help," I accused, glad we were out of earshot of Trent's hut.

Al reached for my arm, his hand falling back before it touched me. "No, we can't," he said with an infuriating sureness. "Trent has overestimated himself, and you won't come out of this alive if you bind your fate to his."

My brow furrowed. "I didn't know you cared."

Fire exploded against my cheek, and I stumbled back, hand pressed to my face as I reeled. Al caught me by the shoulder, jerking me back upright. *He'd slapped me?*

"Don't toy with me," Al whispered. "Trying to shift the elven curse will get you killed!"

He'd slapped me! "Hey!" I exclaimed, almost afraid. He had struck me because I'd used his pain to hurt him. "*You* walked away from *me*. You don't have any say in what I do anymore, and if you hit me again, I'm going to smack you back!"

Al let me go. I tensed, but he turned away, his back bowed as he went to a cement bench. I hadn't even known it was there, so covered in a rambling rose vine it was. Head down, Al waved his hand, brushing aside the vines to find a clear spot to sit. The scent of disturbed roses wafted out—one last bid for beauty before the autumn chill pinched the petals free.

He looked broken as he sat there with his elbows on his knees and stared at nothing. My cheek throbbed, and guilt swam up. I deserved to have been slapped. Using his own pain against him was cruel.

"We need your help," I said, and he looked at me from under lowered eyebrows. My boots scuffed through the leaf mold to find paving as I shifted closer. There'd been a clearing here once—a patio maybe—and I went to sit on a broken statue. It looked as if it might have been a witches' garden, though admittedly not a very sunny one.

"Why do you care about the undead souls? The demons? Me?"

His last word held a painful vulnerability, and I tried to find a more comfortable position. "Because everyone deserves a chance to come back from their mistakes." My roving eyes returned to find him sitting among the roses. "I should know."

"You won't come back from this one," he said. "The elves are massed for destruction. *Our* destruction. The undead souls were the lure and the way. The elimination of the aged undead is a bonus, but it's *us* they're after. We couldn't beat them when we were forty thousand strong. We are four hundred and thirteen now."

His head dropped, and I frowned. Four hundred and thirteen? It had always seemed more than that, but perhaps it was the familiars who filled the shops and parties. "Trent stands with us," I said, and Al sighed heavily.

"It cannot be done," he said solemnly. "Come with me. We're weaving a wall."

"A wall," I said flatly.

The lift of Al's shoulders gave away his disdain for their own cowardice, but his jaw was set. "A wall to keep from being pulled back when they dissolve the lines."

"A wall," I said again, and he bared his teeth at me, daring me to call them cowards. "Al, walls are prisons. You need to break the original curse."

"With four hundred of us?" he protested. "It can't be done."

I leaned forward, trying to cross the distance with my words. "That's why you need the elves' help."

Al looked at me as if I was crazy, and maybe I was, but I stood, unable to sit any longer. "The elves are modifying an old curse, not making a new one," I said, words rushing over themselves. "You told me yourself that was dangerous. All we have to do is end it!"

"And in the doing, we put ourselves in the stream itself," he said sourly. "We will flounder and be lost."

"You don't know that!"

"We do!" he thundered, and I stiffened as I heard Jenks's wings. He was somewhere close, but I said nothing as Al slumped, clearly frustrated.

"We know Landon will be the fulcrum," I said, pacing now. "He's in downtown Cincinnati, right by the square. We know his damn room number, Al! Ivy and Jenks can get us in—"

Al sat up, waving a hand disparagingly. "Why do I even try?"

"If we're with him, we can shift the focus of the charm!" I protested. "Al!" I complained, my feet stopping as he frowned at me.

"There can be only one weaver in a spell that complex—"

"Then Trent and I will be a fulcrum and slant it the direction we want," I pleaded.

"Rachel." Al slumped. "We tried that. Their magic . . . It's too strong."

"Then we can try it again," I insisted.

"Their magic is *too strong!*" he shouted, and I shut my mouth. Sighing, Al held a hand out to me, inviting me to sit down. "It can't be done," he said softly, never letting his hand fall, extending it for me.

Frustrated, I stomped over and sat down. "Cowards," I accused.

"Realists," he countered, but his anger was gone. The silence stretched. "What do you hope to get out of this?" Al asked, startling me.

"To end the war between you. To bring you home!" I said, and he actually smiled.

"No, I mean what do *you* want from the world? From everything?"

"Oh." That was different, and the fire seemed to wash out of me. He'd come here to save me, save me again. "The same thing you do, I guess. A little peace to find out who I am."

Slumped, Al looked out over the broken clearing. "There's no peace but for the dead, and even that we've found a way to corrupt."

It was starting to sound like a pity party, and I stood. "I don't have to listen to you anymore, remember? I have to go. I've got to make a scrying mirror before midnight." Damn it, I was going to have to do this without their help. If I couldn't convince even Al, then the rest were useless. I strode back to the path, arms swinging.

"Rachel?"

His call was so soft, yet it pulled me to a halt. I didn't turn, standing there with my back to him, but he knew I was listening.

"You don't need the mirror anymore to connect to the collective," he said, voice holding a sliver of pain. "Why do you think I'm here?"

Mystics, I thought, shaking as I turned around to see him still on the bench.

"You haven't for a long time," he said, hands clasped between his knees, making him look worried and scared. "We, ah, hate to admit it, but demons are still tied to elven magic."

My feet scuffed a few steps back. "Maybe it's not elven. Maybe it just . . . is."

Al rubbed his forehead. "I don't remember."

My hope flooded back, and I came to him, sitting so our knees almost touched, begging him to listen. "Al, I know we can do this. You may be only four hundred, but you have the gargoyles as anchors now. There's support among the elves, hidden in the dewar. Vivian is trying to sway the witches' coven. Professor Anders . . ." I hesitated. "Ah, she's okay, right?"

Al waved a hand and sighed, his regret that she was indeed okay obvious.

"Well, she's rallying the scientific community," I continued. "You aren't alone this time. Four hundred and thirteen survivors, but *you* are the ones who made it this far. Can't you convince the rest we have a real chance?"

"It was beautiful here once," Al said distantly, eyes on nothing.

"Al!" I shouted, then frowned as Jenks's wings clattered. "I can't walk away from this!"

"Right here, this spot," the demon said, his hands beginning to glow. "The fountain was the perfect blending of sound and motion." I started, eyes wide as a haze shimmered over the broken statuary and realities seemed to shift, focusing in and out until a mossy fountain of fish and antelope took form.

"The moonlight made the water into pearls, and the smell of the night vines was intoxicating," Al whispered, and I could hear the water, see it. "There were pixies then. That bastard killed them all when she died. It wasn't their fault."

He was fingering the pocket where the chrysalis lay, and I couldn't speak as I looked over a memory pulled from the recesses of time. The patio was new and clean, looking like midnight in the late noon sun. I knew without asking that he was talking about Trent's mother and dad. "You were here?" I asked. "You knew them?"

"I knew her."

I leaned forward as the magic faded and reality imposed itself anew and the shattered ruin of the fountain smothered the spell. I could see a fin in the wreckage, and the curve of a graceful leg. All gone. All spoiled.

"Not everything changes, Rachel," Al said as he stood up. "Some things just are."

"So you won't help," I said.

His hand trembled as he set the chrysalis down on the broken statues. "No."

"Then you'd better leave because I'm busy," I said, eyes rising to a faint glimmer of pixy dust coming through the greenery.

Al said nothing, and I started when I turned to find him gone. Grimacing, I stood. Okay, some things changed, and it was up to those who cared to fight for the change they wanted.

"I'm sorry, Rache," Jenks said as he hummed into the clearing.

"Me too." Frustrated, I turned and went back to the spelling hut, hurt and sick at heart.

I left the chrysalis behind.

Chapter 25

The black van was borrowed from one of Ivy's friends, and therefore untraceable past a fictional Hollows address. It smelled like Special K and blood lust under the acidic bite of disinfectant. Between that and the pheromones Ivy and Nina were dumping into the air, my vampire scars were tingling.

Looking across the front seat at Ivy, I muttered, "You need to relax," all the while wishing the side windows would open a little more.

Ivy took a slow breath, stilling her painted nails as they drummed a frustrated staccato on the steering wheel. We'd been here for about ten minutes, and she hadn't let go of it yet.

"This is relaxed," Nina said, but she'd gotten up from her rear seat, moving forward with a pained slowness to avoid touching anyone. Kneeling beside Ivy, she put an arm around her back. Head tilting to rest almost on Ivy's shoulder, she whispered something. Ivy sighed and the tension visibly flowed from her, her head thumping down to land upon Nina's.

Happy, I turned back to retying my boots. I was glad that Ivy had someone and that it was Nina.

Ivy was decidedly polished in black slacks, white shirt with a collar, and a suit coat that was tailored to both show off her curves and scream "desk clerk" all at the same time. She'd even put on makeup. Nina looked even more professional, with bangles and a belt that I thought could be used as handcuffs in a pinch. They were going in first, coming out last, and keeping our way clean and open at all times.

But the *snick-snick* of a weapon being checked jerked my head back up. Nina had slipped into a seat, and Trent stiffened at the little pistol she was sighting down. "I said no weapons," he said, leaning from the backseat with his hand outstretched.

"Rachel has one!" Nina complained as she held it close to her chest like a favorite doll. "How are we supposed to take the front desk if we can't have guns?"

She knew darn well mine was just a splat gun, not considered lethal by the FIB or the I.S. thanks to some clever judicial loopholes. Jenks darted to her, his wings loud in the small space. "David's got the front desk already," he said, red dust slipping over her threateningly. "Ivy, you said she was ready for this. I don't have the manpower to babysit her."

Ivy sucked on her teeth, and with that as an almost silent rebuke, the zealous woman glumly handed the gun to Trent. "Can I keep my knife?" she asked sarcastically, and Trent nodded.

"Be careful how you use it."

I exhaled as Trent put the gun in the van's illegal "safe hole" and shut it. My eyes returned to the one-way back door of the hotel, waiting for a Were to signal us that the sixth floor was cleared; the staff in the break room for an emergency OSHA meeting; and the hotel ready to assume new, albeit temporary management. No guns. That was rule number one, four, and sixteen. This operation had an excellent chance of crashing down before we reached the end, and I didn't want guns cluttering the issue. It was going to be hard enough to survive this.

"At least it's not in the tunnels," Trent said as he checked that his laces were tied.

A quiver, quickly quashed, lit through me. I liked the mix of thief, commando, and lover he had going for him. "You don't like the tunnels?"

Coming up from his soft-soled boots, Trent lined his utilitarian hat with his spelling cap and settled it onto his head. "No. They're damp and make me sneeze."

"And cold," Jenks added, looking just as good in his thief-black tights.

And cold, I echoed in my thoughts, hoping this stayed within the hotel. September was iffy for pixies, even those skilled in staying alive through a street chase as the sun went down, taking the temperature with it.

"There he is," Ivy said, and my attention followed hers to the rear door. "Ready, Nina?"

A Were in a suit with his hair carefully corralled in a trendy ponytail was leaning halfway through the white fire door, beckoning us in. Nina started to get out, jerking to a halt when Trent caught her arm. Her lips pulled back in a snarl, and Ivy hesitated when he tugged her close, ignoring her tiny little fangs, now bared at him.

"No one dies, Nina. Especially if they deserve it. Understand?"

Her brow furrowed, and Trent pulled her closer, demanding an answer. Jenks hovered over his shoulder, and finally she accepted his dominance and nodded. Ivy took a slow breath, relieved. Nina was an odd mix now that Felix was gone, and no one quite trusted it.

"Just give us ten minutes to put everyone in a closet," Ivy said to break the tension, but I could tell she was worried about Nina as she handed me the keys to the van and got out.

"Be right back, Rache," Jenks said, then zipped out the side door with a sullen Nina.

Ivy's pace was held to a deliberate, sexy stride as she went around the front and joined Nina and Jenks. I had a pang of worry that we were here alone and unsanctioned by any police force. But damn it, if we had brought the FIB into it, we'd still be arguing with Edden about vampires getting their souls being a bad thing. Even so, I hunched in guilt, wondering what that said about me. Who had changed, me or Trent? *Stop it, Rachel.*

"They'd better leave us something to do," Nina complained as they neared the building, and Trent chuckled.

I licked my lips, worried as Jenks back-winged in front of Ivy and reminded her to put a box in the door to keep it from shutting. Ivy's singsong "I got it, pixy!" was soft, and I smiled as she nudged it forward, waiting for Jenks's approval before stepping over it. She was gone.

Jenks gave me a thumbs-up and darted after her.

Ten minutes.

"We've got an hour until the undead can be aboveground," I said, checking the clock on the van's dash. "Twenty minutes until the equinox officially begins. We need to be in and out before then." Forty minutes minus ten equals thirty. Why did we always cut these things so Turn-blasted close?

Trent was fidgeting, and I moved in a hunched walk to the back of the van. "Relax."

Trent followed my gaze to his hands and shook the tension from them. "Easy for you to say. It's not your people who are about to flush everything back to pre-Turn chaos. If I'd known they were going to do something this boneheaded, I wouldn't have pushed to come out of the closet."

It was nice of him to say, but I knew I was the real reason he'd lost clout. Frankly, I didn't care anymore. We'd make them play nice in the sandbox, and that would be that. Nervous, I leaned to look at the clock on the dash, then knelt beside Trent to look out the window for Jenks. "They're just scared."

"Scared," Trent scoffed, fiddling with the ends of his ribbon. "My people want a return to power so badly they don't care who they step on to get it."

I slid a sideways look at him. That had sounded kind of familiar, but I wasn't going to say anything.

A sparkle of dust caught my breath, and I lurched to open the sliding door. It was Jenks, and he was carrying something heavy, his path slowly arching to the ground. It had been only two minutes. Something had gone wrong. "What happened?" I demanded, one hand on the side of the van as I leaned out and down to catch him. "Jenks?"

"It's a key," Trent said, holding my shoulder so I wouldn't fall out. "I think we're okay."

With a burst of silver, Jenks rose up, clearly laboring. "Someone take this, will you?" he exclaimed, and a heavy brass key fell into my hand. "Tink save me from the artists! Every other hotel is in the twenty-first century and uses card keys, but no-o-o-o-o! We have to be special. We have to be extravagant! We have to be so far behind the times that it's considered chic! Why the hell did I volunteer to bring it out for you?"

"Is everything okay?" I glanced at the clock. They couldn't have secured the front desk that fast.

"Yeah, we're good." Jenks stood on my palm, wings drooping and a sheet of red dust pouring through my fingers. "That Nina is one scary bitch. Remind me not to stare her down again. The lobby and restaurant are cleared out. We figure he's in 612. It's the only one with a crib, according to housekeeping."

"Lucy?" Trent exclaimed, almost hitting the ceiling as he stood. "She's here?"

Jenks nodded, head still bowed as he caught his breath.

Shit, this changed everything. "Okay. Trent, if we find her you take her and get out. End of story. I can do this with Jenks." His daughter came first. I understood and supported that, even as I was scrambling to adapt.

"Ah, Landon is probably in the adjoining room," Jenks suggested, but his soulful, almost pitying expression told me he was just saying that to try to give Trent something to pin his worry to. We could *not* start a firefight in a room where Lucy was.

"I can't endanger Lucy," Trent said, his worry lines melting into alarm. "Rachel . . ."

"If we find her, she's a priority," I said. "You take her and go."

"Yeah, cookie maker," Jenks said as he took to the air again. "We got this in a can already. We just need to put a label on it and put it on a shelf. Let's go."

Looking ill, Trent rolled the door open.

"Is he going to be okay?" I breathed to Jenks, turning my lips up into a smile when Trent spun to help me out.

"It's the people holding Lucy I'm worried about," Jenks muttered, but I thought Trent might have heard as he wiggled his fingers impatiently for me. "We're burning daylight, people," Jenks prompted, and I grabbed my jacket and put my hand in Trent's. Little tingles of energy balanced between us. The lump of my new cell phone was in a back pocket, and the cool feel of steel from my splat gun that never seemed to warm up was at the small of my back. Jittery, I closed the door, making the sound echo in the small space. Trent and I hustled forward as I shoved first one arm into my jacket, then the other. The leather would give me some protection against spells, both earth and some ley line.

"Which way, Jenks?" Trent asked as we stepped over the box and crept into the back receiving room, and Jenks hummed off at head height, intentionally dusting a thick yellow that would linger. The scent of excited vampire mixed with cinnamon and wine as we followed Jenks's glowing path through the receiving area to the warmer kitchen, and finally into the bar.

I'd been to the Cincinnatian before, and I'd always thought having the bar just off the tiny lobby sort of elegant in the tight confines a city hotel demanded. The new decor—rich with texture and color—made up for the small space. The ringing of a phone pulled my attention to the front desk. Ivy's eyes met mine, but I couldn't smile. Lucy was here. It changed everything.

The light past the front desk was decidedly gray. We were getting close to the mark. My eyes went to the elevators and the Were fidgeting in a borrowed uniform keeping the lift at the lobby for us. The Weres had cleared the building with the understanding that they'd not be involved in a magical firefight. I could understand their reluctance. Even the I.S. didn't send a Were out after a witch, much less a bunch of elves. "Jenks, does Ivy know about Lucy?" I asked, and he dusted a silent yes.

Trent took my elbow. "We don't need Ivy," he muttered as we angled to the ornate elevators, and he frowned when I made the finger sign for "be ready to move."

Ivy's eyes shifted to black. Her motions graceful and holding purpose, she swooped to answer the phone. A professional, polished greeting flowed from her, but I could see the tension growing. It was falling apart even before we got started.

"I said I have this," Trent said again, his voice agitated as we got in the elevator.

"I never said you didn't." I pulled back in the tight confines of the lift. He was sending off sparks, and it was irritating.

Jenks smirked, smacking the button for the sixth floor, and the doors closed. "There's a small contingent of Weres up there, but they won't show unless you scream for them," Jenks said, and Trent exhaled some of his tension. "We're going in blind," the pixy added, miffed.

"Because of the keyed locks, right?" I said.

"Yes, because of the keyed locks," Jenks said, hands on his hips. "Most of the doors fit too tightly against the floor, too. Tink-blasted fire codes. I can go in through the ductwork, but I don't know the layout and it would take at least twenty minutes."

We didn't have twenty minutes, and I caught myself before I chewed on my lower lip.

"That's why I got rid of my card system," Trent said, but his brow was pinched and it was obvious he was thinking of Lucy. "We can't go in spells flying if my daughter is in there."

"We won't," I said as the doors opened.

"Then how are we going to do this?" he asked, tight on my heels as I followed Jenks into the elevator lobby.

"I don't know yet." My nose wrinkled. The scent of Were was thick up here, and there were signs of a scuffle, hastily cleaned up: the flower vase had no water, and there was a petal stuck to the glass that never would have passed inspection.

"Rachel . . . ," Trent prompted, and I hesitated, seeing his worry for his daughter, for me, for his people.

"I don't know, but I'll be taken and beaten before I hurt Lucy."

Jenks was waiting at the end of the hall, and my stomach tightened as I counted down the room numbers. Lucy was in one of them, probably the one with the crib.

"Which one?" Trent whispered as we came to the suite of rooms.

"Give me your phone," I said as I had a sudden idea and held my hand out. "Lucy is probably with Ellasbeth, right?" I scrolled through Trent's numbers called to find her. Trent nodded, eyes widening as I punched a button and put the phone to an ear. "So we find out what room she's in."

"Works for me," Jenks said, hovering between us.

Trent's cell was ringing, and we stared at the twin doors before us—waiting. There was only a muted conversation from a TV. My pulse hammered, and then, so soft as to almost be imagined, the repeated ping of an incoming call rang from a tiny speaker.

It was coming from behind us.

I spun. Jenks darted to one of the doors across the hall, pointing at it with exaggerated excitement. I slid Trent's phone away and took up the smooth feel of cool steel instead.

"No spells," Trent hissed.

"You think I'm going to shoot Lucy?" I said tartly.

Frowning, he took up a position on one side of the door, and I took the other. "Housekeeping," I whispered, trying to keep the key from scraping as I fit it, but it was the master key and it needed some persuasion.

"Let me." Trent wrenched the handle and the key at the same time, and the lock clicked open.

Jenks zipped in before the door was even half an inch out of the frame. "Moss-wipe elf!" he exclaimed, and Trent shoved the door open in a panic. "Tink's a Disney whore. Rache!"

Panicked, Trent lurched in, leaving me to try to get the key out of the lock so I could shut the door. That call might have carried, and the last thing I wanted was Landon to find us.

"Whoa, whoa, whoa!" Jenks shrilled, and I finally got the key free. "I think you got him!"

Flushed, I shoved the door shut and bolted into the outer sitting room. Trent had one knee on the back of a big, blond, and unconscious man. The scent of ozone was thick, and Jenks's dust sparked as it picked up the un- spent magic. Behind them, Ellasbeth watched with wide eyes. She was tied to a chair and gagged, and my lips parted. Ellasbeth was tied to a chair? Oh, she was pissed, too, her face red and muffled shouts trying to escape around her gag. I wasn't sure I wanted to untie her. Shaking with adrenaline, Trent looked up at me, then Ellasbeth. He made no move to untie her either, and the woman jumped in the chair, furious.

"Nicely done, Mr. Kung Fu!" Jenks said, clearly impressed. "You didn't kill him this time!"

This time? I inched in. "Jenks, are we clear?"

"Yep." He was grinning, hands on his hips as he looked at Ellasbeth's fury.

Trent dropped the unconscious man's gun. Face white, he strode to El- lasbeth and yanked the gag down. "Where's Lucy?"

Ellasbeth took a gasping breath. "That son of a bitch!" she raved, blond hair in her mouth, her eyes everywhere. "He's crazy! He's going to kill the ley lines! He's going to end magic!"

"Where is Lucy, Ellasbeth?" Trent demanded, and then his head snapped around at a delighted "Daddy!" from the back room.

I stumbled out of the way as Trent bolted to her. I couldn't help my smile when I heard Lucy calling again, her little-child voice raised in delight. "Daddy, Daddy, Daddy! Surprise!"

Jenks was at the door, looking in at them even as he hovered backward to me. "I love reunions," he said, his dust shifting to a melancholy orange.

I looked at the clock on the wall, my smile fading. "Go get Ivy, will you?" I said, and Jenks's dust shifted gray. Trent was out of it, and I needed help.

"You got it." Jenks darted through the door and into the hallway as I opened it a crack.

"How about some help here?" Ellasbeth said bitterly.

Sighing, I listened to the quiet hallway, deciding everything was okay before I shut the door. "He tied you up, huh?" I asked as I used the downed elf's knife to cut her bonds.

"Landon is a philistine," she said, rubbing her wrists and wiggling her ankles for me to hurry up. "He's tricking his own people into ending magic with the promise of killing all the demons. You can't kill demons without magic. What if they aren't pulled back? How do you do magic without the lines? You don't!" She hesitated at the soft scuff at the bedroom door, her face going white as she looked at Trent standing there with Lucy on his hip, the little girl patting at his frown lines.

"Hi, Mommy," she said, wiggling her feet. "Surprise!"

I blinked when a little purple rocking horse with wings suddenly appeared and Lucy squealed in delight. Al had taught her a new trick.

"Trent . . ."

Ellasbeth tried to stand, and I shoved her back down. Ticked, the woman frowned at me. "He's using the vampires' undead souls as an excuse to break the lines," she said. "We have to stop him. With the lines broken, the ever-after—"

"Will shrink and implode on itself," I said blandly, interrupting her as I freed her feet.

"How do you know that?"

Finished, I rocked back and slowly stood, deciding to keep the knife. "Because I stopped Ku'Sox from doing the same thing. It must have given Landon the idea."

She started to move, and I shook my head. "Stay put."

"I didn't know that was his plan," Ellasbeth said, peeved but flicking nervous glances at the man Trent had downed. "I never meant it to get this out of hand. I only wanted to scare you, Trent. I'm so sorry."

Trent's white face wasn't going away. Lucy was singing as she sat on his hip, and his expression became frightened as his eyes met mine. "I can't," he said, those two words almost tearing him in two.

"Daddy, where's Ray-Ray?"

I swallowed hard as I remembered him forcing Lucy into my arms and demanding I leave, Trent willingly becoming Ku'Sox's slave to save her. "Don't worry about it," I said softly, and Ellasbeth looked between us, her lips pressed as she tried to figure it out. "Jenks is getting Ivy. Get them both out of here."

"What?" Ellasbeth said as I pulled her to her feet. "Hey!"

Angry, I took out a little of my misplaced aggression on her, pinching her shoulder and getting in her face. "You want to be tied up again?" I said sharply, and her anger flashed to fear. "Then get out of here."

The man at my feet moved, and I pulled out my splat gun and shot him in the back. With a little sigh, he collapsed. Ellasbeth looked at him, then me, standing before her with a gun in one hand, a knife in the other. Slowly I handed the knife to Trent, who double-sheathed it with his own longer knife. "I suggest you go fast and quiet," I added.

"Where's-s-s-s Ray-Ray!" Lucy bubbled, clearly not frightened, but hey, the girl had been kidnapped three times now.

Smiling, Trent jiggled her on his hip. "Shhh, Lucy. We have to be quiet to go find Ray."

The little girl bounced happily, then suddenly concentrated on her fingers until she got them to snap. The flying rocking horse exploded into a puff of pink smoke, and the little girl laughed, delighted. If we survived this, I was going to have to talk to Al about the spells little girls should and shouldn't know.

But she was being way too loud, and as Ellasbeth darted around the room gathering her purse, her coat, her heels . . . whatever, I turned to Lucy, worried they wouldn't get down that first crucial hallway. Trent wasn't having much luck as Lucy kept making and exploding winged horses into little pink clouds "Lucy?" I said suddenly. "Do you want to play hide-and-seek?"

Trent sighed as Lucy stopped bouncing, her eyes going wide as she covered them. "Shhh," she whispered, then flung her hands from her, smacking Trent in the face as she cried out, "Here I am!"

Smiling, I tugged her sweater straight. "That's right. But you have to be quiet to find Ray. Shhhh. Ready?"

Trent's free hand touched my waist, and I froze.

"Rachel . . . I . . ."

The door opened and I spun, relaxing when Jenks darted in, Ivy shutting the door softly behind herself.

"Just go," I said, resisting the urge to straighten his hat after Lucy knocked it. "Ivy and I have this."

Ellasbeth shrugged her long coat, looking at us as if jealous. "You can't stop him without elven magic."

"Watch us," I said, my confidence faltering.

Jenks's wings hummed. "Guys, my pixy sense is tingling."

Trent stiffened. "It's the curse. He's starting it."

"Then you'd better get going," I said, shoving him to the hallway. "Ellasbeth, where are they?"

The woman's lips pressed together. Ivy's eyes shifted to black, and Jenks's wings clattered a warning. But then Lucy giggled, and Ellasbeth's shoulders slumped. "He's across the hall," she said. "But you can't stop him. He's got like six men in there."

Jenks snickered, and my eyes flicked to the one who had been guarding her. I was going to miss Trent's help, but hell, I'd been doing this long before I learned he was worth my trust. And to be honest, it would be easier if I wasn't worrying about him.

Ready, I looked at Ivy, waiting by the door. Jenks was hovering at her shoulder, and I knew we had this. "Go," I said, and Trent shifted Lucy on his hip.

"Thank you," he said, eyes glinting as he hesitated briefly in front of me before putting a hand on Ellasbeth's back and hustling her out the door and down the hallway. We followed them in case there was trouble. Lucy was whispering loudly, but I didn't think it would make it past the thick doors and soundproofed walls.

"Just like old times," Jenks said, and I couldn't help my smile as I checked my hopper.

"Old times," I scoffed, relishing the adrenaline scouring through me. "We've only been doing this for three years."

"Yeah, but for a pixy, that's like a decade."

Ivy was testing the edge of the knife Trent had given her. Her head came up and she tossed it, catching it again to hold it properly. She looked at the door and then cocked her head. "After you, Jenks?"

Jenks shrugged. "I can't open it. It's a manual."

"Manual it is," the vampire said, and with a soft grunt, she planted a side kick on the lock, exploding the door inward.

Chapter 26

The thick, supposedly kick-proof door took two blows of Ivy's boot before the lock broke free of the studs and the door slammed into the opposite wall. Men shouted, and Ivy dove in, hands in fists and screaming. Jenks was a hot sparkle of dust after her, and I followed as the thuds of fists into flesh exploded into the snap of a wrist or knee and a masculine bellow of outrage.

Yep, it was going to be one of those days.

I slid to a halt in the well-appointed, low-ceilinged, brightly lit room, half of it arranged as a dining room with a small kitchenette, the other half a comfortable living room complete with big TV and two couches. Ivy was rising from the man she'd just downed, her eyes full and black and her shirt torn. She grinned at the two men by the couch, beckoning them forward.

"Rache!" Jenks shouted in warning, and I ducked, falling to a crouch and spinning with my leg extended to hit the man coming out of the bathroom. He was good, stumbling to avoid contact and going down into a controlled fall and rolling free of me.

I stood up—right into the arms of another man. He smelled like cheese as his arms wrapped around me, pinning my back to his front. Bad idea; I flung my head back, breaking his nose. The man bellowed but didn't let go, and my eyes widened as the first man pointed a handgun at me.

Adrenaline pounded. My head snapped back again as I broke his hold. Breath held, I spun him to stand between his buddy and me. The gun seemed to explode in the small room, and I shoved my living shield at the shooter, not knowing if he was shot or I was shot or we had both lucked out.

Arms flailing, my would-be attacker fell into the shooter and they crashed into the small dinette table. Drawing my splat gun, I shot them both. One last spasm, and they were still.

"Ivy!" I spun, then went down on one knee as another gun went off and fire engulfed my leg. My breath came in with a gasp and my free hand clamped over my thigh. A man across the room was pointing a gun at me. *Shit.*

Howling, Ivy blocked a swinging lamp to jam the palm of her hand into someone's jaw. Hair swinging, she planted her right foot and plowed the other into the man who'd shot me, sending him pinwheeling back into the window. He hit with a thud, shaken but not out. The lamp hit the floor and shattered.

Agony crept up my thigh, throbbing to my skull as I hobbled forward, splat gun pointed. Two puffs of air to put him out—and then I fell almost as fast as he had, my hand clamped to my leg. Light-headed, I sat on the couch, not letting go of my gun as Ivy took a last look around the room and strode forward. Blood was a slow but steady leak from my leg. We'd gotten them all, but where was Landon?

"You okay?" Ivy asked, winding her hair back into a bun as Jenks dusted my leg. There was no exit wound. It was still in there.

"I don't know." I strained to see the other side as the pain retreated into a heavy throb.

Ivy reached to touch it, and I jerked away. "It doesn't look bad," she said.

"Well, it hurts like hell."

"That's good then," she said, her worry lines beginning to ease. "Where's Landon?"

"Look out!" Jenks shouted, and my heart thudded. One of the men

I thought I'd downed was aiming another one of those stupid guns at us.

"Move!" I shoved Ivy and brought up my splat gun. *Please let there be enough propellant,* I begged. I lunged for the floor, aim never wavering as I squeezed. The bang of the man's gun echoed, drowning out the puff of my weapon. I hit the floor, my shoulder taking most of the force as the ugly sound of the bullet burrowing into the couch slid through me.

Heart pounding, I lay on the floor, watching the man's eyes roll to the back of his head. I'd gotten him.

Ivy stood as the man's head hit the floor with a thud. "Should have double-tapped him," she said as she extended a hand to me.

"I was a little busy." With a heave, she had me back on the couch. *Where was Landon?*

Ivy wiped her hand under her nose as Jenks flitted over the room, verifying that they were all down. "None of them used any magic," she said uneasily.

"You noticed that too?"

Jenks's wings clattered as he rose up. A door slid open and Landon strode out, flanked by two men with guns. "Because very shortly there won't be any and I wanted to be prepared," Landon said. "Shoot them."

Ivy lunged for the cover of a fallen chair. I yanked her back to me, tapping the line and throwing a circle of protection around us. Bullets pinged off it, and Landon motioned for them to stop. His lips were in a tight line, and I thought he looked ridiculous in his traditional robes and that stupid flat-topped hat. Newt could get away with it, but not him.

"Landon, you're an idiot!" I shouted, the scent of spent gunpowder making it through the barrier where bullets couldn't. "I'm not letting you do this!"

Ivy grimaced. "Let me out."

She darted her gaze to the doorway, and I dropped the circle.

Ivy was a blur, leaping to the doorway to hide behind a wall as they sprayed it. I rolled to the broken coffee table, peeking out to see Landon standing alone as his men advanced on Ivy. I didn't know where Jenks was. *If you've hurt him, Landon . . .*

Vampire fast, Ivy burst from hiding, diving between the men with guns. One man accidentally shot the other in the chest while trying for her. He froze in shock as his buddy went down in a spray of blood—and then Ivy was on him. A kick to the back of his knee sent him to the carpet, and she tackled him. One leg wrapped around the last man's neck and she began to squeeze. The man fought back, sending them crashing into the walls and furniture.

My leg throbbed as I stood. I had to lean heavily on the couch, pointing to Landon, then me, as if in invitation. Ivy could handle two men with automatics. Landon was mine. *Where is Jenks?*

"Trent chicken out?" Landon said, and I lurched a step closer as the unfocused magic in the room began to build.

"He's taking his daughter and ex-fiancée out to lunch."

His lip twitched as he followed the ramifications of that. "Call your vampire off and maybe you live."

"Oh, I'm dead already," I said, ignoring the pain as I pulled myself up straight. "It's just a matter of how much damage I can do first."

"Call her off, and maybe *she* lives," he amended, and in the split second my eyes flicked to Ivy, his hand flamed with a white-hot fire.

Again pain exploded, this time in my chest. Wide eyed, I fell to kneel before Landon as I struggled to breathe, to keep my heart beating. In his hand was a twisted mass of my hair, taken probably from my brush at the church. He'd made a target-specific spell, and I couldn't fight it.

"Son of a fairy whore!" Jenks shouted, back again. "Ivy! Quit playing with that guy! Rache needs help!"

"No, I don't think so," Landon murmured, and I heard Ivy hit the floor, groaning. The man she'd been choking rose, kicking at her as he screamed. I tried to move, but every muscle sang with fire. Breath fast and shallow, I gripped the carpet, pulling myself closer to him. I would not fail in this. I wouldn't!

"If you're going to be a demon, you should be a demon," Landon said softly, and I twitched, my back arching as I fell, looking at the ceiling, trying to get a clean breath. Landon's hands were glowing, a haze of purple hanging between them. Slowly his hands came together. Struggling, he pulled them apart to show a spiderweb spool of glittering gold hanging in the air. And then he blew it at me.

I could do nothing as it settled over me, seeping in past my aura, winding its way to my core. My heart pounded as it begin to search, little darts of magic moving through me like a parasite. Groaning, I rolled over, but it clung, soaked in. Tendrils wafted out past my skin and then fell back as if the curse was looking for something to use to invoke. A soft, insidious chanting came from Landon, along with the sounds of Ivy's frustrated struggle and Jenks's swearing.

My eyes closed as the chant spun into the humming of my blood, settling into me like water, expanding my mind until it was unable to string two thoughts together. I recognized the spiderweb pattern. It was the curse that tied the demons to the ever-after, ages old and unbreakable—and Landon was trying to fix it on me.

It glittered in my thoughts like a living spell, and as I struggled to keep it from invoking, the sound of the drums quickened until it was as if I had been there at the beginning, watching ancient elves craft in the hollows of a primeval forest, calling upon their Goddess to give it the strength to last forever. And now it was seeking to bind itself to me.

Power slipped around my mental grasp like sunbeams, and abruptly I realized the curse was connecting me to Landon. Until the elven curse fixed upon me for good, we were bound together. There, in the background of his thoughts, was the curse to break the lines. *I can take control of this,* I thought, but not when I was fighting to get this damned binding curse off me.

"Let go," Landon whispered, and I felt his breath on my cheek as he knelt over me while I curled into a ball and fought it. "Submit. End the pain," he taunted.

But to submit would bind me to the ever-after. *How long,* I wondered, *how long had Al fought? Newt?* My breath came in a ragged gasp as the winding wisps of the binding curse seemed to find my soul. "No," I groaned, even as it wove deeper.

The stinging slap of his hand meeting my cheek pulled my eyes open. Landon hung over me, sweat beading on him. "Let go!" he demanded. "Be a demon. Die with them."

My eyes searched until they found Jenks and Ivy, held at bay by my torture.

"No," I forced out between clenched teeth, then screamed when he leaned on my shot leg. Agony arched through me. "Get off!" I shouted, flooding him with a jolt of power.

Landon fell back with a cry of outrage, but the second of inattention cost me, and I gasped again, scrambling to catch the binding curse before it settled in any deeper. It didn't have me yet, but the feel of it was familiar, and with a shock, I realized that it drew its strength from the Goddess's will. *Can I use this?*

"Son of a whore!" Jenks shouted, and Landon laughed as Ivy began to struggle as well, held down by Landon's last man, bloodied but still intact.

Jenks was free, darting madly and scoring on the incensed man. "Jenks, no," I tried to shout, my voice failing. Ivy was down. We were losing, losing badly, and my heart leapt into my throat when, with an ugly snarl, Landon got a lucky strike in and Jenks was flung into the wall.

"Jenks!" I staggered to a kneel, and the binding curse dug deeper. It was the Goddess's magic, but Jenks was in danger, and I didn't have time for it. Lurching to Jenks, I sent a wave of force through me, driving the binding curse to my chi where I bubbled it, the hateful thing hissing and black like living tar. I might not be able to get rid of it, but I sure as hell could capture it—hold it in limbo.

I fell before Jenks, hands reaching. He was breathing, and fingers shaking, I lifted him, wanting him to be okay. His wings sparkled, and his eyes were closed.

"You don't know when to stay down, do you," Landon snarled, and something hit the back of my head.

I reeled, clutching Jenks to me as I fell. Landon hit me again, and I let him, curled into a ball to protect Jenks.

"Get your hands off Ivy, you sons of bitches!" Nina screamed.

"Nina!" Ivy called out in panic. "Help Rachel!"

But it was Trent who pried Landon off me, his smooth unworked hands glowing with a power I could feel. A great boom of sound pulled my head up, and Nina dove at the man holding Ivy, wrenching her free and snapping the man's neck.

"Jenks," I whispered, then cowered, one hand holding him to my middle when a second boom of sound shook the room. Dust shifted down, and a wall fell, showing a bedroom.

"Rachel!" Ivy was shouting. "Go help Rachel!"

But the half-crazed vampire went for Landon. He stood in a circle, fire dripping from his hands. Trent was poised between us, energy licking his feet and sparking from his hair. Nina howled, and as Ivy reached to stop her, the woman dove at Landon.

"No!" I shouted, and with a sneer, Landon pushed a silver-rimmed ball of energy at her.

It hit Nina with the sliding sound of chains, and with a jerk that snapped her head forward, she was propelled backward into a far wall. She hit with a sickening thud and slid down, arms and legs askew.

"Oh God, Nina . . . ," Ivy whispered, coughing in the dusty air as she crawled to her.

Trent stood between Landon and me, shaking in anger. "You use borrowed power, Landon. I want it back."

Ivy looked up from Nina, hatred in her black, black eyes. Landon met them, and I swear he quailed. Everyone he had used to protect him was down. "Right," Landon said, spinning to mark a circle.

"He's jumping!" I shouted. The sparkle of power rose up as if in slow motion, and I lurched forward, Jenks still in my grip. Trent tackled me, and I hit the carpet, my fist holding Jenks jamming into my solar plexus. Tears sprang up as I tried to breathe, and with a nasty smile, Landon vanished.

"Not this time," I groaned, eyes clamped shut as I sank a tendril of thought deep in his mind. That curse he'd tried to bind me with was still in my soul, and we would be connected until it became a part of me and was fully invoked. I distantly heard Trent shouting my name, and I smiled as I felt the real world swallowed up by the imagined, but no less real, world of the dewar. I was on the floor in the hotel, but my mind was elsewhere, surrounded by elves.

Thoughts not my own beat at me, and I hid my mind behind Landon's as he sent a wave of emotion and domination over them all, collecting the rising power to bend it to one will. He didn't know I was there in his soul.

I could feel his fear of what had happened and his relief because he thought he had escaped.

The dewar was exactly like the demon collective or the witches' coven—there but not a joining of minds yet, each one remaining an individual. The sound of drums shifted the beat of my heart, and the chant tickled a memory I'd never had.

The dewar elves were spelling, and as their power rose, given direction by Landon's will, a growing sensation of division blossomed with it, like ink on a blank page. *Vivian?* I thought, then quashed it lest Landon know my soul was here, piggybacked on his thoughts. But it was Vivian, and Professor Anders, and a handful of other bright silver thoughts striding through the ponderous beat of the rising curse. Their song was a half step out of sync as they tried to break the curse and prevent the lines from ending, but their voices were small and easily lost.

Morgan! Landon's thought iced through me as he found me hiding. I gasped as a wave of hatred pinned my soul down. *Now you die!*

I felt my body clench as Landon spun his intent through the dewar to collect his borrowed power to his purpose. The chant for the curse to break the lines continued without him as Landon turned his attention to destroying me. Vertigo spun me as he lit a flame of destruction in the middle of my brain. My throat went raw as I screamed as Landon's curse raced through me, burning.

Almost lost under my agony, a twang echoed through me. It was the first ley line, falling under the dewar's curse.

The dewar drums thundered, and a cheer rose, drowning out the pain Landon had pinned me with. He turned his thoughts from me, and a comforting black presence scooped me up, rolling me in the scent of burnt amber until the pain retreated and I could think again.

Rachel? It was familiar, the cooling burnt amber holding a hint of a British lord's accent. I could feel my body shake on the floor of the Cincinnati hotel, but the pretend world in my thoughts was more real and I slowly focused on those minds around mine. A smattering of souls clustered near, stinking of frustration and broken trust. It was the demon collective. Al had found me.

Al? I thought, and his relief swept me, tempered by sour acceptance. My body was being cradled by Trent. I could smell the broken scent of spoiled wine. He held me as Al held my mind, but it was my mind that was in greater danger.

Thank God you came, I thought at Al, knowing all the demons could hear me. *We have to stop this. Landon is breaking the lines!*

Why do you think we're here? Al thought dryly at me. *You shamed them into it. We're likely going to be trapped in the ever-after again, but if the lines end, everything goes with it.* And then he thought so loudly that for a moment it drowned out the heart-hammering drums, *To me, all free souls! To me!*

Somewhere, pixy dust sifted down upon my bleeding leg. Somewhere I heard Ivy crying for Nina. Somewhere Trent rocked me, begging me not to leave him.

But I couldn't abandon the dewar, and I felt my mind expand as free souls came—demon, elf, witch—so sure and swift that the dewar's confidence faltered.

Trent! I called when I felt his thoughts wrap around mine as his arms were in reality. *No! He's here to help!* I shouted when the demons bristled. *Leave off!* And I gasped, both our bodies jerking when Al yanked Trent's soul next to mine.

Your thoughts smell funny, but they're strong, Al said, and then we all started, faltering as another line snapped.

I felt myself jerk again as my thoughts expanded as if in a hiccup. Trent's presence beside mine grew bright as the demon minds dimmed. Alone, Trent and I seemed to stand with the elves and witches who'd cleaved to us. Confused, I listened to the dewar drums beat against us, furiously renewed by the snapping of a second ley line.

Al! Trent, help me find Al! I thought as the howling of surface demons being pulled back to the ever-after became strong, the scraping of their claws like nails on a blackboard, shivering through my awareness like ice. The vampire souls were being forced back to the ever-after—and I think the demons were going with them.

Help me! I thought, terrified. As the lines went, so would they, reducing them sliver by sliver. *Al!* I shouted, reaching for his presence, but it slipped like silver past me.

I can't help them, Trent thought, frustrated as he hid me from the dewar drums. *They're bound to the ever-after.*

I wouldn't allow it, but the theoretical world made another hiccup as a fourth line snapped. I could feel the undead souls sliding past my awareness, howling as they spiraled back into the ever-after. Determination alone held the demons in reality, and that wasn't enough, for when the last line went, so would they. Landon would have it all.

I gasped as a fifth line fell, and the demon collective began to fall apart in panic. *Don't let go of me,* I thought to Trent. *I'm getting them out.*

What? Trent thought, and I focused on his awareness until his thoughts became clear.

I'm going in after them. Don't let go!

There was only one way I could find and get a grip on the demons. I didn't have time to think about how smart this might or might not be, and I dove deep into my mind to find that tiny ball of black hate that Landon had cursed me with: the original binding curse. *Take me,* I whispered, opening myself to it and willing it to bind with my soul.

I gasped, hearing Al's agonized cry of heartache as the curse gleefully dug its claws into me, molding to me, becoming part of me. And if it was a part of me, then I was a part of it. With a snap that shook me to my core, the demons' thoughts became clear, huddled together in misery.

Rachel, why? Al asked, his presence clearer than the rest. *You were to be the beginning of us anew, with all the best parts and none of the bad.*

Another line snapped with the sharpness of a tension wire giving way. Somewhere I could feel Trent's arms around me, the warmth of his tears on my face. His mind, twining about mine, was fainter. He was losing me. *Grab someone,* I thought at Al. *Tell them to grab someone else. Everyone goes. Hurry! The lines are going faster.*

Another line snapped, and the demon collective cried out as if an elevator had dropped six feet. Panic sifted up through me, pushed by their own thoughts of failure.

Let us go, Al thought, and I focused my awareness on him. If I hadn't taken the binding curse, I never would have found him. But in the doing, I'd lost Trent.

You want me to survive? I asked Al. *Then you have to survive with me! I'm not doing this by myself. Hold on!*

There was only the thinnest thread of hope weaving through them, laced with madness and strengthened with hate. I fed on that, bolstering it as I focused on the binding curse, still hot-iron bright in me. I could feel them all behind me as I ran the lines of the spell, seeing the shades of color and sound, looking for the telltale sparkle of the Goddess magic that the elves had needed to create it. Of course the demons couldn't break it—it was Goddess made. But I could.

Rachel, no! Al protested as he saw my intent. *It will kill you!*

You're going to live forever, you son of a bastard! I exclaimed as I sensed him try to wiggle free of me. My thoughts clenched on his awareness, I held him as I dove to the bottom of the elven curse and found the Goddess, chortling with delight at the mischief she was making. Mystics swirled around her, visible in my mind's eye like purple eyes lidded with feathers.

A mystic saw my thoughts, focusing on me with rapt attention, unable to remember but knowing I meant something. Then another. Oblivious, the Goddess strummed a ley line, laughing in delight as it curled up and vanished, and my temper snapped.

Hey! I exclaimed, and the Goddess's emotion imploded on itself, boiling down to a thought of recognition and hatred.

You! the Goddess snarled, and I opened my thoughts to her, inviting attack. The binding curse was created with the Goddess's strength, and it would take that to break it.

I will kill you! the Goddess screamed into my mind, ribbons of her bright intent coursing through me to snuff out my awareness.

The last ley line lay glittering, overloaded and humming. It would fall soon of its own accord without the Goddess's will, and I wanted to weep for the stupidity of it all. The ever-after was going to fall. I couldn't stop it. I could only keep the demons from falling with it.

You want to kill me? I thought at her. *Try,* I thought, willing the mystics to me, bringing them home, accepting them.

The Goddess screamed as she felt herself disintegrate. I could hear the dewar shaking with her outrage. And in that bare instant before she turned her thoughts to crush me, I wrenched control of the mystics from her.

Power sang through me, a million voices turned to one intent.

No! the Goddess cried, panicked. *Give them back!* But she was helpless as I bent my will to the elves' ancient binding curse.

End this, I said to them, and with no more than my will, the curse that bound the demons to the fate of the ever-after simply . . . ceased to be.

A perfect moment of understanding and purity chimed through the demon collective. It resonated from me, blending into the demons and beyond. I felt them all, their awe, their bewilderment of grace bestowed. The wave washed out from them to leave a shocked silence.

And then the last line between reality and the ever-after broke.

They are mine! the Goddess howled at me, and suddenly I was scrambling to save myself as the Goddess dug at me, reclaiming what was hers.

Fire burned as the mystics rose up, two forces of the same beginning now poised to swamp each other until one was supreme, the other dead. But I didn't want the job.

Al! I called, floundering. *Al, help me!* I cried, knowing he alone could pull me free—if he loved me enough to forgive me for what I'd done. Yes, I had saved them, but I'd used elven magic to do it. I was polluted, a pariah, unclean and reviled.

Please, I whispered as the Goddess dug to my soul, and a sudden smack on my face jolted me to reality.

My eyes sprang open. I was looking at a broken ceiling. Trent was holding me, my head in his lap. Al knelt beside him. The scent of ozone was thick in the air, and my throat hurt. "You're here," I said, voice raspy.

The instant of relief in the demon flashed to nothing, and he pulled back. "Why did you do it?" he said darkly. "Everyone knows you've got mystics in you now."

"You treacherous demon bitch!" Landon screamed, and I gasped as Trent stood, dumping me in his effort to get between me and Landon.

"You will not!" Trent shouted as he stood over me, gesturing.

Landon howled, red faced, as he did the same. But nothing happened. Blinking, he looked at his hands.

Trent became white faced, and Al laughed. "You broke the lines, little man," the demon said, and Landon backed up as Al strode forward, white-gloved hand reaching. "Guess what? I'm bigger than you."

The lines were dead. *Jenks . . . Where's Jenks?*

Landon made a dash for the door, robes unfurling as his soft slippers scuffed.

"Excuse me," Al said, striding out after him.

"Jenks!" I called, sitting up in panic, and then opened my fist, remembering that I'd been holding him. "Oh God! Are you okay?" I asked, seeing him peering up at me with his wings hardly glowing and his narrow face pinched.

"I don't feel so good," the pixy said as he rubbed his shoulder. "Did we win?"

The lines were dead. The ever-after was going to vanish. But the demons would not go with it. "I don't know," I whispered, beginning to shake.

Trent sat down beside me, exhausted. "The hospitals are going to be full. I'm taking you home to get that leg looked at."

My attention darted to my thigh. It was throbbing like the devil, but at least the bleeding had stopped. "Where's Ivy? Nina?"

"About five minutes ahead of us," Trent said as he looked at Jenks sitting on my palm, trembling from the cold and shock.

"Lucy?" I asked as he stood.

"With Ellasbeth," he said shortly as he lifted me to my feet.

The blood rushed from my head and I stood for a moment, wavering. I could hear noise in the street. The lines were gone. Magic was dead. We'd be lucky to get out of Cincinnati before midnight. "You think giving her to Ellasbeth was a good idea?"

Trent tucked a shoulder under mine. "I think you were right about her and I was wrong. Can you walk?"

Jaw clenched, I took a hobbling step to the door. "I might have broke something."

"I think so, too. We should get out of here."

Nauseated and holding Jenks close, I limped to the door. The demons were safe, but I'd killed the source of magic to do it. That probably wasn't going to go over very well.

Chapter 27

I leaned hard against Trent as the elevator lurched and settled. My leg throbbed, and I cupped a depressed pixy tight to me. I knew Jenks was thinking about his kids, scattered over the city, and Jumoke and Izzy at Trent's estate. If he couldn't fly, then they couldn't either. There were no predators in Trent's gardens, but that wasn't what Jenks would be worried about. It was the natural magic from free-ranging mystics that gave pixies flight, and there wasn't enough of them around anymore. The Goddess was pissed, having gathered her untold thousands of eyes to her and gone brooding somewhere, plotting to kill me.

Or at least most of them, I thought as a tingle passed between Trent and me as the ornate doors slid apart. Noise spilled in, and what little zest I had left for the day vanished as I saw the FIB hats and I.S. vests in the lobby. "What happened?" I asked as Jenks perked up, a faint dust hazing him.

"Looks like someone made a call." Trent scooped me up and carried me out when I balked. There were too many people, and I was sure more than one of them wanted to talk to me in ugly, accusing voices. My bleeding leg was obvious, and Trent started for the front desk. Both an I.S. and an FIB cop were interviewing a tearful hotel employee, and the restaurant to the left was full of sullen Weres. One of them caught sight of me, jiggling his buddy's elbow before grinning and giving me a bunny-eared kiss-kiss.

Heads began to turn, and I felt sick. "There's Edden," I said as I looked over Trent's shoulder to the bar. Immediately Trent did a one-eighty, making me dizzy. "Do you see Nina or Ivy?"

Trent shifted his grip on me before taking the shallow stairs up, his jolting pace making my leg throb even more. "No. I think they got out before all this."

"I can't see fairy farts," Jenks complained. "Rache, it's my wings that don't work, not my brain. Put me on your shoulder, will you?"

Someone pointed us out to Edden and he grimaced before turning away again. It wasn't a promising start. "You sure you can hold on?"

"Hell yes," the pixy grumbled, and I carefully shifted him. "I'm not going to yell at Edden from your hand."

"I know how you feel," I said, glancing at Trent. "Ah, I appreciate this, but—"

"You will sit where I put you and not move," he said as he pushed his way through the milling uniforms and into the informal bar area. "'Scuse me. Pardon!" he said loudly, finally setting me on one of the bar stools. It was about the right height, but I almost lost my breakfast at the pain when Trent moved someone's satchel off the adjacent stool and lifted my leg onto it.

"Edden," I called, and the man's ears went red. "Edden!" I called louder, and his shoulders hunched. I debated sliding down and hobbling over, but Trent gestured for me to stay, needing to turn sideways to slip through the crowd to reach him.

"This sucks," Jenks complained from my shoulder, and I waved at Edden when he looked at me after Trent shook his hand. The officers he was talking to broke up, and the short, graying, and overworked FIB captain reluctantly came over, hands in his pockets.

"Edden, did you see Ivy and Nina?" I asked even before he got close.

Edden glanced at the big glass doors, clearly worried. "I saw them into the ambulance myself," he said, then sent his gaze over my bleeding leg, Jenks sitting on my shoulder, and then Trent. "Al said you were going to try and stop Landon." He pulled himself straighter, looking over the crowd. "Paramedic! I've got a non-life-threatening GSW!"

"Gee, thanks," I said, trying to smile. *Al, eh? Interesting . . .*

"The slug is still in her leg." Trent hovered close to keep people from knocking into me. "Can you get her to emergency or should I take her home?"

Edden scratched his shoulder, his expression creased in worry. "It will take an hour to get an ambulance out here. How fast is your copter?"

"An hour!" I exclaimed, and Jenks's wings clattered when Edden took my chin and peered at me.

"You aren't dying," he said distantly, evaluating my pain by the look in my eyes. "The roads are clogged." He let go of my chin and straightened. "This is worse than last time."

An unusually small woman with a Red Cross tackle box was trying to push her way through the taller people. I heard a grunt and the man blocking her way jumped. "Oh, I'm sorry!" She beamed up at him, worming her way closer and shoving people to make a space around me. "My God, you would think they were afraid to go outside," she muttered, eyeing me for signs of shock. "Why are there so many Weres here?"

"They cleared the hotel out for me," I said, and Edden started edging backward and beckoning someone closer. She was poking at my leg, so I looked away, trying not to pass out. If I passed out, I'd never make it to the next fight, and there was going to be another. The vampires' souls were gone. I'd felt them being pulled back to the ever-after, trapped in a universe that would soon shrink to nothing and die. Cormel was going to be pissed.

I looked past Trent—now on the phone with a finger in his open ear— to the night-gloomed street. Traffic was stopped, and the flashes of red and blue lights on the buildings were ominous. "I can't believe you hired Al," I said to get my mind off my leg, and Edden's entire demeanor shifted to a pleased wickedness. "Seriously? Where is he, anyway?"

"Chasing down Landon." Edden almost swaggered, so pleased was he. "He's the one who called us in. We got here before the I.S. Ah, if it's any consolation, Cormel agrees that the elves were trying to kill the undead."

"No, that doesn't help," I said sourly, then jerked, pain stabbing me. "Ow?"

The paramedic looked at Edden, not me. "It's still in there."

"I know it's still in there!" I exclaimed, and Trent smiled as he put a hand over his phone.

"Edden, the surface demons are gone, correct?" he asked, and Edden nodded.

"You need to get that leg looked at," Edden said.

"I am," I said snarkily, gesturing at the woman wrapping a temporary bandage around my leg so it wasn't so awful looking.

"I mean," Edden said, leaning in close, "by someone who can do something about it."

I smiled hopefully at the paramedic, and she shook her head.

"No. This goes to emergency. I don't have the forms to file for taking out a bullet."

Trent snapped his phone closed. He looked pleased with himself and I swear I felt a tingle as his hand touched my shoulder. "My med copter is coming. I'll take care of Rachel. Where did they take Ivy?"

"I've no idea."

"Can you find out?" Jenks piped up, and Edden's "I have things to do" expression softened at the worry in the pixy's voice.

"I'll ask." Edden gave my other shoulder a squeeze. He headed out into the mess, shouting a request to get a name and contact number from the Weres and get them out of here. I thought it sweet that Trent was going to take me to the same facility where Ivy and Nina were. Or maybe he knew I'd never stay at the hospital unless I could hobble down the hallway to make sure Ivy was okay.

The paramedic pushed some pills into my hand and curled my fingers over them. "Pain amulets aren't working. Find some water and take these. You have four hours to get that bullet removed and sutured, or they're going to make it heal open and ugly. Got it?"

"Got it," I whispered as she snapped her tackle box closed and went to tend to someone's crushed finger. I opened my hand and looked at the little packet of pills. I suppose it was better than nothing, and I took the glass of water Trent had reached over the bar for.

"Thanks," I said, words garbled as I juggled the pills around on my tongue. "You know there are a lot of people who need a medical copter more than me." God, they tasted awful, and I swallowed them down and made a face.

"I'm sure there are," Trent said as he kissed my forehead.

"Tink loves a duck," Jenks complained. "You're not going to sift your dust together right here, are you? Take me over to Edden. He's warm."

Edden was stuck in the middle of the floor, and I didn't like the way he kept looking back at me or the shade of red his neck was turning. The Weres were beginning to leave, and Jenks's wings tickled my neck as we both realized that every single one of them was running in the same direction the instant they hit the pavement. "What is going on?" I asked.

Jenks sifted a thin, frustrated dust and Trent fidgeted, his expression wary as we watched three more Weres run down the street. "Ah . . . I'll be right back," he said when Jenks began making a weird whine, Trent jiggling on his feet before lurching into motion and striding to Edden. The floor was clearing out—and it made me even more nervous than the crowded one.

"I don't care if it's the devil himself they got pinned down, you get your ass over there now and stop it!" Edden was shouting.

Jenks's wings clattered, the barest hint of silver slipping down my front. "You just going to sit here?"

My leg was bandaged, and I held it as I moved it off the stool, teeth clenched as I tried not to use my leg muscles at all. My stomach lurched, and I almost lost those lame pills. I hesitated, the bar hard under my hand as I planned my way over, noting every handrail, every chair.

"Come on, Rache!" Jenks urged. "They're almost done!"

I painfully hobbled forward, every step hurting. Trent caught sight of me, his expression shifting to annoyance, and he slid an arm around my back to hold me up as I made the last few steps to lean on the decorative side table. "What's up?" I asked.

Clearly upset, Edden pointed at five more men, and they trooped out. Six more released Weres jostled around them and ran up the street in the same direction.

"Rachel, I'm sorry," the captain said. "Get up to the roof and wait for Trent's copter. I have to go. There's a mob at Fountain Square, and without magic, we can't stop it."

"That's like half a block from here," Jenks said, and my eyes flicked to the door and the new night beyond.

"Which is why you are going to go to the roof until Trent can get you out."

Get me out? Suspicious, I put a hand on Edden's arm and stopped him cold. "Why?"

"Get her out!" Edden exclaimed, his eyes hard on Trent as he pried my fingers off.

Trent's hold on me strengthened as he began to pull me toward the elevators. "Let's go, Rachel," he said, but his worry tripped all my warning flags and I dug my heels in—so to speak.

"Trent, what don't you want me to see?"

Edden's expression became almost panicked, and I squinted mistrustfully at Trent as he soothed me with a calm "It's nothing you can do anything about."

Nothing I can do anything about?

Jenks's wings fluttered and he tugged on my ear. "Rache, they've got a demon pinned down in the square. My wings are broken, not my ears."

"Jenks!" Edden exclaimed, and Trent, too, winced.

"At the square?" I looked at the doors, remembering the Weres running that way. Panic slid through me at the thought of what a human, what anyone, might do if they found a demon unable to do magic. *My God. Al.*

"Way to go, Jenks," Trent grumbled.

"You said she couldn't do anything about it!" Jenks shouted, hurting my ear. "Well, she's not dead, is she?"

"And I want to keep it that way!" Trent argued.

I pushed up from the table, telling myself that my leg didn't hurt that much now that I'd swallowed those pills. "Is it Al?" I asked, and Trent lifted his shoulders, unhappy. "You don't know!"

Edden put a hand on my shoulder and I shrugged it off. "You didn't think this wasn't going to happen, did you?" he said, brown eyes sad as he looked past Trent to the dark street. "Demons have preyed upon humans and Inderlanders for thousands of years, and now that they're helpless, what did you expect? That we'd take them to our bosoms and make cocoa?"

"Something a little better than this." Teeth clenched, I shoved past Trent and headed for the door. It was only half a block. I could hear the noise from here.

"Damn it, Jenks!" Trent swore. "This was exactly what I was trying to avoid."

"Rachel!" Edden called, following me. "You're not in any shape—"

I took a step down, pain widening my eyes. Breathless, I leaned against the stairway railing. God help me, I had two more to go. "I just busted my ass getting them to reality. I'm not going to let a mob kill them! Now either get me over there or get out of my way!"

Both men were silent as they looked at me, both with regret.

"Well?" I snapped, pain making my words sharper than I wanted. "Just how serious are you about this, or is it all only if it's convenient?"

"That's not fair," Trent said, and then I gasped when he scooped me up.

"Trent! Put me down!" I shouted. "You son of a bastard, put me down!"

But Jenks was laughing. "Relax, Rache. Look at his ears. He's taking you to the square."

"You are?" Blinking fast, I put my arm around Trent's neck to distribute my weight more evenly. Sure enough, Trent's ears were red with irritation and his jaw was set. "I knew I loved you," I said, almost crying. "Oh God. Thank you."

Trent's gaze was fixed on the door as Edden dropped back in frustrated defeat. "I hope you still do by sunrise," he said dryly. "This is the dumbest thing I've ever done."

"Kalamack, she can't even walk!" Edden protested as I used my good foot to shove the glass door open.

The smell of the concrete night rose up around us, gritty on my tongue with the flashing lights and the sounds of an angry crowd. "You sure?" Trent asked.

The sound of gunfire popped. I thought of Al. I had no magic, no safety net, and I couldn't walk well. "Yes." I had to, even if fear had me so tense I felt sick.

Trent began to walk, his steps usually so graceful now jarring.

"Okay," I said more to myself than anyone else. "We'll finish this, find out where Ivy and Nina are, and then go to Trent's to check on Lucy. I'm sure they're fine. Trent, I'm sure she got Lucy out of here before the sun went down."

"She did," Trent said as we turned the corner. "I already . . . called. My God . . ."

He stopped dead on the sidewalk as the wall of sound hit us. My mouth dropped as I stared, heart hammering. The square was packed with screaming people, angry, with their fists in the air. The lights were bright and the big TV showed a frightened newscaster, the captions spelling tragedy and fear as the sun went down across the U.S. On the stage in a bright spotlight was a man with a handgun. He was pointing it at a kneeling figure before him, bloodied and beaten. Bound and held from behind by two more men was an androgynous figure with big bony feet showing from under a shapeless robe. *Newt.*

"No!" I screamed, wiggling until I hit the ground. Trent pulled me up, and I reached out.

"Stop!" I screamed as the man on the stage shouted something. The crowd howled, and then I almost passed out as the flash of the gun and the sound of a shot shocked through me.

A wave of sound echoed between the buildings as the mob cried out. I could not breathe, could not believe it as the bound figure fell, dead, on the stage. I. Could. Not. Believe. This.

"At least it smells better than the French revolution," Al said at my elbow.

I spun, almost falling until Trent propped me up. "My God," I said, touching Al in his new suit and lingering on his red, goat-slitted eyes. "Go," I said, shoving him back toward the hotel. "Go! Get out of here! Trent has a copter coming. Go!"

"It's her!" someone shouted, and my heart seemed to stop. "It's her! It's that demon woman!"

"Shit," Trent whispered, and I went cold as people in the streets turned, their faces ugly with fear, hatred, and a mad aggression. "Rachel—"

I gasped as someone grabbed me from behind. My leg gave way and I fell. "Trent!" I screamed, fighting the elbows and hands as I was pulled up and away. "Damn it, let me go!" I demanded, and then screamed when they twisted my arm behind me, forcing me through the crowd. Agony numbed my leg and I fell, so they picked me up, shoving me from person to person, pinching my arms, pulling my hair, tripping me. I couldn't see, couldn't breathe.

"Jenks!" I called out. He was gone. I fought to be free but someone punched me in the middle and I bent double, unaware and struggling to breathe until they hauled me up onto the stage.

Terrified, I hung in someone's grip, shocked and bleeding as Al landed next to me in a sliding thud. Men kicked him to stay down, and he sat where he was, his new suit torn and his face bloodied. Newt still stood, her expression proud and a little wild as she waited beside me, her hands bound with a plastic bag.

"You try anything and I'll shoot you!" the man with the gun screamed at us. The bleeding corpse behind him was dragged off, and the crowd carried it away. My gore rose, and I struggled to keep from vomiting. *Trent? Where are Trent and Jenks?* Jenks couldn't fly. He'd be crushed.

"If you have any ideas . . . ," Al said, sitting cross-legged with his hands laced behind his head.

"No, not really." I pulled my eyes from the slick smear of blood, wondering how many demons they'd killed so far. What the hell kind of an ending was this?

"Get up!" the man with the gun screamed. "I said, get up!"

Al stood, his expression far more placid than I would've expected. "Thank you for our freedom," he said to me as the man with the gun cavorted before us, whipping the crowd up to bolster his own courage. "I will never understand why you cared."

"I don't like bullies," I said flatly, and Newt smiled. The electric lights caught a glint in her eye, almost anticipatory. I knew she longed for an end, but this was wrong, so wrong.

"They will all die!" the man screamed. "All the demons. Magic is dead, and we will be safe! Safe from the freaks and unholy demons!"

They might kill me, but they would damn well listen to me first.

"Shut the hell up!" I shouted, my voice cutting through the noise as if it was supplemented by magic. The crowd heard me, and in the barest hesitation of their outrage, I added, "And get your stinking hands *off* me!"

Adrenaline was a silver ribbon, snapping through me as I plowed my elbow into the man holding me. Weight on my good leg, I spun to break his nose with my elbow, shoving him off the stage and into the crowd.

Al cried out in elation, his expression fearsome as he rose and moved in sharp, decisive motions, flipping the two who held him into the crowd. Like a banshee gone berserk, Newt howled, kicking at everyone who got close. Between them, no one dared try the stage, and in the sudden hush, I realized no one was up here anymore but us, the forgotten gun, and the man who had shot it, now huddling beside a huge amp.

Al paced back and forth, his steps red from stepping in blood. Newt held her hands out to me and I tried to get the plastic knots free. "I was beginning to think you might not make it in time," she said dryly.

My heart was pounding, and I couldn't feel my leg. "Who was that?" I asked, eyes darting to the blood smear. Behind us, the man who'd shot him cowered. His hand had bones sticking out, and the gun, now useless to him, lay tauntingly within reach.

Newt glanced at the blood, then rubbed her wrists as the knots came loose. "I don't know. He wasn't a demon. Honestly, I was simply enjoying the fountain and he was sitting beside me."

Relief coursed through me, quickly followed by anger. "They killed an innocent man because he might have been a demon?" I said loudly, then turned to the crowd, slowly realizing what they'd done, what they'd allowed, hell, what they'd encouraged to happen. "You killed a man and he wasn't even a demon!" I shouted, my voice echoing between the buildings. "What is *wrong* with you people!"

"They're demons!" someone shouted, quickly hushed by those nearest her.

"Yeah? So what?" I shouted back. That didn't go over so well, and the murderous rise of complaint started to gain strength. The crowd, though, was beginning to break up at the back as the I.S. and FIB began to show.

"Demons deserve to die!" another shouted, and I turned to him, feeling both strong and weak with Newt and Al behind me.

"Why, because you say so?" I said, fingertips tingling. "Maybe, but not on my watch. I warned you. I told you taking the easy way out was a bad idea. Did you listen? No! So you're going to listen to me now!"

That went over even better, and small fights were breaking out all over as the Weres tried to get closer to the stage. "You need more practice at this," Al said as two men vaulted onto the stage.

"Go home!" I shouted as Newt waved a cautionary finger at the men.

"Go home, and pray that I find a way to reinstate the lines in Arizona, or demons without magic will be the least of your problems! You all think that security and peace are born from destroying everything stronger than you? There is no safety. There is no peace but what you make, every day, every second, with every choice."

As if that was the signal, the crowd surged forward, swamping us.

Panic iced through me again, and I slipped on some poor man's blood and went down, almost passing out from the pain as my hip hit the stage. "Rache!" I heard distantly, and then I'd had it.

"Enough!" I shouted, and a great boom of sound exploded from me. My fingers tingled, and I pulled my head up as men cried out, falling back from the stage, pushed by a glowing ball of silver light. My hair was floating, and I tried to flatten it, but I couldn't stand up, and my hands were sticky. I felt as if I were glowing, and I looked at Al. He had fallen, seeming as shocked as I was. It had been magic, but how?

"Oh, you did it now!" Newt crowed, kicking that gun under the amp and almost dancing as she lurched to me and hauled me to my feet. Everyone in the square was picking themselves up. It was so quiet you could hear individual people and the whine of a siren.

"Mystics?" Al said, again at my elbow, but he wasn't talking to me, and Newt nodded.

My heart seemed to both sink and expand. Mystics. I couldn't hear them, but clearly they were here with me. And if they had found me, then so would . . . the Goddess.

"Oh no," I whispered, scrambling to hide, to run, but Newt held my arm, forcing me to stay still and face the crowd.

"Just . . . let me," she almost snarled, her lips inches away as she pinched my arm. "Let me in, Rachel."

And panicked, I did, wiggling as I felt her siphon off some of the energy in my chi to shift my aura to hide me for a few moments more. As soon as the Goddess figured out she could find me by the mystics circling me, I was a goner.

"Bloody Band-Aid," Newt said, eyeing the dispersing crowd. "I feel better already. Al?"

Someone in an FIB hat was beckoning us to the stairway. Numb, I shuffled that way. The crowd was scattering now as the cops started arresting them en masse, cuffing everyone and making them kneel in rows.

"Well, I'm not going to say this is a good thing," Al grumped, and I gasped when Newt clenched my arm.

"Not good!" she snapped. "The lines are broken and you're still going to hold to outdated beliefs based on a war that not even you remember the cause of?"

"It's elven magic," he whined, looking pathetic.

"Both of you shut up," I said as I saw Trent. Oh God, he had Jenks with him, and I almost fell off the stage trying to get to them. The crowd was dispersing. They even had an ambulance, and I felt sick as I realized the medical people were clustered about that man who'd been shot. Another, very loud group of FIB agents was reading the rights to the man who'd shot him, his broken hand bound before him, bleeding and ugly. Maybe the shot man was still alive.

"Trent!" I called, and he reached out. I fell into his arms, burrowing my head against his shoulder as I shook. "They were going to kill me!" I sobbed as Jenks's wings clattered. "What is wrong with them!"

"Shhh, you're okay," he soothed, and I pulled my head up, sniffing and sniveling as Al stiffly handed me a cloth handkerchief. "Next time, can we stop the lynch mob some other way?"

"Jenks, you're flying," I said, and the satisfied pixy landed on Newt's shoulder.

"For the moment," he said, sparkles almost vanishing. "Crap on toast, girl. How come you can do magic and no one else can?"

"Because she's got a growing sliver of mystics looking to her," Al said sourly. "That's probably why you can fly. She's a magnet."

I felt like a magnet, all spiky and full of little electrical charges. I looked up at the *thump-thump-thump* of chopper wings echoing between the buildings. What was left of the crowd scattered, even some of the handcuffed Weres sneaking off. It felt good to be alive, and I leaned into Trent even more. "I told you this would happen. And no one listened."

"Can she ever be right without rubbing your nose in it?" Al griped, and Jenks spilled a silver dust that vanished too quickly for my comfort.

The chopper swung into the square, and I smiled up at it, knowing it was going to take me somewhere where I wouldn't have to think for a while, where I could have a bath, wash my hair, and maybe get the bullet out of my leg.

"Oops, she's going down!" someone called, and I felt myself fall into Trent's arms.

And I swear, I heard him singing as the helicopter lifted us up and away.

Chapter 28

The wind whipped my hair into a snarled mess as I inched to the edge of the medical helicopter. In an instant, the scent of antiseptic and bandages was stripped away, the hint of pavement and horse coming to me in the moonless night. Trent reached up, his hand bandaged and a raw red scrape on his cheek where he'd fallen. My heart seemed to skip a beat as I settled my fingers into his. I could have lost him. I could have lost everything.

"She should be in the chair," said the paramedic who'd taken the bullet out and stitched me up on the way over. Trent just shrugged and lifted me down, my muscles aching as his grip tightened on me. My ribs hurt, and I held my breath. I'd rather die than sit in that chair with straps and be lowered down.

Which is a distinct possibility, I thought as my feet hit the parking lot and the resulting jolt of pain broke through whatever mundane drugs they had me on. "Thanks," I whispered, feeling ill as I tucked the crutch Trent was handing me under my arm. It was already sized to me. Seemed he kept them on hand as a matter of course.

I was still trying to wrap my head around the mob at the square. They'd shot that man in cold blood. Newt was going to be next. Then me.

Then Al. Nothing could excuse that kind of mindless panic, and I was shaken, betrayed by the same people I'd risked my life to save.

"Tink loves a duck!" Jenks protested, tugging at my hair as the wind swamped him. "Can we get inside? I want to check on my kids."

"First thing on the list," I said as I looked past Al and Newt, ogling Trent's holdings, to the cluster of people coming down the stairs to greet us. This wasn't the usual way, but the parking lot had been empty for almost three months and apparently there was an issue waiting for Trent in his front office and this was quicker.

"That's one good thing," I whispered, barely heard over the copter blades as I saw Quen, Ellasbeth, and the girls. Ellasbeth held Ray, the little girl solemn and quiet. Lucy was more vocal, but clearly unhappy as she reached for Trent, complaining loudly when Ellasbeth stopped short at the sight of Al and Newt.

Grinning, Al tweaked Lucy's nose, but his smile vanished worryingly fast.

"Trent!" the woman exclaimed, looking frazzled with her hair down and Lucy tugging on it. "There are demons everywhere! Everywhere!"

"None of them can do any magic, Ellie," Trent admonished, taking Lucy before the little girl jumped out of her mother's arms.

"But they're everywhere!" the woman complained, shooting sideways glances at Newt and Al. "Cooking in the bar's kitchen, in the garage looking at your cars, in the conservatory talking to the fairies. I've had to put up a sign to keep them out of your apartments."

"I'll see what I can do," Trent said as Lucy wrapped her arms around his neck and gave him a fierce, little-girl kiss.

My teeth clenched as I step-hopped to the stairs, trying to decide how to get up them. Ellasbeth looked awful, not just tired from dealing with the stress of what was probably four hundred demons showing up on her doorstep, but frightened now that magic was gone.

"You need to do something about Landon, too," she said, taking Lucy back when Trent saw me balk at the stairs. "He's been on the news, talking to everyone with a mic. He's trying to put a spin on this to blame Rachel."

"Me!" I barked as Trent cupped a hand around my free elbow to half lift me up a step.

Ellasbeth looked at me, her words hesitant as she took in the bandages and blood. Not all of it was mine. Most of it wasn't mine, actually, and that somehow made it worse. "Ah, no one believes," she said. "But you need to do something, Trent. He's blaming you, too."

"I'll get right on it," he said wearily, and she scowled, thinking she was being put off, but I honestly didn't know what she expected him to do. According to the news, anti-Landon sentiment was growing among the elves as they demanded answers and he kept blaming me. Even the elves had lost their magic. Either the Goddess was withholding her strength, or the elves needed the lines, too.

And yet I had blown down everyone in the square using mystics. Hurray, me. I snuck a glance at Al and Newt, glad they both seemed to be ignoring it. Newt's cheerful attitude in the face of the-end-of-all-magic wasn't giving me any warm fuzzies, though.

"Sa'han, Dali is waiting for you in your office, and Cormel would like to speak with you at his convenience," Quen said.

Ray reached out, and Trent took her, leaving me to handle the next step alone. "In my office, eh?" Trent said, nodding for Quen to take my elbow since Ray had buried her face in his chest and wouldn't let go. "Tell Cormel he's going to have to come to me if he wants to chat."

Newt and Al were waiting for us at the top of the stairs, and Quen scooped me up. I would've protested, but I'd slowed everyone else down to a crawl. "That was incredibly stupid," Quen muttered, lagging behind as Trent took Ellasbeth's elbow and turned her away from me. "You put yourself and Trent in incredible danger taking the stage like that."

I frowned, not saying anything until we reached the top and I wiggled until he put me down. "I didn't take the stage, they dragged me up there. And what would you have done if you saw Jon on a stage with a gun to his head and a dead body at his knees?"

Quen's eye twitched as he looked past me to Ellasbeth, ushering Lucy inside, Trent and Ray following as Trent argued over something with the frazzled woman. "The same. Are you going to let me help you to Trent's office?"

The helicopter was winding up again, lights flashing over us and making Al look more demonic than usual as he grabbed my arm. "I'll help her," he said, making me wonder at his motives.

"Both of you back off," Newt said as she pushed Al away with a single finger on his chest. "I'm helping Rachel today. She saved my life, the poor dear."

I was starting to feel like a dog's tug toy, but I really wanted to sit down and didn't care who helped me to Trent's office. I leaned heavily on Newt as Al held the door and we shuffled inside. "Thanks," I muttered, and Jenks swore at me as I tucked my hair behind my ear when the wind cut off. I'd forgotten he was there. Ellasbeth was already halfway down the hall, her voice twined with Lucy's as the little girl tried to outdo her mother in volume.

"It was incredibly brave of you," Newt said as we slowly paced after them. "Very brave, but incredibly stupid."

Oh God, I thought my ribs were going to cave in, and my teeth clenched. "I wasn't thinking about rescuing you. I just wanted them to stop killing people."

"Obviously," she cooed, and my steps became even slower as we got to the carpet in the hallway and I couldn't shuffle anymore.

Trent was standing outside his office at his empty secretary's desk. His expression was pinched with irritation. Ellasbeth didn't look much better, and she almost had a cow when he handed Ray to Al. "Quen, I'd like you and Jon to find out where Ivy and Nina are. Apparently they never made it to the hospital."

I spun, my sight dimming when I moved too fast. "What?"

Quen took Ray from Al and inclined his head. "Sa'han," he said simply, turning to go.

The soft clatter of Jenks's wings under my ear shocked through me. He'd been so quiet I'd forgotten he was there. "Hey, Quen," he shouted. "How about dropping me off at the greenhouse? I want to check on my kids."

"Crap, I'm sorry, Jenks," I said.

"Don't worry about it. Go sit somewhere," Jenks said, a thin red dust spilling from him as he took to the air. "Your grinding teeth are giving me a headache."

Ellasbeth and Lucy trailed along behind him, leaving Al and Newt staring expectantly at Trent and me. Trent took my elbow, his expression grim as he angled us to his office.

Ivy . . . "Trent, you don't think Cormel has Ivy and Nina, do you?" I asked. "He wanted to see you." See Trent, not me. The slight difference was the only thing keeping me here and not stealing one of Trent's faster cars, bad leg or no.

"That's what Quen is going to find out."

It was going to be a long night, and I almost cried when we finally got to Trent's office. Dali was in there, and I tried not to lean on Trent as he opened the door. The couch Trent had put in last week for short catnaps never looked better, and I gave Dali a swift nod, heart pounding as I moved as fast as I could and almost fell into it. Leather-scented air puffed up around me, and I thought it smelled wrong without a little vampire incense in with it.

"Dali," Trent said cautiously, and the older, somewhat fat demon turned from where he'd been looking at the colorful saltwater fish in the wall tank behind Trent's desk.

"How very elven," Dali said softly, eyes flicking behind Trent to Al and Newt. "Keeping all his beautiful captives on display."

The rims of Trent's ears went red. "Everything in that tank was captive bred. Nothing came from the wild."

Simpering, Dali settled himself behind the desk as if it was his. "That makes it worse."

I could tell Dali sitting at his desk bothered Trent as he rubbed the side of his nose and went to feed the fish, his motions slow as he took a canister of food from a drawer inches from Dali's foot. "Why are all of you here?" Trent said, his back to everyone as he sifted the food in and the rest of his fish came out of hiding.

Newt settled herself gracefully in the remaining chair, leaving Al and Trent standing. "Last in, last out," she said cryptically. "Dali's line was the last formed, so it was the last to go."

I tried to shift my leg up off the floor, deciding to let it stay where it was when I almost passed out. "What about my line?" I asked when I could think again.

Al harrumphed, fists at the small of his back as he stood before the big vid screen showing an empty paddock at night. "Last line formed while fleeing the ever-after," he explained. "Which might be why you are able to perform magic, and we can't."

"My line still exists?" I said, and Al shook his head. The lines were dead. There was no question as to how I could still do magic, and Dali wasn't happy—even with Al's lie as to why.

"Now, Gally," Newt almost pouted, shifting her robe to hide the welts the makeshift cuffs at the square had given her. "You know that's not why Rachel was able to do magic."

"It wasn't mystics," Dali growled.

"I didn't have any choice," I said in a rush, seeing Al stiffen. "They're dead. All the lines."

Oh God, the lines were dead. I hadn't seen Bis since yesterday. He must be in agony. Ivy was missing, probably in one of Cormel's bedrooms awaiting my arrival so he could kill her and make me save her soul.

"I have to go," I said, leg throbbing as I gripped the arm of the chair and lurched to a stand reaching for my crutch. "I have to get back to the church. Trent, I'm sorry, but I can't do anything, and I need to help who I can."

"Don't be stupid." Newt leaned across the space between us to yank my crutch from me and throw it at Dali. Trent reached to catch it before it hit his fish tank, but Dali was faster, and he glared at Newt as she settled back, pleased with herself for keeping me on the couch and getting Dali's attention all at once. "Dali, you know as well as I that Rachel's line went down first. The Goddess hates her. Rachel can do magic because the tiniest mote of mystics are looking to her, swarming her and creating a field she can tap into." Newt's eyes rose as she looked speculatively at me. "Filling her chi with wild magic . . ."

I sat back down, pinned to my chair by Dali's fierce look.

"That is a lie!" Dali insisted, and Newt looked to the ceiling in false idleness.

"Or any she cared to share it with," Newt finished. "She's like a little ley line hot spot."

"Enough!" Dali shouted. Trent inched in between me and the incensed demon, and Newt bobbed her foot like a twelve-year-old, delighted to rub the demon's nose in something that would get me into trouble and distract Dali from realizing she'd once practiced elven magic, too.

"It's the mystics, you decrepit old demon," she said saucily. "The lines are dead, and the ever-after has until sunrise before the tides shift and it's sucked out of existence, taking everything with it."

Jenks . . . , I thought, looking at the door but helpless to walk to it. He couldn't survive long without magic. Bis either. And the vampires. Their souls would have nowhere to go when they died their first death. Something was going to snap.

"You freed the familiars, yes?" Trent asked, and Dali's expression went sour. "Your slaves? You're abandoning them?" Trent exclaimed, outraged. "Your contract says you'll keep them alive. You can't just forget that because it's difficult."

"Difficult?" Dali snapped.

"And the undead souls," I said aloud, thoughts on Ivy. She'd kill herself twice to keep her soul and consciousness together, even if she believed that would send her soul straight to hell.

Dali leaned forward over Trent's desk, a thick finger pointing at me. "Failure to uphold any contract here *isn't* my fault. I held to the undead curse as well as can be expected." Lip curled back to show his teeth, he glared at Trent. "You and your species are to blame for the vampires' soul destruction, not me."

Soul destruction? I wondered, then pounced on that because it seemed to distress Dali the most. "You promised the first undead that his soul would be waiting, didn't you? That promise falls to all who followed him. And now you can't fulfill it."

"This is not my fault!" Dali shouted, and the fish behind him dashed into hiding.

"You oversaw the curse," Newt said sourly.

"This is intolerable," Trent said, beginning to pace. "An entire population of living, breathing people trapped in the ever-after to die?"

Dali laughed, the bitter sound chilling. "Funny. That's what you had intended for us."

Trent spun, his anger slipping from his iron-clad control. "It was your idea first."

Al tugged his suit coat straight. "Because you made slaves of us and warped our children so far from us they were as imbeciles."

"Hey!" I exclaimed, not wanting to be counted as an idiot from birth. No, I could prove that all on my own.

"Boys and girls," Newt soothed, her pleasant expression faltering when she noticed a bruise in the shape of a handprint on her arm. "We, ah, have all suffered, and though we clearly cannot forget, can we at least strive to forgive each other such that we can . . . survive?"

Trent turned his back on us, frustrated. "There's nothing to move forward to," he said as he looked at his hands to estimate their shaking. "No magic to move forward with. They didn't listen to me, and now we all suffer."

My stomach hurt, but my ribs hurt more, and all I wanted to do was lie down and not move. "I'm sorry," I whispered. "If there was anything that could be done . . ."

"There is, love."

Dali's head snapped up at Newt's soft croon. The demon's hard, unforgiving expression pulsed through me with a surge of adrenaline.

"Newt," Al growled as he stood before Trent's seldom-used wet bar, his shoulders hunched and tense. "Shut the hell up."

Trent came forward a step. "There aren't enough mystics looking to her," he said, but Dali's vehemence as he thumped a meaty fist on the table brought him up short.

"No!" the older demon shouted. "I'll not have it! I'd sooner see us dead than be saved with . . . elf magic!"

Newt's foot bobbed and her cheeks flushed. "Dead is exactly what we will be. Are you blind or simply that stubborn? Demons can do magic through the Goddess. They just don't like to admit it. They think it sullies them."

"It does!" Dali cried. "They're animals!"

Newt simpered. "Aren't we all, old man. Rachel?"

She extended a slender hand to me, pale and unmarked. I could have sworn that her knuckles had been bruised, and I shied from taking it. Smiling, she turned her reach into a flamboyant gesture. "She's modest. The girl can do it."

"No!" Dali exclaimed. "By the two worlds colliding, if I could go back in time, I'd kill her the first time she set foot in my office!"

Al rubbed his forehead before picking up two shot glasses full of an amber something he'd just poured from Trent's bar. "I know the feeling," he said, setting one of them on Trent's desk and giving it a clink before sipping his.

"Then you'd both be dead three times over already," Newt said brightly. "You, Dali, are not yet ready to slip from this life, and for all your pissing and moaning, neither are you, Gally. Not like this—whimpering and sniveling, taken out by an elf's plotting. Rachel can do elven magic. I don't care if you don't like it. So can you, so can you *all,* if you would take that holier-than-thou noose off your necks!"

"Ah, Newt?" I hazarded, but Dali had stood, his face red and frustrated as the already insecure demon came to grips with the fact that he was helpless before a world that wanted to see him dead.

"No more!" the demon bellowed, and Newt stood, robe unfurling.

"You will!" Newt shouted back, and I pressed deeper into the couch. "I have watched your cowardice and unfounded prejudice stain our existence long enough! We share a source of magic with the elves. No wonder they best us time and again when we ignore the source of our strength and take it in the dribs and drabs that exist in tiny pockets."

"Enough!" Dali shouted, and Newt strode forward to put her face inches from his.

"You will *listen*!" she exclaimed, her black eyes flashing and a haze of blue rimming her hands.

Dali's eyes flicked to them and she abruptly backed off, shoulders hunched and eyes down. Al cleared his throat. "This just got a lot more interesting," he said, and Dali's confidence came rushing back. "Newt, where are you getting your magic, love?"

Newt grimaced. I gave Trent a shrug, breathing easier when Dali finally found someone else to be mad at.

"Rachel isn't the only one dabbling in elf magic, eh?" Dali said, clearly disgusted as he pushed back from the desk and stood.

"I don't know what you're talking about." Newt hid her hands in her sleeves. I suddenly felt like two kids having been caught setting off stink spells in the girls' bathroom. Not that I had experience there—much.

Brow furrowed, Dali took a sip of his drink, not as irate as I would've expected. But then Newt was known to be crazy. "You knew about this?" Dali asked Al.

Al shrugged. "I didn't believe her. How could a demon hide that she and the Goddess—"

Newt's head came up. "I won't sit and do nothing as Rachel goes insane trying to hide what she is, what we all are. The Goddess will speak to us, answer us as well."

"And leave us to die," Dali said bitterly. "To fight and scratch out an existence when she turns her back on us? No. Never again. She has her favorites and I'll *not* be played for a fool once more."

It was starting to come together, this bitter rivalry between the elves and the demons, and I watched, silent, when Newt, her robes rustling faintly, crossed to where Dali now sat against Trent's desk, his head bowed as harsh thoughts spun through him.

"You don't have to," Newt said softly as she touched his arm.

A haze shifted between them, and Dali looked at his hands, feeling the energy she had given him, filling his chi with a portion of her own. His breath caught as he accepted that there was a way out of this—if he could let go of a lifetime of hatred. "How long have you hidden this?"

Newt turned away. "I don't remember. So long that the Goddess's mystics don't look to find me anymore."

Her expression was pained, and I started when Trent's hand landed on my shoulder in support. I knew how she felt, and I imagined that the hurt of losing the exaltation the mystics imparted never dulled with time but only intensified.

Dali looked tired as he shifted his attention to me, eyes flicking listlessly to Trent standing protectively beside me. "You taught her how to hide them as well?" he asked Newt.

"I changed her aura so they can't easily find her, but Rachel has a newer bond, one they haven't forgotten yet." She hesitated. "They're still looking for her, knowing that the Goddess must become again. Her eyes have seen reality through Rachel, and the need to partake in it has left the rest predisposed to becoming anew."

Becoming. The Goddess had said that as well, but she'd feared it, as it would destroy her.

"Dali, we can reopen the lines before sunrise with elven magic."

Trent's hands on my shoulder tightened. "I'll rally the dewar and the enclave."

"No."

Dali's word was soft. He never looked up, his mien holding regret as he stood against another man's desk, in another man's house, in a world that didn't want them while the prison they'd desperately tried to escape stood poised to crumble and destroy the very world they wanted to live in but were afraid to.

"You'd have us live like this?" Newt said bitterly, pulling at her clothes as if the tattered and stained remnants were their pride and power. "We can reopen the lines, but it must be done before sunrise. I've been talking with the Goddess—"

"What!" Dali's head snapped up. In the corner, Al clinked several glasses together, and my mouth became dry at the sound of water being poured into them.

Undeterred, Newt lifted her chin. "She's actively looking for Rachel, but she knows that if the lines stay shut, she'll have reduced sight. She's already starving. The only access she has to reality is through failing pixies and Weres who don't even know she exists. She's not listening to the elves anymore thanks to Landon tricking her into destroying the lines."

Interesting, I thought, wondering if this was why elven magic had failed. A tiny wisp of possibility took hold, pulling me straighter in my seat. I could do this, maybe. I had wrestled control of the mystics' individual power from the Goddess's will before. Several times before.

And every time, I ended up fighting to disentangle myself from her so my thoughts wouldn't kill her, change her beyond recognition, make her . . . become something new.

"I cannot live by reality's rules without magic to make it tolerable," Al said. "Dali, we have a chance to not only survive, but in the doing, the world will thank us. Perhaps give us a place again."

"Give us a place?" Dali thundered. "We are demons! We don't take charity, we take what we want!"

"Well, what I want is to belong!" Al suddenly yelled. "I want to try it this way for a while. What the hell, Dali. If you don't like it, you can go back to bartering souls to fill your waitstaff, but I think we can do well here with other people's rules." He hesitated, eyebrows rising wickedly. "Finding our ways around them. Making them squirm within their own . . . laws."

Newt's face was flushed. "But first we need to reopen the lines."

I held my breath, waiting. There was more being decided here than if we should try to save the ever-after.

"We lack the strength," Dali said.

"Then we join our strength with the elves." Newt put her hands on the desk and leaned toward him.

Dali's disgusted gaze flicked to hers from under a lowered brow. "No," he growled.

Trent stepped from me, his breath held and color high. His eyes were bright, and he looked like a leader of people even torn and bandaged as he was—maybe because of it. "Why are we even considering *not* doing this? The dewar is disillusioned with Landon. They'll listen to me. Let's reopen the lines and be done with it!"

"Because she lies, elf!" Dali pushed Newt back off the desk with his voice alone. "The Goddess lies! She tricks! She will kill Rachel outright before allowing the lines to be reopened, and then doom the rest of us to a slow, ignoble death to give herself something to play with for another thousand years. The Goddess will not grant power to us to do this even if it expands her reach. She'll kill us, then do as she will!"

"But we don't have to rely on the Goddess's will," I protested, feeling left out as I leaned forward on the couch. "I can simply take the power we need from her and be done with it! I just need someone to weave the curse and give it direction." And maybe save my ass afterward.

Dali seemed to freeze, only his eyes moving as he looked at Al first, then Newt. Both of them seemed to center in on themselves, avoiding him as he slowly gathered his presence. A chill slipped down my spine, but I'd only said the truth.

"The way is that firm already, then?" Dali said, bewildering me even more.

Al's head bowed, ignoring the question. He looked ill, but Newt's chin lifted as if taking on a burden.

"Rachel almost caused a new becoming on the Goddess twice now and still managed to extricate herself, saving both their lives. The Goddess will strike her dead on sight, but there will be a span where Rachel is unrecognized, and in the battle for supremacy, Rachel could spin enough magic from her to reopen the lines if we were there to take advantage of it."

It was what I already knew, but hearing Newt say it made it sound risky.

Dali's expression was wary. "It would leave her vulnerable to the Goddess's wrath."

As if he cared. He was calm, scaring me more than if he had been shouting. "I can handle it," I said, shaking inside.

"I'll be there with her," Newt said, making me feel worse.

"And me," Trent offered, and I took his hand as he extended it. Seeing us thus, Dali's expression twisted and he looked away.

Al remained pointedly silent, clearly unhappy. His silence was noted by Dali. Hell, it was noticed by everyone, and he set his glass of ice and liquor down with a sharp snap.

"You both together," Dali said, lip curling. "With her. Trying to take over the Goddess."

"It's what we have," Trent said loudly.

My heart thudded as I saw the possible end of my days laid before me. "I can't sit and do nothing if there's a chance. If this works, magic will be restored, the undead will still have their souls in a parking orbit until they fully die, and the thousands of familiars you've got tucked away in the ever-after will still be alive. I'm going to want them to be freed, though."

Dali sniffed. "Of course you do," he muttered.

"Even if the lines hold for only a short time, we can get the familiars out," Newt said. "They will undoubtedly be gathering in the largest space and be easy to move."

But I didn't want a rescue. I wanted a resolution.

"This is a bad idea," Dali said, unconvinced.

"But it is an idea," I said. "Bad or not, we have to try. If I can steal the energy, will you spin the curse? All of you? I can't do it."

I held my breath as Dali sighed, eyes averted as he balanced what was at stake and what it might cost. Pride was his fulcrum, unfairly shifting the weight so that one side had greater force than the other to make a wrong decision more than possible, but likely. *We were going to doom the world to another wave of needless violence because of pride,* I thought, already trying to find a way to make this work without the demons' help. Perhaps the dewar would be enough.

But Dali stood, looking down at himself, stuck in the form he was in when the lines closed. "No one likes this helpless muck we wallow in. I'll ask them. They will decide."

My heart leapt, and Trent's fingers tightened on my shoulder.

"Excuse me," Newt said as she beamed, reaching for Al gracefully. "There might be some dissent that needs to be addressed. Al, will you accompany me?"

Silent, Al picked up his bottle. Not looking at me, he stomped past, his shiny cop shoes catching the light and his pace holding an amazing amount of determination and bad attitude. He yanked the door open, his steps audible on the carpet as he went to the great room.

"Dali?" Newt asked smoothly, her hand now extended to the more powerful, slightly overweight demon.

"This isn't going to be easy," Dali grumbled as they left together.

"Nonsense." Newt looked over her shoulder at me and winked. "You got them to let her into the collective as a student. You even got them to stand up to Ku'Sox when she and Al and that elf of theirs stood up to him. And they didn't kill Trent because of you," Newt was saying as the door eased shut. "Getting them to practice elven magic will be nothing," came through, muted, and then Dali's bitter laugh.

My skin tingled where Trent's hand traced across it as he moved to the wet bar. "Trent?"

He was silent as the enormity of what we were going to try to do fell on us. Still not saying anything, he brought me a glass of water. "Here," he said as the cool glass filled my hand. "You need to keep your fluids up."

"Trent . . ."

"Drink it," he said, and I obediently took a sip, the room-temperature water bland as it slipped into me. Sighing, he sat down beside me, his brow furrowed and his gaze hard on nothing. "I want to say that it's going to be okay," he finally said.

"But you don't know." Ribs ached as I leaned to set the water on the floor. "Trent, the Goddess is looking for me. She's better equipped for a mental battle and she knows how to fight me off. I don't want to kill her, which means I'll have seconds to wrestle control away, and then I'll be fighting to get free before I infect her too deeply for her to shake it off. And then what? I'll be hiding from her the rest of my life."

Trent's eyes touched on mine and he reached for my hands. "You don't know that."

My fingertips tingled where they rested against his aura. I started to pull back, and he gripped me harder. "Don't move," he said sheepishly. "You're getting rid of my headache."

Damn it, I was coated in them even now. No wonder Dali was looking at me like I was a leper. "You too, eh?" I said, giving up on trying to hide them anymore.

"I was so scared when they hauled you up onto that stage," Trent said suddenly, and I held my breath as he carefully pulled me into him. "I saw my entire life with nothing. My money gone, my power stolen. I couldn't reach you and no one listened to me. I thought they were going to kill you."

I could hear his heartbeat as I rested my head on his chest. It felt good to do nothing. "So did I," I whispered, unable to say it louder lest I start to cry. I'd been terrified for him. For Jenks.

"And now you're going to do it again."

His hand gently stroked my hair. I didn't want to move for anything. "Probably."

Trent made a rueful sound. "You were right. As usual. This is hard. But I'm going to do it anyway."

He kissed the top of my head, and I tilted myself so I could find his lips with mine. A faint tingle spread between us, warming and healing even as my leg throbbed.

His eyes were glistening when our lips parted. I wished that this was over and it was tomorrow, and we were having coffee at Mark's before taking the girls to the zoo. "You should stay here with the girls," I said, and his hold on me tightened.

"Just try to stop me."

He was looking at my mouth again, but my besotted smile faded at the sudden rap of a thick knuckle at the door.

"Ivy and Nina . . . ," I whispered, fear causing a spike of adrenaline in me.

"Quen?" Trent said, his brow furrowed as he carefully helped me to sit up while the door opened. His hands were gentle, but I was still grimacing when I looked up to find it was Al, not Quen, standing there—staring at us with the memory of his own loss so clear on him it hurt. Seeing my pity, his face hardened.

"I wanted to let you know that Quen has found word of the ambulance driver and paramedic who picked your . . . friends up. They're both in intensive care with internal injuries."

"No." I fell back into the couch after trying to stand. "What happened?"

"They'll both make it. It helps that they were living vampires," Al said dryly. "But as for Ivy and Nina . . ." He shrugged. "There is no sign of them."

"Cormel." My heart pounded as I turned to Trent. "He wanted to talk to you. He took them!"

Trent rose, pace fast as he went for the phone on the desk. Al cleared his throat to stop him dead in his tracks. "It wasn't Cormel who injured the paramedic and the driver," Al said. "It was Nina."

Tension pulled my shoulders tight as I figured it out. Nina had died on the way. The sun had set and she'd never lost consciousness. She had freaked out, and Ivy had tried to contain her. Shit, where would Ivy have taken her to try to bring her under control? Somewhere safe where Cormel couldn't touch her?

Heart in my throat, I grabbed the arm of the couch and pulled myself up. "I have to go."

"But the demons and the lines . . . ," Trent started, and then he changed his mind, bending to pick up the crutch Newt had thrown, bringing it to me with a sad, determined look.

"Al, tell everyone I'm sorry. I have to go. I'll be back as soon as I can." The crutch fit under my arm, painful as I hobbled to the door. Al stood and did nothing, making me wonder if he'd told me this knowing I'd leave. He knew better than most how close I'd come to losing myself the last time I'd fought the Goddess.

"I might suggest the helicopter," the demon said, voice oily. "The entrance you make in that is almost as good as simply . . . popping in. Besides, the roads are impassable. I'll go with you. No one listens to me anymore."

"I know the feeling," Trent said, but I was already halfway to the hallway.

"Thank you," I said breathlessly as I passed Al.

"Don't thank me." Al looked at his fingertips in speculation. "I just don't want to be there while Newt explains to the collective that we have to work with the elven Goddess to try to reopen the lines."

"That bad, eh?" I muttered, jaw clenched as we found the hallway.

Al leaned close, voice dangerous as he whispered, "We don't forget, Rachel, and it's not as if it was our ancestors who were betrayed. It was us."

Chapter 29

The glow from the streetlight made long shadows against the tomb-stones, and the chopper blades whipped everything not nailed down out and away. I'd never get through my hair tonight without a bottle of detangler, and I made a mental note to check my bathroom before we left—because even if Ivy was here, there was no way we could stay.

"Careful," Trent said, arm around my waist as he helped me over the shallow wall that separated the graveyard from the garden. My stomach was tight, and Jenks was swearing as he looked over the destruction. I couldn't bring myself to look up, even as the helicopter began to shut down and the wind quit pushing.

"What an unholy mess," Al said from behind me, and I suddenly realized he was walking on sanctified ground. The elven curse was well and truly broken then.

One good thing, I thought, looking up.

Breath catching, I stopped, pain stabbing my leg as Trent continued on for a step. Backpedaling, he stood beside me as tears threatened to blur my vision. *I will not cry,* I said to myself, but my chest was tight and my throat almost closed.

"I'm sorry, Rachel," Trent said, gently pushing me back into motion.

I let him, my head down again as we angled to the stone walk and the undamaged wooden fence. "Bis?" I called as we circled around the front, but there was nothing, no cheerful sparkling of pixy dust, no wind-chime laughter, no deep rumbling response from the gargoyle—just the faint hush of traffic a street over. It felt dead here, abandoned.

"I'll find him," Jenks said as he hacked his way through the tangle of my hair.

"You can fly?" I asked as he got himself free and hovered backward, tugging his clothes straight and checking his sword belt.

"Yeah." Expression serious, he peered up at the steeple. "It feels pretty good here, even if it looks like the back room of a troll bordello."

He darted up, wings clattering, and Al pushed past us. "Damn mystics," he muttered, stomping through the gate and toward the front door.

Mystics. I suppose they might have gathered here more than anywhere else, either mine or the Goddess's thousand eyes looking for me.

Guilt closed in. I should have checked on Bis. Okay, I'd been busy, and until the sun went down he hadn't been in any danger, but I was responsible for him.

"He's a grown gargoyle," Trent said, whispering it so Al wouldn't hear.

"How do you do that!" I exclaimed, but Trent's smile faded very fast. "He's just a kid."

Al turned from where he waited in the shadows, his new suit rumpled. "Treble is sleeping," he said, voice low. "I'm sure he's doing the same."

Sleeping or in shock? I mused, stretching out my awareness and finding nothing, nothing at all. Trent's grip on my elbow pinched as he looked behind us at the empty graveyard. Al took the stairs, impatient with our slow pace. Neighbors watched us from behind tweaked blinds, vanishing when he sarcastically doffed his hat at them. "You'd think they never saw a demon before," Al muttered.

"I think it's the helicopter," I said, glancing over my shoulder before starting up the wooden stairs. Ivy had to be here. She was scared, possibly hurt. Vampires always went home to ground when they were hurt. The city was in a panic, but here in the Hollows it was eerily silent as everyone held their breath for sunrise. *Please be okay, Ivy. Please.*

Al gave the DON'T CROSS tape a look before yanking it down to flutter into the bushes. Jenks's wings were almost normal, and I felt the first hints of relief at the bright silver dust.

"I found Bis," he said as Trent helped me up the stairs. "He looks okay. His aura looks like he's just asleep."

"Are you sure?" I asked, and Al grunted as he shoved the door open.

"I told you, it's the shock. If they're lucky, they'll simply not wake up."

Saying nothing more, Al strode inside as if it didn't bother him, but I could tell it did. His grumbling grew louder as he clicked the light switch several times to no effect.

"Jenks, what about Ivy?" I whispered.

The pixy hovered before Trent and me, a worried dust slipping from him. "She's in her room. Nina too. Wait!" he shouted when I started forward. "Slow down. You go in there stinking like fear and you'll set Nina off. Give Ivy a chance to organize her thoughts. She knows you're here. They'll be afraid of Al, but you and Trent look like easy prey."

Oh God. "It's bad?"

Jenks nodded, making my heart sink. "You, cookie maker, need to take a backseat. We know how to bring Ivy down. You don't."

"I know what not to do," Trent said, but his worry was obvious as he helped me shuffle inside. I was glad there was no light as I looked over the soggy gloom. Al was poking about my seldom-used desk, head cocked as he held up a tiny chair Jenks had left there. Jenks was darting about, lighting the candles we had scattered around for when the power went out. Slowly the space brightened as the wicks took hold and wax began to burn. It smelled—sort of a sour, bite-at-the-back-of-your-throat smell, stinking of vampire fear and heartache. *Ivy* . . .

I looked down the black hallway, both afraid and anxious.

"Maybe I should go get Bis," Trent said, and Jenks made a sparkling beeline back to us.

"That's the best idea I've heard out of you since you, ah . . . never mind. You're going to need a ladder," Jenks said, but Trent was already taking the belfry stairs two at a time. Sighing, Jenks pointed at Al, then his own eyes, and then Al again before following Trent.

Al frowned, wearing that same wary, reluctant look he'd had in Trent's office before he walked out with Newt and Dali. He made a "get on with it" gesture, and my heart thudded. Jenks was watching him, eh?

"Ivy?" I called, wanting to give her even more warning. "You here?" It was obvious she was, and I limped to the top of the hallway. There was a thin crack of light leaking from under her door, and I looked at Al. "Why are you here?"

"To catch you when you fall. And you will fall. It's simply a matter of finding the right lever."

Swell. "Ivy?" I called again. "Ah, you okay?"

Breathless, I waited at the sudden slide and thump of something heavy in Ivy's room. A frantic hush of words followed. It was Ivy, and I reached out, finding myself painfully yanked back into Al. I fought to get his hand off me, stopping when Ivy shouted, "No. Nina, no!" I hesitated, Al's grip easing as Ivy added, "It's Rachel. Please. I'll be right back."

"Don't take it away. Don't leave me. No. No!" Nina howled, a desperate pain in her voice. "Oh God. Give it to me!" she suddenly raged. "Give it to me!"

I couldn't move as Nina's fierce demands dissolved into heartrending sobs. Any hope I might have had that the newly undead might survive their souls died. Clearly Ivy had captured Nina's, and Nina was out of her mind to get it back. Everything was out of balance and her second death was the only way to bring it back again.

"Whoever made this curse was a sadist," I whispered, and Al's grip on me fell away.

The light spilled into the cramped hallway as Ivy opened her door. The sound of Nina's heartrending sobs pulled at me as Ivy slipped out and shut it behind her. The newly undead were often unpredictable as their mind reorganized under overwhelming shifts of hormones and instincts while the body fought with the mind, trying to convince it that it was still alive. Hunger usually kicked in when the original aura was depleted to a measurable threshold. But that wasn't why Nina begged for Ivy to return in great gasping sobs. It wasn't blood Nina wanted, it was her soul.

Back against the door, Ivy stared at me with black, haunted eyes, chilling me. "You shouldn't be here."

"This shouldn't have happened." I hobbled forward, tears blurring my sight. "Ivy, I'm so sorry," I gushed, my arms going around her as she began to cry.

Great gasping sobs shook her, and I held her to me, the silk feel of her hair bunched between us. My own tears flowed at the unfairness of it all, the end of her hope that she and Nina might have something normal, that they might have a life, a love, in the fleeting time they were allowed a moment of happiness before the curse came around full circle and took it all away.

"I'm so sorry," I whispered, hardly breathing.

"She wanted me to kill her," Ivy sobbed, her voice muffled. "She begged me, but I couldn't do it. I couldn't even lie to her and promise I would."

"It's okay," I said, and she pulled back from me, eyes glistening as Nina quietly wept behind the door Ivy guarded.

Ivy wiped her eyes, looking more beautiful than I'd ever seen her even if it was grief that brought her alive. "She died in the ambulance on the way to the hospital," Ivy whispered. "There was no way to stop it. And I couldn't finish it. When she begged the paramedic to, I . . . I wouldn't let him."

She'd fought them. She'd beaten them into unconsciousness with the savagery of a lover protecting the one she loved.

Trying to smile, I wiped the tears from my cheek and sniffed. "It's okay," I said, stomach knotting. "I wouldn't have been able to do it either. Remember?" I hated them, hated the demons for this. Of all the curses I'd seen, heard whispers of, witnessed the destruction from, this utter raping of hope by destroying people through their love and fear was the worst.

Ivy licked her lips, haunted eyes flicking past me when Nina sobbed behind the shut door. "I should have killed her twice, but I was so scared that her soul would be lost forever when the lines fell and there was nowhere for it to go. Nina was fine until her soul went into the bottle."

Another heartrending cry of loss rose behind the door when Ivy opened her hand to show me the hazy bottle I'd given her. Nina's moan was so filled with pain it even made Al shift his feet. Or maybe he just wanted a closer look.

"I had to do it." Ivy's hand shook. "I had to. I couldn't let her soul go to that hell."

I took Ivy's hand in mine, closing her fingers over the bottle before she dropped it. Her hands were frighteningly cold. Her head bowed, and I pulled her to me again, hating the demons all the more. But a niggling thought wedged under my heartache. Ivy had used the bottle after the lines had fallen. It had worked with the Goddess's strength. Mystics wreathed her, unseen and unnoticed, my thousand eyes that I'd blinded myself to still working my will for me.

From behind the door, a wail rose, and Ivy sniffed back her tears. "She knows I have it. She wants it, but it will make her walk into the sun. Rachel, I can't."

I jerked when Ivy pulled back, her expression suddenly empty. "You take it," she whispered, pressing the bottle into my hands. "Take it and hide it."

"Ivy, I can't."

"Hide it where she can't find it. Rachel, please!"

"It's mine!" Nina howled, having heard us, and Ivy's eyes went wide. Shaking, I forced the bottle back into Ivy's hand.

"That won't help," I said, hating my own cowardice.

Ivy's head bowed. "I didn't know it could hurt this much," she whispered to me. "I watched my mother die her first death, and then Kisten passed on."

Again I pulled her to me, trying to give her strength.

"This is so wrong," she breathed, but the tears were gone, leaving only an exhausted numbness. "How is your leg?"

"My leg?" We separated, and my heart seemed to break at the distance between us. "My leg will be fine," I said, almost crying again.

"Ivy?" Nina warbled behind the door. "Please, I need it! Just for a moment. I'll give it back. I promise!"

Ivy swallowed hard, empty as she stood before me and glanced at the door. "I've got her tied up. I was hoping . . ." Her shoulders fell, and she glanced behind me to Al. "I decided that she should have it, even if she walks into the sun."

"Ivy . . ."

Tears spilled from her anew as her chin lifted. "Even if it means she dies." Her black gaze found Al. "You all deserve to die in whatever manner the elves can devise. What you have forced on us deserves payment in pain."

Al became solemn. "The elves killed the maker of the curse years ago."

"You let him do it!" Ivy raged, and Nina screamed in pain behind the door.

Al held his hat before him, head lowered. "I agree, but we can't unravel her work."

A woman? I mused. *A woman did this?*

"And even if we could," Al said, gesturing to the door, "enough of the undead would refuse it out of fear, wanting the chance at immortality even if it cost them their soul." His gaze fastened on Ivy, and she quailed. "You yourself can't walk away from it. Or you would have let Rachel take the virus from you already."

"Al, stop," I said as shame caused Ivy to drop her eyes.

"You like it," Al said bitterly. "The urge, the lust, the glorious satisfaction of fulfilling that need."

"That's enough!" I exclaimed, but my neck was tingling with remembered passion.

Expression holding a bitter betrayal, Al shifted his accusing gaze from Ivy to me. "The curse is power, Rachel, and she knows without it her world would be flat and gray. She'd rather live with pain and heartache than no feeling at all."

Angry, I got in his face. "That is a sad excuse to cover your own guilt," I snapped, then dropped back when Ivy touched my arm.

"No, he's right," she said, shocking me. Her hand fumbled behind her, rattling the knob. Never turning around, she pushed open the door. "See what your pride has wrought, demon."

She opened the door to show her bedroom, the cool grays and soothing greens lit by a battery-powered lantern hanging from the dark light fixture. Nina was tied up with soft straps. They were designed for this, but they still cut into her skin as she struggled to be free, her eyes black and wide. Blood marked her clothes, but I think it was from the fight in the ambulance. She hadn't been dead long enough to be hungry. Though her soul was gone, her aura would remain for a few hours yet.

"Ivy, please," Nina begged, straining to be free. "Just for a moment.

You can have it back, but I need it just for a moment." Her eyes flicked to mine, then back to Ivy. "I need it now!" she raged, a muffled scream coming from her as she fought her bonds.

"Interesting . . ."

I spun, reaching for the support of Ivy's dresser when my leg almost gave out. "Interesting?" I snapped at Al. "You son of a bastard! These are my friends!"

Al's eyes twitched, but he never took them off Nina. "I mean," he said as he shoved me deeper into the room, "that she knows where her soul is. Your spell bound it so completely that she recognizes it."

"Give it to me!" Nina cried out, her emotions swinging back to sadness. "Give it to me, it's mine," she sobbed.

Ivy dropped to her knees, taking Nina into her arms and hiding her face. She whispered things I couldn't hear, and Nina's rage dissolved into a helpless, sobbing acceptance.

My stomach churned. I thought of Bis up in the belfry and Trent probably trying to reach him without a ladder. Before me, Ivy and Nina both ached, trapped in a hell of the demons' making. The fear of the people in the square rose up in my thoughts, good people so scared they thought the only way out was genocide.

"We have to reopen the lines," I said, and behind me Al sighed.

"Rachel, I know Newt thinks it's possible, but it isn't."

"To separate them forever from their souls is . . ." I turned to Al, searching. "I don't know a word that means that depraved and cruel."

"To say it would break the worlds," Al said, but I didn't think there could be a word like that, and he turned as Trent scuffed into view with a sleeping gargoyle in his arms, Jenks on his shoulder. Trent's eyes widened as he took in Nina tied to the chair and Ivy kneeling in front of her, trying to ground her, bring her back. Seeing all eyes on them, Ivy whispered something to Nina and got to her feet to stand protectively beside her. Her jaw was clenched and I was so proud of her. Even now she was willing to fight.

"No, this was very well done," Al said as he eased into the room and lifted Nina's gaze to his by lifting her chin with a careful finger. "Very well done."

"You son of a bitch." I shoved Al. He fell back, catching himself on the dresser, his red goat-slitted eyes narrowed.

"Easy, Rachel," Trent said, but Jenks had taken to the air as well, blade pulled.

"I should have let you all die, you know that!" I shouted, shaking.

Al tugged his suit straight. "Yes, you should have," he said mildly, pissing me off. "But you didn't. I have an idea."

"So do I." I shrugged off Trent's hand, feeling braver when Ivy and Jenks fell into place beside me. "It involves you and that crowd at Fountain Square."

Al's dismissive look made my face burn. Speculation heavy in his gaze, he turned to Ivy. "What are you willing to sacrifice for her?" he asked Ivy, and my heart seemed to stop at the thoughtful but manipulative tone in his voice.

Ivy's eyes flashed. "Everything."

I stiffened. Nina's head came up, only it was not hope but my fear that roused her. "Ivy, no," I warned, and Al sniffed derisively, already knowing Ivy's answer.

"Everything!" Ivy said again, almost grabbing his arm.

Al flicked a glance at me, then back to her. "Be utmost sure. Your needs, your desires, no longer yours alone but wedded to another?" he said, and Ivy nodded, grasping at the barest hint of hope. "What another needs, you must attend to. What another craves, you must find. It will be heaven if you love her or hell if there's any doubt. It can't be undone, and you will be responsible for her soul until she dies a second death or you lose yours as well. It's a chance, nothing more."

"How?" Ivy begged, and I could take this no more.

"Ivy, he's a demon!"

"So are you!" she exclaimed, then lowered her voice as Nina began to sob again, calling for her soul. "Tell me," Ivy demanded of Al, her own fear making her even more desperately beautiful. "I will do anything to stop this."

My heart thudded as Al was silent, thinking. "Ask her," he finally said, chin lifting to indicate me.

"Me?" My anger vanished. Jenks's dust was an uneasy red and Trent's face was pale.

"Rachel, please," Ivy said, and I jumped when she took my hands. She was trembling. "I'll do anything. I love her!"

"I . . . I know you do," I stammered, trying to figure this out. Me? Was he serious?

Al took Ivy's free hand, opening it to show that tiny bottle I'd given her. Taking it, he moved it to mine, closing my fingers about it. I swallowed hard at the stirring I felt within it. Tingles cramped my arm, and Nina moaned, voice raw and raspy.

"I can't put Nina's soul back into her body," I protested. "It's going to do the same thing it did to Felix and she'll suicide to bring her mind, body, and soul back in balance."

"True," Al drawled, making Jenks yo-yo up and down in impatience.

"Then what, ash breath?" the pixy snarled. "You hurt any of my friends anymore and I'll lobotomize you in your sleep!"

Al frowned, but Ivy's hope had kindled in me and Al's confidence fanned it to a painful brightness. "To remain sane, her soul needs the stimulation of a stable, living body and aura," Al lectured, as if trying to teach a dull student. "And so . . . ," he drawled, gesturing for me to finish it.

"I need to put it into someone still alive," I said, glancing at Trent when he made an abrupt noise of realization. "Ivy, if I put her soul into you—"

"You can do that?" Jenks asked, his suspicion thick.

"Of course my itchy witch can," Al huffed as Ivy went three shades whiter. "She already put an alien presence in that Were fellow, David, was it? And there was no love there. At least not at first. I think he rather likes it now."

Yes, David liked the focus. It was made to live through another, the symbiosis complete and beautiful. But Nina's soul was hers. To graft it to another . . . was that right?

But as I looked at Ivy's hope and Nina's ragged exhaustion, I figured what was right didn't matter much. "She might still need to take in her aura with your blood," I said, and Ivy grasped my hands. They were shaking, but her need to do this was absolute.

"I don't care," Ivy whispered, alive and filled with hope, more beautiful for having seen her despair only moments before. "I want this. It feels right.

I love Nina. She . . . loves me. I can't see her like this, and I can't end it. Please!"

I felt light and unreal. "I don't know what it will do to you. What happens when you die? Will both your souls perish?"

"I don't care!" Ivy shouted, and I turned to Al and Trent, wanting their opinion.

"It's Nina's soul, free of her consciousness," Al said. "Unlike that ill-fated attempt when you, ah, tried to bind with that soul, Ivy likely won't notice a thing. But there will be far-reaching repercussions from this."

"I don't care," Ivy whispered.

"Well, I do," I said, very aware of how much he liked breaking people with their own desires. "Tell me why you want this, Al, or nothing happens."

"Rachel!" Ivy cried, and I clenched my teeth and faced Al squarely. Behind him, Trent and Jenks waited, scared but trusting me.

Al's smile went wickedly crafty. "Ivy will be the first of a new kind of master vampire," he said, and Trent made a soft sound of understanding. "A living one. The newly undead will look to the living for their continued existence, much as they do now, but it's the undead who will be bound to the living, not the other way around. It should impart a measure of . . . morality that's absent now."

I hesitated, seeing the hope for the end of a long-kept guilt in him, and Al dropped his eyes, embarrassed perhaps that I knew him so well. "The soul Nina sips from Ivy will be her own," Al said. "Where is the guilt in that? Freely given, freely held. The undead will lose their clout. It will fall to the living. Where it should be."

The undead controlled by the living? I thought, seeing the sense of it.

"I want to try," Ivy said, and I turned to Nina.

Nina stared at us, her gaze pained and her desperation shining. "Ivy can have my soul," she whispered, voice ragged, in ribbons. "She already has my heart," she panted, head drooping so her hair hid her face. "Oh God, it hurts. That you might be able to do this hurts. *Please.* Just do something. I can't exist like this."

The need to fix this seemed to warm me from within. My hands shook, and tingles raced through me as Trent slipped an arm around my waist. I felt ill, breathless. "This will break the original curse, won't it?"

A rare smile holding a long-held pain crossed Al's face. "As no other thing can, but it must be done on an individual basis and will be reassuringly slow as it filters through the population and gives us something to pay our rent with."

"The transition will be gradual enough that it won't destroy the current balance," Trent said, his expression hopeful as he saw the possibilities in what we were about to unleash. I thought it fitting we'd do it here in a broken church.

"What do we need?" I said, and Al clapped his hands once, making me jump and Jenks ink a bright sparkle of silver and black.

"Salt," he said, eyes glinting. "Lots and lots of salt."

Chapter 30

We didn't have salt, thanks to my kitchen being firebombed, but we did have pixy dust. Jenks was almost his old self as we readied the charm, feeling needed as we moved the furniture to make a large space in the sanctuary. Candles glowed from the sills of the stained-glass window, and Bis slumbered, hanging from the light over the pool table. He'd never woken when Trent transferred his clawed feet to the cold metal, and he looked like a huge bat hanging there. I hoped he was all right, and I promised myself I'd see this through—one thing at a time.

My stomach hurt as Al finished wiping down the old oak floor, his goat-slitted eyes worried as he threw my silk dress into a corner, having removed "excess stray ions" with it. "Ivy goes in the middle," Al said, sounding unsure. "The spiral is etched outward from her."

"Ivy?" I called, and I heard her coaxing Nina out of their room. She was still bound, but she numbly sat where Ivy put her. Suspicious, I turned to Al. His motions were too fast, too quick. He wanted this even as his regret and worry grew with every moment. "Why are you doing this?" I asked.

"Jenks, dust a spiral, please," the demon said, avoiding me, and my eyes narrowed. "Start at the center and move widdershins. Three arms is traditional. And keep enough space so that if Rachel should fall she won't hit one of the other arms."

Fall?

"You want it flammable?" Jenks asked, and Al hesitated.

"Ah, no, but the longer you can make it glow the better."

Hands on my hips, I frowned up at him. "Why are you doing this?" I asked again, and his eyes flicked to mine.

"You're in the way." Hands on my shoulders, he pushed me closer to the pool table. Peeved, I watched Jenks happily dust a sparkling silver path, skating a bare inch off the floor as he laid down a glow that I could tell would last a good five minutes. Plenty of time to save or damn a species— and my friends.

"Al," I prompted, and he turned fast enough to make his coattails spin—if he'd been wearing his usual green crushed velvet instead of his forties suit.

"I never agreed to this," he said, his distant gaze making it clear he was talking about the original vampire curse. "I maintained that it was unsporting to curse those who had no original intent, but Celfnnah was sustained by bitterness."

Celfnnah. My eyes widened as I remembered. Al had a ring with her name on it. He had loved her. He had loved her so much that he couldn't deny her revenge—her dark bile poisoning a thousand lives, a thousand lifetimes.

"If we're to survive a return to this world we've been exiled from, we need to end this. We need to let the pain go and heal, no matter where the source comes from," he whispered, but his heartache was not for me, but for her.

"Al, I'm sorry . . ."

"And the cost to perform this curse of binding will be exorbitant," he added, gaze going everywhere but to me. "It will keep even Newt in new socks. I swear, that woman can put holes in her socks in one afternoon."

"Al . . ."

"It's a simple curse," he said, ignoring that I'd seen his guilt and aching need to move on, to be accepted. "Most of it was prepped when you made the curse to bind the soul in the bottle. You're simply moving it to a new container. Walk the spiral with Nina's soul. It will draw it from the bottle as you go, and when you get to the end, you peel it off you and bind it to Ivy."

Peel it off me? I didn't like the sound of that. "If it's that easy, why don't you do it?"

"Because Ivy is not my friend," Al said, his hands heavy on me as he moved me to stand right before the beginning of the spiral.

"I'll do it," Trent said suddenly.

"Because you, Rachel, are covered in elf shit," Al amended, dramatically wiping his hand on his suit, "and you're the only one *they* are listening to. Walk the spiral. I'll catch you when you fall."

He wasn't talking about me falling because of my leg, and "covered in elf shit" meant the mystics. I believed him. My fingers had been tingling for the last five minutes, but even more telling was Jenks darting about as if nothing was wrong. Even Bis's color had darkened to his normal pebbly gray, though he showed no signs of waking up. But if the mystics had found me, then the Goddess could, too. *Make this fast, Rachel.*

My heart pounded. Ivy stood at the center. Her hopeful expression almost hurt. She trusted me to do this right. Nina's soul was in my hand, like a promise to be fulfilled.

"Plan C, eh? Bind the soul and run like hell," I said, and Trent tried to smile, failing. Jenks was on his shoulder, and the pixy gave me a thumbs-up. This was for Ivy, for everything she'd suffered, everything she'd told herself she wasn't deserving of. For her, I would risk it all.

And then I stepped forward, placing my foot on the glowing line.

My breath came with a slow intake, seeming to pull with it the memory of drums echoing against a sky faulted by uncountable stars. A slow lassitude spilled into me as I exhaled, pulling a ponderous beat from the spiral to replace the breath within me. I recognized it, accepted it as mine, drew it in to become one with it so I could bend it to my will. *Wild magic.*

The bottle grew ice cold in my hand, numbing as Nina's soul coalesced from creation energy. Far, far older than the Goddess, it emerged, pushed by the waves of sound from the drums into a form that had no shape, a thought that came from no idea man had ever witnessed.

I paced forward as the cold crept up my arms, paining my elbows as I finished one spiral and began another. Within me, the first hints of a low chant echoed against the drums. They twined together, making a new sound to beat upon the soul seeping into me, forcing it into a pattern and shape that it once knew. It was a sound that hadn't been heard for a thousand years. Tears pricked as I realized how much both species had lost in their war. *Wild magic.*

I struggled to keep my breathing even when a cold wash came spilling down my sides. The bottle was empty, and it fell from my numb hands as I gave myself up to the drums, knowing it was the only thing that kept Nina's soul bound to the earth—and the soul rebelled, breathing the cold of death into me. My world was a glowing spiral, but as my will began to falter, threads long left fallow began to glow within my own soul, urging me to pick them up and begin anew. But to do so would be my end.

Dizzy, I began the third spiral. Ivy waited, eyes pinched and hand held out, reaching. I pushed one foot before the other, the heat-stealing soul seeping deeper, making my steps a flagging hesitancy. The seeping cold reached my soul, icing the edges, making me forget until it was only the memory of drums and the whispers of ancient elders that moved me forward. Ivy waited. Ivy waited for me. Ivy believed in me, pinned her life to me, not knowing that it would come to this . . . as I brought peace to her. If I could just move one more step. *Wild magic.*

"Help me," I whispered as Nina's soul sent cold daggers of teeth into me to tear and rend, and Ivy reached, pulling me to her.

Fire exploded in me at her touch and I gasped. Head jerking back, I sagged in Ivy's arms, the drums thundering and the chant winding high through us, through our minds as the soul slipped from me and filled Ivy. We fell to the floor as Nina's soul abandoned me for more delicious prey, prey that wanted to be taken.

"No! Stay back!" I heard Al shout, and a small scuffle. "The curse isn't sealed. Touch them now, and the soul will slip from them both and be gone forever."

"Ivy!" I called as the world rushed back and I was sitting at the center of a pixy-dust spiral, Ivy cold in my arms. I hadn't exploded into flame; it had been the sudden absence of Nina's soul. It was in Ivy, and it was struggling to take Ivy's soul with it.

"Seal it, Rachel," Al demanded. "Now, before it escapes!"

Wild magic whispered through my mind, and with a desperate need to believe happy endings existed among the pain, I gave up and opened myself to the thousand eyes. Wild magic was mine.

"*Ta na shay!*" I shouted as the drums thundered, energy clean and deep coursing into me with the sound of folding wings. "*Ta na shay!*" See me!

My eyes opened wide and for an instant I saw everything from everywhere. My heart made a pained beat, and I choked. "*Ta na shay. Cooms da ney,*" I wept, and I watched with eyes not mine—eyes not of any world—as Nina's soul eased to slumber, dropping the threads that would pull Ivy and Nina both from this world to whatever lay beyond. My throat closed from the sheer beauty, and I forgot to breathe. I thought I'd done it.

"Ivy?" I whispered, and her eyes opened. Their solid blackness shifted, becoming purple as she blinked and wings covered her soul. I could hear the sound of feathers, and my skin tingled with remembered pain.

Panicked, I turned to Al and Trent, but it was Bis whose gaze caught mine. He was awake, his red eyes whirling as his wings opened in fear.

"She found you," he rasped, and both Trent and Al spun to him.

"You're awake!" Trent called in shock before he looked back at me. "Did it work?"

"Ah, guys?" Jenks squeaked in distress as he hovered, spilling a hot dust. "I don't think that's a good thing. I think I'm going to explode here!"

Trent's expression flashed to fear. He looked at his hands, hazed with gold as his aura resonated from the building energy. His eyes met mine, panicked.

"Mother pus bucket . . . ," Al whispered, and then he lunged at me. "Rachel!"

But it was too late, and I cowered as a flash of brilliant light lit the church, burning with an icy intensity. I couldn't breathe. I couldn't *see*! Falling back, I squinted, picking out a darker shadow standing in the middle of the church, swarmed by glowing mystics.

"You!" a voice exclaimed, the hatred echoing in my head as if she'd spoken in my mind. "Your singular thoughts will be ended!"

It was the Goddess. She'd found me. "No, wait!" I cried, one hand propped up on the cold wooden floor as I slid between her and Ivy—and then I screamed as a white-hot knife of anger dove in my thoughts, driving to my core to rip out my soul.

"I will not become!" the figure shouted as I writhed, struggling to escape. "I will not be ended!"

But I couldn't even breathe without taking in her mystics—and I floundered, burning from the inside out. *Ivy. Ivy was beside me—unconscious.*

"Rachel!" Trent cried, and then I heard a sodden thump.

Fear galvanized me, and I pulled my head up. Trent was picking himself up off the floor beside my desk, a spot of cool darkness in the fiery glow. Mystics were everywhere. I got a breath in, then another as my mystics coated me in a protective haze, buffering me and Ivy both. But it wasn't Ivy the Goddess wanted to destroy.

Struggling to sit up, I blinked, trying to find the Goddess in the glow. Mystics coated her so heavily that the body she was in was slowly charring, sending the rank smell of burnt amber to coat my lungs.

"There will not even be a memory of you!" she howled, and I screamed as she flung out a flaming hand. A stream of living magic hit me and I fell, sliding across the smooth oak floor and hitting the wall. My head felt as if it was going to explode from her hatred as the Goddess's strength wiggled deeper.

"Oh God, stop!" I pleaded, shaking as I collapsed. But I was only a singular thought that held many—not many thoughts making one, and she had me outnumbered. The mystics in me were trying, but it was all they could do to keep my lungs clear and my mind my own.

"You can't help her!" Al shouted, and I pulled my head up, shaking as I saw the demon holding Trent back. Jenks and Bis were with him, both frightened. Nina had broken her bonds and was creeping to Ivy with the singular intent of not being noticed. As frightening as she looked, I knew Ivy would be safer with Nina than with me. It had always been so.

"She needs help, you coward!" Trent said, and Al yelped, letting him go.

Trent lunged for me, yanked back as the Goddess shot a bolt of living energy at him, exploding the floor in a shower of splinters—right where Trent would have been.

He fell back, face pale. I managed a clean breath at the brief respite. For all her strength, she couldn't think of more than one thing at a time. I met Al's eyes, knowing this was the end. *At least the demons would survive*, I thought, and then I blinked. *The demons . . .*

Maybe . . . The Goddess was here with all her mystics. I'd need them to reopen the lines. But I couldn't do it alone. I needed the demons. I needed Al.

With a savage howl, the Goddess turned her attention back to me, and I jerked as great chunks of my memory went numb, connections to it sliced cleanly by the Goddess. "Al . . . ," I groaned, hand outstretched, then clenched into myself as the Goddess laughed, her head thrown back as her mystics beat at me, burning me from the inside out.

"I will not become!" she howled, eyes glowing. "You cannot stop me!"

"You can't help her!" Al thundered, shoving Trent behind him.

"Then *you* do something!" Trent raged. "Or have you learned nothing?"

"Fine!" Al shouted, and I gaped, unbelieving, as Al picked Trent up and threw him right at the Goddess.

The Goddess shrieked. A burst of light blinded me as Trent struck her, and then I screamed as the cold of death touched me.

"No! No!" I exclaimed, frantically trying to push away, but it was Al, and I took a grateful sob of air in as he pulled me from the floor and into his arms. He'd reached me. Bis was with him, and a tiny part of me marveled at the glowing glints of gold in his eyes. He was growing up.

"Stay down," Al muttered. "She'll just knock us over again. Trent is fine. Beneath her notice. You, though . . ."

"You both die!" the Goddess shrilled, and I jerked, head spinning. Shit, she was headed right for us, her pace leaving flaming steps of rubber behind her as her shoes burned away.

"Hang on. This might be tricky," Al warned. "I'm not used to this elf slime."

I made a gasping hiccup as his masculine energy dipped into me, using me like a living ley line. "Hurry up!" I shouted as a brighter glow blossomed between her hands and her eyes seemed to shoot fire. "Al!" *Holy crap, she was going to freaking kill us!*

"Someone do something!" Bis exclaimed, wings opening in alarm.

"*Rhombus!*" Al exclaimed, using my word to make a circle, and the world went dark. Panicked, I wiggled. "Al!"

"Don't move, or you're going to break it!" Bis shrilled, and I froze.

I took a breath, then another. We were in a circle. I saw it now. I hadn't gone blind. It was Al's smut, coating the molecule-thin barrier. "Trent . . ." *Oh God, Al had thrown him at her.*

"He's fine," Al said, and all three of us jumped as the Goddess hammered atop the bubble. I could see her now, looking wraithlike as she burned the body she was in, holding it together by sheer willpower. Al's smut acted like sunglasses, and I spotted Nina huddled under Ivy's baby grand, protecting Ivy with her body. Trent didn't look much better, dazed as he sat against one of the piano's legs with Jenks on his shoulder. They were all forgotten as the Goddess focused on me. I prayed that Trent would stay where he was. He looked okay.

My mystics were gathering inside the bubble. I could feel them freely passing in and out, making Al wiggle and squirm even as Bis basked in their warmth. "Al," I whispered, feeling a possible hope. I probably wasn't going to make it out of this circle alive—not with the Goddess standing and waiting to pummel me—but if she was here, and the mystics were here . . . I might as well try. "Al, we can reopen the lines."

"Are you moonstruck!" he bellowed, then winced as the Goddess blew a hole in the ceiling in frustration. Thick beams bounced and rolled, and Nina pulled Ivy deeper under the piano as Trent and Jenks danced back out of the way. "Rachel, we're going to be lucky to get out of this with our lives! The Goddess knows my aura signature now, too."

"Like you really think we're going to make it out of here alive?" I protested.

"And whose fault is that!"

"Help me up," I said, wiggling to get out of his arms. "I want to see if we can give as well as take."

"Rachel, we're trapped!" Al exclaimed. And then someone's foot hit the edge of the bubble, and it fell.

Light burst over us. I gasped as the Goddess howled in victory, then cowered as a blast of white-hot intent washed over us . . . and fell away. Al grunted in surprise, and I looked up.

Astonishment wreathed the Goddess, looking wrong on her glowing face as shock evolved into understanding. "You cloak yourself in your disharmony," she whispered, the body she was in staggering back a step.

"Disharmony?" I echoed, looking at Bis, his feet clamped onto Al's shoulder. There could be no disharmony without lines.

"You're coated in the cost of perverting my will!" the Goddess said, her expression shifting to a hot anger, and Al began to chuckle. "It will not *save* you. I will burn it away, and you both will *die!*"

"Yeah? How much *you* got, bitch?" Al said boldly, standing up and dragging me with him. "*I* have a *lot* of smut."

"It's the smut!" Bis said, red eyes wide. "Rachel, it's smut. She can't get through it."

Grimacing, the Goddess cried out, her wails becoming fierce as her fire raced over me and died. Al and I shared an aura—his smut insulated me. His *smut*?

"Get the rest," I demanded, hope a bright goad. "Bis, go get the rest. We can do this!"

"Got it," Bis said, launching himself out the hole the Goddess had made, pinwheeling to avoid her haphazard strikes.

"Al, don't let her burn me," I said, going still at a memory. Peter had once asked me to not let him burn. But I wasn't committing suicide. There was a chance here. *Wasn't there?*

"What?" Al said, looking from the Goddess for a brief second before throwing out a hand and blocking her desperate attack. "Rachel?"

"I'm going to need all the mystics she has," I said, pulse quickening. "I'm going to let her in. See how many I can convert."

Yes . . . the mystics in me hummed, eager to make a becoming.

"No!" Al shouted, horrified as he understood. "Rachel, it will kill you!"

But there was no other way, and with a deep breath, I dropped the gates to my mind.

She wasn't expecting it, and I felt the Goddess stumble as I flooded her with myself, setting seeds of my thoughts within her even as I swung out again.

You will be ended! I will not become! echoed in me, and I sent more mystics, knowing they'd be crushed but needing to distract her from the growing cancer I'd set festering within.

I will not become. I will not! she screamed, and I turned my thoughts to where the lines used to hum in my mind like great gates. If I could flood them with energy, just one, the way would be open and I could pull on the flow of energy to open the rest.

Bis, I called, finding his presence riding the chaos, his mind dipping and swooping freely in mine. *Where are they?*

They won't come! he thought, his mood chancy as he rose up on the sudden swipe of emotion from the Goddess.

And in my doubt, the Goddess found a small hole in my defenses. *I will not become, I will not!* the Goddess thought. *The other could not make me become, and I will see you gone!*

She attacked with savagery, and I writhed in soundless pain as great chunks of myself were dissolved, taken in and swamped by the Goddess. She was eating me alive and I groaned, grasping at anything as memories slipped away, diminishing me.

You will be nothing! she howled, the sound of wings beating at me as she rolled me into nothing. *I will remain! I am all. They are mine. All of them!*

Fire licked my soul where she tore great chunks of me away. Ice dove deep to fracture what was left and let more fire in. I panicked, feeling myself eaten away, smaller and smaller as I cowered, trying to protect what was left. There was no attack. She had everything. She had it all. I was a fool's thought, a failure, and she coated me in acid, eating me alive.

"Get off her, you self-absorbed bitch!"

I screamed, the sound real as it echoed in my church. The clean breath of nothing cascaded over me, astringent and biting. I was stripped bare, and I huddled in Al's arms as the Goddess shouted and fumbled. Her mind had been ripped from mine and was now fighting great swaths of organized thought that had been strengthened beyond reason by insanity.

I blinked, realizing I was actually seeing two figures in my church, swaying back and forth, locked in a glittering sheath of white that rose through the broken roof to the stars.

"Newt?" I whispered, and Al's arms around me tightened.

"She was the only one who wasn't afraid," Bis said, his leathery tail wrapping about me as he sat on Al's shoulder.

"I know you!" the Goddess exclaimed, her bitterness harsh as a broken knife. "You're slow with disharmony. Your smut will bring you down, and I will feast on your thoughts and make them mine again!"

There was a burst of light, and with a gasping groan, Newt fell backward, staring up at the Goddess from the floor. Panting, she wiped the blood from her mouth. "You're right," she said, her eyes taking on a dangerous glint. "Rachel, hold this for me."

Hold what? I thought, then stiffened when the weight of her five thousand years of imbalance and smut fell on me. I floundered, struggling to keep my heart beating. It was everything and everywhere. Dizzy, I couldn't get enough air as Bis took flight in one panicked swoop. Newt had dumped her smut on me, and I could hardly think.

"Newt!" Al shouted, and I cried out as the sudden vertigo became me hitting the floor. The shock struck through me, and I blearily looked through the hissing glare and darting mystics. Al was gone, really gone! I couldn't tell who was winning. Newt and the Goddess looked the same, blurring together, becoming one.

But no one was looking at me. Suddenly I realized this was my chance. I could hardly string two thoughts together, but if I could reopen the lines . . .

Think bigger! Newt's thought echoed in my brain as she saw my intent. *The lines are dead. The ever-after is dying. Use what's left to make a new one! Use the smut and make a new one! How do you think we did it the first time?*

A new ever-after? I thought, feeling Bis's thoughts join mine. *From the ashes of the old?*

Snarling, Newt fell upon the Goddess, eating through her thoughts even as the Goddess spun about and did the same. They were locked in a spiral like yin and yang, snake eating snake, the balance of becoming held in check as the worlds collided. Flat on my ass, I watched, stunned as the Goddess fought with hatred, and Newt balanced it with a savage confidence, then whipped her thoughts in a dizzying spiral to send the Goddess quailing back until her fear shot spikes of doubt into Newt. Newt patted them out with a dizzying memory of stars and acorns.

No wonder Newt was insane.

"Rachel?"

It was Bis, and I touched his feet as he landed on my shoulder. I could hardly move under Newt's smut, but my mystics gathered, cleaving to me, hazing my thoughts and expanding my reach. As they fought, I took in the forgotten, the wounded, bolstering them with my energy until the mystics hummed with life and brimmed with need.

Find me a thin spot in the balance of mass, I told them, opening myself. Newt's smut was more certain than any protection circle. *Find me a thin spot in time,* I demanded again, and the sound of feathers filled my awareness.

Everything that had been or would be touched every other spot, existed in every time, lay dormant in every being. You just had to know where to look. And I had a thousand eyes today.

Mystics gleefully burrowed through time and space, the sound of their wings piling upon one another until a thin spot in the weft and weave began to fray. I focused on it, made it my all, funneled everything down to that point, that instant, weighing it more heavily than anything else— and with a sudden pop, a wind of thought blew through the spaces between me, sucking nothing into more nothing. I gasped as I felt it widen, expand . . .

And then it vanished and the mystics flooded back to me with images my brain couldn't comprehend.

It hadn't happened.

A boom of sound rocked me, and I pulled myself back to reality. Al and Trent stood before the writhing column of what had to be Newt and the Goddess. Power echoed between the walls, straining the glass and bowing out the wood. My skin tingled, and Bis's grip pinched when a flash of light exploded and Newt tumbled out onto the hard floor.

"It won't hold!" I shouted, and she turned to me, the Goddess occupied for a moment with Al and Trent. Neither of them needed a line to do their magic. The entire church was glowing with the cast-off power.

"Balance it," Newt said, staggering upright and fixing her hat. "You need to balance it. If you get enough mass on the other side, it will stay open."

"With what!" I shouted, but she'd flung herself at the Goddess with a joyous howl.

A sudden pop of high pitch burst the windows. Trent and Al were knocked down and I cowered, Bis's wings shielding me. The very air was glowing, and I inched back until I hit the wall. *Balance it with what?* I thought, palms stinging as they found the broken floor. I could hardly think with all this smut.

The smut! I realized suddenly. Smut was intent to pay back an imbalance in reality created by magic. It was a counterweight to reality. It was . . . balance. Newt had given me balance.

"Bis, be ready," I said, and his grip on me tightened.

"For what?"

"I don't know!" I cried, focusing my attention entirely on one day, one beautiful thought that had held me. I was. I existed, and I would not be ended so easily!

And the weft and weave parted.

Go! I exclaimed to the mystics, and they went, flooding into the tiny hole I'd made in reality. Newt's smut pushed me forward, and I gasped as I felt Bis's thoughts snag mine. His wings beat and he held me firm in this reality as black imbalance pulled over and around me like a shirt over my head, leaving me disheveled and clean. For an instant I watched the new reality quaver, heart in my throat.

And then it began to collapse.

No! I screamed. It would not end like this. It would not!

Hold it open, Rachel! Al shouted in my thoughts, and then suddenly I wasn't alone. The demons. The demons had come!

Streaks of half-heard emotion flowed past me into the new, still-fragile bubble of thought, etching ley lines with the footprints of their mind as they dove into the new reality, cementing into place new lines to keep it alive.

What? What have you done? the Goddess exclaimed, all our thoughts as one for this moment of time. And then Newt pounced, wrapping the Goddess and her mystics up in the smut that polluted the ever-after. Holding tight to it, she dove into the new reality sparkling in our joined thoughts.

I staggered as the balance shifted. Bis floundered, his emotion back-winging in fear as the pull became too great. Like a great rushing wind it rolled our minds to the abyss, drawing us in as well. *Newt!* I called, and then with the sudden parting of a leaf from a tree, the connection broke. I was alone.

My thoughts hit a wall, and reeling, I took a huge breath, trying to figure out what had happened. Real air sucked deep into me, and I coughed out stardust.

"Bis!" I called, but he was with me, his tail wrapped about me and his thoughts twining with mine. New ley lines glittered in our shared mind, singing in perfect balance. The new reality was safe. There were lines again!

The echo of my voice died . . . and nothing rose to replace it. It was silent, and the hush of dust settling whispered over me. My neck hurt, and I shivered in the dark as I looked up to the stars through the gaping hole in the church's ceiling. There was a new hole in the floor, too. Newt and the Goddess were gone. The mystics, gone. The demons—gone.

Gone? "No," I whispered, voice raspy as I looked for Al. I couldn't see him, and I fumbled, falling when I tried to get up. Bis took to the air, landing in front of me with his glowing eyes down in sorrow. They'd thrown themselves into the new reality to balance it out with their smut. It wasn't fair, damn it! I'd worked so hard. It wasn't fair! I couldn't leave them to that hell. Not again! Not now!

"Ivy? Ivy!" Nina cried out, the sound harsh. I was alone, and it hurt.

I collapsed, groaning as I hit the floor. A second crash sounded against my ears, painful and loud. "No, don't," I moaned as something hit me, and then I was pulled away, rocked as warm arms held me, soft words tried to pull me back, telling me to never leave, to stay with him always.

"Ivy, wake up! Please, don't close your eyes. Look at me!" Nina begged, and I managed to open my eyes to see her bending over Ivy. She shook in fear, but her pain-induced savagery was gone, and the first feelings of success began to overshadow my guilt from failure. *Al. Newt. What had it all been for?*

"I'm okay," I whispered, and Trent gasped, holding me so tight I couldn't breathe. I patted his back, smiling as Ivy's eyes opened. They flashed black, then spun back to her normal brown as she found Nina. The glow of their auras was clear, mixing but not, there but unseen. I could see it, but it faded even as I watched.

Ivy began to cry in joy, and she sat up and held Nina's face with her hands as she tried to see past her tears. "Your soul is so beautiful," she sobbed, and they kissed, clinging to each other as if they'd been apart for years and years. But maybe that's the way it felt. I smiled. It was good. It was just.

But the demons were gone. Newt, Al. All of them. And it hurt.

"Are you sure you're okay?" Trent said, and I nodded, grief for the demons welling even as I was happy for Ivy. I'd wanted to do so much more. The demons. The familiars in the ever-after. There just hadn't been time.

"Of course my itchy witch is okay," Al said, and my head jerked up in the new glow of a handheld lantern to find him bending over us, expression wry. Bis was on his shoulder looking proud and exhausted. He'd broken the lines. The two worlds had collided. We had survived? *Where is the Goddess?* "Rachel is a pus bucket full of miracles," the demon added, eyes rolling. "Thank you, Bis. I don't know these new lines yet."

"You're here!" I exclaimed, then hunched into myself, coughing to get rid of the last stardust. Al's light spell glittered with the clarity of a new sun, almost rivaling the demon's good mood. He was here, his smut was gone, and his magic glowed with an amazing beauty. "I thought you were sucked into the new reality!"

"We were." Al set his glowing lamp on the pool table and extended a thick, ruddy hand to haul me to my feet. I felt his strength meet my shaking hand and I rose from Trent's arms as if being pulled from the water. "It was the only way to get everyone across," he muttered, as if embarrassed.

"But . . ." I wavered on my feet, scuffing the bits of ceiling laying upon the floor.

Al grinned wickedly and yanked Trent up as well, the fast motion sending Bis to one of the remaining ceiling supports. "You saw us etch the lines to fasten it to reality, didn't you? You think they only go one way? Stand up. Fix your hair. My God, you still haven't learned how to dress yourself."

"But you were trapped," I mumbled, listing to the right until Trent slipped an arm around my waist. He was grinning. I'd never seen him do that before. Ever. "All of you! Newt and the Goddess!" Fear slid through me and I looked at the hole in the ceiling. "She knows where I am."

"Don't worry about her." Al's eye twitched. "Newt . . ."

His words trailed off and his head bowed. "Gone?" I echoed, looking over the church as if I might see her, praying I would. "She became, didn't she. Newt . . ." I couldn't say it. There was no way that Newt could survive that. She was gone, both Newt and the Goddess destroyed as they became something new. Perhaps it was fitting. Perhaps . . . But I just felt as if I'd lost someone tied to me in more ways than I'd ever know.

Jenks hummed before us, hands on his hips. "Someone better tell me what happened or I'm going to stick my sword into all of you!"

"I think," Trent said as he lifted me to sit on the edge of the pool table beside Al's light, "that Rachel made a new ever-after and the demons etched new ley lines to keep it from collapsing."

"And Newt became the new Goddess," I whispered, tingles coming from where Trent still held me, refusing to let go. I couldn't help but wonder how the demons and elves would handle that: The Goddess was a demon?

Trent frowned in consideration as he figured that one out, but Al was clearly pleased, making me think this might be the only way that the demons' pride would allow them to begin to forget. "I'm going to have my hands full explaining this," Trent said, and I could see him already planning his next speech.

"Perhaps." I played with the tips of his ears, and he jumped, his startled eyes meeting mine as I smiled. "But they're going to listen to you now. I'll help. It will be easy."

"Easy," he muttered, reddening as he took my fingertips and kissed them.

"Must you do that where I can see?" Al harrumphed, but it was all show. "It's a damn small reality, but far more stable than the one we sang into existence last time. Dali did a last sweep before the collapse, but we might have to let the familiars go." He winked, putting a finger to his nose. "Just not enough room for them, the undead souls, and whatever gargoyles had been clinging to the memory of their past."

"And you're not trapped there," I whispered, knowing it was true when he smiled.

"No. Never again, but we have a place to be—if we wish. Have you tasted the lines?" he asked, and I shook my head, eyes widening as I reached out a thought and found them, glittering and silver, like pure thought shining in the night. Newt became the elven Goddess? It couldn't be, and I looked over the church as if expecting her to pop in and tell me everything was fine.

But she didn't.

"I'm sorry, Newt," I breathed, then wavered as my sight seemed to darken at the edges. My heart pounded, and I felt light-headed.

Ivy had stood, Nina beside her holding the grace only the undead possessed, but I saw a new gentleness to it, and I knew why tears still spilled from Ivy's eyes and she refused to let go of Nina's hand even as she gave me a grateful hug.

"Thank you," she whispered, and I couldn't speak as vampire incense spilled over me. Beaming, I gave her a squeeze, a tingling warmth rising through me when I pulled Nina in so I could hold them both at the same time. Nina remembered why she loved—she alone among the undead remembered. She was at peace, and the curse spawned by the hatred between the elves and the demons could be broken. Ivy was no longer afraid to live. I would've done this all for that alone, and my throat closed up as the two of them pulled away, new hope in their eyes.

It was over, and a heavy lassitude began to seep into me. "Can we go home?" I whispered, and Al harrumphed, probably remembering he didn't have one anymore.

Trent scooped me up, holding me as he smiled. "You are done, Rachel Morgan. You hear me? No more."

"Yeah, Rache. Let someone else save the world once in a while," Jenks said as he darted into the air, chasing Bis out through the ceiling and to the graveyard. Limping, Ivy and Nina headed for the front door, and Al gallantly gestured for us to go before him.

Reaching up, I slid my fingers through Trent's hair and pulled him to me for a very satisfying and well-deserved kiss. He was smiling when our lips parted, and I beamed up at him as Al grumbled for us to hurry up, happy with the world. "Right," I said, eyeing Trent's lips and wondering how long it would take to get back to his place. "What are the chances of that, Mr. Kalamack? We just renewed the source of magic. You don't think someone's going to want an interview?"

He laughed, making me feel loved, but my peace came from more than that. I'd gotten Al back, and he was proud of me, even if trusting the elves was going to be as hard as hating them. I'd freed *all* the demons so as to be sun and shadow both once again. I'd proved to Ivy that she was worth being loved, and that would spread through the vampires like a spring's thaw, changing them forever. And though it meant nothing to anyone but me, I'd brought a new understanding between Trent and Ellasbeth, because children should have the chance to be loved by those who love them—always and no matter what.

Trent, though, was mine, and my head fell against him as he carried me through the ruins of the church to see if his helicopter had survived. No one would ever take that away, not the demons, the elves, or even the Goddess herself.

Because for all the changes, some things were immutable truths: friendship transcends all barriers, understanding trumps fear, and great power can always be surmounted by determination. And with Trent, Al, Ivy, and Jenks beside me, we had all three.

I always had.

Chapter 31

The sound of baying dogs over the happy chatter outside the pavilion tent held power over me even now, and I shivered at the thread of adrenaline. Feeling it through my hands, Red blew out, telling me to chill. Smiling, I gave her mane a tug, fiddling with the gold ribbons I'd been arranging. I was fine. I was more than fine. It was going to be a fabulous evening, one that I had planned and waited for—if I could just get these Turn-blasted ribbons to lay right.

"Easy, Red," I soothed, and she flicked an ear at someone's laugh, clear over the hissing lanterns hanging from the high supports. She didn't like the people sitting in the rows of white chairs where she would usually crop grass and roll to rub out the itchiness of a long ride. She didn't like the ribbons I'd plaited in her mane. She didn't like that I'd blackened her hooves, and she really didn't like my dress, swishing in the clean straw and trimmed in open lace. It was admittedly too white and too long to be suitable for riding, but that's what I was going to wear, and she would behave.

"Just a few hours," I coaxed, popping my cupped hand against her shoulder when she threatened to pull out the ribbons she could reach. The old horse snorted, ribbons forgotten at the unexpected sound, and I held her head to me and took solace in her horsy smell, still there despite the bath and brushing. A few hours ago the pavilion had been frantic with last-minute details and rushing about. It was just Red and me now, waiting until almost the end, and the soothing gray of sunset was nice. I really didn't have much of a part to play, but I wouldn't have missed it for anything.

Red's ears flicked, her body young under a youth charm, but her mind old and tempered. If she was tensing, there was a reason, and I let go, turning to where the white cloth billowed, showing the wedding guests assembled amid fire pots and torches just now starting to give off light, but Red was looking the other way.

"Mom!" Ray whispered, and my eyes widened as she came in the back of the temporary pavilion. "Have you seen my spelling cap?"

I dropped Red's head, aghast as I ran to close the billowing curtains before anyone could see Ray. "What are you doing here?" I exclaimed, almost whispering it. "You should be lost in the woods by now!" Elven weddings. I'd had no idea they were so complex. No wonder Ellasbeth had wanted a church wedding.

"I had it this afternoon." Ray swooped about in her lacy wedding dress, and I halted, blinking fast so I wouldn't tear up. She had no idea how beautiful she was with her dark hair piled atop her head and her color high in worry. "I went to put it on, and it wasn't there. I think Jumoke's kids are hiding it."

"Ray . . ."

"Jenks!" the young woman exclaimed, hands in fists as she looked at the ceiling as if the pixy was up there hiding, and Red snorted, stomping at her show of frustration.

"Ray, relax."

"But I can't find it, Mom!"

I won't cry, damn it, I thought as I stilled her, bringing her to a halt as I tucked a stray curl under a jeweled pin. "I love it when you call me that."

Ray stopped short, her flush deepening. "Well, you are," she said, fidgeting. "Ellasbeth is nice and all, but you're the one Dad loves."

Meaning Trent, I thought, giving her a hug and feeling her strength and determination, happy that I might have had a part in that. "Your mother would be so proud of you," I said as I dropped back, still holding her shoulders. "You have her stately beauty."

Ray's eyes dropped. "And my dad's hands," she said, meaning Quen this time. It made sense if you didn't think about it too hard. "Mom, I can't get married without my cap," she said, her momentary calm gone as she began casting about for it again. "Where's Jenks? I know it's Jumoke's kids. They were plotting to hide it as they did my hair."

Of that, I had no doubt. The pixies had been in and out of the pavilion/ stable all afternoon. Trent had banished them shortly before leaving with Quen, and smiling, I began taking out the pins holding my spelling cap on. "Jenks is doing a last security check in the woods. Here." The last pin came out, and I shook my hair free. I wouldn't be doing any magic today. "Wear mine. No one will know the difference."

"I can't wear yours," she protested.

Eyebrow's high, I smirked. "I can ask Lucy for hers. She's sitting with Ellasbeth."

Ray winced, her eyes flicking to the shifting walls as if able to see the large glen beside the river where her mother had last stood upon the earth. The last I'd looked, Lucy was sitting directly between Ellasbeth's stately snobbery and my mom's loud refusal to let anyone think Ellasbeth was better than she was. Takata was enjoying himself immensely, sitting back and watching the show before the show, as it were.

"Ahh, I'll wear yours, thanks."

My heart almost broke from happiness as she all but flopped onto a linen-covered bail of straw and I carefully used my hairpins to fix it among her elaborate braids. Ellasbeth was not happy, making no bones about her disapproval of Ray's marrying a Rosewood baby, even if that baby had grown into a powerful demon who'd turned his thoughtful studies into researching aura mechanics. The field was relatively new and massively funded by an ever-decreasing but desperate segment of the old undead. It had never occurred to me that Ray might marry one of the kids that Trent and I had saved from Ku'Sox. Funny how things worked out.

But I think Ellasbeth's disapproval stemmed more from the coming lack of grandbabies than from Keric's being a demon. While elves and demons had finally learned to live together—in part because their new Goddess was a demon and she wanted it that way—the biology remained static. There'd never be a successful demon-elf pairing. The magic fought the science, and the science undermined the magic. There were some things, apparently, that even a crazy Goddess couldn't fix.

Ray wound her fingers around themselves, fidgeting as she looked to the billowing drapes and the coming sunset. "Maybe I should've asked Loo to ride with me. Mom looks ticked."

Mom meaning Ellasbeth this time, and I sighed, fixing her hair and knowing it would be the last time ever. "She's not mad at you, she's mad at my mom. To tell you the truth, I think Lucy likes sitting between them. If she can keep them from throwing curses at each other, then she can convince a hanging judge that the sun is black and the moon is green."

Ray snorted, reminding me that under the finery and glam, she was the same little girl I'd spent the last twenty-seven years helping Trent and Quen raise, putting Band-Aids on cuts, making unexpected cupcakes at dawn before school, cheering from the stands in the rain, and drying tears when a boy was mean—missing her when she was with Ellasbeth. If that wasn't being a mom, then nothing was. It had been glorious, even if Trent and I had never made it official. With Ray getting married, it felt as if a tie between us was being cut.

"I'm so glad you're standing with my dad," Ray rushed on, and I kept arranging her hair, knowing she needed soothing as much as that flaky horse did. "I can't imagine Ellasbeth doing it."

I laughed, but it sounded almost like a cry. "Me either." I had to stop. I had to let her go. "Go on. You need to lose yourself in the woods. Keric knows where you'll be, right?"

She stood, looking like grace given substance, breathless with action and promise coiled up in her, ready to be loosed on the world. "Yes. If you see Al, tell him if he doesn't wear the pelt, I will turn his ears into snakes."

I nodded, my hand trailing from her as she paced quickly to the back of the pavilion and slipped into the twilight. "Hi, Ivy!" she called, already out of my sight but heavy on my mind. "Jenks, your kids are butt-hats!"

"Yeah? Tell me something I don't know, short stack!" Jenks shouted, and I spun to the makeshift door. *Ivy?* The sun was still up. I hadn't expected her to make it until the reception when Nina could come with her.

Pulse fast, I wiped my eyes as she walked in, gray about the temples, wrinkles about her eyes, but moving as slinkily and smoothly as always.

She made the fifties look good. Really good. "You made it!" I said, glancing from her to the saddle. I had to finish up and get out of here. I needed to be on the hill overlooking the glen by sunset, and it was almost that now.

Eyes glittering, Ivy pulled me into a quick, heartfelt hug. My eyes closed as the scent of vampire incense and contentment washed through me. Okay, maybe I needed some soothing, too, and I smiled as I pulled back, thinking she looked better than great. And she'd made it before sunset. I'd thought she'd be too busy.

"Rachel, you are as radiant as Ray," she said, and Jenks hovered between us, his silver dust graying about the edges. He was due for another rejuv charm, but was resisting.

"You mean wild," the pixy said. "Love the hair, Rache."

I touched it, not caring that I'd ruined the elaborate upsweep by taking my cap off. It was frizzing already, and I took the last of the pins out. Trent liked it better wild anyway. Though I'd not seen or heard the Goddess since Newt had become her, Jenks said mystics still coated me from time to time as she turned her thoughts my way. I knew every time she did because my hair became impossible. It happened a lot, and maybe that's why my life had been so perfect.

"You said you couldn't make it until after sunset," I said.

Ivy smiled as if knowing something I didn't as she made kissy noises at Red and petted her soft nose. "Nina told me to leave. Apparently I was fidgeting. Getting the office excited."

Jenks snorted, and I thanked him when he dropped a pin into my hand.

"Nina keeps them in line better than I do anyway," Ivy said, eyes wistful. "The old ones don't like me much. Not like before."

I can't imagine why. Ivy and Nina had flipped the vampiric power structure. Not a week went by without a protest or incident, but it was contained within the vampires, living and dead, and the world was content to let them figure it out.

"They just don't know you like we know you, Ivy," Jenks said, darting back when Ivy idly threatened to smack him. It was an old game that neither tired of.

"Nina will make the reception, won't she?" I asked as I went to drop the saddle pad on Red. The music had shifted, both the baying of the dogs and the quintet. I was going to be late. No help for it now.

"She wouldn't miss it." Ivy held Red's head as I placed the saddle, and my lace rustled as I leaned to bring the cinch up. It was good to see Ivy out of the office. Being the head of Cincy's I.S. had taken her out of the church about the same time I'd given up trying to be two things and moved in with Trent, though to be honest it was the girls' pouting that moved me more than Trent's heavy sighs. But all things change, and we both loved our lives.

"*I* wouldn't miss it," Ivy whispered as I leaned into Red for leverage to tighten her cinch. "You deserve this, and I wanted to be here to see it."

"Yeah, it's your big day!" Jenks said, wings clattering. "Make-it-or-break-it time!" he said, gyrating wildly. "Time to crap or get off the pot!" he added, and Ivy shot him a look to shut up.

Excuse me? My motion to cinch Red's saddle hesitated. "I suppose," I said. I'd miss Ray, but Trent and I had been empty nesters before when both girls had been at school.

"He means this wedding is a big step," Ivy said, glaring at him. "The demons and the elves formally joined and their war officially ended."

"It took me forever to convince Dali to help with the vows," I said, glad the grumpy demon had finally agreed to it, threats and promises aside.

"Tink's last will and testicles, you should have been there, Ivy," Jenks said, and Red flicked her ears, threatening to snap if he got any closer. "She *laid down the law.* Started every other sentence with 'Look, you,' and had a list a mile long just to get him to come."

"You do what you have to do," I said, smiling. Al had been there, and I swear I'd felt Newt's laugh in my mind. I was smart enough not to tempt fate with trying to contact the Goddess directly. Newt was gone but not dead, her spirit showing itself when elven magic spun out of control and into something unexpected and not always nice.

"Jenks . . . ," I protested as he teased Red, but Ivy just smiled and shrugged. Seeing Ivy happy was all I'd ever wanted, and she was happy. What would happen when she died was anyone's guess, which was probably why Ray was an expert in auratic physics and Lucy had focused on business law with a heavy slant toward vampiric living wills and trusts.

"I still say *I* should be with the elven emissary and *Dali* in the woods wearing this rag," a low, cultured voice with a hint of a British accent said, and I started, not having felt Al pop in. "My God, it still smells like wolf. You're looking well, Ms. Tamwood."

Ivy's eyes slid to Al as the demon brushed at the wolf pelt he wore over his extravagant suit. It almost rivaled Takata's in marks for "Look at me! I don't care that you're staring!" the fabric almost glowing from silver threads and dark dyes.

"And you look ridiculous," Ivy said, making Jenks snort in agreement.

"It is the required uniform." But still, he winced as he took off his hat and hunched, pleading with me. "Rachel, love, talk to Ray. Tell her this is undignified. It's a wolf skin, and not a very big one. She said she'd turn my ears to snakes if I took it off."

"Then maybe you shouldn't have taught her that curse," I said, remembering getting that call at three in the morning. It was the last sleepover Ray had been invited to. Mothers of fourteen-year-olds have no sense of humor.

"She listens to you!" Al protested, and Ivy let go of Red when the horse got a whiff of Brimstone and tossed her head.

"Al, just wear it," I said. "And get your ass back out with the wedding party. You're going to make them late coming in."

"I will not," he said stiffly, frowning as Ivy gave me a kiss on the cheek. "Quen has my steed. I have plenty of time to pop back. Listen, they haven't even found her yet."

It was true. The hounds still bayed, and I shivered. I'd asked Trent to forgo that part, but Ray had insisted. The dogs wouldn't be allowed to follow them back to the glen, though.

"See you at the reception," Ivy said, turning to stand right in front of Al until he moved out of her way.

"Damn cheeky vampires," he grumbled as he moved. "Thinks she owns the world."

I soothed Red before reaching for her bridle. "She's in love," I said softly. "She does own the world."

Al was silent, and I turned to see him staring at me, the wolf pelt hanging half off his shoulders. "You took your hair down," he said, his voice shifting, deeper and less flamboyant. "Is that for your elf?"

"No." The pelt was slipping off his shoulder, and I stood before him and tugged it straight. "Jumoke's kids took Ray's cap, and I gave her mine." He wasn't jealous—not really.

"I suppose if you have stood with him this long against all the forces of nature opposing you that you'd be afraid to do anything . . . else?" Al said, his tone rising in question at the end.

Jenks's wings clattered in warning that I was going to be late, but it was Al who grimaced. "I'm not afraid of anything except missing my cue," I said. "Will you just wear the pelt?" I grumped as I adjusted it. "It's only for an hour. Pretend that it's a job. I've seen you wear worse." A horn blew, and I frowned. Damn it, I was late.

"It's undignified!" Al moaned, his usual mood restored.

Jenks's wings shivered against my neck. I hadn't even felt him land. "This coming from the demon who let a live *Tyrannosaurus rex* eat him so he could blow him up from the inside during the last ten minutes of the film?"

Al frowned. "I do my own stunts. It was in the script."

Which was true. Al had five Oscars to his credit and had produced and directed movies that had earned twice that many. As he had said, Al did his own stunts, and the dinosaur had been real, reengineered from old DNA using sophisticated magic and some of Trent's more illegal machines. The one they didn't blow up was on loan to the San Diego Zoo.

"Can you get me tickets to the premiere of *Mesozoic: In Time, No One Can Hear You Scream*?" I asked, and when he winced, I shook my head. "Wear it, big man, or I'll change something other than your ears to snakes."

He leered, making Red's ears pin back. "How do you know someone hasn't beaten you to it?"

"Al!" I shouted. "Wear. It."

Sighing, he tugged it back into place. Jenks was laughing, his dust looking gray in the lamplight, and I hustled forward to adjust the pelt before Al could take it back off. "He looks like a Neanderthal in Armani," Jenks said, laughing merrily.

"It's not that bad!" I soothed, pulling Al down to kiss his cheek and make his ruddy complexion shift even redder. "You look like the big bad wolf. Now go. I have to meet Trent and Quen on the hill."

"Quen is with the hunting party, and if it wasn't for Ray, I'd never do it."

"Then I have to meet Trent. And she loves you. Go!"

Grumbling, Al backed up, but he hesitated before he winked out, a familiar, crafty glint to his expression as he took a breath and his eyes opened wide.

"Tink loves a duck," Jenks said loudly. "I think Brimstone breath just got an idea."

"Yes!" Al exclaimed, and Red bobbed her head, agitated when the demon was suddenly coated in shimmery silver ever-after. "I have an idea!" he cried again, his voice distorted as the energy field fell away to show that Al's silver-threaded overdone finery was gone, replaced by thick boots trimmed in fur and an elegant coat with shadings of tree and field. The wolf pelt worked with it, especially in the graying light and the smell of horse, and I smiled. "If I'm to be a huntsman, I will *be* a huntsman! They will tremble in fear, and that whiny Keric will think twice about stealing my beloved Ray!"

"Go get 'em, Al," I said, weary as he jumped and his shiny afterimage fading to nothing.

Jenks snickered as he took to the air. "I think you might have just birthed the idea for his next film."

"Just as long as he leaves me out of the credits. I got hate mail for three whole years the last time."

The dogs' song shifted, and I looked at the graying walls of the tent. I had to go. "Come on, Red," I coaxed, and she obediently took the bit, noisily moving it around until it felt right.

"You're late," Jenks said, helping enormously, and I led the horse over to the mounting box. I normally didn't need one, but I normally didn't ride wearing twenty pounds of lace. Red didn't like it, and she shied.

"Hold still," I muttered as I swung my leg over. Red squealed, and I pulled her in tight, bashing my chest against her as I lurched on. We spun in a tight circle, and breathless, we came to a halt.

There in the flickering light of the gas lamps was Trent. He was sitting atop Tulpa, a bemused expression on his face as he took in my hair, the mane of it going everywhere. "I thought you were going to wear it up?" he said, and I flushed.

"Jumoke's kids hid Ray's cap, and I gave her mine," I said, thinking he looked fantastic in his father-of-the-bride finery. My God, Ellasbeth would be kicking herself tonight.

"Quen decided to stick with Al to keep him from going out of bounds," Trent said, gesturing for me to hurry up. "It's just us on the hill, and you're making us late."

"So I heard," I muttered, meaning about three different things. My pulse quickened as the horns sounded again, closer even as the dogs' singing became faint. Tradition said the bride and groom were to come in with the groom's parents and the bride's protector. It was only after the vows were spoken that the bride's parents joined them. I thought the ceremony uncannily like the pixy's tradition of stealing the bride when there wasn't enough dowry.

"I don't think we can make the hill, but we can hide at the edges of the glen," he said, and I nodded, bringing Red around and heading for the back door. My heart was pounding, and I thought it silly that he could still do this to me. He was a little wider across the shoulders with maturity, and the first hints of silver were in his hair, but you had to look close. The stress of maintaining his species-friendly industries was taking its toll, but he'd made his way back from almost nothing even with me beside him. It felt good.

"Rache, if you've got this, I gotta go," Jenks said, and he darted off before I could raise my hand in acknowledgment.

Tulpa bobbed his head as we came alongside, and Red gave him a look to behave. The stallion was ancient by horse standards, the father of five of her offspring.

"Ah, you haven't seen my cap, have you?" Trent said, and I realized my being late wasn't why he'd come back down.

Leaning across the horses, I gave him a kiss, pulling his cap out of his back pocket at the same time. "Want me to pin it to you?" I said saucily as I put it into his hand.

Trent blinked at it, then leaned forward to hold the fluttering drapery out of our way. "I had it all the time?" he muttered, then dropped it on his head, looking heartstoppingly charming.

I took a clean breath of the sunset-gloomed air, bringing Red back under my tight control when she tensed, wanting to run and leave the noisy throng. It was sunset, and I stifled another shiver when the approaching party called and the assembled guests answered them with their own horns, guiding the wedding party in. The faultless sky had shaded to black in the east, pink and blue in the west. Birds took flight at the noise, and I settled more firmly on Red. Maybe the elves had something here.

"I'm glad you're with me," Trent said as he pointed out a sheltered spot where we could watch from under the trees and still be unobtrusive. "I don't know if I'm coming or going today."

Beaming, I shifted a strand of hair from his eyes as the horses walked to the edge of the glen. We'd been noticed, but everyone was focused on the empty space between the chairs and the river where the ceremony would take place. "I'm happy for you. I know this means a lot. That Ray have a traditional elf wedding, I mean."

The rims of his ears reddened, and he gave me a sidelong look. "It's that obvious, is it?"

I angled Red closer and let my head drop against his shoulder. It was awkward, but I made Red stay there for at least a few paces. He was happy, and that made me happy. If not for that dumb tradition about ruling elves needing to marry someone fertile, he might have had a wedding himself, chased his bride down among the trees, defended her against her parents, and triumphantly brought her home to his family. But it didn't matter. I had everything I could ever want.

"Look, they're coming," he whispered, and I followed his gaze to the far end of the glen where Keric and Ray rode in on Ray's black stallion, the shaggy monster high-stepping and excitable. They looked beautiful, waving at the assembled people when they stood and cheered. Behind them came Quen, Al as the huntsman, and Keric's parents, the two looking proud and tearful. I knew how they felt.

We spun Tulpa and Red to a halt, holding back as tradition dictated until their vows were said. It might be a while as they were swamped by well-wishers. Trent was beaming, his eyes never leaving the couple as they dismounted and graciously touched hands and cheeks to everyone.

"I can see why you'd want this instead of Ellasbeth's church wedding," I said, and he jerked, eyes flicking to mine. "It's beautiful."

"What I wanted didn't matter," he said, pausing to bring Tulpa's head up from the grass. "It still doesn't," he said, leather creaking as he leaned across the space between us and kissed me. His lips were warm and his touch sent a wave of tingles down to my core, but guilt kept me from enjoying it.

Seeing my downcast eyes, Trent took my chin in his hand to make me look at him. "Rachel, it's not too late. The demons won't stand in our way. The elves either. Why don't you ever say yes to me?"

To marry him? Sighing, I dropped my gaze. "I don't know," I whispered, and then frustrated, I pulled my head up. "Trent, we've been over this. You can't marry a barren woman and maintain your hold on the dewar and the enclave."

Trent slumped, making me angry.

"What is wrong with what we have!" I exclaimed, careful to keep my voice from carrying. "I thought you were happy!"

"I am happy." Trent's eyes held a mix of heartache and anticipation that I didn't understand. "Rachel—"

"I'm happy you're happy," I interrupted, a growing feeling of frustration joining our old argument. "The girls have grown up beautifully. I don't know how they keep it straight, but I guess as long as they're loved, it makes sense to them."

Our eyes lifted to the river as the head of the dewar and Dali waited with Ray and Keric. The chairs were empty now as everyone stood around the couple in a protective circle—everyone who cared for them, loved them, wanted to see them happy. My frustration sort of left.

"It makes sense to me, too," Trent said softly, but I felt a hesitation in him, something he hadn't yet said. From the river, Al shouted and gnashed his teeth, falling down as if dead amid cheers as he formally gave up his protection of Ray, the huntsman defeated by a token blow from Keric and his mother, their hands joined on a ceremonial sword. It would go to Trent as the symbolic spoils of war.

"You're happy?" I asked again, and he reached out and set his hand atop mine as I held Red's reins.

"More than I've ever been in my life," he said, but still I heard a doubt, a lingering niggle of worry.

"Then nothing could make this more perfect," I prompted. He said nothing, and I shifted Red's reins to my free hand so I could take his hand more firmly. "Trent . . ."

Dropping his head, he whispered, "A new little boy or girl would make this more perfect."

My breath caught, and I forced myself to not shift my grip, making it neither less tight nor more so. He wanted another child, and I couldn't give it to him. "You know I'd never stand in your way."

He pulled my hand to his chest, drawing my eyes to his. "I'm glad to hear you say that."

He was smiling, bursting almost. My heart seemed to break, and I pulled away. Behind him, clouds of blue butterflies rose up as the couple became one. *Sunset.* "That's our cue," I said, a lump in my throat. He wanted another child, and I couldn't give it to him. Hell, what did I expect? It was my own fault, really. It wasn't supposed to matter. I told myself it didn't matter, but after twenty-seven years, it did.

"Rachel, no!" Trent exclaimed, leaning in a jingle of tack to grab Red's bridle and bring me to a halt. "Not with another woman, I mean you and me! Us!"

From the crowd, a soft sound rolled out as the butterflies rose, symbols of love and war all wrapped up in one, for as butterflies seek out flowers, they also seek carrion.

"What do you mean, us?" I asked, and Trent took my hand, nudging Tulpa into motion and drawing Red into his wake. My head hurt, and my shoulders were stiff. Why was he bringing this up now? In front of everyone?

He was totally self-satisfied, sitting with that damned smugness that irritated me, eyes forward and smile fixed. His eyes, though, were dancing. "It's our present to Ray and Keric," he said. "Al's and mine. We've been working on it for over three years. We both thought a child, one that was part of each of them, would be a fitting expression of their love. But if you don't want to . . ."

"Present?" I breathed, and Red began to prance as my seat shifted. My thoughts went to Ivy's cryptic mood and Al's odd question. Hell, even Jenks had been acting weird. *They knew?* "You found a way? When?"

Trent turned to me. Everyone was watching us now as we slowly approached. "It wasn't so much the nuts and bolts as it was—"

"Viable children?" I interrupted, my pulse fast. "Between elves and demons. Trent. You found a way?"

We were almost there, the crowd parting to show a clear path to where Ray and Keric waited with knowing eyes, the curve of Ray's smile saying she had been in on it, too, but Trent stopped us, turning to me and taking both my hands. "Rachel, I appreciate that you respected my duty enough that you refused to marry me to prevent the dewar from turning from my counsel, but you have some thinking to do, Ms. Morgan. With the possibility of an heir between us, you can't hide from me behind duty or a technicality of convenience anymore."

I couldn't say anything, stunned. I'd been saying no for so long that I didn't know how to say yes.

"We'd better go," Trent said, the rims of his ears becoming red as he realized everyone was looking at us with delight. Pixies had joined the butterflies, and the entire glen began to glow in the rising moon. A great shadow of leather and angles cut across it as Bis back-winged, shifting his flight erratically until I heard Jenks swear when the gargoyle caught him. His red eyes blinked at me across the distance, and he gestured for me to say yes even as he kept Jenks from butting in. Damn it, did everyone know about this but me?

"Trent." Breathless, I pulled him back to me. I knew I was flushed, and Red bobbed her head, a clear barometer of what I was feeling. "I don't need to be married to be happy. I don't need to have a child . . ."

He leaned in and kissed my forehead, and from before us, I heard my mom sigh. "I know that," he said, looking deep into my eyes. "We've tried it your way now for over twenty-five years. Can we spend the next twenty-five my way? And if you don't like it, you can always . . ."

With a little cry, I slid my hand behind his neck and pulled him to me for a real kiss. The assembled people cheered, and I closed my eyes as the sound of pixy wings wreathed us. *Give up? Leave?* echoed in my thoughts as his lips met mine, holding both a promise and a desire. *Never,* I answered myself as we parted and, hands still connected, turned to those who meant most to us and were welcomed in between the pixy dust and the blue butterflies.

THE BEGINNING

Dear Reader,

Never did I imagine that the Hollows would become what it has, starting from the humble beginnings of a short story to evolve into the thirteen-book, multiple short story, graphic novel, and lavish world book series that it has become. It's a rare honor to be able to play within the same world for so long, the luxury of time to slowly evolve the principal characters a gift.

The success of the Hollows comes from all corners, starting from the ever-skillful editing of Diana Gill, to the stunning covers designed by Larry Rostant, to the uncountable folks at Harper each doing his or her part to bring one person's imagination to another across distance and time. It truly is magical.

But it's the readers who are the lifeblood of any artistic endeavor, those who wait a year for the next tome and eagerly scoop it up to live a little while outside themselves, who talk over the characters and argue over their choices, who bring the words alive and make them real. It's *you* who make that happen, and for that, I thank you.

All my best,
Kim

About the Author

New York Times bestselling author Kim Harrison was born and raised in the upper Midwest. Her bestselling Hollows novels include *Dead Witch Walking; The Good, the Bad, and the Undead; Every Which Way But Dead; A Fistful of Charms; For a Few Demons More; The Outlaw Demon Wails; White Witch, Black Curse; Black Magic Sanction; Pale Demon; A Perfect Blood; Ever After;* and *The Undead Pool,* plus the short-story collection *Into the Woods* and *The Hollows Insider.* She also writes the bestselling Madison Avery series for young adults.